MADDALENA

Book One of *The Golden Tripolis* Trilogy

MADDALENA

An Illustrated Novel

EVA JANA SIROKA

SEMELE
BOOKS

Princeton, NJ

Copyright © 2005 by Eva Jana Siroka.
Text, cover painting, illustrations, and map © 2005 by Eva Jana Siroka.

All rights reserved. Printed in the United States of America.

No part of this book may be used, reproduced, or transmitted in any form or by any means, including electronic, mechanical, recording, or by any other information storage and retrieval system, except in brief quotations in literary or critical reviews.

For information contact Semele Books, Princeton, New Jersey.
www.semelebooks.com

Maddalena is a work of fiction. Names, characters, places, and incidents are used fictitiously. Any resemblance to actual events, locales, or persons, living or dead, is entirely coincidental.

Book and Cover Design by Nancy Webb Graphic Design
Cover painting, illustrations, and map by Eva Jana Siroka

Library of Congress Cataloging-in-Publication Data
Siroka, Eva Jana.
Maddalena: an illustrated novel/Eva Jana Siroka. 1st Semele Books ed.
1. Maddalena—Saint—Rome—History—Alessandro Farnese, 1520-1589—Northern Artists—Fiction.

Library of Congress Control Number: 2005901089

ISBN 0-9764937-0-5

10 9 8 7 6 5 4 3 2 1

First Semele Books Edition: May 2005

*This book is in the memory of my father,
the sun that would not set.*

Table of Contents

La Fioraia *1*

Venus *5*

Servus Domini *25*

Jewish Queen *39*

Berti *53*

Neophyte *69*

Don Alfonso *79*

Healer *89*

Urbi et Orbi *99*

Alba *111*

Credo *117*

Scholar *123*

Limbo *133*

Devil's Apprentice *147*

Excelsior *163*

Manus Domini *171*

Klara *179*

Nemesis *183*

Inferno *195*

Angel of Mercy *213*

Fallen Angel *229*

St. Magdalen *251*

Author's Notes *271*

She was a flower woman, but not an ordinary fioraia.
He wanted to become pope, like his grandfather.
Rome, the eighteenth of June in the year of Our Lord 1567.

La Fioraia

onna Rebecca sat on her flower cart, waiting for the sunrise. For years, the men on Campo de' Fiori had desired her, struck by her perfect oval face and the rich, dark hair that framed it with flair—so heavy it pulled her chin up, giving her a dignified, imperious stance.

They called her *La Maddalena*, and one by one, Messer Ephrahim sent them away.

"They're not one of us, *Tochter*."

The men in the ghetto came nearer her heart, but they were too common for her mind.

Monna Rebecca did not mind living with her parents. The hot Roman sun darkened her skin and her father's library sharpened her thoughts, where she discussed Josephus' history, argued Plato's philosophy. But she was not proud and humbled herself to help every creature. No man had stirred her, and she resigned herself to live unwed.

With her *gamurra* tucked under, long legs dangling, she peered through the morning haze trying to recognize faces, wondering if Don Theophilos would send for more herbs. His Eminence Cardinal Farnese was ailing, and his physician kept her family busy.

Rome was waking up. Oxcarts rattled on the cobblestones. Farmers set up their stalls in Campo de' Fiori. Boatmen's voices drifted from the Tiber.

Monna Rebecca heard a dry cough nearby.

"Would you like my wrap, signora?" she called to her neighbor. She could almost touch, but barely see, the old flower woman. The cough finally subsided, and a strange scent cut through the odor of fresh dung that dominated the farmers' market each morning.

Monna Rebecca hopped down and reached for her oil lamp. A ring of light spread through the fog to the next stall and lit Monna Chiara's face. Wrinkled by the elements, stooped from years of toil, with a clay pipe down the corner of her mouth, she looked like a sorceress.

"Are you well, signora?" the young woman asked, seeing dark stains on Monna Chiara's *camicia*.

"It's nothing," Monna Chiara replied, quickly covering the spots on her blouse with a scarf. "Let's talk about something important. Isn't it your special birthday?"

Monna Rebecca nodded her agreement.

"Can you believe it? Today, I'm twenty-five."

"Best wishes, signorina. Do you want me to cast your fortune again?"

Seeing the Tarot deck emerge, Monna Rebecca pinched her nose to stop laughing. "We can hardly see and my horoscope is always the same. Are your cards marked?"

"Folly." Monna Chiara pointed to the sun rising above the hills. "Who knows. A new life may begin for you right now."

Monna Rebecca trusted Aristotle. She valued Herodotus. But a reading on her birthday? Another fool's journey into the world of shadows?

"Signora, you know how much I honor your judgment."

"Sit over here"—Monna Chiara pointed to a wooden crate—"and set your lamp there. Right there. And this time, on your special birthday, I'll let you shuffle."

Monna Rebecca scrambled the cards all over the board, piled them high before cutting them. "The inverted cards don't count!" she said, wagging a finger.

Monna Chiara nodded, closed her eyes, and mumbled a quick incantation.

"What do you really want?" she asked, surrounded a fresh puff of sweet scent. "Security? Wealth? Children? They all come with marriage." Her worn fingers, crooked from splitting hemp stalks and removing the tough fibre, slowly turned the first card.

The reading had hardly begun and Monna Rebecca already felt vexed.

"The Empress. Always the same song. Of course I want to be happy and make others happy. And I do love Mother Nature. We both do. Isn't that why we sell flowers?"

"Be patient." The finger pointed to the second card in the circle of her horoscope, but Monna Rebecca didn't look. Instead, she listened to the cock-vendor across the lane bartering with his first customer, whose loud voice she recognized. A maid from Cardinal Farnese's kitchen. Distracted, she looked at the card without thinking and reflected only on the fourth.

"The Ten of Pentacles. My past? A safe harbor. I am a *fioraia*. I sell flowers and read my honorable father's books. What else is there?" Monna Rebecca closed her eyes. An image she could not identify burst in her mind. Powerful, it overcame her.

"What do you truly desire?" Monna Chiara asked as she turned over the Nine of Cups.

"I want to enter a world beyond my wildest imagination. I'd like someone guiding me, wiser, stronger than my father, someone I could ... "

"But you have it. Right here, in this card. Your dream will come true. But I warn you, child, there's no such thing as love ... Let's see how you are going to get there."

The sun rose vigorously, its warmth reassuring. Noticing her lamp flickering, Monna Rebecca extinguished it.

"The passage of light—human to divine," she mumbled, focused on the next card. "Adonai, you are holy, and in you I trust. This is my very special day. Please, give me a sign."

Monna Chiara turned over the Sun, but the card was inverted.

"That card doesn't count."

Suddenly pale, Monna Chiara closed her eyes and reached for the next card as another bout of coughing consumed her. The pipe fell from her mouth, spilling smoldering specks of hemp over the damp ground, and a small spattering of blood colored the board.

"*Signora!*"

"It's nothing, my dear," Monna Chiara wiped her mouth and hid that hand below. Staring in their face was a striding skeleton with a scythe over its shoulder.

Monna Rebecca froze. She'd seen the Fool in her readings. Does not everyone venture on the path of folly once in a while? The Tower made her humble. And while the Hanged Man gave her goose-bumps, she lived honorably, responsibly ...

The Death. She'd never seen that card in her fortune. Was she to die? Soon? Terrified, she crossed her arms and locked her hands in her armpits to prevent them from shaking.

"*Sì. La morte.*" Monna Chiara continued after clearing a trickle of colored spit from her chin, staring directly into Monna Rebecca's eyes. "The death is merely a transition to an eternal life, far better than most of us have here. You, at twenty-five, are still young and healthy. This card tells you that you must put your past behind for a new life here on earth."

"And now, let's see where your hopes lie." She crossed the next card over the last.

"The Lovers," Monna Rebecca broke in, relieved. "This is silly. I've seen that card in every one of your readings. It brings me nothing."

"This time, since the Lovers's card is coupled with Death, the outcome's quite different," Monna Chiara objected. "The pair is about neither love nor desire. It's about a journey that will lift you to heights most of us will never know."

Monna Rebecca hardly breathed. "A journey!?"

Amid the market's raucous noise, the silence between the two grew unbearable as Monna Chiara turned her gaze back to the deck, almost as though she had not heard the question.

Monna Rebecca examined the old woman's face. It was blank, but her voice gained strength as Monna Chiara topped the last pair with one, final card.

"You see? You'll be like the Star, bright and serene as Venus, like the wondrous star of Bethlehem over the Christ child, born to release the fear in us. Believe in Him, and you will be blessed. This is an extraordinary reading, Rebecca. Your own dreams will seem like a trifle."

Monna Rebecca stood tall, overwhelmed.

She knew. Like her father, she'll help people.

She would be a healer.

Venus

Alessandro Farnese awoke late. He stretched in his huge four-poster bed with gilded columns, silk drapes, and embroidered bed linen, feeling lonely in his colossal palace staffed by hundreds. He lay in austere splendor, reflecting on the immortality of his soul.

The sun was already past the horizon, climbing through the haze and dappling the church steeples and palace roofs with warmth. Bright light shot into the cardinal's bedchamber through the shutters moving in the morning breeze, across his silvering beard, past a curio cabinet, to Titian's *Penitent Magdalen,* bathing the saint in her naked glory.

Every morning, Alessandro admired the beautiful woman in the painting and could do nothing about the arousal he felt. Every morning, Padre Carlo, a man made lean by a life of forced piety, dressed his master, little twitches around his eyes betraying his disapproval.

"Your Grace," the padre began, holding a large scroll, "have you a decision on *Il Gesù?*" The first Jesuit church in Rome had preoccupied Alessandro longer than the Vice Chancellor of the curia cared to remember.

"Look." Alessandro pushed the proffered plans aside. "Messer Tristano is a capable architect, but he's unoriginal. I promised Monsignor Borgia twenty-five thousand gold *scudi* for the construction, but the design must be more innovative."

Alessandro shifted his gaze back to the Magdalen, seeing her as if for the first time, wondering who had inspired such incredible beauty. Could she have been real, with her innocent eyes and creamy face, her lips open in prayer?

"But … " Padre Carlo began.

"No buts."

"Will Your Grace see Monsignor Borgia?"

Alessandro's head felt dense. Should he ask Don Theophilos to bleed him again? The man was a useless leech. He needed gentle hands, like those in the painting.

"Maddalena, are you still alive or did the master steal your image to let it live for me here in my bedroom?" In the brilliant light, everything was clear—the gentle face, the slim neck, the hair like a waterfall cascading in deep waves around the white promontory of breasts.

"Oh, Maddalena, you are lovelier than dawn," Alessandro murmured, frustrated.

"Your Grace? Are you ill?" A wave of horror struck the faithful padre.

Alessandro shut his eyes. "I'm exhausted," he muttered. "Lord, can't I just be a man?"

At last he replied. "I'll see Don Francisco. Tomorrow. Before vespers."

† † †

A swiftly passing thunderstorm painted the grass fresh green, and the torrential downpour left muddy pools. Alessandro stood above the Forum on the Palatine, cutting a tall figure over his architect with a giant head and gopher-like expression. Thick hair lay limp on the cardinal's collar, slick from the humidity. Just for a moment his spine arched, protesting the weight of his water-drenched vestments.

Below, in the Campo Vaccino—the cows' meadows—the Arch of Titus framed old temples and basilicas, and broken archways and columns hinted at their glorious past. But the air resounded with the sound of bells, pealing a melody of Christian Rome as men unloaded stone blocks for the ceremonial gate to the new casino. Alessandro's litter-chair rested nearby, its attendants waiting, the master complaining about the slow progress on his casino.

"Your Grace," replied Don Giaccomo bluntly, "I need more money."

The cardinal, a red pillar, stood silent, unimpressed.

"You spend more than you have—your church, villa, palace, Excellency."

"So?" came the curt reply.

"So, Your Grace, until we get at least one project finished, both men and finances stay tight." The architect inhaled sharply. He never won. Why did he even try?

Alessandro squinted in the oblique light and diverted the conversation.

"How are the foundations for my casino coming?"

Don Giaccomo exhaled and pointed at two diggers on the hill.

"*Eccelenza,* you see what I do." Curling his hand into a fist and lifting his index and little fingers above the others in the sign of horns, he nodded. "The men do what they can. The river's back to its banks, and the ground is slowly drying out. The winds have been favorable."

Don Giaccomo's fingers shot up again to ward off evil, as a loud cry ended in a scream.

"Ay, Madonna, I'm falling!"

"What in hell? Begging your pardon, Your Grace ... What *is* the problem *now?*" Don Giaccomo stared, horrified, as the diggers' heads vanished below the surface.

Alessandro lunged forward.

"Your Grace, stay calm! I'll see what happened," Don Giaccomo gasped, watching a cloud of dust rise. He scuttled on his short legs toward the muffled cries drifting down the hill. Alessandro followed, burdened by his wet cassock. Cautiously, they positioned themselves around the lip of a huge pit.

"Madonna, save my men," gasped Don Giaccomo, wiping the dust from his face as it belched up, volcano-like. He grabbed Alessandro's arm. "Excellency, this isn't a place for you!" he begged as the dust settled to reveal the hazy outlines of a deep stone chamber. Buried in rubble sat the older digger, Beltraffio, coughing and gasping for air, unaware that he and his friend had fallen through the earth into an ancient shrine.

"Marco, I think the Lord has punished us for prying! But I've got your hand, and I'll pull you toward me. *Uno, due, tre!*" Beltraffio yanked hard and fell backwards, holding a beautifully carved stone arm. "*Amico,* answer me! Where are you?" He stumbled around, looking for his friend. "Marco, answer me!"

Dust continued to rise. The men at the edge of the chasm looked at one another.

"Do you see what I see, Your Grace?" Don Giaccomo asked, stunned by the sight below.

Alessandro nodded, shocked. He could not tear his eyes from the pit.

As a white arm with sensuous fingers appeared, his head began to spin.

"Excellency, no one must come near. I'll get Archimede. He can be trusted." The architect called down the hill for someone to fetch the giant stonemason and then turned back.

"*Venere pudica?*" he asked, peering through the dust and pointing to the hand still in Beltraffio's grip, its marble fingers spread wide in the gesture well known in classical sculpture as concealing a figure's breast or private parts.

"Yes. Chaste Venus." Dumbstruck, Alessandro could only nod.

The huge Greek, a cubit taller than most Romans, but with wits the size of a grain of rice, jumped into the pit to clear fragments of blocks and tiles away from the half-buried Marco, before cobbling a makeshift staircase from the rubble. As he picked up his body, a few stones shifted, revealing first a woman's breast and then the entire statue.

"St. Nicodemus! Mercy! The she-devil!" Archimede shook fiercely.

"Stop it!" Alessandro's temper flared. But he too succumbed, as the statue swayed in the settling dust, calling him.

"Your Grace … You are deathly pale."

"It's nothing. My humors, I think," he whispered. "Don Giaccomo, help me down the hill and then look after the men."

Carefully, they walked the muddy slope, and the architect waited until the cardinal's litter-chair left. Soon after, Archimede pushed the wounded Beltraffio up to the surface, and Marco's dead body followed.

"Well, Beltraffio," Don Giaccomo calmed the poor digger who was dripping with blood. "I thank you in His Grace's name for your service. We'll get your back straightened and your head stitched up! As for your friend … Archimede!" he yelled. "Get these men into the oxcart!"

As the cart bumped down the hill and work resumed, Don Giaccomo turned his attention to what he knew best, serving his patron with devotion.

† † †

Long after the late evening bells of San Lorenzo stopped ringing, with his back to the Tiber, Alessandro presided over a banquet table covered in the finest damask, dreaming about his new Venus. Now as the excitement wore off, he began to feel a sinking sensation.

I have everything. Everything, *except* the papal tiara.

Grateful for a breeze, he watched his guests—young, old, rich and not so rich, the buffoons and drunks, the dwarfs, dogs, and cats—wondering how some of them managed to appear at his feasts.

A voice drifted in the mist from the river, through the open arches. "Alessandro," it called, the sound sweeter than a mother's lullaby.

He shook his head to erase the voice, but its echo persisted until a living Venus hovered above. Dazed, he raised himself to meet her, staring, until he was drenched in sweat.

"Oh, my Lord!" he whispered and crossed himself, finally seeing the image dissolve in the rising moon.

He wanted to eat, but only a few oysters remained on the golden platters. Seeing that the alabaster vessels were nearly empty of marinated sea creatures, he signaled for more food, but strangely, no one noticed. The silver candelabras needed new candles and the exotic flowers fresh water. Liveried servants stood at attention, too busy guarding the blazing torches transporting the lively company into a world of pantomime to notice the commanding hand.

Elegant young couples waited in the candle-lit loggia, ready to amuse the company with another dance. The musicians, armed with lutes, recorders, and violas de gamba, struck up a lilting tune. Alessandro, charmed by the dancers, exhilarated by their youthful energy, became envious. Even their lacquered manners could not disguise their mischief.

Across the floor, Berti Spranger bowed to his partner, bracing against her smile.

Alessandro studied him. He had first considered hiring the young artist when they met in San Oreste. With an alluring face framed by a shock of black curls, talented, personable, and obliging, he was certain to go far. All things beautiful moved the grand patron of the arts, and his Flemish servant cut a striking figure. Perhaps he should keep him.

More food appeared, until the banquet table was smothered with bowls, tureens, and platters, as if the evening had only started. Forgetting his servant's corkscrew tresses and the apparition, Alessandro attacked the next course. Wild game lay stylishly arranged on silver platters. He chose one tender quail, a chunk of partridge, a roasted duck breast, and a stuffed pigeon for company, leaving room for sweets.

The scent of the Farnese lilies mixed with pungent sweat intoxicated everyone, even *il gran cardinale,* and the dancers' limbs became galvanized, despite the dignified pace of the *pavane*. Face after face, the men and women radiated their passion for life. When the lutanists varied the pace for the brisk *gaillarde*, Alessandro's tense fingers caught the beat.

One quick step, then another. Bow, bow again, turn, and another deeper bow.

The partners switched and repeated the steps to a grand finale. Bowing to his young lady, Berti withdrew to a table where people of his rank were seated. The hall grew hot. Restless, Alessandro rose and moved across the hall, bowing to his guests, until, suddenly, he stopped.

Berti wondered about the comely young woman near his patron. Perhaps they're friends.

Judging from his laughter, Alessandro had found his bright side. He stretched an arm draped in red silk and his hand, heavy with precious rings, waiting.

She straightened the string of pearls in her blond coiffure and smiled.

"Your Grace," she offered with a clear voice, "I'd be honored to see your gardens." As the musicians played the last notes, Berti mouthed Alessandro's answer. "Your servant."

"Ridiculous," Berti thought. He was the servant.

The Farnese gardens were unfinished—a web of paths and new shrubs—but the pair headed toward the grand staircase and the courtyard. Berti picked up a leg of pheasant, filled a clean goblet with wine, and strolled to the garden façade of the open loggia. Grateful for the fresh air, he watched the clouds skirt the rising full moon.

The couple passed Alessandro's famous Hercules, pausing by a small marble of Eros. For a few minutes, the moon's long fingers played mischievously with the androgynous god and the couple. Alessandro's laughter pierced the air as he stroked the curls of Venus' son.

The waxed torches blazed brightly in the loggia, but the path to the garden was unlit. Only a few sculptures and a small fountain stood in the center. Guiltily, Berti slipped behind an arch and watched as Alessandro's arm curved around the woman's waist.

As mist began to rise from the river, they merged with it.

† † †

A large, yellow moon hung over the city, illuminating the river façade of the Farnese palace. As it rose, Venus reigned supreme over her pale sisters.

Alessandro sat in his study, far from the clamor of the banquet hall, his brown eyes cloudy, his hands fidgeting. Plush tapestries bordered with Farnese lilies covered the upper walls. Carved wainscoting accented the lower third. A frescoed chimney-piece divided the wall, lined with family portraits in ornate frames. Although the ensemble evoked a sense of extraordinary luxury, the cardinal, worried by the stalled construction of *Il Gesù,* could not appreciate it.

"Lord, give me a sign," he murmured to himself. "What kind of church would honor Your Son, Jesus Christ?"

He was thirsty, but the wine jug was empty. He thrust his fingers into the crystal bowl by him, grabbed a handful of sugared nuts, and finished them greedily. Spilling sugar crystals on the desk, he picked up the bowl and probed its ice-smooth surface with a lover's passion.

The candle sputtered as the knot collapsed into a pool of wax. In the shadows, the contours of the bowl swelled into alabaster breasts. Alessandro began to tremble, his mouth dry, breath short.

"Fie, devil, leave me alone!" he cried out. Groggily, he ran down the moonlit corridor into his bedchamber, his mind in the grip of Venus. Haunted by her voice, he fell into bed, forgetting to draw the curtains.

During the night, he tossed and turned until a sharp pain stabbed his head. He awoke, finally and fully, grabbed the bell, and pulled with the fury of a man who has hardly slept. The sound echoed urgently down the hall.

"How may I serve you, Your Grace?" Padre Carlo emerged, hastily straightening his cap, looking alarmed.

"Get my physician!"

"Immediately, Excellency!"

The petrified man bowed out. Alessandro faced the draft wafting through the wardrobe, his head an ugly knot of pain. Dragging himself to the washstand, he splashed water in his face.

"*Mater dolorosa!*" he said, looking at himself in the glass. "What's that awful lump over my eye?" He braced himself on the stand.

Don Lodovico Tedeschi, his majordomo appeared, panting as usual. Not enough hours ever permitted the rotund man to serve to his master's full satisfaction. With a forehead stained by sweat and a bulbous nose prone to excitement, he kept a large kerchief at hand and used it.

"Begging your pardon, Your Grace, Don Theophilos is not here. Don Clovio is unwell and … "

Don Lodovico hesitated. He was sure the cardinal did not want to hear the details.

"Monsignor Borgia wants to speak to you about your new church; Don Giaccomo must have your new instructions on the casino; and Monna Chiara wishes to know … Christ have mercy!" Don Lodovico choked as Alessandro dropped his arm.

"What evil has befallen Your Grace?" the majordomo cried, as his patron staggered back and crumpled into bed. A hairy spider hung from the baldacchino, not far from the cardinal's head. Don Lodovico crossed himself and raced to the bed to pull on his master.

"Holiness! There's a huge tarantula but five cubits above you!"

"Why should I move?" Alessandro demanded. "Some day, something else will get me." He did not budge as Don Lodovico flung the covers over him and hit the insect with a pillow.

† † †

The bells of San Lorenzo tolled nones. Confused, the cardinal squirmed in bed, rubbing his bandaged eye. He could feel cool air moving despite the summer heat, and his teeth began to chatter as a bout of shivering overcame him.

"Don Theophilos, where are you? Prop me up and uncover me! I'm not dying, not yet!" He groaned, one moment chilled to the bone and the next roasting with fever. "God knows why I keep him. I'm dying of agony, my eye is in a spasm, and the idiot tastes my urine! What does sugar in my urine have to do with this bite?"

"Don Fulvio. My favorite antiquarian." He smiled at the newcomer, a short, rather gaunt man with thinning hair and dignified posture.

"Calm yourself, Excellency. Don't let ill humors take hold of you!"

"How can I?" Alessandro muttered, still shaking. "I called that stupid quack. Where is he? Do you know that I actually had to *order* him to cut the carbuncle?"

Don Fulvio panicked. "Shouldn't Your Grace rest?"

Instead, the patient fumbled for his robe and half-slipped off his bed. "Get me some spiced wine," he demanded. "My *nonna* swore by it no matter what the malady. Damn all doctors!"

Don Fulvio rang for service, and the cardinal calmed somewhat. As always, he was glad to have his friend with him. If only he had some pleasant news to cheer him up. He looked across the room, his eyes widening in surprise. A bronze putto grinned at him in the candlelight.

"Where did he come from?" he demanded. "And where's my Venus? I want to see her."

"They found many little objects, but *two* large statues, Your Grace," Don Fulvio explained. "I had them stored with your Farnese Bull. Then, on second thought, they were moved to the secret chamber."

A full decanter appeared. The cardinal helped himself generously.

"Ah. The true ambrosia. I'm ready, my friend!"

Alessandro rose, dizzy from the laudanum. They made a strange sight, the cardinal anchored on his antiquarian's arm, the white bandage drooping across his eye. Together they descended long staircases, until the vaulted ceilings began to hang low. After countless turns with only mice as occasional companions, they faced a dark corner. The air was distinctly musty.

"My friend, what *exactly* did you find?" Alessandro asked, a knot of excitement in his stomach.

"See for yourself, Your Grace." Don Fulvio slowly inserted the large key until most of the shaft disappeared in the lock, turned it a full three turns, pushed on the heavy chamber door, and paused to light two oil lamps waiting by the door. Two rats scampered into the dark landing.

Across the small room littered with antique marbles, the statue of a nude woman lay on a pallet of straw, her face turned, one arm shielding her virginity, the other broken away. Holding his breath, Alessandro looked at her, straining his good eye. He could hear his heart thumping. The lamp trembled in his hand and cast warm shadows over the immobile marble body, tickling it with soft nuances of gold and pink. The pale flesh looked alive.

Alessandro's knees shook, but not with weakness.

"Oh, I must touch it, feel it, love it." He knelt in reverence before the pagan idol, running his fingers down her dimpled shoulder, cupping it in his hand, the warmth growing within, sliding his palm down to the broken limb.

"Beautiful goddess," he murmured. "Mother earth cradled you in her arms." As he explored the budding breasts, he spilled his seed down his thighs.

"You fool," he told himself. "You should know better."

"Greek? Aphrodite?" he mumbled stupidly.

"Venus. A stunning first-century Roman copy."

The cardinal lifted the lamp higher. More figures lay on the straw, a drunken satyr and a boy with grapes.

"Look, Your Grace. The infant Bacchus with his tutor Silenus," Don Fulvio said, pointing to the group. "The goddess of love and the god of wine go hand in hand."

"Anything else?" Alessandro chattered in response. Exhausted and ill, he still wanted to make love to the statue. Never before had such a mysterious urge assaulted him.

Perhaps the goddess of love had spoken and confused his senses.

"Numerous small objects," Don Fulvio replied as he helped the cardinal back to his sleeping chamber. "We can see them later. Isn't that more to your comfort?" he added soothingly as he tucked the cardinal into bed. "And Excellency, there's something else. Don Lodovico extended Monna Chiara's contract. I think she's waiting in your *guardarobba*."

"Eh?" The feverish patient squinted through his good eye.

"Don Lodovico thought you might enjoy some flowers in your room."

"Fine," he acquiesced. "Send her in, but then let me rest!"

† † †

A dress rustled. Suddenly Alessandro's room was filled with such a fragrance he imagined himself dead and in heaven. Focusing his good eye on a graceful figure spreading clusters of jasmine at his bedside, he felt himself falling into an abyss, as the fear of final judgment gripped him.

"Man's salvation rests on the grace of Jesus Christ," he reminded himself. "But are we, weak human beings, also responsible? I'm no better than the rest! I've tried to follow His teaching but failed."

The towers of Paris misted before him, as he contemplated his life as it was before the vows, when he was a young papal legate defending his grandfather Paul's interests. But at night, over and over again, perfumed fingers enflamed his skin.

Women had always been his life—as his children proved.

"Your Grace!" A sonorous voice penetrated his drifting mind as his breathing grew laborious.

Maybe he was not dead after all. He struggled to stay alert, squinting at two dark eyes, each a sea of onyx and solid as if inner strength could flow out but nothing could penetrate.

The longer he gazed, the more the long legs shadowed through the *gamurra,* the face carved more exquisitely than the most precious cameos in his cabinet, mesmerized him. But what fascinated him was the woman's patrician posture, the tilt of her head, weighed by the locks coiling defiantly from her coiffure like serpents.

"Are you a goddess?" he demanded, at the same time aware that the scent was unmistakably a woman's. "Lord, don't let me die. Don't deny me this last pleasure!"

A cool hand rested on his forehead, as spiking fever overcame him.

Caught by an unexpected affection, the woman lingered, her eyes on Alessandro's face, seeing only loneliness. Age had lifted the hairline, touching his forehead with nobility.

She stretched her fingers over the bandage, resetting the fabric, and fingered the proud bridge of the aquiline nose, resting momentarily on the exposed lid. Sickly and pallid, it was huge, like one of the all-seeing eyes of the pagan heads scattered in the Forum.

The face twitched. Startled, she drew back, took a deep breath, and left.

† † †

His Most Reverend Excellency, the Cardinal Farnese, was delirious. Four days had passed since his visit to the secret chamber. His

Holiness Pius V dispatched his personal physician, but neither Don Mercati nor Don Theophilos could agree on a treatment, wasting hours in lofty exchanges, ignoring an unseen complication.

Gluttony, a privilege of the rich and powerful, was a sin, not an illness.

"Anyone who awakens in a stupor with his eyeballs tinted the color of honey," Don Theophilos argued, "but manages to keep his private organ up must be under the influence of Venus." The cardinal's hunchbacked physician could hardly cure the fatty pustules on his own face, but still he was a devoted servant.

"Nonsense!" Don Mercati replied contemptuously. "What makes you think that?"

Don Theophilos snickered. "Why that powerful planet could have designs on our most reverend cardinal, I'm not sure. Not without consulting the patient!"

"An elixir of sweet musk, crushed coral, and gold, pulverized with lapis lazuli … "

"But, Excellency, consider the potency of my physic in which rose water is prepared with no less than one hundred roses that have blossomed under the sign of Virgo."

"*Signore,* please continue."

"The heart and spleen of patients under the sway of Venus produce too much sweetness in their blood," Don Theophilos protested, "but my medicine fights that exact malady, especially when made worse by a spider bite! When suspended in the extract of alcanet water, be it even the patient's final moment, he'll emerge young and healthy."

Don Fulvio and Don Lodovico, in the background, felt lost.

"We must trust Don Theophilos," the majordomo opined. "He might rub His Eminence the wrong way, but he knows infinitely more than Pius' fool, too busy collecting minerals."

But Don Fulvio was already on his knee, head bowed in salute to a frail, white-robed monk of the Dominican order, who came striding resolutely toward them. Figures around the two men sank in salutation to the pope and his retinue of cardinals, bishops, and acolytes.

Pius V paused by Don Fulvio and addressed him candidly. "We are troubled by Cardinal Farnese's health. He has not confessed for three days! Only confession and absolution can open Our Lord's way that looks favorably on the shrine in which the soul dwells with his blessing."

The pontiff's words rang with kindness and conviction.

"Don Mercati, you are free until the patient confesses. *In nomine patri*."

The pontiff began his prayer kneeling by the patient's bed, his long white beard caught in the folds of the cardinal's coverlet, his dirty feet exposed to his retinue.

"Amen," came the responses to the petition for Alessandro's soul.

But just as God once turned away from His son, Pius' prayers bore little fruit. Although the danger from the spider bite had passed, only rarely did the patient emerge from his stupor, poisoned by too much sugar and wine.

☦ ☦ ☦

The city boiled, the heat penetrating even the thick palace walls.

"Water!" Alessandro propped himself on an elbow. The room whirled and filled with divine light, spinning like a kaleidoscope. He licked his parched lips.

"Your Grace." The hands that lifted his head were strong but softer than the petals of roses. "Open your mouth. Drink slowly," celestial voices coached him as drops settled on his tongue and moistened his throat.

"Water," Alessandro sighed gratefully.

Each hand pulled a blue flask, the glass more brilliant than lapis lazuli, and filled a spoon with a dark, aromatic liquid, gently trickling in the potion. He tried to focus. The hands merged.

"Your Grace"—the voices also became one—"a few more drops!"

Alessandro's face softened. His breathing strengthened. He opened his eyes for the first time in days, only to imagine himself on Olympus, for his Venus stood beside his bed.

The tall woman looked at him with a compassion absent in the women who flattered him and seduced him without sharing their hearts, their faces forgotten by him—had it not been for the children they bore.

"Who are you?" Alessandro demanded, examining a hint of Moorish blood in her face.

"My name is Monna Rebecca, Your Grace," the maiden replied and bowed. "I brought an elixir of life which has cured His Eminence."

She looked at him, suddenly timid before this man who ruled the church and Rome, confused, not in charge. That much she knew. Nothing else was clear, except for the cardinal staring at her, thinking that she must be the loveliest woman in the world.

A tinge of carmine stippled her cheeks.

"Apelles was said to have created the perfect image of woman," Alessandro recalled. "He took the most beautiful features of many and fashioned them together on vellum, as God created Eve. But this woman is real." Fully conscious now, he was drawn to the unknown maiden, who seemed so reluctant to meet his glance.

Rebecca sensed a new kind of fever as she straightened his covers. She stepped away and hid her hands behind her back. Never had she been truly interested in men, too plain, too tame, without spirit. She knew girls married for propriety and security, dying without knowing love. But, she refused to be one.

Then there was the prophecy at her birth. And Monna Chiara's reading.

"Monna Rebecca. How can I thank you?" the cardinal asked and smiled encouragingly.

As her eyes finally met Alessandro's, a wave of heat flushed down her breasts and left her disarmed. Stupidly she stared at the short, curly hair framing his neck, wanting to press her face against it. The indignity of such an urge threw her emotions under a spell.

She fought her fate, not knowing that he was fighting his as well.

Alessandro wondered what moved him. Her beauty? But beauty, as he knew too well, was transient. His smile broadened, filling his gaunt face with joy. Could it be the beauty of her soul?

She smiled back.

"Come closer, daughter."

Rebecca's knees buckled as he raised himself to see her better.

A blush darkened her face fully, and for the first time in his life he wondered whether the foolish emotions he called love were real.

Neither had known such feelings, beyond a poet's dream. Their emotions captured them instantly, completely. He wanted to reach out and touch her but hesitated, infected by her shyness. Instead, he pointed to the flask.

"And where do you take the authority to prepare such potions?"

She wanted to tell him about knowing Latin and Greek, but modesty ruled.

"Begging your pardon, Monsignor, but father reads books."

Alessandro studied the color of her skin. "Who, pray, is your father, Monna Rebecca?"

"Ephrahim Ben Shuham di Ferrara, an apothecary in *platea judea*. Our people live there."

As she pointed, her body arched. He could not remember when a woman had ignited his loins so forcefully. So the old devil in him was still alive.

"*Platea judea?*" he asked, looking past her, taking the meaning in with a new breath.

"Yes, Your Grace. It is not far from the river and here. Your Grace … " She reached out but drew back quickly, resisting the urge to touch.

So she was just a pretty Jewess. Has he not heard of her father? The family must have gained special status under Pius V's predecessor, since apparently they walked freely, unmarked by an ugly yellow badge. But Alessandro knew how Pius hated Jews.

He cleared his throat to regain command. "But your elixir is far from ordinary!"

"It is," she replied, and having regained her strength, raised herself without permission. "Herodotus wrote that the mastic found in the stomachs of goats and sheep, kneaded and suspended in an extract of orchids and half a dram of musk and amber, produces a physic which cheers up ill humor and fortifies the brain."

Why was she telling him that? Alessandro wondered.

"Your Grace, my elixir also instills the heart with love of life."

She was so exquisite that Alessandro could not stop staring. Beside, he had never had a Jewish woman. He closed his eyes as her cool hand rested on his forehead and quickly opened them again. "Tell me," he asked, "how did you come to be here, in the first place?"

"Monna Chiara's ill." She backed away, leaving the scent of jasmine lingering. "I'm your new *fioraia*."

† † †

The Farnese courtyard pulsed with activity.

A long row of oxcarts shifted as each loaded wagon turned about, heading for the Via Recta and the papal town of Viterbo. The majordomo presided over the organized turmoil from the shade of the arcade.

He marked tasks completed on a scroll, sure that nothing was lacking at the cardinal's summer villa at Caprarola. Chests of tapestries, coverlets, blankets, and other household items weighed each wagon that joined the train.

Alessandro stood by his study window, absorbed in thought, gaunt, his robust frame barely filling the drooping robes, his olive complexion pale, marked by illness.

Duties of office prevented him from leaving at once for his summer residence. The entire day before he held a tiring audience to resolve the most pressing matters, ending the day in the asylum of his bed.

One further matter remained. For that he awaited the General of the Jesuit order, the proud Don Francisco de Borgia, Duke of Gandia and descendant of the powerful Borgia pope.

"I should treat him with respect," he reminded himself. "If *nonno's* sister hadn't slept with his great-grandfather, *nonno* would not have worn the papal tiara nor I my cardinal's biretta. I was fourteen and barely knew Latin and Greek!"

Side by side in his study hung the portraits of two beauties, Giulia Farnese, who slept with Pope Alexander VI Borgia, and the enchanting Silvia who kept his grandfather's bed warm. He stared at them as they changed into a single, immediate image, troubling his thoughts.

The door creaked, and he turned to face a visitor, wishing to get this over quickly.

"Don Francisco," he said stiffly, knowing precisely why the General came. "Money's not the issue. I've been disputing with Don Altieri about his land for four years. His stubbornness stands in the way of my … ahem … our grand vision of a new Jesuit church. Monsignore, are you listening to me?"

Don Francisco gazed at the portraits. "Lovely, wasn't she?" He pointed to Giulia Farnese.

The cardinal nodded agreement, bent on his course. "Where were we? Yes. If Padre Tristano is unable to follow my orders, I'll use my architect. God bless your cause."

"And yours. *Reverendissimo signor padrone mio, vester servus humilis,*" the Jesuit replied and bowed out, wondering how many more years before his vision would come true.

Alessandro sighed and rang. He was almost finished at last. An aide appeared.

"We wish to have a word with our new artist, the painter from Antwerp."

"I saw him talking to Don Fulvio about half an hour ago, Excellency. I'll find him. Immediately." The padre understood his superior's gesture.

Alessandro leaned out the window.

The heat was intolerable, yet he welcomed it, feeling the chill of the stone in his feet. The air was as insufferable as the city at times, but Rome was bound to his heart. Every summer he was glad to leave it and content to return in the fall, as he had done every year since he returned to Rome from exile twelve years ago. He hated to think about that time when his *nonno* died and the new pope confiscated all his benefices. He and his brother fled Rome as their family struggled to survive.

Calfskin shoes padded gently across the floor. Was it Rebecca? As he turned, a head of black curls briefly bowed over his hand.

"Bartolomeo." Alessandro quickly revived in the presence of the painter to whom he was drawn on the night of the last banquet. Dark locks over chiseled brows framed the look of a person who demanded his way. Luminous eyes sparkled with life, like Lago di Bracciano at the height of a storm. But when the sun finally descended on the lake, painting it golden-green, the waters mellowed, just like the young man before him.

Alessandro cocked his head. "But for his Flemish nose, he could be Apollo's twin," he thought, amused.

"I've heard great praises from Padre Bernardo of your new fresco," he said.

"I am deeply honored, Your Grace," Berti replied humbly. Although he had been in Italy less than a year, his fine training helped introduce him to Don Giulio, Alessandro's miniaturist who arranged for him to paint the *Last Supper* in the cardinal's church in San Oreste.

By the glow of an oil lamp, he sketched local men as he remembered them at the long table in the tavern—discussing politics, new crops, family life, exclaiming and gesticulating—perfect models for his apostles. Awed, the people of San Oreste knelt before the powerful fresco in which the apostles, men like themselves, came to life.

"Come closer." The command was sharp, but the eyes welcoming.

Why was he so frightened? After all, Archbishop Massimi liked his work.

Before he crossed the Alps, Berti had never made a big decision in his nineteen years. He could have come to Rome as the son of a flourishing merchant and the gentleman he was, but he was still naive. More than once he found his money pouch empty because he trusted people. Then his luck changed, and he could hardly believe he stood before the great art patron.

"Tell me something, for I like your work. Why do your apostles look so real?"

"Eminence, they are but the men in the town—the blacksmith, the shoemaker, and … "

"Son, do you realize that your method may be seen as blasphemous?" the cardinal exclaimed, surprised. A hedonist at heart, he followed norms.

"A thousand pardons, but Peter was a fisherman, Paul a soldier, and Matthew a tax-monger. As for the figure of Our Lord—he came from my heart, as only he could inspire me."

"But how can you be certain you painted the true Christ?"

"God moves my hand. That's how it is, Your Grace. I spent days praying for your recovery, but I also made some sketches for you." He pulled sheets from a folder, charcoal drawings, sketches, and finished studies.

"Where did you learn to draw so well?" his patron asked him, studying with pleasure the familiar road to San Oreste and to Caprarola, the site of his new country villa, the walled town propped high in the background of one of the drawings. "You did this so clearly and precisely from memory? That's extraordinary."

He turned to another sketch. In it stenciled brows crowned a boy's delicate face.

"And this, is it also from memory?" the cardinal asked, staring at the face of his son.

"Yes, Your Grace," Berti responded unassumingly.

The cardinal then asked, "Do you know?"

Berti's entire career rested on his answer.

It seemed as if he had first met Alessandro Farnese only the day before. It was in Caprarola, and his new patron was standing in his

Black curls framed Berti's face.

(Page 9)

Map of Rome in the 1560s.

ST. PETER'S
BORGO
PALACE
VIA GIULIA
VIA dei BANCHI VECCHI
VIA dei BANCHI NUOVI
HOSPITAL OF SANTO SPIRITO
PIAZZA PAOLA
TOR DI NONA
NAVONA
S. M. dell' ANIMA
CASTEL SANT ANGELO
PORTO
VIA RIPETTA
TIBER
M. AUGUSTUS
VIA RECTA
VIA TRINITATIS
SS. TRINITA Dei MONTI
S. M. del POPOLO
SAN FELICE

Alessandro's wine jug was empty.

Come closer, daughter.

(Page 18)

Alessandro stood in his winter garden.

(Page 22)

Rebecca wore a white camicia and golden gamurra.

(Page 25)

Alessandro kissed the statue of Venus.

(Page 29)

winter garden, bathed in light. Berti bowed, but Alessandro ignored him and turned toward Don Alfonso, the little boy from the sacristy at San Oreste where Berti had painted frescoes in the church, meeting him half-way, his cape trailing in the thawing snow. Picking the boy up, the cardinal threw the boy high into the air.

"*Padre zio!* Father Uncle!" the boy addressed the cardinal confusingly, the *father* referring both to his clerical title and, unwittingly, to his paternity. He screamed with delight, rubbing his nose into the silvering beard. "Look, Berti made this horse for me, and he's my best friend!" he shrieked into Alessandro's ear with the urgency of a child receiving rare attention.

Standing there, watching the two, Berti compared their faces and two sets of penciled brows and vibrant eyes. Astounded, he solved the riddle that puzzled him since he first came to San Oreste and befriended the seemingly fatherless boy.

"Do I know?" Berti nodded in response, afraid to look up. "I believe so, Eminence."

Alessandro was impressed. He cupped Berti's chin in his hand and raised his face.

"Virtue is a gift from heaven," he said, "being also endowed by the Grace. How would you like to enter my service, signor *pittore*, serving me and Our Lord as I see fit? You'll live in the Cancelleria or wherever I choose and have a monthly stipend of four *scudi*. Agreed?"

Trembling with excitement, Berti could barely answer. Such fortune appeared too good for anyone, much less an unknown foreigner. But had he not slaved for meager wages, painting frescoes in Parma and decorating Archbishop Massimi's bathroom in Rome? Had he not been poor for too long? Now he had proved himself. He had earned the trust.

"Most Reverend Excellency, I beg you to keep my drawings as a meager and truly insignificant token of my boundless gratitude." Having found the right words, he spilled forth superlatives which surprised him and satisfied his new patron.

"*Il fiammingo.*" Alessandro caught him backing toward the door. "See Don Fulvio about a contract! Tomorrow we leave for Caprarola." And having already heard about Berti's love for his son and his fatherly role, Alessandro whispered, "My boy's honorary *papà*."

When Berti first came to San Oreste, he met Monna Brunella, the boy's nanny with a bosom like the Milky Way. But she did not understand why Don Alfonso became ill after she weaned him. Only when Berti fed him a mush of grains and boiled water sweetened with honey did the child begin to trot again around the yard with rosy cheeks, riding his new stick pony that Berti made from *papier mâché*. With a mane and tail of sheep yarn, it looked real, scaring all the chickens and the sacristan's dog.

Berti recalled the boy's chatter. "Totti, tell me about Ercole. I want to be big and strong like him. No, I want to be like you. You are my *papà,* aren't you? Every boy has a father."

Don Alfonso won Berti's heart quickly. He loved Berti's stories and his affectionate embrace. Berti shuddered now, remembering how he nearly died, like Brunella's baby. Had it not been for the red berries that old Cecchino gave him to prepare an elixir …

"*Ave Maria, gratia plena.* Mother of God, protect the little boy, now and forever. Amen."

Berti finished his rosary, for the memory still conjured fear. And Berti owed much more to the old plasterer who taught him how to lay the daily base for a fresco without making it flower and crack. Each day the three of them met in the church while Berti worked and Cecchino talked about the great Titian whom he knew when he was young in Venice.

Now Berti was to see them both again, as soon as he could settle into the servants' quarters of the cardinal's villa in Caprarola. He was ecstatic.

Servus Domini

The following morning a long, colorful cortege left the palace, headed by the cardinal's personal cavalcade of high-ranking servants and clerks and ending with a gaggle of stable boys, extra horses, and mules carrying provisions. The caravan trailed northward, passing through streets lined with Romans eager for a spectacle.

Alessandro rode in a private carriage with Farnese insignia, leaning forward, searching for Rebecca. He peered through red velvet curtains that barely moved in the static air but saw only lines of peasants, pilgrims, soldiers, and priests, arguing and pushing for the best view.

With each day, the image of the mysterious Jewish maiden haunted him increasingly. She fired his senses still and beckoned him to become their slave. Forty-seven summers sat on Alessandro's shoulders, but they had not brought him the wisdom he lacked during his youth in the arms of desirable women.

Rebecca's image now occupied him constantly, without reason or mercy.

Finally he saw her, standing on a gray stone by the sunlit façade of the Palazzo Sforza, away from the crowd. She wore a white *camicia* and golden *gamurra*. Her black hair tied in plaits danced about her chiseled features, and she held a branch of jasmine. Her Moorish eyes searched the procession for Alessandro's chair. Their glances met, and he caught their longing before the cortege rambled on through the city, passing through the city gate without stopping.

Rebecca dawdled, torn by an urge to pass by the Farnese Palace. She did not come to sell flowers to the crowd. The vision of a helpless, ill man brought her, even though she knew that he may never need her again. She was not a gentile, and the cardinal aspired to the papal throne. She battled her feelings, looking north, imagining the cardinal's standards fluttering in the air as the cavalcade crossed the Tiber on the Milvian Bridge.

Alessandro's mind was also troubled. He rested on the plump cushions, listening to the clatter of the horses on the cobbled Via Cassia and the guards' steady chatter.

Annoyed by the occasional bounce, he played with the golden tassels hanging from the drapes, his pious thoughts colored by the memory of Rebecca's alluring body. The dream of unlacing her linen *camicia* and replacing it with a cloth fit for a queen vexed him for the rest of the journey.

By the time the cortege approached Monte Scimino by Caprarola, the day was past compline, and the cloudless sky had lost its sanguine streaks. The trip was long, for Alessandro refused to ride far in his horse-drawn carriage and changed often to the litter-chair. Even there, his constitution protested the jolts of the powerful runners. But he was determined to reach the villa without an overnight stop.

As night set in, the June sky seemed as if lit by the Northern Lights. Starlight met the torches, candles, tapers, and oil lamps and cast deep shadows against the crumbling façades of the houses, the leaning fences, and the tired faces of the townsfolk, who waited for hours for the arrival of their lord and master. Here and there the sharp call of an owl answered the distant cry of wolves and the wailing of infants, suddenly awakened by the cheering crowd as the procession snaked up the path toward the town and the villa.

Later, Alessandro stood in his dressing room, his nose filled with the smoke of ceremonial musket fire, listening to the bagpipes, trombones, and trumpets, aware that few mortals witnessed such pomp, but just wanting to sleep.

Berti, riding at the mid-point of the procession and followed by other servants, was stunned by the journey's grand finale. As they approached the first terrace below the fortress, a façade opened up, mounting high toward heaven, with huge arrow-headed bastions pivoted on the corners. The beauty of the five-bay loggia marked by elegant Ionic pilasters ablaze with colorful banners was beyond anything he had ever seen.

The first night he shared a room with a tailor in the top floor quarters, spending it in the window seat overlooking the valley, peeking through the slits in the shutters into the star-lit town below. Nestled tightly against the cool wall, he waited for dawn to color the air. Nothing, absolutely nothing he envisioned, could disturb his state of bliss.

† † †

Alessandro's court took days to settle at Caprarola as work continued on the interior decorations. The process was slow, and Alessandro found the details trying. But he felt better, and his voice reverberated throughout the villa, as he met with papal legates and noblemen.

Each morning, after saying the first Mass, he paused in the room of the Farnese Deeds, where frescoes depicted his ancestors as the guardians of Christendom. He had himself painted negotiating with the mightiest sovereigns on the continent, promoting Christian ideals and glorifying Holy Mother Church, hoping that was how he would be remembered.

It was one of those days in mid-summer when the azure of the sky reigns supreme, and the sun's scorching rays crisp the ground. A siesta in the coolness of his summer apartment was what he needed. As the evening set in, the wood's moist chill signaled a pleasant change.

"Padre Carlo!"

"Your Grace?" His aide stood far enough to preserve his *padrone's* privacy and yet close enough to respond. Colored by fresh country air, his pasty face looked surprisingly cheerful.

"I've been thinking about paradise," Alessandro mused aloud. "Do our deeds on earth merit such compensation?"

"Excellency?"

"You have my permission to leave your post."

"Excellency?"

"I wish to take a stroll in the woods. Alone."

"*Però, signore* … wild animals … vandals … you cannot … "

"Cannot?!"

"Begging your pardon, Your Grace, is it not unwise?"

"You have a point. Should I change my mind, I'll ring for you."

In minutes, Alessandro found the overgrown path to the virginal land where he wanted formal gardens some day. Treading carefully, he was accompanied by a flock of wild ducks overhead. The occasional barking of his dogs broke the silence.

"Oh, my Lord, to be alone with You!"

He breathed in the evening moisture. His ears, accustomed to city clatter, ached with the silence of small sounds, the croaking of frogs, the rasping of insects, broken by a splash in the brook. Every time the dogs dove in, the silvery shadows were gone.

Alessandro found a clearing, sat on a split trunk covered with moss and vines, content to exist in his small paradise. The dogs dropped by his feet, their noses trembling with occasional wheezes. He sat, listening to the calls of the forest, the wind playing with his hair.

Across from him, a bush moved and a pair of black eyes appeared. Slowly the branches parted, and a doe stood calmly in the clearing. Stunned, Alessandro heard her calling him with the words of the Song of Solomon: "A dark girl I am, but comely, oh you daughters of Jerusalem … Do not look at me because I am swarthy, because the sun has caught sight of me."

Bewildered, he looked around and answered, "Look, you are beautiful, girl companion. Your eyes are those of doves. Like a lily among thorny weeds, so is my girl."

A branch cracked, and the dogs raced yowling after the creature, but Rebecca's presence still hovered over the empty clearing, her voice seeking him out: "I have sought the one whom my soul has loved, but I did not find him."

And he responded, "Come with me, my bride. Come to the land of lilies."

Startled by the sound of his voice, he looked around, caught by the memory of the vision. The stillness of the woods surrounded him, the dusk molding heavily around his shoulders.

Finally rising, he ran, slowly at first and then faster, without caution, following the path to the villa, pushing against the stray branches which struck his face and left angry marks on his cheeks. They snapped back like furies pursuing his conscience, whipping in the rising wind and beckoning him to return to the land of his lost paradise. When the villa's garden façade emerged, Alessandro slowed to smooth his hair, wipe his face, and regain control.

Entering the villa, he hurried to the service staircase to the underground floor where he picked up a lantern and strode on. Having found the door he sought, he inserted a large key hidden in the folds of his tunic, entered, and locked it, leaving the key in place.

The soft light of his lantern danced over the body of Venus, brought there from the city, coloring her flesh pink and gold. She stood bound to her plinth, the reattached arm protecting her breasts. Setting the lantern down, he stepped forward to meet her gaze and with one motion, pressed his lips to hers. Her lips tinted the carmine of his blood.

"Rebecca! My love and my damnation!"

He remained only briefly. Locking the door again, he marched to his apartment and rang the bell firmly. The padre appeared instantly.

"Padre Carlo, seek out our new painter, Bartolomeo. He's to depart for Rome. At dawn. Tell him," he said, suddenly unsure, "I wish to see him after dinner."

Once alone again, Alessandro took the silver crucifix that hung at his side and, kissing it passionately, cried out, "Lamb of God, who takest away the sins of the world, have mercy upon us. Have mercy on me, for the day of my judgment is near, wretched sinner that I am."

† † †

Long before the sun bathed the hills around Caprarola, two horsemen sped along the path toward Via Cassia. The steeds were fresh, their bodies stretching forward with the resilience of the finest of their species, speeding toward Rome.

Their riders were a peculiar pair. A young peasant in a plain dun-colored *camicia* hanging casually over cotton britches sat the gray horse. An older, bearded Jesuit rode the chestnut. As the city drowsed in noonday heat, they approached the gates at Santa Maria del Popolo and roused the guards from their game of cards.

"Padre, what's your hurry?" The fat-bellied man wiped his moustache with a hairy arm, reluctant to part with his half-filled tankard. "Ay, fellows, come and see our holy man. I bet he can't wait to visit the Borgo!"

The two men waited patiently.

"Seriously, padre," the guard demanded, "how go matters with these stallions? They don't fit the likes of you. What might you be doing with them?"

The peasant leaned forward and produced the papers. Soon the bored guards returned to their posts and a new game.

The shadows were short and the city deserted. Even the cats and dogs hung back in the shady overpasses. The horses' hoofs clattered with urgency as the riders neared Palazzo Farnese, only to find it barred.

"His Excellency is not here." The window on the main portal remained half-shut in the travelers' noses. "He's in Caprarola."

"But he isn't," the peasant claimed adamantly.

"Get your face from this door before I call the guards!" the watchman cried.

The Jesuit shoved a cardinal's signet ring under the man's nose. Swiftly, the portal creaked open, admitting the riders to the asylum of the deserted courtyard.

"Have our horses looked after," Alessandro commanded, "and find someone to look after me." To his companion, he added, "I'll expect you upstairs."

The palace, stripped of tapestries taken to Caprarola, looked forlorn. "What am I doing here? I am a painter, not a confidante," Berti wondered for the thousandth time, meandering through a sleeping palace.

They had spoken little. Alessandro burned with a fever different from that caused by the spider bite. He was kind to Berti, bought him a fine meal, but himself hardly ate. Tension hung in the air, but Berti had no idea what his *padrone* wanted.

"At your service," he called outside Alessandro's bedroom.

"Enter!" the cardinal commanded in a voice that sounded surprisingly rested.

In the middle of the room stood a copper vessel, its back high like a sleigh. His Eminence sat in a pool of tepid water, his head on a cushion, next to him a stable boy waving a large feather.

"Barnabo, another goblet and another bottle. Quick! And you, Bartolomeo, sit." He pointed to a chair. "Tell me if you're happy in my service. But first, where do you come from?"

Berti wondered why he asked. Petty details hardly concerned the Farnese cardinal, but then Berti did not understand Alessandro's liking for him and his apparent need to build a bridge between them.

"I am Flemish," he began, somewhat uncertain, "and my family comes from Antwerp. My father is a merchant. He passed many days in the Eternal City. When I finished the apprenticeship with my master, papà resolved to send me here."

"*Capisco*," Alessandro responded, "but you haven't answered my first question."

Berti's Italian was far from perfect, but there was more to the story.

"*Eccelenza*," he responded, "I don't know what you want. I kiss your hands, and I remain your obedient servant, most happy in your service."

Barnabo appeared at the door. Alessandro motioned to Berti and nodded. "Since we finally understand each other well … "

Berti took the wine from the servant and returned, ready to pour. "*Signore,* how might I serve you? Command me, and I'll do anything you say, willingly!"

Alessandro scratched his head. "I've come to *Roma* on business. A personal business. In Caprarola"—he shifted in the bath—"I told you I wanted new miniature portraits of those in my family who are closest to my heart. I still want them, but not before you paint another picture."

Berti bowed. "Your obedient servant *sempre, signore.*"

"A woman saved my life. I hardly know her, or she me, but I … "

"So that's who she is," Berti thought. People in the palace whispered for some time about Alessandro's miraculous recovery. Berti's pulse livened as he topped Alessandro's goblet.

"This woman is beautiful, and Our Lord has enriched her with wisdom."

"*Capisco.*" What else was he to say? What else could he say? He faced a man who hoped to succeed the frail pontiff. This man was interested in a woman?

The room was tranquil. Occasional splashes echoed against the floor.

"The water's cold! Get me my robe!" Alessandro said with sudden anger, stepping out of the tub, leaving a puddle on the stone revetment. Berti moved quickly, for a tremor shook his patron despite the heat.

Wrapping himself tightly with an unexpected blank stare, the cardinal began to speak.

"Bartolomeo, much against my wisdom and calling, and against my better judgment, I want to see that woman. And I need your help."

"As you command," Berti replied, his face blank. He was stunned.

"Do you dare to judge me?" Alessandro walked back, forcing Berti to look at him.

"I confess to being confused," Berti admitted.

"I want you to be my friend," Alessandro told him.

"But, Excellency, you've already been like a father to me."

Berti actually felt a far greater attraction to the cardinal, who was about the same age as his father, than Alessandro did for him. Alessandro Farnese was married to Mother Church as much as his father was tied to his mother. For either man to sin with another woman was not fitting. But Berti needed Alessandro more than his father. *Il gran cardinale* could help his career.

"Be my brother, Berti." Alessandro implored him, pacing the room like a caged animal. "I'm sure that some day I will come to understand myself. Meanwhile what I want you to do is to go to *platea judea* well before vespers. Seek out Ephrahim Ben Shuham di Ferrara. You shouldn't find it difficult to locate his shop."

Alessandro looked away from the crucifix above the bed.

"Your Grace?"

"The apothecary is the young woman's father. Ask his permission. Yes, do that. Speak with his daughter and have her come to me under cover of dark." His coarse voice died abruptly. "And Bartolomeo, we rely on your discretion."

"*Servus.*"

"You do serve me and well. Now, let me make my own reckoning."

"Yes, Your Grace." Berti left dazed. The address of the apothecary rattled in his head, bouncing off the palace walls: "*Platea judea, platea judea, platea judea.* Lord, have mercy. She's a Jewess." The truth struck him square. "How can I face You on the day of my judgment, if I am to be the cardinal's instrument?"

Under his father's roof, Berti heard nothing about Jews. The proper gentleman guarded his talk, especially before his wife. But he warned Berti to stay away from them. "They're different," he said. "That's all."

Berti had no idea what his father meant. Long before vespers Berti left through the back gate toward the river. The heat was so oppressive that he turned back into town, seeking the silhouette of the old synagogue. He was not sure if it still stood. He had heard that it burned.

Ripa judeorum, the Jewish ghetto, was quiet, and he felt strange entering it. The area centered on an odd collection of banking houses whose owners tainted their reputation by lending money at interest. Living quarters leaned one against another, and dirty ruins of classical Rome, where people kept to themselves, clustered around the church and Piazza del Pianto.

Berti saw no one.

Long lines of clothes flapped in the breeze that rose occasionally from the river, eventually finding its way into the squalid corners where sunlight was rare. He found the shop in a large square not far from the church, but the doors were locked. A goat tethered to a ring bleated in response to his knock. Finally a window opened above the shop, and a tousled gray head with sinewy jaws and pigeon eyes appeared.

"Messer Ephrahim Ben Shuham?"

"Who wants to know?"

"I bear an important message for your daughter."

"I've no daughter for the likes of you," the apothecary cried and slammed the shutters.

"Maybe the old man has a point," Berti sighed, wondering what to do next. "I wish I were, but I am not bold enough to lecture another man about his sins. Certainly not my powerful master." Going around the corner, he waited, sitting with his back against the crumbling plaster and picking at the dry weeds in the cracked walls. When the shadows lengthened, he tried the shop door and found it open.

"Please, *messere ebreo,* help a miserable messenger. That's all I am," Berti said to the Jewish apothecary, a shriveled man with a surprisingly strong gait, and handed over a sealed envelope. "I've been commanded to give this to your daughter. I must wait for her answer."

A scruffy parrot sat on the apothecary's shoulder, ruffling its feathers to the sound of the young man's voice. It flapped its clipped wings, lifting a bit, and dropped back.

"Must wait! Answer, answer, cah, cah!" it screeched like a broken clock.

"Is it possible that all men were created by God alike?" Berti mused.

The Jew took the note and vanished into the rear. The sun shone obliquely across the river, bathing the walls of the shop in amber. The dusty flasks on the shelves glistened, casting an aura of mystery over the labels carefully inscribed in the Jewish tongue. People marked by the yellow badge came in, waited a while in the empty shop, and left.

"If Pius had his way," Berti thought, "he would purge the city of Jews and whores alike. They're a curious lot. If they'd cut their hair like Christians and change their attire and their tongue, they might even be like us." He stared at each visitor. Was it truly possible that God created all men alike? He could not fathom how Alessandro, after the pope the holiest man on earth, could bed a woman like those he saw in the shop.

Standing by the entrance of the shop, looking at the darkening sky, trying to make sense of the few clouds hovering over the river, aware of someone approaching, he turned and stared, shocked at the newcomer.

Monna Rebecca, unlike most Roman women, was tall, regal, and swarthy. She stood there composed, clutching Alessandro's crumpled letter. Berti stepped back, his gaze embracing her figure, aware that few women are born to such beauty.

"Don Bartolomeo," she addressed him calmly. "That is your name?"

Berti nodded, dumbfounded.

"Please, tell your master that I am honored by his invitation, but the custom of my people forbids me to respond." She paused, her eyes holding Berti's. Her lips opened and closed, battling to liberate feelings.

Suddenly he saw her with the eyes of a painter.

"I beg you to convey to His Grace that my decision does not come easily," she continued. "It was made long before he asked me to come."

Her logic was beyond him.

"I implore you, tell His Grace that I honor him, but I may not shame my parents, my family, and my people by leaving to join him."

"Monna Rebecca." Touched by her dignity, Berti tried to master his own confusion. "How can you profess such feelings? You hardly met His Grace. Not only do you not know him, but …

You are not Christian, he wanted to say, but the words would not come.

"But … you couldn't be attracted to him so quickly."

"It was said at my birth that a man will smite me with his love and that he will suffer for it. I never married for that reason. But His Eminence ... He's good-hearted and alone."

"Except he's not one of my kind," she thought, "and it would destroy my father's feelings." She paused and spun about.

"I'll wait for you by the river façade of Palazzo Farnese," Berti said, "when the bells toll compline and the dusk begins to settle. Here's your pass back into the ghetto, should you change your mind. Signorina *ebrea,* may the Lord guide you to the right choice."

But she was already gone.

Berti felt like a traitor. At the palace, he found Alessandro in his study.

"What news do you bring me, son of Hermes and Athena?"

"Your Grace, my heart breaks for not bringing you good tidings. Your fate is in God's hands. He will know how to answer your call. Your humble servant, Your Grace."

"You may be right," Alessandro responded, more to himself than to the young man who closed the door behind him. "Let the Lord decide. It's not for me to choose."

† † †

With Alessandro's note, Monna Rebecca lost her peace.

Since her flowers and salves were appreciated in many noble palaces in Rome, her world was often Christian, and she was comfortable with the ways of gentiles. But after she met Cardinal Farnese and saved his life, the encounter came to haunt her.

The pair is neither about love, nor about desire. It's about a connection that will lift you to heights few of us mortals will ever know. What did Monna Chiara's prophecy mean?

The star shines over the ill-fated lovers until death parts them? Destroys them?

She shook her head in frustration. "*Follia.* I sound like Boccaccio."

Fear paralyzed her. Yet on the eve of Sabbath, which brought her peace in the circle of her family, in the kitchen lit by the setting sun, Monna Rebecca slowly reached a new decision.

Through half-open shutters, one by one, lighted candles announced the advent of the Sabbath in the ghetto. Monna Tamarra, her mother, leaned across the window ledge above her husband's shop to check the sun's course. The walls of Messer Ephrahim's house, facing west toward the river, breathed the heat of the passing day. Below, the entrance to his shop was barred, and Monna Tamarra heard her husband's footsteps on the narrow staircase.

"Is the fire down and the kitchen swept?" She turned to Rebecca, putting the broom away.

"Honorable mother, everything is ready."

Monna Tamarra checked the horizon once more for the rapidly descending sun, hooked the shutters slightly ajar to let air pass through, and returned to the table.

She was still a woman with sparkle, although the toils of motherhood had marked her. Three of her children survived, her two daughters standing by, their hands folded for the traditional blessing offered by Jewish women since time immemorial, Rebecca with her mother's looks and her father's wisdom.

Monna Tamarra raised her candle toward heaven, set it into the holder, bowed her head, and began the prayer: "*Baruch ato adonai, elochenu melech holum.*" She lit the first of two candles for her husband, and in her eloquent communion with God, she asked him to bless her family with health, prosperity, and peace. Rebecca lit another candle for her mother and siblings and repeated after her mother, "Blessed be He, Lord, Our God, and King of the Universe."

The words pierced her conscience with fear. The eldest of Messer Ephrahim's children, she disappointed her father by being a girl. But none of the others gave him the joy his first-born did, and after Adonai, he loved her best. But tonight as the family gathered and Messer Ephrahim recited the traditional blessing, his face was constricted. Instead of breaking the bread and signaling the family to lift their heads, he said, "Bad times are falling on us, people of Zion. Pius and the Holy See scheme for our destruction. We must stand united, for alone like Jerusalem, the daughter of Zion, we shall fall."

Rebecca looked at her father, but he turned the pages of his book and began to read, his words drifting in and out of her mind, alternating with Alessandro's face. His lament overcame the table, creeping slowly into the mind of each member of the family, instilling a sense of doom.

"Oh, father, please don't judge me hard," Rebecca wept silently.

The meal was cold when the apothecary broke bread. Rebecca ate hardly anything and soon excused herself. In the room she shared with her sister, she sat on her straw pallet and pulled her knees up to her chin. Resting her head on the pine chest behind her, she broke into her own lament.

"Adonai, I call you, and you don't answer. You are holy and in you I trust. Forgive my trespasses, for I am but a worm you may crush." Then with the same breath she recited aloud, "Holy Virgin, please take me to your bosom. I love him, and I hope you understand."

She scribbled a note begging her parents' forgiveness, and when darkness descended, she crept out quietly without looking back.

Jewish Queen

Never before had the Jewish flower maiden walked the streets of Rome at night.

Never before did she dare leave the house after the Sabbath blessing. The streets of the ghetto were deserted and panic engulfed her. She hurried toward the Ducal Square in front of Palazzo Farnese, turning sharply into Via dei Farnesi toward the garden wall and then once more. It seemed to her that hours had passed since sundown. The long Via Giulia was empty.

Rebecca found the right gate, but only barking dogs greeted her. She stared at the dark mouth of the portal incredulously, realizing what she had done.

How could she have been so reckless? Without the cardinal's pass, she could not cross back into the ghetto after dark. She could not face her parents. Her note was final. Certainly her decision to embrace his faith was final. Her family's door was closed to her forever.

The palace gate was also shut. No friendly face greeted her. Thanatos laughed at her, beckoning her with his crooked finger. She stumbled across the paved street, ready for his dark embrace in the river. Only a few steps to the smelly, boggy Tiber.

A rat ran over her foot. She sprang away, stumbling over the root of a sycamore tree, and landed in the soft reeds by the water. The earth felt moist, comforting, and full of life.

"Wake up, you fool!" She sat up and slapped herself hard and again and began to cry.

"Don't just walk into the river. Think! You want to see him? Good. First, find shelter!"

Rebecca knew only of the house of Saint Martha which took in prostitutes. Desperate but more in control, she climbed up the bank and crossed back to Via Giulia. In the distance, a light glowed in front of the church of Saint Catherine of Siena. As she approached, a monk sitting on the steps against the closed portals freed himself from the shadows like a specter.

She feared strangers, but on that dark night he was her only hope. Timidly, her heart pounding so loudly in her chest that it nearly burst, she came closer. He looked at her, raised his lantern, and called out, "Blessed be the name of Jesus Christ!"

Rebecca crossed herself and responded, "Amen and peace be with you, Father."

"And also with you. What brings you here at a time when only scoundrels, robbers, and whores walk the streets?"

The torments of the night came out in one breath.

"Father, forgive me, for I have wronged my family. I left my people for a man who holds my affections," she blurted out and threw herself at the monk's feet, burying her face in the scratchy folds of his tunic. "But I came too late. Now I have nowhere to go,"

"That *is* a great sin. But who is this person for whom you have fallen so low?"

"I'm sorry. I can't tell you. His name must not cross my lips."

"Why has the young man abandoned you?" The monk placed his hand on her head.

"He's not so young. Like you?" She looked up into the monk's face but saw little.

"Forgive me. I meant as old as you are. That is, from the sound of your voice."

Suddenly she feared she might have revealed that Alessandro belonged to God, like the monk, but his hand was comforting. "Be it as it may," she sighed, "the fault is mine. I couldn't decide. When I did, I came too late." She lifted her face and hid it again in the monk's tunic.

"Sit by me and tell me what troubles you." His hand patted her back.

"Father, I am a Jewess. Perhaps now you might not want to talk to me."

The monk hardly moved. "And the man you love, does he belong to your people?"

"No," she paused, "he's a gentile."

"Our Lord's ways are mysterious. Can you truly give yourself and profess His religion?"

"I believe I can. I want to. Otherwise I wouldn't have come."

"Why did you do this?" he suddenly asked in a stern voice. "For if you try to benefit from your choice falsely, you'll be damned."

"Father, long ago the ways of your Lord and His holy mother spoke to me, and I wanted to become a Christian. But I could not find the right path to reach Him."

A group of noblemen passed Via Giulia headed north and turned the corner toward the thriving houses of prostitution. They raised their lanterns high, illuminating the pair on the steps, their rude calls echoing in Rebecca's ears, "Signorina, make sure first his pouch is full!"

She covered her ears, but the monk slipped her hands down.

"Daughter, do you really love him as you have just told me?"

"I do, as the Holy Virgin the Mother of God is my witness."

The monk picked up a lily and laid it in her lap.

"A virgin flower for the fairest of virgins from the lord of Farnese lands to his beloved."

The cowl dropped from the monk's head as he reached for her hand. Rebecca jerked away, stunned by the cruel joke, but the monk held her.

"Rebecca, I am Alessandro Farnese!"

She would have been less surprised if Diana came down in her chariot on a moonbeam, since she had given up on seeing the cardinal. She pulled hard, fighting him, wanting to stay, wanting to flee. On the verge of yielding, the arm around her released its grip.

"Go. You're free to go!"

"Forgive me, Your Grace. I beg you. I don't know what I'm doing." She collapsed in submission, sobbing. His arm circled her waist again, firmly and yet more gently than before. For a brief moment, their faces met, bodies touched, rose to a spark, and then parted.

"Shall we walk?" Alessandro pointed to the Tiber.

Rebecca only nodded. His arm was comforting, and she wiped her father's image from her thoughts. Each step was easier as she felt new warmth surge through her body. They followed a path to the river and stood on its bank, watching the last lights on the other side.

"Have you ever been across the river in the house that once belonged to Messer Chigi?" The cardinal broke the silence, pointing to the dark structure behind a high wall.

"Your Grace, I haven't."

"The divine Raphael immortalized his mistress in that villa where the painted gods now feast in perpetuity in the loggia. It is mine now." Alessandro paused, peering through the vapor rising from the stagnant waters. Suddenly he wanted to take her there and join the gods in the joy of having found her. When he spoke again, ardor tinged his voice.

"You are more charming than Galatea painted on the walls of my villa, more breathtaking than my Venus, much lovelier than Aurora, the fresh dawn that greets each day." Alessandro raised his lamp to her face, but the night was dark and the oil running low. Rebecca shivered.

Alessandro spread his cowl around her shoulders and his own, feeling her hips close to his. She was nearly as tall as he, and they walked toward the palace in the eloquent understanding of feelings between them. The dogs fell silent as Alessandro inserted his key into the back gate. In the garden, God's servant pulled his goddess to himself, and kissed her virginal forehead.

† † †

The palace was dark. Rebecca followed Alessandro through the endless corridors and staircases, as if she had never been there before. She dared not lift her head for fear her cloak would fall and reveal her identity to the few guards stirring. Even when Alessandro picked up a second lantern from one of them and the walls brightened, she felt lost. Finally they paused at his chambers. Fear of the unknown almost stifled her.

He closed the door behind, softly, but the sound reverberated in her ears with the finality of her choice. She faced it, afraid to turn and look at the bed where she once nursed her patient.

Alessandro removed the cloak and embraced her, feeling her warmth, his face lost in her hair. He aligned his legs with hers, leg to leg, rib to rib, breast to breast, knowing once again the joy and closeness of a woman, breathing her scent, lingering in it, inhaling in tranquility.

He walked to the bed, took the scarlet cloth that lay on the pillows, and covered the crucifix overhead. He watched her, wondering where his mind had been when he imagined that the new Venus resembled this precious being. Like an Amazon with her head tilted high she was, hair cascading down her back.

Alessandro moved closer, reluctant to break the mystery of her presence and whispered, "I don't wish to hurt you."

"I understand, Your Grace," she muttered.

"Rebecca!" he cried. "Call me by my name!"

She stared. "Oh, Virgin Mary, give me strength," she muttered to herself inaudibly.

"I love you. And may God forgive me my sins," he replied, beginning to unlace her *camicia,* untying the waistband of her tunic, leaving the clothing in a soft heap.

She stood as he left her, watching him light the candles. As the radiance about her increased, so did his passion. Years of training and self-control restrained the thirsty pilgrim, having discovered his spring. He now desired to drink from it slowly, almost wishing that the moment of his fulfillment would never come.

By the light of the candles, his living Venus took his hand and led him to Titian's *Penitent Magdalen.* Here Rebecca found her voice.

"Do you think I am like her? Do you want me to be like her?"

"Psh! The guards have ears." Alessandro laughed, as he had not for a long time, while she sat him on the bed and removed his sandals. Bringing the water basin, she washed his feet, and then dried them as the Magdalen had Christ's, with her abundant hair.

"Yes, you are like her," he said, pulling her closer as he kissed the hollow of her shoulder. "An image which men like me shouldn't keep on their walls."

"My Lord. Forgive me! Alessandro, who is the woman in that picture?"

She pointed to Titian's Danaë, her knees wide, awaiting Zeus.

"I'll tell you about her another time," he replied, laying her gently in the bed. Striking the pose of Danaë, she smiled and asked, "Am I as beautiful as she?"

He knelt by her. "More beautiful than chaste Diana, more striking than proud Juno, and infinitely lovelier than Aphrodite, you are my Jewish queen."

Rebecca understood. She wanted him, but her body went rigid, fearing the unknown. Alessandro descended to her, first feeling her ripe breasts, their points driving him insane, kissing every spot between them down through her tufted virginity to her toes. She mellowed, slowly, tingling with pleasure, responding to his lips burning her skin.

He pulled himself back up and kissed her, tasting her lips, moving his tongue around their fullness, then more searchingly. She learned to respond to his game, to return his caresses as her body softened under his. When he thrust his tongue deep into her mouth, her electrified body met his, willingly and passionately, with no need to cover her mouth when he pierced her. Her eyes mirrored the pain of her fulfillment.

"I love you, Alessandro," she barely whispered, overcome by joy.

He groaned as they moved together like one, the cardinal and his Jewish queen, fighting the battle of love, giving and taking, returning and returning. Neither God nor time could make them stop. As the stars broke over the canopied bed, neither the proud servant of God nor his humble woman regretted their decision.

"Alessandro?" Rebecca blew out the candle and laid her face against his warm abdomen.

"Yes, my queen?"

"I also want to love Christ."

"Lord, have mercy," the exhausted man sighed.

"You belong to God, Alessandro," she insisted. "You can never be fully mine! I too want to belong to Christ. I want to be a Christian."

"Lord, your ways are inscrutable. You give me a mistress, and then you take her away."

"I will always be yours. Remember my words some day," she said and fell asleep.

Alessandro studied her face. "You *are* more beautiful than my Venus," he whispered, "and you make me happier than all the riches my grandfather bestowed on me." He watched the candles burn low, and as the dawn streaked the skies and she rolled over, he could not resist the curve of her spine.

Moving closer, he breathed the scent of the oil in her hair and pressed his lips against her skin. She awoke willing, and when their cup overflowed, the sun's first rays descending on the city found Rebecca high on the pillows, her head against the foot of the covered crucifix. In the light, she grew bashful, her nipples shadowing against the sheet.

"You are lovelier than the dawn," Alessandro told her. "Your eyes behind your veil are like those of doves. Your lips are like a scarlet thread, and even your thoughts please me."

"Umm?"

"Nothing, my queen. How would you like to have our supper for breakfast?" Playfully, he threw a fig at her.

"Don't!" she cried. "Beside, didn't you eat enough of those last night?"

Alessandro kissed her and slid down her willing body with the passion of a man who has starved too long. All day till darkness claimed their chamber, they remained imprisoned between heaven and earth, sustained by the ambrosia of love until sleep overpowered them.

When Alessandro woke, he realized that for the first time since he took sacred vows, he had not said Mass nor even remembered to utter a morning prayer.

† † †

Berti hurried to keep up with Alessandro. The cardinal's stride was vigorous, like that of someone prepared to serve God again but on his own terms.

"Your miniatures delight me," he told the young man.

Berti turned to Alessandro. "Your Grace, it is my honor to serve you."

"After you finish the study of Monna Rebecca," Alessandro continued with a smile, "look around in Don Clovio's workshop. You'll find there all you need to finish the miniature."

"*Eccelenza,* I don't feel ... How can I put this delicately?"

"No problem." Alessandro quickly understood that Berti felt uneasy entering his bedroom with his mistress there. "Should we find my Venus asleep, you could work on a sketch of Jupiter finding the sleeping Antiope. A fitting subject for my new bedroom." He laughed at his idea.

Berti nodded, baffled by the feeling that he should not be there in the first place.

Rebecca, sleeping like God created her, jumped at the hinges' first squeak. Seeing two men enter, she pulled the sheet up to her chin.

"*Buona giornata, angelina.*" Alessandro walked over and kissed his mistress' back.

Berti, still confused by the role he was forced to play, fixed his eyes on Titian's *Magdalen.*

Bella Maddalena.

Alessandro traveled the length of the room and threw the shutters open. "What's all the fuss? Wouldn't you like Messer Bartolomeo to paint you as Venus reclining?" he joked.

Rebecca looked dubious. "Your Grace!"

"*Regina mia,* this is my new painter. His miniatures are even finer that Don Clovio's," Alessandro explained, turning her face toward the light. "Sit quietly. After I send you to Sister Cecilia, all I'll have left will be his miniature of you."

Berti's eyes grew soft. She was as lovely as he remembered. Even more beautiful.

"We've already met," he said. "Isn't that so, signorina *ebrea?*"

Tongue-tied, Rebecca only shook her head in agreement.

"Alessandro, you're already sending me away. So soon! And where?"

"Assisi. Just for a few months, until your baptism. I thought you wanted to go?"

Berti felt awkward. "Your Grace—the sleeping Antiope—is it a passing thought?"

"Yes. A miniature is more appropriate now," Alessandro agreed, watching his mistress braid her hair. "I've matters to attend to. And now, to work!"

He spun on his heels and left.

Minutes passed before Berti could concentrate on anything other than averting his gaze from the tempting forms under the sheet.

"I hope you slept well," he said to Rebecca, hoping to break the silence while sharpening his chalks.

"I did," she said, trying to keep her composure, "but don't make me talk. I don't want to have my mouth open in my portrait!"

She smiled with her mouth closed.

"It makes no difference what you do. Even if you were to go away, I would remember your face."

"So why do you need me here?"

"Well, signorina *ebrea* ... " the man inside the painter began, but she interrupted.

"Please, don't call me that. I hope to belong to Christ soon."

Berti fumbled for a response. "Forgive me. I'd no idea." It was his turn to feel lost. Momentarily his gaze dropped to the drawing paper. She turned her head slightly toward him, then a bit more, and smiled fully, the diffused light reflecting off every lash which lined her eyes. He looked up, surveyed her profile, the high cheekbones, the gentle cut of her nose, and the full lips. As he soaked up the glow of her skin, the book of Esther came to his mind.

"King Ahasuerus loved Esther and made her his wife. Esther, more lovely than Queen Vashti. Would Alessandro's mistress replace Mother Church in his heart?" he wondered.

Rebecca straightened her spine and tipped her chin back.

"How regal. Like that!" he cried, catching the dimple at the corner of her lips. "Signorina, who were your parents?"

"My mother's family came from Andalusia. They were *moriscos*, Arabs from Barbary, from northern Africa. Then my grandmother married a Jew. She"—Rebecca smiled at the complexity of her family's religious history—"she converted and married a *marrano*."

Berti was trying to keep up. "What's a *marrano?*"

"Jewish converts in Catholic Spain."

He was speechless. "Shouldn't you be a Christian already then?"

Rebecca looked disturbed. "No. Many converts only pretended to be Christian. My great-grandfather was caught one day practicing his own faith, and his family was expelled. First they went to Provence, then to *Venezia*. I was born in Venice. Were you ever there?"

"I came here through Lyon and Parma." For a few brief moments, Berti felt himself transported back to Parma. "I nearly died there, drinking lime water from the bucket."

"Actually, I don't remember Venice much," Rebecca continued. "I was eight when we left. My father took us there in search of a better life, but here we are in Rome, not having found it yet."

"Wasn't Pope Paul hostile to Jews?" Berti asked.

"My father is learned. His Holiness needed my father's remedies." Emotion colored Rebecca's voice. "It's true. We received a dispensation."

"All this uncertainty, is that why you want to become a Christian?"

"Doesn't everybody want to be a Christian?" Rebecca smiled inwardly.

"Do you not know that the Catholics and Protestants in my country are Christian," he said wondering that she could ask such a question, "but they kill each other in the name of Christianity?" He tried to explain the events in his homeland, but she clearly did not want to hear. In her agitation, her coverlet slipped, revealing breasts as ripe as melons bronzed in the hot August sun.

Berti lost his train of thought, and his glance was more than cursory.

"I know nothing of the ways of your people," Rebecca announced with a shrug, "but I've always felt alone. One day, the mystery of the Trinity overwhelmed me. It was then I first thought to become a *conversa,* but I was not strong enough to leave my faith."

"Why not?" Berti gawked as the sheet slipped even lower.

"What are you doing?" she exclaimed, horrified, tugging on the tangled sheet.

"You'll see for yourself!" Berti licked his dry lips, unable to tear himself from the curves he drew against his will, the chalk crumbling in his fingers.

"See what?" A stentorian voice interrupted the pair.

"Your Grace," Berti bowed, offering his drawing to Alessandro as Rebecca sprang from bed, the sheet wrapped around her, and looked at the sketch. "Oh, heaven! Could that be me?"

Alessandro did not look at his mistress' face, which appeared in the upper corner. Instead he saw two sketches, one aborted as Berti tried a more pleasing angle of the naked woman stretched across a bed, a courtesan with bold eyes.

Rebecca stood transfixed. "Alessandro, I didn't pose like that."

Laughter convulsed the men. "*Amorino,*" Alessandro said, pinching Rebecca's mouth to plant a kiss, waving Berti away. "The Muses call that an artistic inspiration. *Un'idea.* I call it artistic license. Wait by the door," he said to the young man. "Our lunch is coming."

Picking up the habit he wore that first night, he slipped it over Rebecca's head. "You'd make a fine nun," he announced, pleased by the sight. "A fine Catholic."

"Your Grace," Rebecca began, unsure of her lover's plans. She did not want to be a nun.

"Don't fuss!" Alessandro laughed, pulling her close. "We'll let the holy abbess look after your soul, and when you're ready come six months, I'll baptize you."

Rebecca's eyes rolled in horror. "*I will die* if you send me away that long."

Alessandro laughed teasingly. "I'll ask the abbess to let you write."

"Be serious!"

Berti stood at the door with large baskets, unsure whether to enter.

"Over here!" Alessandro commanded. "On the bed!"

Rebecca paled, horrified by the lavish arrangement of pork, ham, pungent cheeses melting in the heat, and oysters swimming in the juice of a split melon.

"I can't touch that," she thought as Alessandro sliced a piece of smoked ham and brushed it temptingly against her lips. "I can't." Overcome, she threw herself at his feet.

"May I beg leave to go?" Berti said, pained by Rebecca's distress.

"Go, but get us peasant clothes," his master said. "I can't stand my own garb today."

Berti sighed inwardly. "As you command, Your Grace."

"We'll have a long day," Alessandro grumbled, used as he was to traveling in comfort. "We'll go as a family," he added as Rebecca and Berti stared at him, baffled. "It's for our safety. You and Monna Rebecca on one horse as husband and wife, and I on the other. Don't look at me like that! I'll be your father-in-law, my love."

Rebecca's sobbed, already bemoaning the long separation.

"Do stop wailing, *cara*," Alessandro suddenly exclaimed, impatiently. "We'll take you to the inn behind Ponte Milvio. You'll continue by post-chaise."

Rebecca was overwhelmed. This was not what she imagined when she left her family. She had acted foolishly.

"The papers are ready," Alessandro continued. "You'll be well taken care of. Berti, have our horses ready by noon."

He waved his servant away.

"And now get up and sit next to me, so we can we finish our meal in peace."

Settling back, he offered Rebecca bread and cheese. She smiled indulgently as he popped oysters into his own mouth and bit into a slice of melon, washing it down with long draughts of wine. As Alessandro tried to cut a large piece of roast pork, the greasy bone slipped from his fingers and fell into his goblet. Rebecca laughed like a lark in paradise.

"You think that's funny," he said in jest and ripped off her garment.

"Alessandro!" she cried with sudden apprehension.

"So you'd like some more." He took a slice of melon and pushed it into her mouth, moving it up and down like the bow of a violin. As she bit, he pushed her over, removed the pulp and squeezed it over her breasts, rubbing it until the juices polished her skin.

As she arched in pleasure, Alessandro took a handful of oysters, swollen from the juice of the melon, and lined them up in the valley of her breast. She stared as the roundels disappeared into his mouth.

"Here, my queen." The mischievous Adonis dropped the last oyster into her mouth.

"I shouldn't!" she protested but bit eagerly. "That is delicious. Can I have more?"

"Certainly," he cried and steered his flesh with the movements of a camel grazing for the barren journey ahead until his spring burst, and he fell back completely exhausted. For a while, they just existed, the heat of their passion ebbing away.

"Alessandro, will you visit me when I am shut in that far-away place?" She ran her palms down his spine, feeling him in her power. "Promise?"

"I will." He clasped her once more before the long journey north. But it was months before he could keep his word.

* * *

The summer passed swiftly, while the decoration of the winter apartment progressed, covering the walls with charming grotesques.

"Your Grace, I hope these frescoes *all'antica* meet your full approval." His chief painter, Federico Zuccaro, raised elegant eyebrows in mock concern.

"Umm ... enchanting," Alessandro finally uttered, searching for a meaningful word.

Federico motioned haughtily toward the wall. "Didn't we agree on a light subject to keep Your Grace cheerful during the winter?"

"Cheerful is one thing and vacuous another," Alessandro thought, tugging at his beard, streaky with frost. He looked around, day-dreaming of Rebecca, but instead inquired about Berti.

"*Eccelenza,* would you like to see for yourself?" Federico pointed to a scaffold where his partner stood working. Next to him was Berti, filling the wet, empty plaster with a landscape depicting Alessandro's new villa, its mass towering high and broad under billowing clouds above the main street of the town. "He's learning fast enough," Don Federico offered bitingly.

"And what's vexing the *capo* maestro today?"

"Pardon me, Your Grace. This young Fleming likes to do things the way he was taught across the Alps. Who ever heard of painting the hills blue and lavender? Here in Caprarola our hills are green, and our clouds are white." Alessandro looked at the landscape, found it pleasing, and said so. "Indeed," Federico agreed with hesitation. "As I've said, the man learns quickly."

Alessandro turned away. "These decorations are taking too long. Arrogant men, dust, and one obliging servant. Bravo, Bartolomeo."

"Maestro," he said, "I've no vested interest in your *garzoni,* and young Spranger is just an employee. But I do have other plans for him."

"Your wishes are my commands, Your Grace." Federico replied, cutting his bow short.

Alessandro had little patience with the self-indulgent Federico and did not mind showing it. Berti ignored his *capo* maestro as much as possible. As the autumn slipped away in the company of Don Alfonso and old Cecchino, he finished the watercolor miniatures for Alessandro who hid his dark-eyed mistress in a gold medallion on his breast.

Although Berti loved being in Caprarola, he was overjoyed when he presented the cardinal's letter to Don Federico, ordering him back to Rome. The Eternal City pulled him more than he could ever have imagined.

Berti

A week had passed since Berti returned to Rome, and he enjoyed every minute of it, settling in his new quarters next to Don Clovio's in the Cancelleria—the Papal Chancellery—Alessandro's business residence. A Renaissance gem more impressive than the cardinal's still unfinished family palace, it had a huge Doric courtyard and more rooms than Berti could count.

The fall reigned in full glory, nowhere more clearly than in the colorful produce in the peasants' market on the Campo de' Fiori. Walking between the two palaces instead of following the direct Via dei Farnesi, Berti often went around the market square, turning back at the southwestern corner toward the Ducal Square and the majestic façade of Palazzo Farnese beyond, which the great Michelangelo himself designed.

Even when clouds appeared by surprise and rain tinted the stone pavement, the morning skies were colored lemon, cream, and peach. As Berti admired the heavenly glory he waved to the matrons young and old, opening shutters, shaking out carpets and wall coverings, hanging out laundry, and throwing food to the stray cats and dogs below. Many were young and pretty, turning the walk into a pleasant diversion for a handsome man and an observant artist.

One bright morning after All Saints' Day in the year of Our Lord 1568, the air was bracing and chill as farmers moved about briskly, sleeves rolled down and vests buttoned. Their faces and the stalls crammed with interesting produce made Berti want to stay longer. He always started at the baker's counter on the northwest corner, just past the Cancelleria, giving himself time to finish his large butter tart flavored with bits of dried figs, lemon rind, and raisins.

"*Pane, pane fresco! Pannini e biscotti! Signori, prego!*" Messer Toffano, the baker, praised his fresh bread, buns, and dunking cookies, inviting passersby into his shop. Even on cold days the shop's wooden shutters were fully open, the oven's heat steaming the air with a haze that drifted over his baked goods, laid out enticingly on the counter.

"*Misericordia,*" pleaded a gaunt young woman standing by the shop with one boy in her arms and three other children by her side, all eyeing his plump tart, their dirty palms out in the beggar's painful gesture.

Berti stopped in mid-stride, feeling guilty. The family looked pathetic.

"*Signore,* for the love of God help us," the woman whispered, her voice racked with a dry cough, her hand barely strong enough to tug at his damask doublet. "We haven't always been like this. My Beltraffio used to be strong. And a fine worker he was, too, till he lost his job as a *muratore*. But you know those Bergamaschi. They work for next to nothing."

She paused, shaking.

Berti heard stories about Lombard masons flooding the peninsula by the hundreds as far as Naples, cutting stone and then returning home. Many locals had lost their jobs. His eyes clouded with concern.

"My Raffi worked at the Farnese gardens," the woman continued, "but one day last spring, he had an accident. They brought him home crippled, leaving us a bit of money and some medicine."

Berti trusted no beggars, especially children with nimble fingers. He wanted to go, but the woman would not let him. "*Signore,*" she pled, "we *are* hungry and cold. The money the cardinal gave us is long gone, and we have nowhere to go."

Berti understood. He had been hungry, too, crossing the Alps, and nobody helped him.

But the oldest child's face reminded him of Don Alfonso, and he could not help himself.

"Take this and be well." With his half-eaten pastry he also offered the small coins he had.

"God bless you, young man," she thanked him. "My Raffi worked at the Farnese gardens. The money the cardinal gave us is long gone."

Striding away he realized what the woman said, and returned. "Which cardinal?" he demanded, but the woman was too busy dividing the tart into crumbs to respond. So Berti marched on to the sounds of the new day, bracing himself against the streams of shoppers.

In the center of the busy square a wall of heads, elbows, and backs surrounded the stalls. Men and women cut strings of sausages, sliced sides of bacon, counted eggs, laying them carefully in the shoppers' overflowing baskets.

Dead game hung head down. Live animals fretted in cages, attracting children who fed them weeds. Melons and squashes were piled next to crates of onions and olives, and the pungent smell of pears accompanied the buzzing of wasps eagerly rolling in their bruised parts.

"How much?" Berti fished in his vest for a lost *baiocco* and bought a handful of figs, biting expectantly into their grainy centers, careful not to let the juices stain his new doublet, too busy to notice a cloud of feathers over him. "Cock-a-doodle to you, too!" he exclaimed, removing the fluff that settled on his sleeves, and shook his fist at the beast flying wildly about the cage.

At the end of the square by the old theater of Pompey, he covered his nose and averted his sight from a gallows where the smelly corpse of a man hung, barely held together.

Just the week before, he heard about the poor creature from Don Giaccomo.

"It's not a crime to lie with a whore, is it?" Berti wondered.

"Nay, it isn't." Then the architect explained. "But, Madonna Justina testified she saw them 'in the French way.'"

Berti shifted his gaze.

"Where've you been, son? Everyone knows the French do it unnaturally. That's why God struck them with the awful disease. The man who fornicates with a whore from behind is to hang until his flesh drops off. She was found guilty of witchcraft and condemned to burn."

Berti shuddered down to his toes, and goose bumps erupted all over his body.

"Right you are. Stay away from women. They can't be trusted," Don Giaccomo warned.

"I should run," Berti thought, seeing the sun rising briskly, but instead he turned his gaze to another man wearing only a loin cloth who rattled about in a wooden cage, glaring like a savage, swearing obscenities at the crowd throwing rotten food at him, mocking him in delight.

"Honorable signora *nonna*," he heard a young boy ask an old woman, "is that the wild mountain man who lives with the wolves, the one who gets all the bad little boys who don't listen to their grandmothers?"

"No, my little one, the sign says he robbed a bishop and left him to freeze in the street. If it weren't for a Good Samaritan who gave his cloak to the poor wretch he would have died."

"Hee-hee," two scullery maids giggled behind Berti's back. "She didn't say that His Grace the bishop forgot to pay Monna Lucretia for her little favors."

Berti thought he had heard about the caged man, but he couldn't place him, even though he looked familiar. Finally he gave up wondering and walked across the square to buy a pear, the warm sun already over the church of Santa Maria in Grottapinta by the Theater of Pompey, burning his back.

A little monkey wearing a string of silver bells danced on a small table, jingling to a rhythm that reminded Berti of the *misericordia* cart taking away the dead. He listened to the monotonous piping of the shepherd who owned the beast, observing his crooked fingers on the holes, his slippers tied high over muscular calves. Worried about being late for his meeting with Don Fulvio, he threw away the unfinished pear, wiped his sticky fingers on a fine kerchief, and ran—only to find His Grace's antiquarian unexpectedly called away.

† † †

Alessandro's court had been back in Rome nearly four months. As the *tramontano* hissed through the city's narrow alleys just before the feast of *Natale*, Berti decided to thank St. Anne, the Virgin's mother, for his new job by painting a small picture in which she meets her cousin Elisabeth at the Golden Gate of Jerusalem. For inspiration, he bought a print of the same subject by Albert Dürer from Herr Manfred. He always enjoyed visiting the book and print merchants' stalls by the Trevi fountain and listening to the round-bellied German's affectionate laugh.

But before starting on the votive painting, Berti visited Santa Maria dell'Anima, the church of the Netherlandish people, to say his prayers. There as he met Adrien Floris, an old friend from Antwerp, he found himself remembering with amazement how, when he first got to Rome, penniless, jobless, and homeless, Adrien took him to his place in Via della Croce. Berti was desperate, a stranger in Rome, but Adrien soon introduced him to the city and his friends at the church. And now, as usual, the merchant's copper mustache was gingerly turned up, and he was his elegant self.

In fact, Adrien was an epitome of perfection from head to toe.

"Hey, stranger," he said with a hint of sarcasm. "I've not seen you for a full week! Remember? I now live close by, on Via dei Banchi."

Berti mumbled an apology, but the sociable Adrien hardly heard it.

"Look, why don't you join me for dinner? At Monna Piacenza's."

Berti cleared his throat. It seemed a lifetime but in fact only a year since he visited the famous courtesan's house, desperate for a woman. Although he never forgot Monna Piacenza's warm hands, when he fell in love with Monna Alba, Adrien's landlady's daughter, he tired of the place, scented with the effluvium of men's yearning.

"Not tonight, my friend."

Adrien hopped impatiently. "I want you to meet someone. If you don't like the madam, I'm sure there'll be others."

Berti coughed pointedly.

"I understand. But since you've abandoned her, Monna Piacenza has a new admirer. *He* wants to meet *you*."

Why did he not say that in the first place? "I'll be there," Berti assured his friend.

How strange to come back to one of Rome's most sought-out houses of pleasure. How mature he felt and how far removed from the inexperienced lad who literally fell onto the madam's ripe bosom! Monna Piacenza was not alone in her private quarters where Adrien sat amusing himself with a pretty wench.

"Finally!" he exclaimed as the door closed behind Berti.

Next to the stately courtesan sat a blond lad in bishop's vestments, his eyes so colorless, they seemed without lashes. He nodded at Berti in a friendly way.

"Pleasure to know you at last," the cleric said in guttural Italian.

Adrien winked at Berti repeatedly.

"This is His Highness, Prince Albrecht Wilhelm. He's studying for his vows in Bologna. He normally wears his clerical garb, except for that one time I had to help him with my cloak."

"Berti, I wish you'd listen when I'm telling you something very important!"

Berti played nervously with his doublet. In a flash, he knew who the caged man was. But when Adrien told him how he had rescued a shivering, naked wretch in front of another brothel, he was too preoccupied by a new painting.

Berti displayed a smile of recognition.

"We've been trying to meet with you for some time, Herr Bartholomäus," the prince-bishop announced in a nasal voice, his *rs* rattling like chestnuts against a stone wall. "How wonderful would it be to surprise my honorable lady mother with a miniature of myself that you do so well. Perhaps this gracious lady will consent to entertain me while you work on it."

"Excellence," Berti responded, eagerly. "I work from memory. I'll send you a sketch."

"Splendid. It's all arranged." The young German turned his attention to the first course.

The evening passed swiftly for Berti, surprised to find the young scholar an avid collector of art. He was even more dumbfounded when the courtesan sang French songs, accompanying herself on the lute. He thought whores couldn't see past their breasts.

"Are you absolutely sure?" Adrien turned his attention to his friend when only bones and crumbs remained. "You break my heart."

"Thank you, my friend. Not tonight. I prefer to be alone."

"Come and see me at my house. I can introduce you to a few new patrons."

"But I need no one, Adrien," Berti argued. "I'm well looked after at the Cancelleria."

"You never know which way the wheel of fate may roll," the young merchant replied, clearly aware that fortunes are made and lost with the passing wind.

"Thank you, truly." Berti embraced Adrien but did not look in the direction of Monna Piacenza who was attending to the young man, although he apparently needed little guidance. Wondering how someone so young could be a bishop, Berti left by the back door, pausing to gaze happily at the stars and breathe the clean December air.

The night was windless. The Tiber flowed quiet and steady, but Berti's thoughts were jumbled. Why had he not asked Adrien what became of Monna Alba?

He regretted now that he raped the girl and never saw her again. But he was preoccupied by his new post, and his bright future overshadowed the transgression. After all, raping a woman was more a subject of crude jokes than of conscience. But Alba was different, and Berti felt sorry, though—he claimed—he was unduly provoked.

At thirteen, Alba had already blossomed into a woman, but her soul was pure. When Berti first settled into Adrien's household, she had no idea what was happening to her but thought it must have been something divine and preordained, for a handsomer young man she had beheld neither in church nor at the farmers' market by the Cancelleria.

At twenty, Berti's curiosities were long satisfied by city maids and country wenches, but Alba enchanted him the way a pure stream beckons a thirsty wanderer. Something about her reminded him of when he was a child. Like a cherry tree bedecked with blossoms, she shone with virginal purity.

He watched her moving sprightly about the house, singing airs. Her gentle face bathed in an aura like that in pictures of the Virgin. Her neck, arched under pale braids, rose from the lithe body he wanted to hold close. Yet she was like the Lamb of God, and he didn't want to hurt her.

A year later, the night was young, and Berti stared into the placid river. He was restless, just as he was that night when Alba first walked into his room at Via della Croce, an apparition in a white robe, wrapped in a long trailing scarf.

"*Signore,* please forgive me for disturbing you," came a stifled whisper.

"My gentle lady, is that you?" he asked Alba, who stood not far from his bed.

"Signor Adrien left after vespers," she mumbled. "He said … you won't be staying with us long." Her voice choked in her throat. "You'll be leaving for Monte Soratte the day after tomorrow to paint in a church in San Oreste. That's what he said."

He remembered how her voice broke, its echo momentarily suspended in mid-air.

Berti's swung his legs over the side of the bed. His heart ached for her. "Would you miss me?" He paused, throwing the covers aside. He strode to the barefoot girl standing in a heap of fallen cloth. Without words and without hands their lips met, tentatively and searchingly, with the thirst of mutual desire and the purity of a moment forbidding to them both.

Alba sneezed. The spell was broken.

Berti picked her up and laid her on his bed, rubbing her hands and breathing warmth at her frigid feet. He covered her with blankets and sat on the edge, not wanting to disturb the sacred moment that came to him so unexpectedly in his lonely chamber.

She reached for his hand, her gaze strangely detached, but renewed warmth flowed between them, feelings connecting them with currents known only to the young and in love.

So much tenderness overwhelmed the young man. He adored the young woman with a devotion worthy of a Pygmalion turning cold stone into the living Galatea. As dawn suggested itself, he scooped Aurora into his arms, carried her to her tiny attic chamber, and tucked her into her small bed like a child.

The following night, while he was still in shock from the nocturnal visit, Alba's mother told him how she found her daughter moon-walking, far from her bed.

The next evening was even stranger. The afternoon heat blew in from the south, and the opened shutters in his room clattered and banged against the crumbling stucco. The sky grew black, and bright flashes terrified him. For a while that night it seemed as though all the demons joined in an infernal dance. Then the sky cleared, and the first stars appeared.

Berti was already packed for San Oreste. He desperately wanted to see Monna Alba, to talk to her, to feel her near that last night, but he didn't know how to reach her without her mother knowing. He couldn't even draw her face, because all his tools were wrapped.

He drank heavily at dinner and now breathed hard as he saw the apparition emerge. Again. Facing him, lit by the full moon's radiance, was Monna Alba. She stood motionless like a salt pillar, her cap askew, her nightshirt wet and torn across her blood-spattered thigh.

Berti drained his wine flask. Ripping the edge of her torn gown, he dipped the rag into his water jug and cleaned and bound the wound. Moonstruck, Alba seemed surreal.

Once more Berti laid her on his bed. Her arms and legs spread wide, like a Lamb of God ready to be sacrificed, and Berti went mad with desire. No longer could he control his emotions, nor could he subdue the onslaught of his blood.

With one motion he finished the rip in her tattered garb and sank on her, senseless, aware only of entering her and pounding her with a diabolical passion that matched the forces of the evening's storm. Monna Alba's face was bloodless, like that of the heathen goddess in Palazzo Farnese. Her head tilted back, her mouth open in a kind of trance, she gripped the bed-posts, accepting her agony and ecstasy with the resignation of a sacrificial animal. So this is how Teresa of Avila married Christ, the confused maiden dreamt, also wanting to be His bride. The force that filled her was infinitely sweet as she lay moonstruck, with a dark head slumped over her breasts, the young man beside her in a coma of oblivion.

When Berti awoke, his only companion was the curtain, blown by cold gusts from the open window. He saw from the shadows in the courtyard that it was late and rushed to make arrangements to pick up his trunk.

When he returned, the house was in turmoil. Adrien, who stopped by from his mistress' house to bid his friend a safe journey, told him the cook found Alba in the courtyard, the shreds of her clothing scattered about the house—on the open shutters in her room, on the balustrade, on the open window in the kitchen.

When Berti left the house, no one bade him farewell. Little could he have foreseen that Monna Alba would sever contact with her native land and join the followers of Teresa of Avila at a place near the Escorial, the austere residence of his Most Catholic Majesty, King Philip.

† † †

Frequently on the road, since his diverse mercantile interests sent him in all directions, Adrien was glad to be back in Rome. Now well-settled in a splendid palace on the south side of Via dei Banchi Vecchii, the street of the old banking houses near the river where the old artery merged with the street of the new banks, the residence, although not his own, was his to enjoy freely at the cost of being honorary major-domo for Prince-Bishop Albrecht Wilhelm.

In a frescoed hall overlooking the wintry landscape Berti sat with Adrien and his newest mistress at yet another feast, enjoying each other's company. Stormed by Berti's questions, he dallied, vexing his friend to the point of a squabble.

"I've no idea what my old landlady's precious daughter is doing in Avila," Adrien answered, twisting the corners of his waxed moustache until they were properly in place.

Berti breathed heavily, in and out. "I thought you stayed in touch with Monna Galbani."

"I didn't. Can't stand her new husband. He acts as if he made her fortune. I made it for *her,* in my ventures and with a good return."

Berti brightened. "But I thought you were in Spain last summer."

Adrien shook his head. "Mostly at the coast."

Berti looked perplexed. "Haven't you been to Cordoba?"

"Not on this trip, and Cordoba is not Madrid or Avila, my donkey of a friend."

"Damn you! You're making a fool of me." Berti's knuckles sharpened.

"Calm yourself!" Adrien returned to fingering his beard. "Beside, what do you want? You've been back to Rome for at least two months. Whenever we meet, you pay me little attention, and now you want to know if I have news of Monna Alba, whether I have a new gold mine to afford this palace ... and this little treasure." He pinched the girl's cheek. "And you want to know how fast I can make you rich. All of that requires time."

Adrien drained his goblet, refilled it, and beckoned the musicians to play.

Soothed by the tinkling sound of mandolins, Berti relaxed. "When I first looked for you after you left Via della Croce," he tried to explain, "Monna Galbani told me you went to Bologna to become a priest! What was I to think?"

Adrien's goblet hit the surface of the table as he doubled over at the ludicrous thought that he might ever have chosen clerical garb. "Spare me the pain! No, you fool. I was taking the rich neophyte to Bologna after Monna Lucrezia's henchman robbed him." Adrien explained how the prince-bishop returned his cloak weighed down with ducats. "So, you see, not long after that the fledgling looked me up, begging me to set up a cozy nest in the city for him to recover from the exhausting curriculum."

"And this is it?" The incredulous Berti looked around.

Adrien winked at his lady companion. "Yes. The rules are simple. I live here cost-free for seeing to the prince-bishop's private needs."

"And this?" Berti pointed to the bottle of fine Portuguese Madeira.

"From his cellar."

"And her." Berti sized up Adrien's companion with an artist's eye. "Is she his too?"

"That's another story. The prince's reward came back to me in a horn of plenty," he said and leaned toward Berti. "Mostly ammunition and trinkets for the New Indies. I'll tell you more another time."

Berti was skeptical. "New Indies? I thought your ships went only as far as Malaga."

"They do. Andalusia is a merchant's Mecca. All of Italy wants her grain. The vineyards and olive groves abound with rich crops, and I pick up the salt in San Lucar."

Berti cocked his head, surprised. "You trade in salt?"

"And how do you think the Britons and our landsmen preserve their cod? And would you like your porkpies without salt?"

"I thought you traded in Flemish cloth."

"I used to, and I still do."

"But you have so many ships?"

"I buy shares in some."

"Why?"

"Berti, stick to your own trade! What if my ship bound for Rome is blown to the coast of Barbary, and the corsairs sell my grain to the Turks and feed my crew to the fish?"

Berti blew his nose to conceal his astonishment.

"You're amazing! Did your father teach you that?"

"No," Adrien laughed. "Lady Fortuna whispered it in my ear when

I did not want to listen. I burnt my fingers once, then once more, and finally I learned to divide the pie into many small pieces. Some grow into new pies, and others get eaten by the wolves."

The door opened, and a young woman entered, short and full-bodied, with the light stride of a fox. The two young women embraced and giggled behind their fans as the newcomer made herself comfortable next to Berti.

"It's nothing like that my friend." Adrien patted Berti as his friend stood to leave. "But it's not healthy for you to be deprived of nourishment for too long, just as it is not good for a businessman to make deals on an empty stomach."

Berti was reminded that their last such conversation ended as a quarrel about the celibacy of the clergy. Berti tried to protest Adrien's allegations, but his friend shot back. "This cardinal of yours, didn't you tell me he has a lewd painting in his room?" he asked, raising the subject Berti always evaded. "I bet you my entire investment in the *Phoenix* your pious *padrone* and the protector of the Jesuits keeps a woman! We all know how it goes with men, *il gran cardinale* included. He's certainly no saint. All Rome knows that!"

But this night, Berti just left and lingered in the church of San Damaso after vespers ended. Yet even reciting the rosary brought him no relief. A worm of doubt about his patron's sanctity rooted itself in his heart.

† † †

The late December sun set briskly. Berti lengthened his stride along the narrow Via dei Coronari, leaving behind streams of pilgrims returning from the Vatican. The unpleasant odor of mold and human excrement saturated the air, and he shuddered involuntarily as he passed the column of Marcus Aurelius without checking on the construction of the palace at the end of the piazza and turned sharply toward Adrien's place.

"*Sera, vagabondo!* Where've you been?" Adrien greeted him impatiently.

Instead of replying, Berti looked askance at a portly older man next to Adrien. Dressed in traveling clothes, he gave the impression of a merchant.

"This is my friend, Maarten de Waal. He's here on business."

"From where?" Berti inquired after they exchanged pleasantries.

"From Florence," Maarten continued, shaking Berti's hand warmly. "Working for His Eminence, the Archduke of Florence. Delivering one of his manuscripts."

"For Alessandro," Adrien broke in.

"What kind?"

"A missal. From King Matthias' collection." Adrien clarified the matter.

"Whose?" Berti had never heard of the Hungarian king.

"We'll explain more on the way," Maarten cut back in. "But since you know a thing or two about manuscripts, I'll let you have a peek."

Adrien stood aside. "Animal hides, after all," he snickered.

Berti came closer as Maarten unfolded a length of soft cloth rolled around a codex. The oil lamp illuminated the finest lacework patterns, page after page, each executed with greater skill, color, and design than Berti ever saw in any of his masters' shops.

The stiff rustle of vellum, the sputtering of candles, and the thudding of Berti's heart filled the air. As the gilded letters rose out of the lapis lazuli ground on the last page, Maarten closed the book, carefully tucking it back into its soft cover, and laid it with other packages in a padded chest.

Maarten turned to Adrien. "Paints and doodles. Is that what you're thinking? You're right and wrong. And don't give me a hard time. You're a businessman, too. But now, let's go."

The evening was young, but the air was dank. Across the Tiber, thick fog engulfed a procession of donkeys, porters, and servants carrying litter-chairs, accompanied by loud calls and flickering light from torches and lanterns. Nearby, the old port of Ripa Grande was quiet; faint lights shadowed the docks sunk into the murky waters.

The trio descended to the grassy banks, and Berti and Adrien waited while Maarten instructed the captain of his ship about the cargo. As night closed in, an unpleasant chill embraced them. Finally Maarten emerged from the darkness. A misty rain chilled their joints, picking up strength every minute, ending in a cascade of biting needles.

They hastened their steps, not noticing that they had passed the Piazza Nicosia until they made a sharp turn onto Via Orso toward the Piazza Colonna and the Fontana di Trevi quarter. Finally, a warm, friendly tavern materialized before them. Their teeth chattered in the steady downpour. At the Black Rooster—*Al Gallo Nero*—the evening was in full swing.

Whenever Berti felt homesick, he visited Meneer Santvoort's inn, a gathering place for northerners in Rome. That evening a few regulars sat on the steps, but a larger group stood in the main hall. As Berti approached the gesticulating men, he realized the subject was serious.

The voice of Anthonis, Meneer Santvoort's stout nephew, dominated the conversation.

"A holy war, you say? To hell with the saintly apostolic chamber!"

Waves of murmur rose and fell as a whining voice chimed in. "No! It is a crusade. His Holiness will destroy the infidel and bring Europe back to the bosom of Mother Church!"

"They're all vultures, shameless leeches, you imbecile!" came another.

"We all know that Pius wants his Catholic Netherlands back," Anthonis shouted.

The room fell silent, only the involuntary hiccups of a fat drunkard filling the air.

"*Ja*," finally came a reply in a different, stentorian voice. "From the day that Borgia rat was clad in purple, we've had nothing but taxes: tax on flour, tax on salt, and now Pius wants new *monte del carne!* Let him have porridge! May he drop dead eating the gluey mess!"

"Hush, be careful," voices hissed through the room.

"I want my meat, but I won't pay more for it." The voice grew agitated. "I want to enjoy it without paying Pius' second *quattrino* on each pound I buy. I can't even pay the first!"

"Damned right!" Maarten gnashed his jaws as he broke in. "First, Paul cried poverty, but got seven-hundred thousand. Then comes Pius who talks with the poor as with his equals. So I say to myself, Maarten, good times have come to us, hard-working men. There'll be money for taxes and some left for our hungry families. And what does this saintly man do? He pats heads, smiles sweetly, and raises taxes! *Domine deus*, this time I need two-hundred thousand more!"

"Control yourself!" Adrien squeezed his arm. "This is heresy. You could burn for it!"

Maarten ignored him. "What if I do. 'It's for you, dear Lord—Pius smiles and prays—we need to get the Catholics back. We've lost half the world to the Protestants. England and much of Germany are gone. And Scandinavia, Switzerland, half of Poland, and much of France.'"

"Take hold of yourself," Adrien pleaded, laced with fear.

But Maarten went on. "I'll bring the Low Countries to their knees. That'll please King Philip. He may even line my coffers with New World silver. And then, Lord, your word will reign in the new Catholic Europe."

"That's enough." A giant of a man stepped forth with his greasy apron flying. "Meneer De Waal, even if I've tolerated your opinions before, keep your heresy to yourself. Observe the rules or get your ass out of here!"

Maarten suddenly seemed to realize that he endangered everyone in the room. The Inquisition had henchmen everywhere. He hesitated, but only for a moment. "Please accept my apology," he mumbled. "I don't know what possessed me. Must be the wind. My ship's stuck in the harbor, the grain will rot, and that rat wants more money. You understand my position, don't you?"

"Maarten!" Berti tugged his sleeve from behind. "Look, we ... I understand. But think of yourself. Don't you see?" Berti continued in soothing voice, "There's been enough trouble! We didn't come to Rome to be part of it! We came to work and enjoy ourselves!"

Maarten nodded in agreement. "You're right. Can't change history, so let's smarten up."

Afterward Berti chatted with the proprietor and his nephew Anthonis, who arrived from the Low Countries after Berti. When they and Adrien mulled over the evening's events, they all concluded that the news from their native land was bad. The new war in the Baltic grounded the merchants' grain ships, and the poor starved.

"Adrien, do you recall how *papà's* business suffered when the troubles with the English started? People lost their jobs, and hunger spread in the land."

"*Ja.*" Adrien was grateful his family had their ships in the Levant that winter. While the religious wars in Europe were bad news for all, the tensions between William of Orange and the King of Spain would bring grave sorrow to their native land.

"God keep us all," they all said to each other and parted, but not even the bright moon meeting the dawn dispelled their gloom. The next day, Maarten stopped briefly at Berti's studio after delivering the manuscript. He brimmed with gratitude. "Thanks for yesterday. If you ever need help, look me up, any time, no matter what. I'll be there for you and your friends."

As the fog lifted and the winds shifted, his ship left for Genoa, and he for Florence.

Neophyte

Months passed in frenetic activity, and yet another slipped by after Alessandro returned from Naples and Caprarola. Despite his promise to Rebecca, he resisted the pull of Assisi, reasoning that traveling over Monti Martani was uncomfortable and time consuming. But why her last letter lay unanswered in the secret compartment of his scriptorium, he couldn't say.

He felt uneasy.

He stood by his curio cabinet, staring at the two landscapes Berti finished during his absence, looking past the walls of the fortified villa deep into the lush, virginal growth around it. A clearing in the woods and a doe appeared in his mind, causing him to grip the picture so hard that his knuckles became tinted with the blue of the sky in the paintings.

"Great art Thou, Lord, and Thy love has no end, but how can I find rest in Thee? I am just a sinner, like all the rest."

Alessandro dropped Berti's painting on the bed and looked at Titian's lovely Danaë. She drove him insane, her legs spread wide, awaiting her lover in a shower of gold. Shaking with frustration, he fell on the bed and buried his head in the covers, smelling them, seeking the scent of the enchanting woman who appeared in his life just as he tried to reconcile himself to his fate as a servant of God. He rose and walked back to his study and sat at the scriptorium, looking for Rebecca's last letter.

"*My Most Reverend and Illustrious Monsignor and My Most Worthy Benefactor,*" it began and continued in the Latin she commanded so well. Perspiration quickly pearled on Alessandro's forehead, but he read on.

I await that moment to kneel at your feet in gratitude for educating me at the convent of Poor Clares, my soul lighter in the anticipation of becoming a child of Christ, worthy of your approval. Begging a thousand pardons, but there are also times, my Lord and Master, when I feel tormented over a matter that concerns us all.

God made Adam in His own image and gave him a soul. May God punish me for my perverse desire also to be made in His likeness, as was man. But, my kind Benefactor, is it not true that Our Lord made Eve out of Adam's side while he slept, from a rib, which was divinely made in his own image? Does it not follow that the woman who was created thus was already made equal to man? Does it not follow that God is both man and woman in one divine being?

Begging your pardon for my boldness stemming from my ignorance, I continue to be moved by your wisdom, Your Most Reverend and Illustrious Excellency, and I thank God for every opportunity to lie at your feet with devotion.

Your most humble servant, and daughter-to-be in God and Jesus Christ Our Lord and His Holy Spirit, Monna Rebecca.

Alessandro put the letter back on the tall stack, tied the ribbon around it, and locked it in the hidden compartment of his cabinet. His hands shook and his thoughts raced.

He imagined Rebecca washing his feet and drying them with her abundant hair, like the Magdalen. That woman he desired carnally, but this new person, an outright heretic who suggested that women were made equal to men, left him in turmoil. With thoughts equal to those of men greater than himself, she shocked him. For the first time—although he could not admit it—she excited his mind by stimulating his curiosity.

He slammed the cabinet shut and rang the bell, trying to control his hand in his lap, mindful of the bulge that had annoyed him most of the day. He took his quill and scribbled a note, sealing it with his ring. Carlo appeared instantly, a Lamb of God, ready to please.

"Padre, have this sent to my daughter Clelia. I'll come to her dinner tonight. And take out that painted *maiolica* plate with the infant Christ sleeping in his mother's lap, the one she admired during her last visit." Alessandro detached a key from his waist. He watched the padre unlock the chest and look for the plate.

As he followed the marked curvature from the patch of exposed skin of the young priest's neck down his robe to its terminus, suddenly the troubled man found the answer to his misery. While the bells tolled for vespers at San Damaso, the precious objects in the chest rattled objectionably as the poor man's backside provided a solution. When the trembling padre escaped Alessandro's bedchamber, he clutched a warm coin.

† † †

Another summer slipped by, and finally the day came when the cardinal baptized his mistress, giving her the Christian name Maddalena.

Monna Lena, as the *conversa* became known, the woman who returned from Assisi, was not the same person Berti remembered riding behind him through the gates of Popolo the summer before. Not her baptism but rather the long months of confinement behind convent walls whitened her skin. She was leaner, starved by the strict regime of her Catholic education. When Berti examined his study for her portrait, he saw that her face was almost boyish. But her eyes remained unchanged, true heralds of her new spirituality.

Even Alessandro found her changed as she lay in his arms.

"Lena, the lily of my heart." He kissed her fingertips one by one.

"Monsignor." She smiled back as she stretched by his side.

"Did you mean what you wrote me from Assisi?" he asked, touching her hair, cropped short at the shoulders by the abbess. Then he traced the outline of her face and her prominent high cheeks and suddenly thought she looked like a hermaphrodite—and said so.

Monna Lena tried to pronounce the strange word. "What did you mean by that?"

"I intended to say, *cara,*" he said, tracing her slender arms down to hip bones liberated from the usual softness that beautified the loveliest Roman concubines, "that you look almost like a boy. But"—he kissed her bosom—"you're still a woman. A person called by that name looks like man and woman put together."

Monna Lena was frightened. "Does that mean that you'll no longer love me?"

"No, *cara*. It means that I like you the better for it," he said and moved over her, feeling her slim shoulders unencumbered by hair. "Roll over, my sweet," he commanded, "so I can enjoy you both ways." He murmured, feeling the curve of her spine undulating under his belly.

Later, when their skin cooled and their minds refocused, Alessandro returned to his unanswered question: "Did you mean that God created men and women equal?"

Monna Lena snuggled closer. "Umm."

"But you know the scriptures deny that—absolutely!" he argued for control.

"They don't, and even St. Augustine says so. Would you like me to find the passage?"

"Woman, spare me your learned ways right now," replied the vexed cleric, fearing she might be right—although that seemed impossible.

Monna Lena kissed him. "Beside, you have just proved that women can also be men."

"Maddalena, God has blessed you with more wisdom than is good for you. Watch your tongue, or some day even I cannot help you."

"Forgive me. I didn't mean to annoy you," she said and turned to safer waters. "Before I left for Assisi, you said that I look like your new Venus, but she is plump and lovelier than me. Are you still going to put her in the *sacro bosco* behind the gardens?" she asked, referring to the place Alessandro called the sacred forest.

"Yes. But first I must ask Don Giaccomo to find me craftsmen who will carve the rocks by the clearing into sleeping nymphs and build a little temple nearby. Would you like to see it?"

"But it's dark outside. The moon is not out tonight."

"You're right. And it would be hard to get you past my guards," he said, gathering her cropped head to his silvering chest. "When the court leaves for Capodimonte tomorrow, I'll stay behind. We'll go then," he muttered satisfied and soon drooped into a pleasant slumber.

When the last wagon of his enormous entourage cleared the town for Lake Vico and his old summer residence the next day, he remained to show Monna Lena the sacred woods. In the moonlight filtering through swiftly moving clouds in the cooling northern wind, she stood in the clearing, her sparkling golden gown suffusing a surreal presence.

Suddenly Alessandro knelt by her.

"Lena, *mia cara,* you are my breath, the nerve of my being, my vigor, my life. All my life I have resented being the first-born son, obliged to follow my grandfather's path. The tonsure I wear chains me to God, whom I love but who keeps me away from the woman I revere most. If only I were free to take you, my goddess, for my wife," he lamented.

She knelt by him and smiled, the corners of her full lips tipped provocatively, her eyes bright with understanding. He reached behind her head and bunched the luxuriant hair. His other hand lifted her chin, and he kissed her dimple.

"So vulnerable," he whispered, tasting the little dip. She raised her arms around his neck and kissed him back, for the first time with the appreciation of being a woman. Then she slid down, her cheek against his thighs, submission releasing her own passion for the man she loved.

"Alessandro, have you ever thought about sharing life with someone else?"

He didn't reply. Instead he pulled her close and kissed her lips, tasting of the summer that breathed about them in the sky and in the earth redolent of the fragrance of dark berries. Her skin was taut like a ripe melon's, flavored by her joy. He breathed deeply, intoxicated by its perfume, flushed in the night's radiance.

"Alessandro, could we not marry, blessed by the divine rays of the moon?"

"The chaste Diana would not approve our union any more than Our Lord would."

Monna Lena gathered branches of wild jasmine into a bouquet, plaited a wreath from the black oak that towered above them, and raised it over Alessandro's head.

"My lord, do you promise never to have another woman, keeping my image forever pure in your heart as if I were your true wedded wife?"

"I do."

She set the wreath on his head.

"Maddalena, do you promise never to look at another man and be true to me, like to a wedded husband, till death us do part?"

"I do, my love, I do," she replied.

Alessandro removed the chain with a gem-studded cross from his neck and slipped it around hers, bending to kiss it as it coiled into the fold of her bosom.

"I'll never touch another woman. May God Almighty punish me if I do," he proclaimed, buckling them quietly into the soft grass to reconfirm his claim on his new bride. Like the roots of the ancient tree he felt under his knees, he delved his own treasure, regaining strength with each move, reclaiming his status as a man.

† † †

During the summer months Berti found himself longing for the exciting bustle of Rome, forgetting the city's oppressive heat. Life was still a kaleidoscope of experiences.

Shortly after Rebecca entered Alessandro's life, the great art patron decided to strike a coin to honor her. His own grandfather, Pope Paul, had been open about his mistress and their four children, building Lady Sylvia a villa in the hills of Rome and striking a coin to celebrate her, but now such open practices were risky.

Berti occupied a peculiar place among Alessandro's staff. Above all a servant, but unlike others in service he was bound to his patron by their shared secrets.

"If I may offer my opinion, *Eccelenza*," Berti began, standing behind Alessandro, watching the sun's reflection on Lake Vico's ruffled waters, "might not some clever image serve your purpose without betraying its real meaning?"

Alessandro's eyes scrutinized the two blank circles on a sheet of paper.

"Lena means breath, vigor. Life—candle; lilies—the Farnese family; and *legno*—wood—growth." Berti's mind remained focused. "Why not a Farnese lily growing from your cardinal's hat, winding around a wooden pillar resembling a candle. And on the obverse, Athena's profile merging with yours, a great art patron united with the goddess of wisdom?"

Alessandro smiled, turned, and left the room. Soon he reappeared with a large diamond.

"I appreciate wisdom not expected even from my learned mentors. Take this, and when you return to Rome, you may take it to my jeweler to have it set."

Afraid to touch the hand that gave such a gift, the speechless Berti bent to kiss the feet of the man who had already changed the course of his life.

When Alessandro's court returned to Rome, Maddalena was quietly established in an unpretentious house near the Tiber at the end of the Via dei Banchi Vecchii in a busy street not far from the bridge connecting the old city with Castel Sant'Angelo among rows of dwellings unfrequented by great men. The houses were not numbered, but her neighbors quickly learned that she lived where stray cats, her first friends, assembled.

Maddalena missed her family. Uneasy in papal Rome where Pius ostracized the Jews, her father sold his shop and moved to Vienna at the invitation of the emperor, who heard of the apothecary's fame. Still, she blamed herself for breaking up the family. With Berti as her only friend, she was lonely. One morning when he stopped by, he gave her an idea.

"Alessandro," she pled with her lover later that evening, "please understand my position. I shouldn't live here alone. If Messer Beltraffio and his family move in, they'll protect my reputation. And with their help I can open a small apothecary."

"But, *cara*, who are these people? Can we rely on them? They may talk."

"They're trustworthy. Berti met Beltraffio's wife, Monna Crispina, begging in the market. You remember what happened to him when your men found the Venus?"

Alessandro did, vaguely, unconcerned about Beltraffio's broken back. His secretary paid Beltraffio and his dead friend's family to keep quiet about the discovery of his Venus. Pius forbade owning heathen sculptures, and the cardinal didn't want any interference from the curia in matters that pleased him. The rest was unimportant.

Maddalena wondered if he was listening. "Berti vouches for the family and says they'll be loyal to us," she proceeded insistently. "People will think you come for my help as a healer."

Alessandro quickly learned to accept his mistress' suggestions, especially when they made sense, and Monna Crispina became the housekeeper. Her hunchbacked husband performed the small tasks he could, and their children filled the air with pleasant chatter.

Soon, Maddalena's home became a house of mercy. Even those who could not pay left with good advice and a bundle of herbs to bring them relief, if not a cure. By Advent, even Pius, exhausted by walking among the seven basilicas, accepted Maddalena's treatment.

And so it came to be that the humble *conversa* kissed the pope's feet, daily returning to the palace to soak his ulcerated legs in mineral waters from the hills, bleeding the putrid fistulas and covering them with a dry paste of birch bark. The irascible old man grew agreeable, and the curia began to breathe easier. And quite unexpectedly, Alessandro earned the favor of a pontiff who showed no special attention even to the closest members of his own family.

Strange were those visits when Maddalena tended his ulcers, and the Shepherd of Rome and the once complacent Jewess discussed St. Augustine in the purest Latin. Thus when another Feast of Nativity came and went, Alessandro's paradise on earth would have been complete, had his master painter Federico been a trifle more cooperative.

One frigid February afternoon in the year of Our Lord 1569, Monna Lena sat on the settee in her *gran salone,* plucking gray hairs from Alessandro's crown. He rested his head in her lap, smelling the abundant scent of her hair.

"And if I let that miserable scoundrel go," he said, meaning Federico, "who's going to finish the decorations in the Hall of Hercules?" He grumbled, but languidly in response to her soothing fingers.

"Why don't you send the young Parmesan to Caprarola?" she suggested softly.

"Master Bertoia is not mine to keep. My brother only lent him to me, the same way he sent his Flemish artists. Remember that Ottavio is also anxious to complete his palace in Parma."

Monna Lena was surprised by Alessandro's vacillation. "But it's simple."

"That I need Jacopo Bertoia, and they should be content with others to finish their job?"

"Of course." She wondered why he even asked. "You are *il gran cardinale,* are you not?"

Soon Berti had a new master in Caprarola and continued visiting Don Alfonso in San Oreste, long after Alessandro returned with his court to Rome in the fall. He loved Jacopo's virtuoso pen drawings, especially of the lithe dancing nymphs, but when Berti returned to Rome, eager to practice drawing on paper in pen and ink, he could not have foretold that another talented artist, a newcomer from Brussels, would be his true teacher.

Don Alfonso

The Tiber rose day and night. While the city nursed a false security, Berti awoke to the roar of the angry torrent fed by spring rains. Don Clovio paced the floor of his workroom, limping aimlessly between the tables, carts, stacks of boards, and piles of paper. A distinguished gentleman with chiseled features, sunken eyes, and a pair of spectacles hung around his neck, he customarily dressed in somber black.

"It must be hard to be nearly a century old," Berti thought, watching the old man fold his gilded horn into his cloak and wondering how much it helped his bad hearing.

The miniaturist looked his age, tired, frail—almost transparent.

"But why is he worrying about the river?" Berti mumbled, his thoughts churning as he stirred hot varnish. "Ouch," he gasped, licked his hand, and rubbed it against his work jacket. "At worst we'll have muddy water in the courtyard and the gardens. The servants will move some statues to the *piano nobile* and when the water goes down, they'll clean up the mess."

Berti had never seen a deluge like those that plagued Rome, and he had no other worries. Occasionally he thought about Monna Alba, but since his *Visitation* was blessed and placed in St. Anne's chapel in Santa Maria dell' Anima, his life was a tapestry of success.

But he missed Don Alfonso. During summers in San Oreste, full of laughter, stories, and pony rides, the boy rewarded him with kisses and hugs. Now his arms felt empty.

He set the varnish on a table by the window where he could watch it, stirring occasionally before a skin formed, and returned to his corner to work on illustrations of Ovid's tale of Psyche. The image was clear in his mind, but he still needed a pleasing outcome.

Bending over a charcoal study, he blew away the dust, took a piece of bread from a tin plate, and balled it into an eraser to correct Cupid's offensive proportions. Suddenly the familiar herbal scent of Monna Lena filled the air, and little fingers pressed on his eyelids.

"Guess who, Totti?" cried Don Alfonso's clear soprano voice.

Berti whirled around to behold a tall boy, wearing for the first time the britches of the lad of eight he'd soon be. Olive-skinned, with features set, he now clearly resembled Alessandro. At first he hesitated, unsure of himself with Don Clovio and his two gawking assistants, but the child in him jumped into Berti's lap, smothering the painter's face with kisses.

"*Papà, papà,* I missed you!"

"And I you!" Berti thought as he smiled at Monna Lena's bright face. "My sugarplum!" He embraced the boy affectionately and then pushed him gently away. He loved Don Alfonso and understood he needed a father, any father, but still wished the cardinal's son wouldn't call him by that name. *Doesn't everyone know he is Alessandro's boy?*

"What are you two doing here, of all places? I didn't even know you knew each other!"

"I miss my family," she explained, "my little brother and sister. His Grace was kind enough to let me look after this child until he's ready for his new tutor. When he finishes his primary studies, His Grace is going to send him to Padua." Momentarily the boy froze with fear, and she quickly added, "But that won't be for a long time, child."

Berti looked around to see if anyone was listening. "Why don't we all go for a walk," he suggested. Turning toward Monna Lena as they left, he asked, "When did he arrive?"

"Yesterday quite late, with Monna Brunella. Why don't you take him out alone? But have him back early. He needs to rest. His lessons begin tomorrow just after dawn."

Berti nodded briskly at Don Alfonso as if to ask his approval.

"Yes, Totti, let's go! Now!" he squealed mischievously, pulling his hand from Monna Lena's and running down the grand staircase to the open courtyard and the street.

"*A presto,*" Berti called back, hoping to be punctual.

The wind howled across the yard, swooping dry leaves in tall spirals toward the two levels of open loggias. The boy ran to catch them, splashing through great puddles. "Up, up, up they go!" He traced the loops of the open arches with his pointing finger. As Berti was about to grab him, he slipped out and ran toward one corner of the arcade. "Ugh," he gasped, pointing to a face on a heavy pillar, hair streaming in every direction, the angry mouth bellowing. "That looks like Monna Brunella!" he yelled and stuck out his tongue.

Berti wanted to ask about his nanny, but Don Alfonso ran away to the other corner. When Berti caught up with him, he found the boy's head upside down between his knees looking up at another face. "What are you doing? You'll get dizzy!"

"I want to see if this lady looks happy even when I look at her this way."

"And does she?"

Don Alfonso scrambled up. "Yes, much prettier than Monna Nella, but not as nice as Monna Lena," he pronounced decisively, pointing to the happy face on the pillar. "Can we get her some flowers? They tell me she used to be a flower lady, isn't that right, *papà?* And ... "

"Child, don't call me that. You've become quite a chatterbox!"

Don Alfonso tugged on Berti's jacket. "Totti, they also tell me she's your lady now. And you're my father. Isn't that right?"

"What am I to tell him?" he wavered indecisively. "Why don't we go to the river? A lady sells flowers by the bridge there. We could get some for Monna Lena, *va bene?*"

Don Alfonso's face brightened in expectation. "No. First tell me if she's your lady!"

Berti's eyes rolled in defeat. "She's my *amica,* my little friend," he admitted. "Now you must hold on tightly to my hand. Remember, this is not San Oreste!"

The morning was well on its way, and the streets throbbed with life, the usual litter of discarded boxes, meandering crowds, puddles of water, heaps of muck, barking dogs, and riders. The wide-eyed boy kept pointing excitedly, not waiting for answers to his questions.

"Watch out!" Berti yanked the precipitate child back toward the wall of the palace they were passing as two horsemen clattered by. "This is where your honorable *padre zio* lives." He pointed to the Palazzo Farnese.

The boy looked excited. "Can we go in and see him?"

"He has visitors." Berti pointed to the two riders dismounting by the front gate. "They come from His Holiness the Pope."

"What does that mean?"

"That means that your *padre zio* is going to be very busy today."

The boy pulled a long face. "Can you tell me a story about Ercole instead?"

"I can." Berti tried to scoop him up into his arms before they stepped down to the banks of the river, but he was too heavy. A strong gust of wind blew across the water, snatching Don Alfonso's fine green *biretta* and sending it spiraling over the river.

"That's my new hat!" the boy cried. "My new *bambinaia* will be mad at me."

Berti shrugged his shoulders. "She won't. I'll buy you another one."

"With a big feather too?" The boy watched his feather sink into the seething water.

"Sure. As big as you like." Berti rattled his pocket, taking one last look at the current. "Maybe the river won't flood this year," he thought. "Saint Anne," he prayed, watching his step on the wet banks, "please don't let it flood. The boy is here, and I want us to be happy." With effort, he picked the boy up and buried his face into his chest to protect him from the wind.

"I'm hungry," Alfonso announced, glad to be out of the wind. "Can we get the flowers later? I had nothing to eat this morning."

Berti puffed under the boy's weight. "Why not?"

"I couldn't eat. I wanted to see you, *papà*," the child whimpered, rubbing his wet nose against Berti's jacket.

"Tell you what, my pet"—Berti offered to wipe his nose—"I missed you too. How about if I buy you a sausage and a *dolce* at the market and tell you a story about Ercole? We'll also get you a new hat and then some flowers for Monna Lena." They walked the street, chatting about Caprarola and its new decorations.

"Do you mean that you painted *padre zio* in it like the real Hercules?" the boy asked, balancing the large sausage in his small fingers.

"Yes, but he's even wiser and stronger," Berti agreed, promising himself to ask his patron if he could show Alfonso the new Hall of Hercules.

Don Alfonso looked up at him. "But why is he wiser and stronger?"

"Because he chose better than Hercules."

"Chose what?"

Santa Anna. This is complicated.

"He chose between Lady Pleasure and Lady Virtue."

"What does that mean?" The boy clung to his thoughts. Berti scratched his head. "Wouldn't you like your pastry now?" Unsure, Don Alfonso offered him the half-eaten sausage. "I think so." Berti turned toward Messer Toffano's bakery. "Yes," the boy continued, biting into his new treat. "But what is *pleasure?*"

Berti sighed, beginning to feel impatient. "It's like having your sweetmeats."

"Did *padre zio* get all his sweetmeats?"

Berti thought about Monna Lena, but only for a second, and replied, "No, he chose Lady Virtue, and don't ask me who she is. Eat your cake without getting your new jacket dirty!"

The wind stirred a few late afternoon clouds as they walked the market square, looking at the stalls, enjoying a show with a dancing bear, and listening to pipers, until the tired boy could walk no more. Finally, near Messer Toffano's bakery, Berti picked him up again. He could not remember when he had been so happy.

As he straightened out, he nearly tripped over two goats running by. Then, a few steps away, he heard Anthonis Santvoort making fun of the old baker's apprentice, and spotted Antonis' new friend. "Hans Speckaert—from Brussels and Berti Spranger—from Antwerp." Antonis said, introducing the two.

Berti quickly scrutinized the newcomer of medium height. His plain, angular features framed by thin dark brown hair wouldn't have stirred an old maid, but the warm smile earned a friend swiftly. Berti couldn't shake his hand since he was holding the sleeping boy and Maddalena's flowers, but he smiled back. "Welcome to our circle!" he exclaimed instead.

Hans shot back a quick glance, obviously looking Berti over. "I'm honored," he replied, a bit too formally. "See you at the inn!" Anthonis called and waved good-bye. "To be sure," Berti nodded in agreement, watching Hans catch up with Anthonis.

"What a day," he thought as he shifted his position. The sleeping boy grew heavier by the second. When he finally delivered him to Monna Lena's, he realized he had a hole in his shoe.

"Life is going to be interesting again," he thought, squinting across Don Alfonso's darkened room. With his hands folded across his slumbering chest, the boy looked angelic and Berti tiptoed back to his bed to kiss him. Sweet dreams, *angelino*. Sweet dreams.

† † †

Berti stood in a spacious, brightly colored hall, surrounded by puppet-like figures in endless painted staircases, niches, arcades, and vistas whose ingenious design amazed him more than did their natural appearance.

The Cancelleria, the colossal chancellery where Berti lived, bore the artistic imprints of Alessandro's predecessors, but the decorations in the great Hall of a Hundred Days were recent. They illustrated a complex theme of Alessandro's illustrious family centered around a pontiff resembling Paul III, though Berti did not understand it. So he walked around hastily, trying to analyze the style at least, when Don Clovio appeared at his side. A bit more breathless than usual, he perked up as always when asked important questions.

"*É la sala di cento giorni* painted by maestro Vasari da Firenze, the archduke's painter," he said and explained to Berti how this enormous hall was done in *cento giorni*—a hundred days.

Berti stood transfixed. Surely it was not possible to finish a task so enormous so quickly.

"Done, yes," the old man reiterated, "but not to master's *soddisfazione*, though it's true that His Eminence pressured the Florentine to complete the hall while he was away."

Still, Berti was mesmerized by the deed. "Might I ask what His Eminence does here?"

"It's an audience hall, recording the great deeds of his grandfather who gave the Farnese family power, prestige, and wealth."

Berti listened hungrily.

"I recognize the personifications of architecture, painting, sculpture, and geometry," he said, "and this must be the Vatican, surrounded by seven *putti* for the seven hills of Rome. Wisdom and providence must have guided His Holiness' devotion to such a grand undertaking. But why the strange attire of that high priest?" he asked, hoping to impress.

Don Clovio pointed to the entry. "Those too curious will grow long ears like King Midas. Let's hasten pace. His Eminence wants his new missal completed before the next full moon."

"But if that's Paul III, why is he depicted as a rabbi? Or is he?"

Don Clovio tapped Berti's shoulders. When required, he moved at an amazingly brisk pace, and soon they found themselves in the workshop. Berti had hardly begun illuminating the last page, when the sound of stamping feet disturbed his concentration. Fortunately, Don Clovio was no longer there, and Berti felt free to respond to his unexpected visitor.

"You can wash later," the little figure announced breathlessly, "and today I want to hear about how the boy Ercole killed the snake by himself!"

Maddalena stood behind him, shrugging her shoulders.

"He's like Zephyr, here one minute, and gone the next. He keeps us moving."

Berti was not surprised. The boy had grown swiftly since the cure of his malady in San Oreste. Handsome in his blue velvet britches and golden doublet, his noble blood clearly pulsing with even greater determination.

Resigned, Berti wiped his hands. He had misjudged the time. Nearly an hour had passed since the bells of San Lorenzo tolled nones and Don Clovio left for afternoon prayers. "But child," he warned, "we can't be long. I've too much to do."

Don Alfonso's tiny hand slipped trustingly into Berti's broad one, warming his palm and tickling it with his little fingers. Ready to tease the child a little, Berti laughed at his intense face.

"I've told you the story of Hercules a thousand times—or more. How about the one about brave Perseus who killed the bad Minotaur? He was a great hero too!"

"No, Ercole! I want to hear about Ercole! I'm going to be like Ercole. No, wait. Greater than Ercole!" the boy shouted as he hopped along on one foot. Soon they were outside and heading toward the river.

Berti looked at Alfonso with the sweet indulgence of someone clearly besotted.

"I'm going to be like my *papà*," the child told him breathlessly. "I'm going to paint pictures all over the walls and have everyone come to me and kiss my hands like you kiss *padre zio's*. You *are* my *papà*, isn't that right?" Don Alfonso stopped and tugged hard at the seam of Berti's dirty work jacket.

"Well," Berti replied in the same light tone, "if you destroy my jacket, I certainly won't be famous, for I have nothing else to work in. And no"—pausing with a hint of sadness—"I am not your *papà*." He feared the next question, which came like lightning, as they often did.

"But everyone has a father. If you're not mine, who is? Where is my *papà*?" He started to whimper. Berti hoisted the small, sturdy body and pinched its streaming nose.

"Heroes don't cry. Which part would you like to hear today? About Hercules carrying Mother Earth on his shoulders?"

"No, I want to hear about Ercole killing the bad centaur who wanted to steal his wife. That's not nice," the boy wriggled in Berti's arms, in an attempt to slide down and wanting to skip again. "I like having two legs, don't you?" he asked. "Only creatures that hurt others need four to run away."

Don Alfonso's intelligence gave Berti pause. He pulled out a piece of string that he normally used as a plumb line and tied a handkerchief to it to fashion a simple slingshot. Then he told him about the bad hydra and the river god Acheleos who, like Hercules, also wanted Dejaneira for his bride.

"I don't like King Eurysteus. He's a coward. He can clean the stable all by himself!"

They stood near the water. Berti picked up a stone and put it in the sling shot.

"I'll do it by myself. I'll be a great hero like you. And you *are* my *papà*. It's just a big secret, isn't it?" He took the sling and swung it, but the stone fell out into the water. "I'll do it later," he announced, tired but stubborn, asking to be picked up.

The long Via Giulia was empty.

(Page 39)

Alba shone with virginal purity.

(Page 59)

Berti finished the rip in Alba's garb.

(Page 61)

Berti spotted Anthonis and his new friend at the market.

(Page 83)

The heat at Castel Sant'Angelo was intense.

(Page 99)

Pius assessed Berti's Last Judgment.

(Page 110)

Berti visited the Sistine Chapel.

(Page 118)

Alba became heavy with Berti's child.

(Page 144)

Later that evening, long after Don Alfonso was tucked into bed, his cheeks salty from parting with Berti, Monna Lena and Berti argued about the boy for the first time.

"He'll have to know the truth some day, better sooner than later." Berti maintained.

"The boy is not old enough to understand. It's better this way," she argued back, amicably. God knows she tried to persuade Alessandro to see him oftener, especially now that his son was near. But the cardinal had eyes for her only.

Healer

Maddalena raised herself from a low footstool. Picking up the exquisitely bound copy of Virgil she had been reading aloud, she set it next to her Bible and book of recipes. Contented, Alessandro dozed lightly, his arms hanging over the sides of the bath, the fire's sparkle dancing on the spreading silver of his crown.

"Oh, Madonna, I'm so happy." Maddalena murmured, riveting her gaze on her lover.

She examined his hands, covered by curly black hair. Usually they rested in his lap when she read to him, but he was too warm to keep them in the water, and they hung languidly outside. The hands she liked the most had no signet ring, firm to grip but gentle to touch, and when they embraced her, she burned under their command.

"In the book you gave me for the feast of my name day … "

"Which one?" came forth a sleepy voice.

"The one by Signor Nostradamo. There's a recipe to rejuvenate men," Monna Lena teased out of the blue, shocking her dozing visitor.

Alessandro sat up. "Have I ever failed you?"

"On the contrary. But I did not mean that," she mumbled apologetically, fumbling with a bottle of Venetian glass, trickling a few drops into the tub and topping the bath with more hot water. Musk, sweet lavender, and cinnamon lingered in the air, relaxing the bather. He breathed in deeply, his chest heaving with the pleasure of warmth creeping back, and lay back.

"Woman, do stop that!" He jumped again, vexed.

"Two more, *carissimo*. Won't you let me?" Monna Lena quickly extracted the two offending silver soldiers from his dark brows and lathered her cloth with the soap she prepared, following the great physician's recipe. The lingering pungent aroma around them grew stronger—a hint of cloves, coriander, and sweet almond oil. She lathered his thick hair and beard, the oily emulsion penetrating the skin, softening it, leaving it sparkling clean after the long ride from Ostia, one of many bishoprics the cardinal held *in absentia*.

"Why couldn't you send one of your Jesuits in your stead?" Monna Lena demanded, perplexed. Why should *il gran cardinale* take it on himself to inspect the activity in the diocese?

Alessandro wiped the suds from his eye. "His Holiness is tightening his grip on priests who fail to say Mass and engage in activities contrary to the laws of the Catholic Church."

Monna Lena was surprised. "Does he suspect anything about you?"

"You trouble your head about matters that don't concern you. Since my role ties me to Rome, he commanded me to inspect the diocese personally. That's all."

Monna Lena poured fresh water over his head and studied him. "Signor Nostradamo's soap does whiten the skin and brighten the hair as his book asserts. You look like a new man," she exclaimed, wondering if Alessandro had already succumbed to her mulled wine.

"Bring me the looking glass!" He examined himself in the mirror. "What *are* you talking about!" The misty surface revealed no surprises, although he looked better than in years.

"A simple sublimate, although Signor Nostradamo says he used Medea's recipe."

Alessandro recoiled. "Wasn't she a witch accused of making old people young?"

"Don't take matters so literally! I've analyzed the recipe. Beside the natural herbs, he used juices made from green walnuts, cypress cones, and acorns collected underneath withered oak trees. So you see, *tesoro*, it's fine."

Alessandro glanced at her suspiciously. "How do I know this sublimate works?"

"The book says that the slaves of Gordianus used the recipe on the old emperor, and all of Rome wondered how sprightly and young he looked at the ripe age of sixty-three!" Maddalena dried Alessandro's back and covered him with a soft linen cloth.

"Let me see that glass again," he said, ready to reconsider. "I see what you mean." There was more snow in his hair than he liked. He wondered if extra vitality might help him in the next papal election. *Il gran cardinale* was, after all, but six months away from his fiftieth birthday!

"If you're sure ... " he started and paused, wavering. "And how long to brew it?"

"Only a moment," she said with a pleased wink, "if you'll sit patiently by the fire and let your hair dry." She ran to the front hall where her herbs, powders, bottles, and vials of potions were. Next to the container with the powder to clean Alessandro's teeth was the dye.

Monna Lena swirled the dark liquid. Alessandro viewed it cautiously.

"Let me see your book!" He snapped his fingers. "This is not an elixir of life! It says 'How to Darken White Hair or the Beard.'" He pointed to the title and flipped the vellum pages.

Monna Lena stood expectantly: "Shall we try it?"

"Certainly, *cara*," he acquiesced, still uncertain. "Let's. But only if we try these goodies Signor Nostradamo recommends for the benefit of his noble readers." Alessandro winked playfully toward a chapter not intended for good Christians.

The following afternoon, he attended a session of the *camera apostolica*. Afterwards a group of cardinals gathered, moved by their curiosity about His Grace's sudden rejuvenation.

"His cook must have switched the oil. Everyone knows French olives are inferior to ours," Cardinal Cesi sneered. "But I understand that Alessandro's lands in Avignon produce the finest oil for his household."

Cardinal Montalto had to put his word in. "I am not so certain. I heard from my majordomo that Alessandro's cook did switch to the olive oil from his property in Veletri, now that he no longer holds the post in Avignon."

"Only the oil from Veneto revitalizes the skin, for it nourishes the liver without causing ulcers which bring the yellow tinge to the skin." The Venetian legate offered his opinion.

"I've heard that the waters from Tivoli bleach skin young, but I have little respect for those cures and the men who take them," Cardinal Alciati snickered, for he hated Alessandro. "I've tried that remedy, and I still need another," he added, acknowledging his sagging chin.

"But my illustrious colleagues, it's his new barber, doing the French cut! You do recall how successfully Alessandro negotiated with King Francis?" Cardinal Thiano reminded his colleagues of times bygone and nearly forgotten.

But none of them discovered the secret of the potion that returned the brown to Alessandro's lustrous hair. Suddenly proud of his son, the rejuvenated man often stopped at Monna Lena's solely to check on Don Alfonso's new conquests in the wilderness of Latin grammar while Maddalena's concoctions lay forgotten on the shelf.

† † †

Bartholomäus Spranger, His Grace's humble servant at the height of success at a youthful twenty-four years, was tired, suffering from too much ambition.

He was often seen at Meneer Santvoort's inn with Anthonis Santvoort and their two new compatriots, Hans Speckaert and Cornelis Cort. Over beer and meat pies, their conversations turned at first to the Duke of Alba's recent invasion of the Low Lands. But soon they settled on a pleasant topic and moved, even at a late hour, to Cornelis' shop nearby. The gangly man with a big Adam's apple and a head of flaming curls could have fallen out of one of Titian's paintings, and Berti teased him, knowing that Cornelis came to Rome directly from his studio.

"Are you now planning to operate your own press?" Berti asked one night, looking around the room stacked with paper, printed sheets, and drawings for the engraver's copper plates lying carelessly about on shelves, tables, and benches.

The lines in Cornelis' forehead deepened. "That kind of business is costly."

"I thought you made a pile of money working for Titian. And beside, why so much? All you need is a press, paper, some ink, and someone to run your shop. Couldn't you train Anthonis?" Berti pointed to the innkeeper's nephew, shuffling through a stack of engravings.

Cornelis checked his pocket for a piece of chalk and replied, "I couldn't compete."

Berti arched his eyebrows, unconvinced. "Are you two partners?" He pointed to Hans, drawing nearby.

"No," Cornelis replied. "Hans and I became friends in Venice when I worked for Titian. Then we parted ways for a while and met again here."

Berti crossed his arms. "But why is he in your shop?"

"When he came to Rome he had nothing to do. Hans is an excellent draftsman, which I am not. We both do our trade well. He traces the pictures on the plates, and I engrave them."

Berti looked at the engraver's callused hands, marked by nicks and cuts and an ugly singed scar. "Fire?"

Cornelis shot a cursory glance at his hands. "Acid. I use it to bite a design into a plate."

Berti glanced at Hans working. "I can't draw well with the quill. Could you teach me?"

Too engrossed in work, Hans did not reply, although Berti could have sworn that he heard him.

"Come here." Hans pulled out a blank sheet and a drawing depicting the *Finding of Moses*. Berti examined the surface of the sheet, admiring the gnarled tree trunk, sprouting dense foliage, and under it a group of maidens bent over an infant in a wicker basket on the river bank.

"Sit!" Hans cleared a spot across the table. "And don't think you can learn to draw like this in one shot." Although Hans appeared not much older than Berti, indeed closer to thirty, the man's sheer confidence impressed the pupil.

"First draw the composition in chalk." Though tired, Berti perked up and began to copy Hans' composition. When he was done, Hans showed him how to highlight the chalk drawing with the quill. Berti touched up the features, the arms, stressing the points of the fingers, the folds. Finally he did the entire tree in ink, working lightly, right from his shoulder, and finished the drawing without a single blemish.

That night when the guard raised his oil lamp, Berti's face shone with joy, for God and Hans Speckaert had finally taught him to master the quill. For the next two days Berti worked for Don Clovio. Then came Sunday. After church, he hurried with Hans back to Cornelis' shop.

"*Vino?*" the engraver asked the pair, enjoying the day in his own way. Berti heard a young woman singing behind the workshop.

"Do you realize you should have heard Mass today?" Hans admonished Cornelis even though he little expected a response.

"Hans, do you have a woman?" Berti asked pointedly.

Hans pushed greasy thin hair out of his pudgy face. "There's a German girl I've seen in the congregation at the Anima, but she isn't interested."

"Why not?" Cornelis broke into the conversation.

"She's pretty, and I'm ugly. But her father won't have me either."

Berti scratched his nose. "Did you ask? Who's he anyway?"

"A book vendor. He runs a shop around the corner. And, no, I didn't. I've got little to offer. Why should he want a foreigner from Brussels who can't support himself?"

"Nonsense!" Berti retorted, pointing to the stack of drawings. "These are ten times more precious than any woman! How do you do this?"

"Like this." Hans opened his lesson, but Alessandro's liveried servant entered and interrupted their conversation to summon Berti to the Cancelleria.

Before long he was bowing before the cardinal, who finally looked up from his desk: "We were turning over the events of when you first entered Our service, but We can hardly remember. Much has happened since."

"What did really happen?" Berti wondered. His *padrone* was mysterious.

"We hardly know where to begin," Alessandro blurted, twisting the signet ring around his finger. "To better serve Our Lord, We have reached the conclusion that We must step aside for a cause infinitely more noble than Our own."

Berti had no clue. He began to fidget with his hands. "Do you want me to work for Your Eminence's brother, the Duke Ottavio?" was the brightest response he could manage.

Alessandro's eyebrows arched. "No, no, no. It appears that I've misled you," the cardinal replied less formally, pointing to the letter in his hand. "See for yourself."

Berti blushed. "Excellency, I cannot read Latin well enough," he mumbled, shocked by the pope's signature which he *had* deciphered.

Alessandro's brow rose as he handed the letter to Don Fulvio. "Would you oblige Us?"

Monotonously, his antiquarian translated the letter, first a detailed passage relating the sender's poor health and his need to contemplate spiritual matters in preparation for the world beyond. Berti had no idea where the letter was heading. Soon it focused.

We now beseech you to send Us the young Fleming at your earliest convenience, offering Master Bartolomeo full contract with Us. We shall pray most fervently that God may be always with you and grant you good health to serve Him with as much zeal and dedication as you have been known to serve Us.
Pius V, Pont Max.

Berti gulped. The news overwhelmed him and left his mouth dry. While the prospect of entering the pope's service had never entered his mind, the thought of leaving Alessandro and all the people who had befriended him tore at his heart. He barely could ask how soon he was to enter his new post.

"In two days, young man. But tomorrow we are both to see the pope. Make your ways expeditiously," Alessandro commanded as Berti staggered out to tell his friends.

† † †

In July only the city's poorest remained in the city. Anyone who had a chance to exit Rome was gone, certainly all the nobles—except His Holiness, Pius V. No wonder His Grace, Alessandro Farnese, grumbled to find himself summoned by the pontiff, hoping to find him rested after his noon meal, wanting to return to Caprarola as soon as possible.

He was in a foul mood, sitting in the corner of his litter-chair, silent, the heat weighing down his chest, wondering what was so important to require his presence in a city where no one willingly exposed himself to the malaria which plagued Rome's summers. He sorely missed Monna Lena, for he found increasing spiritual solace in the company of the woman he loved rather than the physical gratification that initially dominated their love with such force.

These days unpleasant thoughts regularly deprived the great cardinal of his sleep; for after his love for God and the church, he hoped for nothing less than the chair of St. Peter. While loving Maddalena with his entire being, his mind dictated caution, distance from the woman he adored and his son in her care. They were becoming an unwanted burden to an ambitious man.

With his daughter Clelia, on the other hand, he maintained an easy bond. She was the offspring of steamy days at the height of his *nonno's* power, when he was young and times were more generous to prelates without scruples. Visits to Clelia, tucked away in a marriage of convenience, provided him with occasional pleasant diversion.

Berti sat quietly in the other corner, careful not to intrude on his patron's thoughts. Alessandro's litter-chair entered the Cortile di San Damasso before mid-afternoon. Seeing the Farnese crest on its pleated, red velvet curtains, the papal halberdiers bowed to the great cardinal and his companion and let them pass.

"All Rome is in deep slumber," Alessandro hissed. "Everyone but Holy Father is taking a siesta." Sensing his displeasure, Berti let him talk. "I fail to understand how his constitution endures trials that would consume a far more robust man." In vain he tried to peel the soaked robes away from his well-nourished body, as his feet crossed the heat-drenched courtyard.

"I hear, *Eccelenza,* that *Papa Pio* spends days visiting the poor, frequently feeding them with his own hands and reading to them from the scriptures, never pausing to look after himself. He must be of strong constitution," Berti offered, needing to fill the void.

"His Holiness awaits you in his private apartments." Signor Cirillo, the Pope's secretary, bowed at the portal and beckoned the pair to follow him through the maze of the inner palace.

It was Berti's first visit to the sacred asylum, and he desperately wanted to pause for a moment to admire some of the art; but inside the thick, cool walls the papal secretary moved at the pace of one totally unaware of the scorching heat surrounding the palace.

The room they entered at last was more like the cubicle of a penitent monk than a papal chamber. Refreshed by the cool air, Berti left the limping cardinal behind, half expecting further directions from an old scribe seated in a corner.

"Brother in God, may I ... " he began as a narrow ray of light unexpectedly lit the large signet ring on the withered hand clutching the rail. Berti went soft with fear, overcome at his own ignorance. *"Nobilissimo e sanctissimo Signor Padre, pietà, per amor di Dio, pietà!"* he choked, begging the pontiff's mercy.

The veined hand dropped the quill and slowly rose toward Berti. Only after his lips had touched the venerated ring did Berti permit himself to look at the man who beckoned gently and was about to engage him as court painter.

The small, shriveled man, looking older than his sixty-six years, sat in a simple pine chair next to a worn scriptorium. The weight of his heavy vesture twisted his body, the coarse wool covering all but the bluish veined feet and the hem of a simple flax shirt. The exterior spoke to the man's character to such a degree that the whole room radiated his kindness and warmth. With unmistakable authority, the pontiff first addressed Cardinal Alessandro.

"We wish to promulgate a new decree which will punish sinners for violating the Sabbath and for blasphemy." Fervently the pope tugged the snow-white beard streaming down his chest.

Cardinal Alessandro shifted his weight, feeling momentary relief in his legs.

"Would the Holy Father ever consider that worrying about men's souls even in the middle of a scorching summer is inhumane?" He mopped his forehead.

Aware of Alessandro's weaknesses, the pontiff resumed his thoughts.

"Monsignor"—the pope's knuckles grew white—"in Our continuing concern for men's salvation We wish to enact a new law that all men repent their sins daily, reminding them that their bodies are but weak shrines in which their immortal souls dwell on earth only temporarily. We shall forbid all physicians to attend sick patients without proof that they have confessed."

The cardinal went limp. Had Pius heard anything about Maddalena?

Seeing his discomfort, the pope relaxed his grip on the chair and rang the bell for a chair: "Sit down and take some refreshment, my son, and we shall discuss the matter in greater detail."

"Maestro Spranger," Pius continued, "Our soul is willing but Our body failing. We desire that you prove the skill of which your benefactor kindly informed Us by copying Fra Angelico's *Last Judgment* for Our grave in Bosco by Alexandria. We have seen your paintings, and they speak of great talent. But above all, We wish to see an obedient Catholic."

Bellicose words of a relentless warrior against sin, of a shepherd to lost sheep.

"We command you to begin your work by your most sincere confession to Our Father, to Christ on earth and in Heaven, and to the Holy Ghost. And now, leave Us!" the pontiff concluded as he sank before the plain wooden crucifix in deep prayer.

And as the bells of St. Peter's tolled nones in the summer of 1570, Berti found the joy of tranquility.

Urbi et Orbi

The heat at Castel Sant'Angelo was so intense the stones seemed almost to melt. Even the giant angel seemed to watch over the fortress with reluctance. Below, people filled the shaded streets like busy ants before taking refuge inside the labyrinth of their dwellings.

Berti stood at the top of the bastion, watching the city awaken.

"*Roma: Urbi et Orbi.* To the city and the world you speak," he whispered, "and Meneer Bartholomäus Spranger, the excellent painter to His Holiness Pius V stands at your apex." He bowed gallantly in all directions, his emotions mounting with the heat.

The sun shifted a bit, and sweat freckled Berti's nose. "Ay, it's already hot!"

He turned around. Behind him to the west mushroomed the fortress of the Vatican built by a succession of popes, its various wings, the Sistine Chapel, and the long Belvedere Court surrounded by lush gardens. The vast fabric of St. Peter's gaped, its massive drum and cupola unfinished. Across the Angel's Bridge below, long streams of pilgrims trudged toward the holy ground of St. Peter's, pale northerners and dark southerners, people from Genoa and Naples, from Augsburg, Avignon, Paris, and Prague, white Gauls alongside dark Berbers, *conversos* from Spain, men on foot and animals, all unified by a common vision.

Past the elbow of the river where a man watered his donkey, a procession of mourners moved from the hospital of Santo Spirito toward the cemetery, accompanied by a doleful clanging from the nearby church of Santo Spirito in Sassia. A bit further upstream, near the Mausoleum of Augustus, the Port of Ripetta shimmered like a beehive, vessels opening their holds to the waiting merchants. The fortress occupied several large buildings with wide stairs cutting its slope up to the arcaded court of the customs house. Behind, the round mausoleum of Augustus marked the quarter where whores peddled their wares.

Berti looked at the sun. There it was, one moment on the horizon over the Alban Hills, the next seeming to stand right above his head. Had he passed that much time in reverie?

He walked closer to the parapet over the river and his thoughts changed. He wondered if Monna Lena had already opened the doors of her apothecary and if Don Alfonso had learned his new lines from Virgil. From their dwelling he traced the straight line of Via Giulia toward the Bridge of Sixtus and past it toward the little island in the middle of the river and the ancient hospital of Fatebene Fratelli.

Opening the small portal, he descended the narrow staircase. A pleasant chill met him on the widening spiral to the huge gate that opened to the drawbridge connecting the fortified castle with the Angel's Bridge. From there he passed the Vatican, St. Peter's, and the Gate of the Light Cavalry to report to His Holiness.

It was Berti's first trip on the old Aurelia road, the coastal path which had hugged the Mediterranean toward Livorno since the time of ancient Rome. He was curious about Pius' country villa, built while he was a cardinal and about which odd remarks circulated in the palace.

When he dismounted he was so busy brushing the dust that he nearly missed the villa. It was small, hardly able to accommodate a papal retinue. "Without a coat of arms at its gate," he mused, recalling the magnificence of Alessandro's villa in Caprarola, "the owner of this place might be a lowly bishop."

But when he walked among the exotic plants in the fine gardens, he realized that Pius' love of God was bound to His nature. As he entered the *casaletto,* loud chatter radiated into the front hall. The sight of the pope kissing an elegantly clad man's hand left him speechless.

"Come closer to Us, maestro Spranger, and meet the finest painter that heaven ever blessed with talent and dedication to a holy cause."

The Pope motioned Berti to come nearer the window where two men, one old and the other younger, stood.

Intimidated, Berti hardly moved.

"Maestro Giorgio," the pope nodded slightly toward the older man, "may We introduce to you Our new painter, a young Fleming from Antwerp?"

Berti bowed. Only one man named so could have taken the pope's fancy.

"Maestro Vasari comes from Arezzo, and Our friend the Archduke of Florence has kindly lent him to Us," Pius explained. "And here"—he motioned toward the confident man, only slightly older than Berti—"We are also pleased to accept into Our service a fine new hand."

"Call me Jacopo," the assistant replied warmly.

That's how Berti first met Giorgio Vasari, a sun that never set over the city of Florence, and his disciple Jacopo Zucchi. During their Vatican days, Jacopo's elegant style inspired Berti's female figures, but unfortunately the grand master meddled too often in Berti's private life.

† † †

Piety came to Berti naturally. That aspect of his mind recommended him to Pius above his other credentials, as Berti learned from Monna Lena. She warned him not to stray from his calling, for the pontiff had no patience for apostates, especially under his own roof. Thus when Berti received Adrien's frequent invitations to dinner, the young painter was wont to crumple them in his pocket.

He was working exceptionally hard. Each day, Pius grew more anxious to see the epitaph finished before he died, but the work progressed slowly. Several hundred figures and heads in heaven, earth, and hell had to be copied from Fra Angelico's *Last Judgment*.

With a position of honor and respect, life in the Vatican palace was rewarding. Yet Berti lacked something. When he confessed, he actually wished for some great sin to atone for. Aside from helping Alessandro with Maddalena, he succumbed only occasionally to gluttony.

Soon his piety turned into a mandatory prison. Having to watch when he got up, what he ate, how he dressed, and what he said and read, his religious fervor began to wear thin, at first imperceptibly, then more swiftly. Then he wondered about moving, perhaps to Florence, meeting new friends and working for the young married archduke who kept many beds warm.

For Berti had his own frustrations, and no amount of flagellation or fasting bridled them. He had tried some of Monna Lena's purges, though not many, for she specialized in rejuvenating men's egos. He drank the virgin water from the hills and said his rosary, but his willpower weakened steadily. The Jesuits' recommendation of self-gratification left him miserable.

He looked out at the rectangle of grass between the two wings of the Belvedere. There the ground was parched and the grass withered after the dry summer. The fall rains shunned the sterile Vatican lands. "Strange"—he stepped away from the window—"that is exactly how I feel—burnt out, not full and not empty, wanting, fighting something without understanding it. Then ... why not? A dinner with Adrien would cheer me up." He reached into his pocket and pulled out Adrien's note: "For the sake of our old friendship, do come. Adrien."

That evening at the appointed hour he dismounted by the front gate of the palazzo Adrien kept for the prince-bishop and patted his horse, a luxury he enjoyed as a papal servant. Although his piebald had a slight limp, Lucia's lustrous coat made up for all imperfections.

He followed the fine-liveried servant up the stairs to the newly adorned hall illuminated by tall tapers and bedecked with tapestries that would not have shamed Alessandro's palace. Carved furniture, tall chests, cabinets of curiosities, silver candelabra, and bronze statuettes peeked at him from everywhere, but what surprised him most was the crowd thronging the space.

"Jesus, Mary, and Joseph!" Adrien turned to his reliable list when words failed him, his whiskers turned up to perfection. "You came. I'm so glad!"

Berti returned his embrace. Adrien stepped back, baffled by Berti's attire.

"Don't they pay you in the stingy pope's big palace?" he demanded, sneering openly at Berti's somber clothes, enhanced by a starched white collar embroidered in black.

Berti scrutinized Adrien's silver-laced doublet embroidered with pearls. "What a parakeet!" he laughed as he sniffed Adrien's perfume. "A white *camicia* with a lacy collar and pumpkin-colored britches soft enough for a lady's bottom!"

"Fine business, my friend," Adrien sniffed back. "Haven't I begged you to come in on my new-world business, and what have you done instead?"

Berti's mood turned sour, as he imagined how well he could have done with Adrien.

"Look, don't worry about it. Enjoy!" Adrien picked up a silver plate, in its center a drunken Silenus drowning in a stream of wine. A few grapes remained when Berti took a bunch and uncovered the lascivious pose of two other satyrs. "And where did you get this?" Berti pointed to a lamp that stood nearby, its base composed of satyrs cunningly interlocked.

"Forget that." His host thrust a silver goblet into his free hand. "Meet my friends."

All the faces were new, many quickly engraved in Berti's mind, but their names and connections instantly fused into a jumble of gaiety—men and women of all stations, business associates, gambling friends, servants, but no couples bound in holy matrimony.

The crowd was huge and the hall too small, and even gallant Berti felt uneasy. Loose women and tipsy men coupled without shame, and the air stank with their passion. When the bell rang for the feast in the grand hall, Berti was among the first to sit.

Refreshed by a breeze from the open loggia, he looked around, amused by the tightly laced corsets pushing women's bosoms up to their chins, smelling their sticky perfumes, watching their empty flirting. Alone in the crowd, he tried to strike a conversation, but the exchanges were senseless.

The musicians in the courtyard strummed a sweet tune; first came the plucked chords of the guitars, then sounded the singing mandolins, and finally—heaven above—Berti rose to see what instrument was producing such rich sounds.

"It's the double harp." Adrien tapped him on the shoulder to sit. "When he honors us with his presence—though not today—the prince likes to be entertained, and some new thing takes his fancy. As you can see, it's enchanting. To your health, my friend."

Berti tipped his beaker back but took only a small sip.

Adrien grinned. "A bit out of place? I thought you might like to meet an old friend."

Berti's interest sparked as he traced the pattern of the woman's dress up to her face, but when Monna Alba removed her veil, he was stunned.

"I'm glad you two need no introduction," Adrien laughed at the two blank faces and moved to the head of the table. He picked up another goblet and lifted it above his head. The room quieted, and the guests stopped squirming long enough for his brief address.

"To you, my dear friends, and to our true guardians, Venus, Ceres, and Bacchus! May they never freeze alone and keep our spirits especially high tonight!"

The company greeted its host with raucous laughter. Only when the meal commenced and the company dipped into their plates did Berti stop shaking and looked at his companion.

"I thought you were still in Spain with Sister Teresa."

Monna Alba hardly looked up. "I was, but I came back. Not long ago."

Still in shock, Berti fumbled with his food. "Your mother, is she well?" he finally asked.

"As can be expected."

Berti's brows lifted, but Monna Alba lost her tongue again. "Why, so … Is she ill?"

Monna Alba took a deep breath. "It's my stepfather. He beats her."

Berti looked at her quizzically, amazed that the shrewd, enterprising widow let herself be fooled by a simpleton like her foreman. "Women are so stupid," he asserted. "The only intelligent woman I ever met is Monna Lena. She has to be a man in a woman's body."

He took another sip and touched Monna Alba's hand, inviting despite the callused palm.

As for her, she wondered how she ever left Rome without him. In the days when he lodged with Adrien in her mother's house, she resisted imagining his lips, the sensuous messengers of carnal thoughts, which in her presence deliberately uttered only noble words.

Alba tried hard not to imagine the rest, aware that as she washed and ironed his shirts and breeches with blind affection, her mind whirled in turmoil around the body filling them with clear, masculine definition.

He broke into her thoughts. "Why did you return?"

"I wasn't well." She looked at him briefly, trying to forget what people in Spain told her. It was not Christ who visited her in his divine love but a mortal man who raped her. But she did not believe them, because a Spanish doctor found her to be a virgin.

Her gaze flickered, then grew dull again. "Do you know I have the moon sickness? During the day, I helped Teresa look after the sheep, and we walked the thorny roads of Sierra de Guadarrama, and I flinched not for a moment, nor did I ever stray from my path."

"I never doubted you would." As Berti watched Monna Alba, his feelings for her awakened. He moved closer, loath to miss a word in the noisy company.

She continued with hesitation. "But at night, those bright nights when the ground was frozen with snow or parched with dust, when the full moon shone brightly, they found me far away, sometimes not for days. She is a holy woman—St. Teresa some call her. But then one day we went to Madrid, all of us, to plead our cause at the court of His Majesty King Philip."

"Don't stop!"

She exposed a jagged scar below her shoulder, and Berti touched it. "Is that why you came back?" But she only reached for her goblet without drinking from it.

"Why did you come here tonight, of all the places in Rome, to Adrien's?"

She picked up her courage and replied. "Adrien heard I was in Rome. He came by a few times. I don't know how or where he learned I was back."

Berti scrutinized her face.

"You're wrong," she warned him. "I don't care for him. He wants me for my body, to be tossed away like the one they found in the Tiber last week."

Berti was horrified. "You must be mistaken! Adrien would never do that."

Monna Alba closed her eyes. "Perhaps not. But I heard the wretch was with his child."

"I don't understand you. Why would you have gone to such a man's house?"

Alba slowly found her breath. "I ... I hoped that if I accepted his invitation I'd find you here. I tried at the Vatican, but they wouldn't let me in."

"Alba, look at me!" Berti held her chin between his fingers. She looked angelic. "I did not mean to hurt you ... then. Would you like me to take you home now?"

"No!" Alba fought her confusion. "I mean, *you* did not hurt me. Yes, please take me home. But not in the middle of dinner. I don't want to attract attention."

But the meal was long. Finally they left, unnoticed by a company ready for the revelry of the Bacchanal. Many women had already exposed their pretty legs for the symbolic stamping of the grapes in the yard. Neither Berti nor Monna Alba looked back.

Berti walked with her to the gate, swerving now and then to keep the drunken guests away. Lucia trod patiently as he mounted her. "Why do you stand there?" he asked the girl. "Won't you ride with me?"

She paused, struck by the question. "*He* has asked me," she thought shyly and nodded.

"Then leave your torch behind!" he commanded as he swept her up behind him.

Silently they rode through the dark streets, her warm body pressed against his back, her arms circling his waist, her head against his shoulder, nestled close to his neck.

Silently Berti dismounted by the gate of her house and helped her down. He leaned closer, arms at his sides and, as he did that first night in the moonlit room above, he kissed her good night.

Silently she met him half way and entered her mother's house without turning back. But that night there was no moon, and Berti knew that well.

† † †

Alessandro sat in his study in the Cancelleria chewing on a quill. When the tip finally broke, he dropped the feather on the floor and picked up another to finish his correspondence. He was about to meet with Pius, both of them greatly worried by the Turkish advances in Christian domains.

For months the Holy Father pled for help. But Venice was busy trading with the Levant, and Spain was troubled by her rebellious Northern Provinces. Only when the Venetian arsenal was blown up did the Republic agreed to join the league with Spain and the Papal states. Pius, worried about his health, needed Alessandro.

But his Vice Chancellor, the grand patron of the arts, had his own problems. He checked the new quill's tip, dipped it in the well, and continued his letter:

Don Francisco, We wish to remind you that Our revenues are finite. Our treasury has already paid out over eight-thousand scudi toward the construction of Il Gesù, which has not even reached the stage of the dome. We are neither pleased with the models of the façades that Messer Giaccomo provided Us, nor do We take pleasure in the manner in which the colossal order of pilasters is crowned by the ungainly attic story.

Alessandro further informed the Jesuit General of his demand for a more dignified façade and then delivered him to the care of Jesus Christ and His saintly mother. Sealing the letter, he rang the bell.

"Your Grace?" Padre Carlo appeared swiftly.

"Take these." The cardinal handed over a stack of sealed letters. He raised himself slowly, burdened by the corpulence caused by Maddalena's cooking. Of late, there had been too many oysters and not enough movement, not to mention too much correspondence and too much fretting over the papal succession.

When he entered Don Clovio's studio unannounced, the miniaturist's assistants quickly dropped their brushes to bow.

"How does my exalted prince fare this grim day?" Don Clovio inquired shakily.

"With God's grace We float in His presence, sustained by His divine will. I'm well, very well indeed, my dear old man." Alessandro patted his belly. "God bless you for your devotion to Us. We have seen many days together, you and I, not so, Don Giulio?

"And how fares our Flemish servant?"

Alessandro turned to Berti, standing over an unfinished cassone he was illuminating, a landscape in which a maiden sat with a horned animal, pushing its head into her lap. He had borrowed Berti from Pius for a few days. Now he studied the unicorn, assessing the direction of the animal's tusk, wondering if he should scold his artist or laugh at his invention, fitting a kept woman's gift.

Struck by his gaze, Berti attempted to clarify the image: "Your Grace, as you see, I have painted the very same landscapes I painted for you in Caprarola on this *cassone*."

Alessandro waited.

"I also painted the maiden sheltering a unicorn in her lap, the animal which only a virgin can protect from its enemies."

Once again Alessandro assessed the direction and the angle of the animal's single horn.

Berti felt a chill. "Well, Your Grace, how can I place the head of such a large animal in a small, confined area without diminishing its horn—at least in part?"

Don Clovio limped over, dragging the stiff leg, broken long ago during the Sack of Rome. He pinched spectacles onto the bridge of his nose to examine the figure of the maiden lost in the lush landscape. "You fool!" he muttered.

Alessandro's eyes twinkled. "*Don Iulio!*" The cardinal addressed the old man in Latin. "Do take your rest now," he suggested gently but firmly. "We take no offense with the Fleming. He is inexperienced in the art of perspective, although your lessons show most finely in his work," he quickly added, realizing he had overstayed the time of his meeting with Pius.

So it came to pass that when the glazes dried and Alessandro and Maddalena stopped laughing over the amusing design on her new chest, he lost a bit of weight, imitating the unicorn landing in the sweet lap of his virgin-at-heart mistress.

† † †

Berti, terrified by his emotions as he thought about Alba, saw his life change overnight. During the day, his work kept him busy, and at night he frequented Meneer Santvoort's tavern with regularity, hoping to meet new friends. But the summer of 1570 left many merchants fearful, for in July the Turks captured Cyprus.

For Berti those were distant concerns, and when a discussion grew heated, he visited Hans instead. They became good friends, since Berti helped him meet the girl with whom Hans fell in love. Impressed by Berti's credentials, and even more by his promise to help Hans get established, her father, who sold Berti the Dürer print, happily released his daughter's hand with a small dowry. Berti could not have been happier for his friend.

But still he was miserable, yearning to see Monna Alba until finally he met her by chance in the hospital of Santo Spirito while getting salves for Maddalena. A frequent visitor in the Borgo, Berti watched with interest the construction of Pius' new hospital wing.

Far down the Sistine ward in the long corridor filled with beds, Berti paused by a fresco with the boy St. Francis receiving his habit. While he examined it, a nun in a novice's habit passed him with a child in her arms. When she lifted her head, he recognized Monna Alba. Startled to see her there and in a nun's habit, he ran after her, catching up with her by the niche with St. Francis. "Listen, I beg you!"

Alba's eyes were wary. "Let me go! This child's sick."

Berti looked desperate. "Will you see me?"

Alba winced. "I'm not free. His Holiness has allowed me to join the Carmelites."

"Why did you join another order?"

"I had to. Life at home has become hell. I didn't know what else to do."

Berti could not believe his bad luck. "Will you not see me one more time?"

Weighed down in arms and soul, she asked, "When?"

"Tomorrow, at sunset."

"Where?" She stared blankly at the child in her arms.

"At the bottom of the steps at the Aracoeli church." He hesitated as she moved on. "Wait!" He caught up with her again. "Behind the old town hall."

The walk back to his studio in the Belvedere was short. Instead of painting, he paced the space and finally faced the large Fra Angelico altarpiece he was copying. He saw the calm face of Christ, seated high in the central panel, surrounded by the almond-shaped mandorla.

"Oh, Lord, you must have loved a woman other than your blessed virgin mother! Surely you understand my feelings." Berti fought with himself addressing Christ like a friend. "You took her away from me before when she went to Spain. Please, show me the right path now!"

The sun shifted across the room and rested on the figure of Christ, gilding the surface around him in a supernatural aura. "I understand."

Berti lowered his head peacefully. "I'll wait for your word. But in my painting, I'll paint you as you have shown yourself, surrounded by the golden haze of divine wisdom and mercy."

For the rest of that and all the following day, Berti worked feverishly, finishing the cartoon of the figure he had feared to start, Christ in the pose of mighty heavenly judge. When Pius came to assess the progress of Berti's painting, he turned and said, "Now, young man, there is but one more thing I desire."

The pontiff bowed his head.

"Lord God Almighty in heaven and on earth." He prayed feverishly, his fragile fingers tightly clenched. "In Thy heavenly wisdom wouldest Thou now guide me to crush the infidel? For I have little time."

Alba

The bells of Santa Maria in Aracoeli had long since chimed mid-afternoon when Berti rode by the church and up the long, steep ramp toward the Capitol. In Michelangelo's piazza stood the equestrian statue of Marcus Aurelius, and behind it towered the façade of the City Hall, framed by crenellated bastions. As he rounded the left tower, a stream of senators poured down the central stairs and pushed through the onlookers. Berti cursed his choice of a meeting place.

Behind the City Hall, the path was nearly empty. But for a few men and donkeys passing and two cows grazing nearby, most of the Forum was devoid of people, as if all Rome was on the Capitol behind him. When he reached the rear of the massive building, he checked the height of the sun. Shuddering with foreboding, he jumped off and leaned against his mare.

"It's late and she's gone. Perhaps she never came. What do you think, Lucia?"

His filly neighed in affirmation, but she also might have just stumbled as he crossed the grassy space and stopped in front of the columns of the temple of Vespasian, scanning for Monna Alba. Two men stood to the left by the colossal antique statue of Marforio. Otherwise the vast meadow rested peacefully, untouched by movement.

Lucia neighed again, and Berti laid his hand on her trembling nostrils. Hearing his own heart thump, he rubbed her soft ears to calm them both down. Ahead the mighty Colosseum rose against the horizon, and midway where the column of Focas obstructed the bell tower of the church of Santa Maria Nova, a small herd of cows ambled toward him.

But there was no sign of a woman. Berti looked toward the back of the Forum and the Arch of Titus but saw only a child with an infant tied to its back, harrying a flock of geese toward the Capitol.

He checked the sun again, ready to leave, when he imagined he saw a gray habit flashing through the Arch of Septimus Severus. Remounting Lucia, he raced down the meadow and through the half-buried archway like a lightning bolt to find Monna Alba studying the crumbling reliefs. Startled, she looked up and whispered, "Have you been looking for me?"

Frustrated, he answered curtly, "I have. And what in hell are you doing down here? I thought we agreed to meet behind the old palace!"

Surprised and hurt, the young woman started to run.

"Alba, wait! I'm sorry. Please, listen. I've been looking everywhere for you!"

Monna Alba paused, her expression now more receptive.

"Forgive me," Berti apologized again. "It's simply that I was afraid I'd never see you again." Jumping off Lucia, he walked along a few paces without a direction and then suggested, "Shall we walk across?"

She nodded, clearly feeling too exposed in the open meadows. Behind the colossus of Marforio they turned east toward the Tower of the Counts. Berti dropped the reins over Lucia's back and picked a tiny late blooming daisy, one of the thousands that graced Roman meadows in the spring, to offer her.

She refused it, but Berti doubted she wanted to. He dropped the flower into his pocket, trying to collect his thoughts. "Did you know, my sweet lady, that when you left for Spain I was so crushed I wanted to become a Jesuit? Why did you join the Carmelites?"

Monna Alba frowned. "I was unhappy when I came back. I also wanted to help poor women and girls like me, so I begged Monna Lena to speak on my behalf."

"But you weren't poor when you went to join Sister Teresa and her followers," he recalled. Aware that Maddalena frequently spoke with the pope, Berti was not surprised she helped Alba.

"Whatever I had, I took with me to help Sister Teresa nourish her dream. Nothing is left."

Berti looked surprised. "But how did Lena meet you?"

"Adrien took me to her," Alba replied. "Nino threw me out after you brought me back from Adrien's that night. He saw us kissing and called me a whore."

"Are you telling me you walked back to Adrien's place that night alone?" Berti did not want to imagine what might have happened. Alba nodded, and they walked on.

As they left the Tower of the Counts behind, the road sloped up steeply. Alba tripped over the root of a giant chestnut tree and winced in pain. She stepped aside to catch her breath in time to escape a covered wagon rambling down the hill at full speed.

"Watch where you're going, you bastards!" Berti screamed after two peasants riding at its open back. Seeing an elegant cavalier and a nun on the slope of the Esquiline Hill, they laughed and threw rotten figs at them. "Scoundrels!" Berti picked up a chestnut in its shell and threw it at the men. Alba picked up another one.

"Look!" She pointed to the hills undulating in the distance, already darkening in the shadows of the setting sun. As the sun settled, the heavens filled with streaks of gold and carmine, changing the huge rotunda of the temple of Hadrian into a fiery pit. The entire sky grew red, consuming even the distant Castel Sant'Angelo in its crimson robe, the oblique light catching every stone, every tree, every blade of grass, down to the pebbles under Alba's feet, bathing the two lone figures in the color of blood.

Even Berti's beard glowed afire. Alba screamed, dropped the prickly nut, and reached for her neck, leaving her tall white collar bloodstained. She stepped on the shell and picked out the smooth fruit through a crack in the skin.

"Do you see this Berti? We women are like this chestnut. As long as the shell protects us, no one can hurt us. But you see how smooth the chestnut is?" She moved her fingers over it and gazed into his face.

"Hard on the outside, as long as we can resist, and soft within, so that every man desires to feel us and to possess us at least once for the sake of victory."

Berti watched her, riveted by the blood trickling on her hands.

Alba exhaled, determined to tell her story. "Do you understand what I am talking about?"

Puzzled, Berti shook his head.

"He wanted me from the moment he saw me, and nothing could stop him," Monna Alba broke into sobs, the darkness circling them like a vulture.

"Alba, for the love of God, who are you talking about?" Berti cried, afraid she meant the night he took advantage of her.

"His Excellency Don Pedro de la Siguenza del Alhambra. He followed me everywhere, to the chapel, in the gardens, destroying my peace. I turned to Sister Teresa. 'Child,' she said, 'soon we'll be back in our hills. Pray to the Lord and he will answer.' One morning I heard Don Pedro had left the Escorial on a mission." Alba's voice quivered. "I was ecstatic with relief."

The darkness grew heavy over them, and the branches of the chestnut tree rustled in the growing wind, dropping the thorny fruit in a circle around them as if to cast a spell.

Alba stepped away. "I spent that evening in prayer. When I left the chapel, Don Pedro's servants abducted me." Berti tried to see her face, but the darkness consumed it. She calmed herself and resolved the unbearable. "He defiled me, and I killed him."

Berti drew back, horrified. "In cold blood?"

"No," she replied calmly. "He first raped me and ... " She could hardly utter the word. "When he wanted to sodomize me, I kicked him. He reached for his dagger, but he was in pain and missed my throat. The dagger fell out of his hand."

Alba's hand crept across the folds of her habit toward her neck.

"I picked up the dagger and ... " She fell at Berti's feet, a mound of weeping cloth.

He bent down and held her tightly until she stopped shaking. "Alba, I love you." He dried the tears dripping onto her wimple, picked her up, sat her in the saddle, and walked on.

They descended side-by-side, warmth between them. When they

reached the meadows of Campo Vaccino, he mounted behind her. Feeling her safe in his embrace, he turned her toward him and pulled her headdress off to see the reflection of the crescent moon in her face.

"I am taking you back to Monna Lena. You cannot return to your nuns, not tonight, and not in this state. I love you, and I won't let you go."

CREDO

Life became ever more complicated. Each day Pius grew frailer, kept alive to witness a Catholic victory over the Moslems. He visited Berti's studio, patiently observing the figures emerging slowly to populate the copper panel gaping with blank outlines.

In six months Berti painted only one quarter of the composition and completed the figures seated by Christ's hand blessing the souls in Paradise. His figure floated in golden light like in Berti's vision, the pink of Christ's *camicia* and the blue tint of His gown pallid in the first glaze over the umber under-drawing.

Below Christ, Berti drew three angels holding the instruments of His passion, the cross on which He was crucified, the lance that pierced His side, and the column where He was flogged. They were Berti's invention, born the night after he saw Alba in the Forum. In the delicate, almost androgynous, face of the middle angel, her features shone through.

Lovingly he imbued her skin with delicate pinks, tinted her cheeks with the gentle flush of her once-guarded virginity, and painted her locks like molten gold burnished in the glow of Christ's aura, her lips like unblemished cherries. After the meeting in the Forum, they met again and again under the cloak of darkness and the protection of bustling crowds, their emotions dormant but ready to burst forth volcano-like at any moment.

Berti stepped away to inspect her figure as he mixed pale creams to highlight the peachy tones of the cloak draped in soft folds over the bluish gown underneath. Ready to kiss her, he balked only at the panel's wet surface. He existed sustained by Alba's image in his painting, thus paying her tribute, and so he awoke in anticipation of celebrating the birth of Jesus Christ at the Sistine Chapel that night.

The morning dawned gloriously. But with its passage mist fell over the palace, and the city glistened in sleet. Berti picked up Don Alfonso after the bells tolled vespers at St. Peter's. Exhausted by his fast and the excitement of participating in the Mass, a great honor the pope bestowed on him, the boy fell asleep over Berti's shoulder in the Belvedere's long corridor.

Berti spent the evening quietly, watching the face of the boy he now blindly adored. When he bent to arouse the child, he considered the resilience of youth, oblivious to the bells' loud ringing and the commotion of people preparing for the evening liturgy.

"*Angelino*, do wake up." He tickled Alfonso's cheek with the fuzzy quill.

A deep sigh, and the boy responded. "Is it time, *papà?*" he asked brightly.

Berti no longer protested his sham paternity. As they marched briskly through the palace's breezy corridors in step with the hail rhythmically pounding the frozen shutters and bouncing off the stone floors of the open loggias, his heart swelled with pride.

No longer a child and dressed in the habit of a nobleman, Don Alfonso wore an embroidered doublet lined with sky-blue taffeta, his little sword dancing under his flying cape as he tried to keep Berti's pace.

"Totti, please, not so fast," the child in the boy pled as his cheeks grew redder. He was tall and lanky for his eight years, but his legs were no match for Berti's.

"Do you want me to carry you?"

"No." Don Alfonso put his hand in Berti's as they joined the stream of men passing through the courtyard of San Damaso toward the Ducal and the Royal Halls and into the Sistine Chapel. Behind the great iron screen separating the sanctuary of the chapel from the nave, papal staff already filled the space. Berti nodded to a few of his new friends, bowed to the Florentine Vasari speaking with a stranger, and joined his assistant Jacopo busily conversing with Hans.

The two Florentines shared guest quarters in the Belvedere not far from Berti's, decorating the Chapel of St. Michael for Pius. "Blessed be the name of the Lord," Berti greeted them all, and they responded with smiles, especially for Don Alfonso.

They regarded the boy with curiosity, unaware of how his angelic voice and intelligent mind charmed the old pope who invited him to hear the finest choir in the Papal States.

"Who are they?" The boy hid himself behind Berti's cloak and peeked at the spikes with axes on top forming a double-sided corridor to the gate in the screen.

Berti's eyes grew soft. "That's the Swiss Guard. The captains are on the other side." He pointed to the double row of eight colorfully clad men and lifted the boy over people's heads.

"Look Totti, there's my *padre zio!*" the boy screamed, seeing Alessandro on the pontiff's right in the regalia of the Archpriest of St. Peter's and the Leader of the College of Cardinals.

"Hush!" Berti covered the child's mouth, looking to see if anyone noticed, but as the murmurs around them rose in crescendo, only Hans had.

"Totti, I'll be quiet now, I promise," the boy said, pointing to the tall, canopied papal throne. Pius sat there in majesty, yet looking crushed under his regalia and the tiara, leaning feebly against his shepherd's crook, his unsteady hand shaking.

Berti picked up Don Alfonso and together they admired the splendor of the papal court, the cardinals seated against the left wall, the patriarchs, bishops, and deacons against the right, and the chancel filled with liturgical celebrants and the master of ceremonies. Below the box with the cantors and the choir, Berti recognized Don Giovanni Pierluigi, the greatest composer the city of Palestrina had yet produced.

"Be careful," the boy whispered as Berti let him down, avoiding the long sword of the man pushing past him. "Why can't he wear a little sword like mine?"

"Silly boy," Berti thought as he smiled. "He is a nobleman, so he needs a big sword." Berti bowed to the Duke of Urbino, Alessandro's brother-in-law, giving a good poke to the boy to follow him. "And now you must hold your tongue," he ordered.

The Mass was magisterial, moving under the invisible baton of the master of ceremonies, attaining such a level of piety that Berti brimmed with emotion, breathing deeply, overwhelmed by his thoughts and feelings. The boy's fingers squirmed in his hand; he patted his head. The pope rose and returned to the throne, addressing the congregation from a lectern illuminated by the sacred candle of the Nativity, a slight man whose voice bore the word of God into the remotest crevices of the chapel and into men's souls.

Most moving was the music. Berti had heard about maestro Palestrina but had never heard his music. Its spirituality and majesty filled him.

The silver of the bells filled the chapel, and a solitary male voice wafted through the silences. "I believe in one God. *Credo in unum Deum.*" It arched in the simplicity of a musical line, "*Patrem omnipotentem, factorem caeli et terrae.* The Father Almighty, maker of heaven and earth, of all that is seen and unseen." The choir embellished the syllables with florid passages rising gently up and falling, making Berti's skin tingle.

He confirmed his own faith in the silence of his heart.

I believe in one Lord, Jesus Christ, the only begotten Son of God. Berti looked at the imposing figure of Christ in Michelangelo's *Last Judgment* over the altar. Next to him, the boy recited in perfect Latin, as befitted a cardinal's son. Silence followed the music, broken by an occasional cough from the rows of senators and conservators at the foot of the choir stalls.

Berti's emotions drifted. He saw how the candlelight illuminated Michelangelo's painted triumph, revealing the frescoes one by one as candle smoke drifted up to them, from the reclining Jonah over the altar through the large panels depicting scenes from the Old Testament to the prophet Zecariah above his own head. Don Alfonso stood perfectly still, locked under the crook of the guards' elbows, watching the light flicker on their halberds, forgetting to shift from foot to foot, which he was wont to do when bored.

The bells jangled again. Berti shivered, despite the fact that the large hall full of bodies and burning lights was warm, the air perfumed by well-dressed men, burning wax, and incense. The boy looked up but found him lost in thought, the sounds of Palestrina's *Credo* filling him with faith, sadness, and hope, the voices of angels of light and darkness filling the void of his being with unaccustomed intensity.

I believe in one Holy Catholic Apostolic Church. I acknowledge one baptism for the forgiveness of sins, and I look for the resurrection of the dead and the life of the world to come.

The voices rose and fell and rose again, their gold mixing with crystalline silver as they sang the final low *Amen*. Berti looked at Hans, who seemed more to feel the Mass than hear it, a man so deeply steeped in faith that he left Berti ashamed, particularly as the vision of Alba sprang suddenly into his head.

"I want her but I can't marry her, not in the pope's service. Look at Palestrina, who lasted but a few weeks in the papal service and was dismissed because of his marriage."

He was at a crossroad but knew that his direction was clear. Glory and fame beckoned. The plainsong of the *offertorium* drifted gently across the space, a simple melody carrying the text with crystalline purity, while to the right of the altar the rite of preparing the sacred elements for the Holy Communion unfolded.

As the music shifted from *Benedictus* to *Agnus dei,* Berti's entire being was submerged in the voices, soaring and strengthening in religious conviction, ornamenting each melodic phrase with harmony, transparency, and purity of line. To the lilting voices of trebles and tenors he envisioned rivulets of water streaming down the terraced hillside in Tivoli, merging with the basses to form a powerful cascade of molten sonority.

The Mass ended and Berti stood silent, overwhelmed. The bells of St. Peter's pealed again, resounding with joy over the Vatican and the City of Rome. "Happy New Year," he finally said in Flemish and embraced Hans. "My fondest wishes to your bride and her family."

Don Alfonso slept on Berti's shoulder as they left the chapel in the triumphal procession of men, forgetting for fleeting moments their ambitions, desires, and animosities as the year of Our Lord 1571 opened.

Berti hugged the boy closer. It would be a good year. Cataclysmic events at last brought Pius victory over the infidel and marked great changes in Berti's life. Whether those events were truly happy, only God could fathom.

Scholar

Monna Lena had much to be thankful for. There was Alessandro, although she saw him less and less; there was Don Alfonso who'd go away with his father but come back; and there were the people of Rome, who visited her more and more frequently, trusting their lives to her.

Her life was radically changed, but she was too preoccupied to pine for her past. She had no time to miss life in *platea judea,* although for twenty-five years her own was rooted there. She returned once to her father's shop, run by another man, but felt like a stranger. The people who knew her held her in contempt and called her vile names.

Now as she walked the ghetto streets, she was shocked by the dilapidation of her former world: shabby lean-tos on the ruins of pagan Rome, seemingly held up by clothes lines strung between them; dirty, tattered children running half-naked in the streets; toothless hags lying in the ditches. When she lived there, she hadn't noticed them much. They were simply part of the ghetto. Now she wanted somehow to stop and help them, but she knew she could not.

To them, she was a traitor.

Maddalena did miss her father at times. For so long she enjoyed the wisdom he shared with her, watching him care for people and heal them with his remedies. She had to remind herself that no matter how much he once loved her, to him, too, she was dead.

But like her father she was blessed with a gift for making people feel better. Unlike him, she also had the faith which blesses newly baptized Christians. Those attributes not even cantankerous old Pius could resist. Surrounded by his own trusted physicians, he admitted her to his presence, but her ministration to the chronic sores on his legs was less important than their discourse on the science of horticulture.

"*Cicoreum.* Chicory." Pius pointed to a picture of a plant enjoyed for the soothing hot beverage it yielded. "Do you know that there is a new plant, *coffea arabica,* which can invigorate a man like me and give him the strength of Adonis?"

Monna Lena turned away, ostensibly to search her packet for another sharp tool to puncture the offending ulcer on the papal leg, but truly to hide her smile, imagining the shriveled man wooing a woman. The pope as Adonis? Impossible.

"I do," she replied in Latin. "Meneer Floris visited that country and told me about the dark potion that brings fire into the veins, but I prefer his stories about the small onions that grow in the Arab soil. Once a year, when Persephone returns to earth from her dark prison and greens the land, they grow into lovely flowers covering the countryside with all shades of color."

The pontiff looked doubtful. "Are you sure that plant is not from the Arabian myths?"

A faint smile broke on Lena's face. "Holy Father, hasn't Don Mercati told you about it?"

"I don't recall. He's too busy collecting his minerals." Pius resettled the open herbal manuscript in the folds of his lap and turned over a few pages to one illustrating another group of plants beginning with the letter *r*.

"*Rapum, rosa, rosemarinum, rubus, ruta.* Turnip, rose, rosemary, blackberry, rue." He fingered the meticulously clean strokes of the plants' names drawn in red paint. "Young woman"—he turned to Monna Lena—"you should have been born a man so you could join Don Mercati in the ranks of my favorite physicians."

She blushed at the reference to her inferior sex but managed a lighthearted reply. "Holy Father, I *am* only a woman. Begging Your Holiness' pardon, but if I married Don Mercati, we could give you a family of children dedicated to the science of medicine and horticulture."

The Pope, amused, grinned unexpectedly but only for a moment as she pierced the infected pustule, and brownish sap ran into the receptacle, followed by a stream of dark blood.

"*Oddio,*" he sighed against his will, gritting his teeth and clenching his fists.

"I am sorry for hurting you, Holy Father. If you only would let me come more often, as I begged you, I could bathe your ulcers and keep them from growing putrid."

"Bandage my leg, daughter, and sit by me," he invited, the worst behind him.

"Who taught you to paint like this?" He pointed to the rotund, fleshy white root with a crown of healthy leaves and touched the delicate foliage of the rosemary painted next to it.

"The Fleming in your service, maestro Bartolomeo. He comes to my house to take my ward for walks, and one day he caught me trying to teach myself how to use the watercolors."

The pope thought momentarily to press her again about the boy's paternity but reconsidered and instead asked, "And you did these by yourself?"

"Yes, Holy Father."

"The writing and the pictures? Who taught you to work so neatly?" He flipped back and forth between the pages filled with skillful, anatomically precise drawings of plants and flowers.

"My father, Your Holiness, Messer Ephraim di Ferrara." She reminded him of her roots.

"White rose, red rose, and the wild rose." The pope turned to the glossary explaining the medicinal properties of each, ignoring her answer. He felt deep contempt for Jews, vacillating between his Christian duty to love all men and his desire to cleanse the Eternal City of them; but Rebecca, the lost sheep, came voluntarily to the bosom of Mother Church.

"And you have compiled these writings by yourself?"

"It was nothing. Nothing at all," she replied modestly, recalling some of the stunningly illustrated books in her father's library.

With great interest Pius read the Latin inscriptions on the stiff vellum page. "Red rose. Haven't you forgotten to include at least one medicinal power of this noble plant?"

She blushed again, but for a different reason, and recited a quick prayer to arrest his repeated assaults on her maiden state, but without success.

"And tell me, daughter, how is it that no man has captured you?"

"When I became a *conversa,* I gave myself to Christ, Holy Father." She lied as she had many times before, trying not to remember Alessandro's warm lips on her body. The past week he was an unexpectedly frequent guest at her house, his vigor renewed with the increasing hope of capturing the papal throne as Pius' health declined.

"Madonna, can you ever forgive my trespasses?" She prayed hard but, ignorant of her turmoil, Pius closed the manuscript and lost his train of thought.

"We will ask Signor Mercati to put your gift with Our valuable manuscripts in the library on nature's wonders, and thank you for your noble dedication to Us and Our good health. God bless you, daughter." Tracing the sign of the cross over her head, Pius motioned her away.

As Monna Lena crossed the bridge back into Rome she wondered what Pius would say of her anatomical drawings, which she did not dare show to Berti, much less to Alessandro. They were not many, but Monna Alba had managed to sneak her into the anatomical theater of the hospital of Santo Spirito where she studied the dissected cadavers in the dim candlelight of the mortuary chamber.

"If only I were a man," Monna Lena habitually sighed while trying in the darkness of night to recreate the anatomy engraved in her mind.

Deep in her root cellar, wrapped in a length of soft cloth and buried in a wooden casket, she hid a book of Vesalius. Her latest acquisition was a book of Juan Val Verde de Amusco, *Anatomia del corpo humano,* which she bought, cautiously dressed as a man, in the shop of Antonio Salamanca. She always opened it reverently first to page sixty-four, where a man cheerfully exhibited his flayed hide.

"I wish I were a man," she sighed again as she entered her front *salone* to find Alessandro fidgeting impatiently on the settee in the warmth of the open hearth.

The closed shutters darkened the room, and she quickly lit the lantern. The furniture in her *salone* was sparse, two large armchairs and a settee and a small desk by the window; but they were of the finest quality. The house was built from stone blocks, so even in warm months three sheepskins were piled high to keep Alessandro's gouty foot comfortable.

"*Carissima,* where have you been so long?" He sprang up and pulled her close. "You're looking thin and tired." He pushed the sweaty locks away from her face. "How's the old goat?"

"Alessandro!" she gasped, but quickly forgetting the tone of his question she reported on Pius' health. Alessandro winked. "Not yet? We'll have to give the old man his victory first, and then let him join his maker." He was in a hurry and had no time for details as he bent to kiss her. "Your Grace!" She choked, surprised by his speed, her mouth filled with the bite of his passion. Alessandro pushed her over and moved in impatiently as he tended to do lately, and his arrogant heat quickly melted into her warm, generous sea of renewed joy.

"Are you leaving me so soon?" She felt his passion ebb within.

"Sorry, *carissima.*" He smoothed his robes absentmindedly and muttered, "Duty calls."

Maddalena did not bother straightening her *gamurra,* for he was gone before she thought about it. She still loved him, even more than before, and it pained her to see the object of her adoration poisoned by a greed for power. She drew her knees tightly to her chin, still feeling Alessandro's warmth spreading and trembling within, and fell deep asleep in front of the hearth.

† † †

Berti sat by Don Clovio. It seemed an eternity since he worked under the old man's watchful eye, and much had happened since. Berti had ways of recounting his good fortune, but the best was Monna Alba, even if she would not talk to him. He considered marrying her, but that would damage his career. Taking her against her will would surely displease the Virgin.

Berti still wanted Monna Alba, but he did not know what to do. Don Clovio seemed the right person to ask, but as he tended to do when the subject was not appealing, the old man quickly changed it.

"Did I tell you that not long ago Meneer Lampsonius wrote to me, recommending your friend Cornelis highly to our noble patron?" Don Clovio showed Berti the respected scholar's letter, florid and full of praise much deserved, as Berti knew.

"Is His Grace going to take Cornelis into his service? You know my friend could use Cardinal Alessandro's support for a new printing shop. There are so many good artists in Rome, and Cornelis could add their work to the cardinal's collection by engraving their images permanently on paper. His prints would be considerably more refined than studio copies!"

"I know, son. Meneer Lampsonius writes that your friend should engrave Michelangelo's masterpieces just as he did Titian's works in Venice. But look over here." Don Clovio pointed to a passage in the letter." He also says that your Cornelis can work directly from paintings but that he's incapable of drawing copies for the plates by himself. That's a shame!"

"Hans can do them for him. I've seen his fine hand."

"Who do you say?" Don Clovio took out his gilded horn and leaned closer to Berti.

"Hans Speckaert, the other friend I told you about, would do them for Cornelis. He's a marvelous draftsman! And I am sure His Grace has many drawings he'd like to see engraved. Cornelis could do them all."

"I don't know. His Grace, may God give him many more years of health, many more than I now have left, is too busy with his new church."

Berti bit his lip. "Would you consider talking to him? Hans is getting married next month, and I must help him find a patron who appreciates his talent."

Don Clovio smiled. "I'll see what can be done for your friends. May God be with you."

Berti was managing his career admirably, so long as he stayed out of the way of the snob Vasari, who continually complained to the Holy Father that Berti was lazy. That was not true, of course, but if his work did not progress as rapidly as the conceited Florentine demanded, it was because his heart was not in it. Copying the large *Last Judgment* was tedious, and he amused himself by filling little panels with landscapes and figures copied from prints. He sold them before the paint dried, and his belly started to round off like his money pouch.

But no amount of money could buy Monna Alba. She simply would not talk to him. Whenever he could, he hurried down to the hospital of Santo Spirito and tried to catch a glimpse of her returning to the convent. He also quarreled with Monna Lena.

"Do you love her?" She confronted him one day after he brought Don Alfonso back. "If you do, go to Pius and beg his pardon, and ask him to give her dispensation to marry you."

"I couldn't do that."

"Then you don't love her," Monna Lena replied sadly and walked away.

"What's bothering you today?" Berti grabbed her arm.

"Nothing at all." She averted her face.

"That's not true." He pulled her closer. "You've been crying. Is it His Grace?"

She pulled away and crossed the room.

"Lena, you can tell me. Could he have abandoned you so hastily?"

"No, but he's always so busy, and he has less and less time for me. He won't take me with him to Naples, but he'll take Don Alfonso," she complained, jealous of the boy who had grown close to her heart.

Berti followed her. "Lena, look at yourself!" Berti demanded, offering her a looking glass. "Have you seen yourself lately? You only work. You wake up grinding and blending powders and go to sleep exhausted from taking care of everybody who needs you except yourself. How do you imagine you can keep yourself pretty for Alessandro?"

"He told me he loved me for my soul," she replied, but Berti was unimpressed.

"And the dark rings around your eyes, where do they come from? Too much contemplation is no good even for saints. Right now, you're far from sainthood!"

"Damn you, conceited man! What do you know about that? Once you told me you wanted to be a Jesuit. Do you know that the first love of the soldiers of Christ is to give, to speak from heart to heart. Can't you at least give yours to a woman and take her honorably instead of stalking the poor thing like a criminal?"

"And what do you know about giving?" he snorted. "Yes, you do. You give yourself to every upstart, every scum of the earth who needs you, but not to the man who raised you from the dirt, who put you on a pedestal and adored you better than all of his treasures put together."

Berti became so angry that he nearly smashed the looking glass against the floor. Horrified by the consequences of his foolishness, he controlled himself swiftly.

"Maddalena, he doesn't want a smelly woman ready to argue the scriptures with him with an obstinacy that borders on the criminal," Berti continued urgently. "Can't you understand that? His Grace wants a pet that will keep him young in other ways than coloring his hair and beard with Signor Nostradamo's recipes.

"And damn you too, woman! You know how to please all, anybody, but not Alessandro these days!"

Monna Lena braced herself against Berti's accusations, but anger disabled her reasoning.

"Out of my house and don't ever come back! If you want to see the boy, talk to Alessandro. My doors will be locked to you."

"So be it!" He slammed the gate and rode to Gallo Nero, crossing the bridge back toward the Vatican in the nick of time, but he soon forgot about his quarrel with Maddalena.

The next day was Hans' wedding, and what a splendid occasion it was!

Don Alfonso would miss it, but nothing on earth could stop the boy from going to Naples with his *padre zio*. Berti and Cornelis stood as witnesses for Hans and admired his bride, the only moment when the people stood motionless. After the ceremony at the Anima church, all souls born north of the Alps gathered at Meneer Santvoort's inn and danced and drank the night away. When Hans joined his wife in the back quarters, Berti was suddenly envious.

A few guests still remained, reeling tipsily across the dance floor, some snoring under the benches. The square in front of the inn was almost empty. As Berti looked around the darkened space, he felt the same, very alone.

"Why ... Why don't you spend the night with me," Cornelis stuttered between hiccups. "We won't see each other for a while!"

"To maestro Tiziano!" Berti saw the bottom of his tumbler. "Excuse me, my friend." He relieved himself suddenly under Lucia's belly. She snorted in surprise. "Don't worry about anything. I'll come and visit you in Venice, and maybe the great Tiziano will teach me how to paint ladies' bosoms with peaches and cream. Ha!" He tried to scramble up into the saddle. His filly stood patiently, and her inebriated master made it on the third try.

The night was dark, but the rapidly clearing clouds gradually revealed more and more stars. The cool spring air worked miracles for Berti's head. As he passed a fountain, he slipped down and stuck his head in the frigid water.

"Wake up, you dunce." He slapped his face till it burned and stung, knowing that if he returned in this state, the guards would not let him in.

When he realized it was too late to pass through the Vatican gates, in no matter what condition, he wondered where he could go. To Adrien's. Go back to the inn? And most certainly, Monna Lena would not have him.

The thought of a woman, any woman, enraged his senses. He mounted and rode on. But when he slipped off Lucia again, he found himself not in front of Monna Piacenza's but facing the rear gardens of the Carmelite convent. Nothing stirred, except from time to time a creaking branch. He looked around anxiously, but the entire place looked asleep.

It was then that he knew he must see her, must explain to her that she must be patient until the pope dies. Then they could find a way, a way for what he had no idea, and for the moment, that seemed unimportant.

The wall was high but the vines sturdy and long. Unused to physical exertion, Berti found the climb hard, and his hands burned. A dog ran to him, sniffing suspiciously, ready to bark, but Berti quickly emptied his pockets of sausage bits from the feast.

Where next? Was anybody stirring? Berti thought he saw a candle flicker on the upper floor. The only shutters that were slightly ajar led to the cellar. Forcing them open, he climbed through, falling onto a pile of grain sacks. Rows of smoked ham stared at him like sleeping, wingless bats, and as he found his bearing, the mice scurried away from him. Finally he found a door out of the cellar, but it was barred, and the lock was tight. In the distance, the night watchman cried the late hour, but Berti did not understand him.

The sacks were heavy, but he managed to pile a mound to get him up to the window and out again. Finally he stood on firm ground, the crackled walls against his back and the night chill filling his nostrils.

"Where's the dog?" He scanned the courtyard suspiciously. Slowly he circled the walls, trying to imagine the layout, carefully separating the dormitories from the chapel and the service buildings, somehow hoping to find Alba.

A small loggia opened its archway, covered by the dense foliage of a broad tree. Berti reached to the lowest branch and recoiled as he touched something. A bat swooshed by his head; its noisy wings momentarily paralyzed him. A cloud of them descended on him, attacking him for disturbing their peace, scratching, going for his face and neck.

Berti fell like a sack. Hardly noticing that he sprained his ankle, he hobbled for cover toward a dark gate in the side façade. As if by miracle, he found himself inside.

Ave Maria, gratia plena. His lips chanted a prayer. The creatures had nearly killed him.

The damp hall was deserted, a long corridor of groin vaults propelling him bay-by-bay, door-by-door, to the nuns' tiny cubicles. Limping painfully, he peeked into a few but dared not inspect the pale, motionless bodies breathing on the straw mats. He looked in both directions, hoping for a clue, but none appeared.

He desperately wanted to see, to talk to Monna Alba, but how? Suddenly, he felt hot breath against his leg. The dog was back, licking his hand. He patted it to keep it quiet. The hall felt cool, and he trembled with fear.

The animal led him toward the end of the corridor and a small light that grew larger and larger as he approached, finally revealing a small chapel with a simple crucifix on its back wall. A young woman knelt at its foot, her back rent by the whip lying at her side. When she turned her head, the face lit by the tall taper was Monna Alba's.

Her hands, folded in prayer, dropped leaden by her side as she gasped and turned ashen.

"You ... here? How did you find me?" In vain, she tried to close her ripped garb.

All Berti's life turned toward this moment.

Ignoring the dull pain in his sprained ankle, he embraced her with the passion born of months of denial and separation, and picked her up in his arms. Resigned to fate, and lost in her embrace, he followed the corridor back to her cell.

Like the time when Monna Piacenza first taught him the pleasures of the world, Berti remembered nothing of the night with Monna Alba, except that no one, neither Pius nor God, could separate him from her again.

LIMBO

Berti took the brush out of his mouth and passed it from his right hand to his left, burdened by his palette and a cluster of brushes. Was it hot inside? Or did the heat radiate from the painting? The hell in the *Last Judgment* was a fiery cavity in the gut of a jagged mountain topped by rugged boulders. It steamed and brewed with men and women eaten by lust, avarice, gluttony, and greed.

"Yes?" He voiced his question again, unsure what the messenger had said. "Can't you see I'm busy?" He picked up the brush and then realized that the messenger was Jacopo, Beltraffio's eldest. "Signor *pittore*, Monna Lena said it's very, very urgent."

What did she want? He had not seen her for weeks since she threw him out. As far as he was concerned, he would not return until she apologized!

But he saw Don Alfonso at his father's palace after he came back from Naples and admired the treasures that filled the boy's pockets on the journey, including a digit of St. Alfonso. "Now look, *papà!*" Don Alfonso showed Berti a chain with the bone as a pendant.

Berti looked dumbfounded. "Where did you get that?"

The boy hopped gingerly. "*Padre zio* got it from the monks. They were terribly nice to me. I also met a boy, and he shared his pie with me."

Berti gave the boy a nod. "Wasn't he jealous of your new keepsake?"

"No. He said his daddy told him it's all goats' bones."

"Impossible!" Berti exclaimed, horrified. "Goats don't have fingers!" He did not think much of Don Alfonso's treasure, but if Alessandro thought the relic would protect the boy, he must have had his reasons. Berti had heard of far lesser objects performing miracles.

"*Signore* ... " Beltraffio's boy shifted from one foot to another.

Berti put his tools down on the cart and wiped his hands on his work coat.

"Urgent, you say?" and he ripped the note open. The words danced unsteadily on the paper. "Come quickly, the boy wants you."

Berti recognized the handwriting. "Run! I'll be there as soon as I can." Struck by a premonition, he ran down to the stable and saddled Lucia. He passed Jacopo in the second courtyard and arrived at Monna Lena's before Jacopo approached the Castel Sant'Angelo bridge.

"What's the matter?" Berti inquired breathlessly, sunblind in the dark corridor. The familiar house was filled with a threatening smell of medicine and oppressively stale air. Darkness hung low, wrapping all in deep shadow. Not a sound stirred the air.

"Lena?"

Hearing her wailing hysterically, Berti ran to Don Alfonso's room. A squat candle by Alfonso's statue of the Virgin was almost burned down. The boy lay still, his face unnaturally bloated. Then Berti saw his neck. Despite the stifling air, he shivered.

"Lena, what happened? Is His Grace here? Does he know?"

She shook her head, barely able to speak.

"He's in Parma. We sent a messenger."

Quickly, Berti assessed the situation. "Why didn't you tell me the boy was ill? Get Don Mercati! If you can't find him, ask for an audience with the Holy Father. I don't care what you do, but we must have his blessing. If his prayer does not work, the child has no chance."

Monna Lena struggled to regain composure.

"I thought he was fooling me at first, not wanting to eat or study his Latin. 'Your uncle won't be pleased with you when he returns,' I told him. Then he started coughing and choking. I thought something was in his throat. There was a lump on the side."

Her voice was thin, as if choked by hands gripping her throat. "I gave him purges to make him throw up. That made him worse, and his throat started to swell more and more. Look!"

Asleep, the boy gasped for air with a thin hissing sound, his face turning blue. Berti felt his burning forehead, threw off the covers, and removed his long shirt. "How long has he been like this?" The question trailed from his tongue as he saw the swellings in his armpits.

Berti grew numb. "Maddalena, look at me! Did he bring the plague back from Naples?"

"I don't know." She shuddered. "I … I honestly don't. I've never seen anything like this. It's not the plague. I helped people when the pestilence struck Rome the year you came here. But this is as if the devil is in his throat!"

Berti shook in anger. "I thought you didn't believe in that kind of quackery."

"I do now! Can't you see that even the Holy Virgin has abandoned the child?" Monna Lena pointed to the statue. Her words sliced through Berti's mind like a knife.

"It was not the Virgin but I," he said. "When I stole Monna Alba from Christ, I took the mantle of her mercy from the boy." He sank before the statue. "Heavenly Virgin, please give me this once, and I'll never, never fail you again!" Maddalena stared at him as if he had lost his mind. "Are you sick?"

"Don't you remember? Fonsi nearly died from the fever that took his nanny's baby."

Bewildered, Maddalena only shook. "What does that have to do with the Virgin Mary?"

"Plenty!" he replied hoarsely. "I gave Fonsi a brew of red berries, but it didn't take fully. So I prayed to her to save the boy. She did, and I promised her to join the Jesuits to honor her son. But I didn't. I couldn't. I cheated her then and again, when I stole Alba from her."

"But why?" Maddalena shook her head violently. She knew all about Monna Alba. If Berti wanted to marry, why did he not beg Pius to dispense her from her vows? Yet she felt compassion for everyone. "It's not your fault!" she offered in reconciliation. "Alessandro didn't beget his son in a holy union. He, of all men, should have known better!"

Berti's empty stare finally galvanized Maddalena. It took forever before she came back from the Vatican, Don Mercati following closely. No matter how hard they all prayed, no matter how hard the Pope's physician tried, the boy hung between life and death without change.

Berti did not want to understand Don Mercati's explanation. "Choking sickness. It makes the throat swell until the child can't breathe. God punishes all naughty boys for playing with themselves by letting the devil enter to torment them in the world beyond."

"But Don Alfonso's innocent! He's a child!" Berti blushed. "Please, Don Mercati, don't bleed him. He's exhausted." But Don Mercati insisted on purging the child of the spirit that was taking his breath away, because all other methods had failed.

Then, unexpectedly, Alfonso's breathing became stronger, and his waxen face picked up a hint of color. He opened his puffy eyes. "Totti," the boy moaned softly, "can I go outside and play with my horse?" His frail hand fumbled at his side.

"My love, you cannot," Monna Lena pleaded. "You must get better first."

"But I want to." The boy began thrashing around. "I want my *papà!*"

Maddalena and Berti looked at each other as the boy gasped for air.

"Your father's in … " Monna Lena forgot herself.

Berti pushed her aside and scooped the boy into his arms. "I am here, child."

"*Papà,* can I have my horse?"

"Sure, my boy, sure you can." He bent gently to pick up the tattered remains of the toy horse he painted for him in San Oreste.

"Totti, I'm very sick, am I?" The boy panted for air as the swelling tightened his throat. "Do you think God will let me bring my horse into His garden?"

Berti chest constricted with pain. "Sure, Fonsi, of course He will."

"Will you come and visit me there?"

Berti averted his face. "Of course I will," he whispered. The boy grew lighter and colder in his arms. Helplessly Berti watched the boy's face grow more and more ashen.

"Totti, I see *nonno*. He's waiting for me by the gate." The dying boy looked for the old sacristan from San Oreste who waited for him in heaven. "And there are Monna Brunella's boys and her little girl," he mumbled deliriously.

"Madonna, why do you punish the child?" Berti wailed as Don Alfonso's contorted face quieted. Fonsi gone? Never again to ask him for a story of Hercules, never smothering his face with wet kisses? Berti did not understand. But could it be true? In the agony of his realization, he took one last look, kissed the still warm forehead, gave the dead child to Monna Lena, and ran.

As if pursued by the Furies, he staggered through the streets, ready to throw himself under the wheels of carriages. At length, he found himself in a familiar street and pounded on a gate that opened swiftly. Wild cries and loud laughter surrounded him like a snare.

"Welcome back, maestro. We missed you." Monna Piacenza arched herself enticingly. Berti examined her scornfully. Why had he not noticed how old and fat she was?

The madam smacked her lips. "Shall I be of service to you tonight?"

"I want another!" he growled back.

She called out. Three women appeared.

"Here, Lucretia the Greek knows the secrets of divine Aphrodite. Just admire her fine legs!" Monna Piacenza lifted the girl's gown and pinched her to show off her plump wares.

"And *Simonetta veneziana* over here knows the art of her mother and her grandmother like you have never dreamt."

The madam squeezed the plums of her bosom toward Berti until his face was sticky with her sweet nectar.

"But here, Conchita from Andalusia will certainly not fail you, for once she shares her wisdom with you, you will never seek another. She claims that even the devil cannot resist her. So which one will you choose, maestro?"

Berti stood, the ghost of the boy hovering about him. Still stunned, he stared dully at the three women, his own Aphrodite, Hera, and Athena, and unlike the Greek shepherd Paris, he made his own choice. "All three, great Madam!"

His defiance filled the room. The candles hissed ominously. Monna Piacenza came closer, unsure of his answer. He broke the silence, laughing like a madman, louder and louder, until the air chilled and horror made hair stand on end.

"I want all three, for neither Pius nor God can save me now."

† † †

But Pius *was* interested in helping Berti. After all, he was the Lord's shepherd on earth. Saddened by the death of a boy whose talents promised that he would live to serve the Church, he lamented Berti's loss, navigating the complicated web of the young man's frayed emotions. "We grieve with you, but he was not your child, for all the pet names he had for you, was he?"

Berti sobbed uncontrollably. "He was like my own son, Holy Father."

"But you're young. You can have your own sons, as many as the Lord grants you!"

Berti wondered what Pius could know about having and loving sons. "I believed Your Holiness wanted me to serve the church," he said and dried his face with a kerchief.

"Come closer, son, and look at me," the Pope beckoned. "Is your heart truly open to the sacrifice I myself made so long ago?" Pius' gaze riveted him, and Berti felt uncomfortable.

"Holy Father, I love a woman, but she is not free. She is a nun."

Pius shifted in his chair to look out the window into the calm splendor of the gardens. Then he asked, "Would you marry her if she were free?"

Berti gulped. The question found him unprepared. Maybe this was the way the Virgin was testing him. He cleared his throat and replied, "I would, if that were your wish."

The pope spun around and shocked him with the next question: "Is Cardinal Farnese the boy's natural father?" Somehow, against his will, Berti replied, "Holy Father, he is, but … "

"It interests Us not whether the Farnese cardinal fathered his child before or after he took his sacred vows," he said grimly, "for he will answer for his sins on the day of judgment."

Berti nearly stopped breathing at the frightening words. The pope tugged his skimpy beard with visible satisfaction. Alessandro Farnese would not warm the pontifical chair after his death.

"As for you, Our painter, We give you permission to marry Monna Alba."

How did he know? How did he know her? Berti could not understand, but then it dawned that Maddalena was the pontiff's reliable source of news. He also had his own insight.

"Yes. We believe God wishes it. She can leave the order and join the household of Our servant and your friend Maddalena, since her own flesh and blood will not look after her."

Berti was reluctant to demonstrate his apparent gratitude. Did he want to marry Monna Alba? Did he want that sweet girl enough to make her his companion for life?

"But ... " the Pope continued. Berti cringed at the light, razor-sharp voice.

"But, maestro *fiammingo,* God and We wish to test your love first. You may take Monna Alba for your wife, but only after Lent."

Berti's chin dropped. "Holy Father, that's nearly a year away!"

"Resign yourself to the wisdom of God, and your days will be blessed for ever." The voice paused on each word as the hand inched forward in a sign of dismissal.

There was no one to turn to. Cornelis was in Venice, engraving Titian's masterpieces onto copper plates. Even Hans accompanied him for a while to help him prepare the studies. Beside, Hans was besotted with his wife, and when he came back, why should he listen to the sorrows of a friend instead of enjoying the nuptial bed? Anthonis was lost in work too, running the inn after his uncle's death, and Adrien was away, busy as usual making fortunes.

But then of course there *was* the Casa de' Fiori of the aging Monna Piacenza, the offspring of great courtesans, illegitimate granddaughter of Lorenzo the Magnificent and illicit daughter of Lorenzo's own bastard nephew, her line exotic and her erudition commendable. In her, Berti discovered the comfort of a mother's soft touch and a father's wisdom. Stunned by grief and crushed by guilt, he justified his visits to the whorehouse as lessons, which, as it was to turn out, engraved his future career in stone.

"You must learn Latin and know the ancient authors," she advised him, paging through a beautifully embossed leather-bound manuscript. "Without Homer and Ovid you'll go nowhere in your profession," she advised him.

At first he viewed the madam's words as foolish, but soon he realized that the pope would not live forever and that he had to expand his own horizons to include temporal princes, such as the profligate prince-bishop. Berti did a couple of pen drawings of Mary Magdalene for him, one of the penitent woman seated, longingly gazing at a wooden crucifix. Nothing but her streaming golden hair and a bit of cloth covered the alluring Monna Alba.

"Make me a version of the Magdalen standing so I can admire all of her," demanded his particular patron. Berti drew her in a contraposto, one knee bent forward, the other firm on the ground, pointing to a skull next to her feet, the other hand holding the holy scriptures away from her body. He drew her disregarding post-Tridentine Rome's rules of propriety, the starched cloth failing to cover her budding breasts, hoping the libertine cleric would never meet Alba.

She was his and could belong to no one else. Berti did not know what mesmerized him other than her virginal beauty. Naïvely pleased to become his wife with the pope's blessing, she finally acquiesced to his pre-nuptial demands.

They often rode out late at night, when summer spread the secure blanket of darkness across the city and the woods carpeting Rome's outer hills, away from the house where she lived temporarily and where the boy had died, to drink unashamedly from the spring of their love.

One such night, Berti lifted his head from the soft cushion of Alba's bosom. "I can't even begin to imagine how I could survive the summer here in the city without you," he murmured tracing her form with his lips and pulling himself closer to her face. She wound her golden locks around his ear.

Alba puckered her lips. "Do you like me in my new gown?"

"You look purer than Diana, my beloved, but I like you better without it." His fingers inched over her face, his eyes drinking her moonlit features.

"Aren't you lonely in Maddalena's quiet house?"

"She's a good woman," she replied, "the sister I never had. And I'm busy helping her look after the house, feeding the chickens and milking her goat."

Berti took her hand and sucked each finger separately with great relish.

"You were born for love and not for work, my beloved."

"For love?" She sprang. "You promised to wed me with the pope's blessing!"

Berti ignored the question and pushed her back in a long kiss.

"You're like the dawn that graces the Alban hills," he whispered. "Pure like the mountain lakes of the Alps I crossed, and enchanting like the blossoms that grace your golden hair."

"How can a man bear so much love?" she whispered, quickly forgetting her question.

His skin tingled with desire, and he covered her skin with more wild kisses.

"Here in the sacred woods," he said, breathing hard, "lives the child of Aphrodite. Alba, my dawn!" he cried out as he felt for her deepest spring. "You give me strength. You can restore the peace of my soul, here in your earthly paradise." He trembled, spent.

"Berti, I've something to tell you."

"Can't it wait?"

"I have to leave Rome." Disturbed by his lack of interest, Alba pushed him away.

"Christ!" he cursed, burying his face in her warm lap.

"I won't be far, to the hills east of Rome. My great-aunt Monna Cecchi is old and ill. You see, I've no dowry. Nino won't give me any of the money my father kept for me."

Alba's money was the last thing on Berti's mind. He kissed the tip of her nose. "What does your great-aunt have to do with your dowry?"

"She's very old and alone. She wants her own kin to look after her. If I do and she dies, she'll leave me her homestead. Wouldn't you like that?" Alba stood, pulled her gossamer dress over her naked breasts triumphantly, as she did in his drawing of the penitent Magdalen.

"Wouldn't you like living up there in the hills of Monte Gennaro, close to God, hearing His voice, letting Him show us our way?" she asked swirling about, looking for her petticoats. "The shepherds winter in the hills near my aunt's land, and the bells of their cows and sheep will wake us in the mornings. We could be so happy."

Horrified, Berti tried to imagine the rugged, rustic houses, the mountain streams with rough boards for bridges, and the sounds of the bleating sheep and mooing cows instead of the angelic voices of Pius' choir.

"Come closer, my treasure." He pulled her down and pushed her dress and unpleasant thoughts far away. "I see eternity right here, where I can keep you to myself," he moved his elbow into a more comfortable spot over his shirt, bracing his knees firmly against her legs.

"My beloved." She resisted a bit. "You will have me for your wife, won't you?"

"As the Holy Virgin is my witness," he lied shamelessly.

† † †

The distant hills of Rome were rugged and the summer hot. Berti often rode the old Nomentana road toward the hostile cliffs of Monte Gennaro.

The religious storm in the Mediterranean had reached its climax as new activity stirred the calm. The Holy League was reality. Don Juan, bastard son of an Emperor and Commander-in-Chief of the Christian fleet, was finally planning an offensive against the infidel, and Pius was too busy to worry about his epitaph. Berti, freer than usual, escaped the city at every opportunity.

The cozy nest the lovers built far from the tiny mountain hamlet was hidden deep in a cave where a pleasant chill welcomed bodies scorched by the torch of love. Monna Alba could not get away easily from the watchful gaze of her old relative and the villagers, for her beauty attracted the attention of all the marriageable men.

"Berti, I am afraid tonight." She huddled near him for protection without knowing why. The bats were particularly troublesome that night, but she was used to them. Berti lit a torch and chased them away; for a moment his dark outline was shadowed against the mouth of the cave like that of a crooked vulture.

"You are more beautiful than the moon, more perfect than the evening star," he called and rushed back to his love.

Alba covered herself, like the Venus Pudica discovered in Alessandro's gardens.

"I waited more than an hour for you, my love."

He pushed her hands away. "I've waited for an eternity for you. In my dreams your face appeared to me."

Alba shuddered, overcome by his ardor.

"My darling, you fill me with emotion, desire to live, to have you, to possess you. Why do you cry, my love?" He embraced her.

"Not tonight, dearest, please forgive me. I'm afraid." She pushed him away, seeing the bright disk of the full moon edge across the grotto's opening.

Annoyed, Berti challenged her. "But what can you fear?"

"Sin. I'm afraid of God, of his anger and his punishment. He sees us. Consider my words. He is judging us right now."

"Don't worry. You belong to me. You always have, even before I met you!" he muttered wildly without hearing her, unable to control himself.

"What do you mean?" she whispered, frightened by his intensity.

Berti's eyes glowed. "I've loved you ever since I was a child, perhaps always."

"I don't know what you mean. Please let me go. I must return to Monna Cecchi!"

"You're like the Virgin in the painting in Antwerp. I want you Alba, I must have you!" Berti cried, clutching at her.

"Please, not tonight. I'm afraid!" she begged, even as his embrace swallowed her.

The full moon guided their path back to the hamlet and Monna Cecchi's house, Alba's face streaked with tears.

"*Tesoro*, I'll talk to Pius, I promise. We can wed soon, sooner than he wants us to," he said and almost believed what he said.

But the pontiff had more important matters on his mind. Weeks passed as Berti returned to the rugged mountains, overwhelming Alba with empty promises and boundless love. The blazing sun dried the ground to a crisp, but the same force patiently bronzed the vineyards that graced the gentler terrain south of them, the taverns spilling out their old supplies at a fair price.

As September came to its slow end, life bloomed once again for Berti. Daily, more and more figures taking on life and color inhabited the altarpiece; the pope moved quickly in the hope of defeating the Turks, and Alba was sweeter than ever. Berti grew richer by the day, and the ink on his contract with the church of the French people in Rome was barely dry when he passed the city gates onto Via Nomentana. The days were shorter, the dusk earlier, and with it a chill settled into the barren hills, making their love nest uncomfortable.

"I hope she isn't late tonight," he fretted as he filled his backpack with flasks of wine at the inn by Nomentum, but to his great surprise he found the young woman sitting at the edge of the cliff near the path that led to the mouth of their grotto.

"Did you miss me that much?" he asked as he kissed her salty face.

Alba was pale. "It's not that. You will take me for your wife? Soon. As you promised?"

He hugged her and walked on.

"You *promised!*"

He turned. Losing his footing for a moment, he faced her, suddenly filled with a premonition. He looked at her waist. Alba lifted her chin, trying to control her voice as she spoke.

"I'm with child, and you know the truth. Now will you marry me soon?"

"Alba, my tender star, I want to but I can't! The pope won't even see me these days. You know I can't anger him by marrying you without his permission."

Alba's face turned to stone.

"Darling, we'd be lost!" Berti blurted without thinking.

The stone wept.

"Didn't you hear about the fall of Magusta?" he argued dispassionately. "All of Rome is talking of nothing but the news from Cyprus, and Don Juan of Austria is sailing for Corfu to meet the Turks. You do understand the importance of our victory over the barbarians, don't you? This is more important than you and me. We must wait till the time is right."

"But people will know that I am with your child."

"It won't matter. I want you to give me a boy. We'll call him Don Alfonso. Be patient."

Alba was patient, waiting and waiting, gently letting out the stays of her *gamurra*, attending her failing great-aunt. She hardly saw Berti, who was busy with Pius' altarpiece.

On a crisp day in late October, staggering news reached Rome and Berti in his workshop, where he was touching up the group of angels around Monna Alba. God had finally granted the Catholic victory over the infidel in a shattering battle at Lepanto, and the news spread through Rome like wildfire. All the city rejoiced as bells tolled, announcing the great miracle. As Berti knelt at the foot of his painting to offer his own thanksgiving, Adrien appeared.

"Did you hear?" Berti turned to embrace his friend joyfully, but Adrien stood stiffly, his face drawn. "Are you well?" Berti asked, foreboding marking his own face.

Adrien could hardly look at him. "Do you know? Who told you? I just saw Maddalena."

An unspeakable fear gripped Berti.

"Monna Lena? What did she tell you!?"

Adrien's jaw nearly locked, as his emotions broke loose.

"You must be brave. Alba's dead. They found her under the cliffs of Monte Gennaro."

"Dead? Alba dead!?" Berti cried incredulously.

"She was looking for her aunt's lost goat, that misfit Dura who hardly ever gave milk, and her foot slipped off the path. We must hurry. The funeral is tomorrow."

Berti hesitated but only for a moment. The words about to come were to change his life, for not one but two people weighed his conscience. He straightened his back to face the reality.

"She was with child. My child."

Adrien's face grew ashen. "Mother of mercy! You must be strong and brave."

Feeling doomed, Berti no longer cared.

Devil's Apprentice

They sat down at the Black Swan. In the smoky room lit by squat candles in tin holders and a few oil lamps a dirty curtain moved and the innkeeper's sallow face emerged.

"You're all my guests!" Adrien's coins clinked on the table. Voices hushed under the low ceiling, the regulars seeing the prosperous newcomers. "Go home and sleep," the innkeeper laughed, watching the cavalier balancing himself on the worn bench. "Go and bed yourself, old fool!" replied the merchant, full of wine and Monna Piacenza's girls.

"Let's have another feast!" Berti added his share.

"What a paradise!" exclaimed a man with a pox-marked face. "What joy to drink without worrying about the *scudi* trickling away! Don Diego, open the taps! Didn't you hear these gentlemen? Bring us something to eat!" he shouted, encouraged by the others.

A gypsy woman with a cross around her neck squeezed in, putting her head coyly on Berti's shoulder. "Excellency, I'm thirsty. Order some of Don Diego's best!"

"Esperanza, my treasure, you are working fast," laughed Berti's neighbor. "Don Pascuale here, at your service. Any time you need a notary you can find me right here at the Black Swan." He prattled on with a leaden tongue. "You've already forgotten me, haven't you?" he added, pinching the gypsy's bottom.

Berti laughed as she jumped.

"Here, Excellency. My friend Michele the cobbler can attest to my honesty." Don Pascuale guarded his face against the gypsy's claws as he made way for the procession of food and drink, ready to dive in as the shabby table creaked under the unexpected burden.

Succulent rabbit legs swimming in spicy wine sauce landed under Berti's nose, followed by tender mutton chops with sausages lost in roasted onions competing with bottles and bottles of wine among large crusty loaves of bread.

"To our dear Pope Pius! May God bless him with many good years! And here's to my friend, His Holiness' first and finest painter. May his career continue to shine!" Adrien proposed the first toast, struggling to keep his full tankard up.

"To the pope's first painter. May he keep our souls merry and our bellies full!" The company responded heartily, attacking the food ferociously.

Berti offered his tankard to the dark gypsy, and she puckered her moist lips open, ready for a kiss. Instead he took her cross and put it in her mouth.

"Black pusscat, have you been to confession lately? I like them sweet and pure!"

The hall shook with laughter.

"She confesses all the time, many times a day, to Franciscans, Dominicans, Carthusians, and Benedictines too!" The innkeeper bowed. "They come in all sizes and colors, and they certainly like her confessions. They keep coming back to us. Isn't that right, my little virgin?"

"Music, strum the guitars and the lutes!" the drunken Adrien commanded. "And you, *putana nera,* dance for us!" He swept the empty dishes from the table and motioned her up.

"Flamenco, will that please you?" the burly Don Diego inquired, eagerly pocketing the tossed coins. He moved fast when his pouch commanded. "It's the devil's dance, and our Esperanza here is Lucifer's best friend. La-la-la, la-la-la," he mouthed in a false baritone, clapping in time with the guitars' warm chords. "Catana and Michaela, where are you lazy sluts? *Vino,* let's have more *vino* for our illustrious guests!"

The crowd formed a circle around the table, more bodies pushing from behind. Like a nimble cat, the dark gypsy jumped onto the table, her dusky legs arched wide apart, ready to begin. Her castanets chattered against the fiery rhythm of the guitars, the black mass of her tight curls whipping through the air.

"*Vino! Vino!*" The voices sped with the music as the beakers rose into the air.

"Aurora, Basilia, Francisca, Rosina, Rufina, Sabina! Where are you damn girls? Can't you see we have customers?" Don Diego clapped louder as Esperanza's naked feet, full of hellfire, drummed the table.

"Higher, higher!" the crowd called as her dirty skirts inched up her firm, naked legs.

"Money, money!" signaled her upturned palms as coins rolled onto the table, clinking and clattering under her feet.

"Lower, lower!" the men cried in unison as her greasy *camicia* slid off her shoulders, revealing her ebony forms. Berti tipped his head back as he emptied another beaker, his blood pulsing into his mouth. The circle of onlookers joined hands and swayed with the music.

Sensuously, the gypsy whore moved like a cat, arching her breasts, breaking all the rules of the dance to capture her audience. The men responded like savages, the stamping of their feet echoing against the low barrel vault.

"Esperanza, where is your *caballero?*" they cried. "You must choose one!"

A rose dropped at Berti's feet, and the men around him pushed him up onto the table.

"To love," he toasted without knowing what to do. He swayed, stamping, clapping—a willing captive to the music and the smell of her body.

The night watchman called the seventh hour after sundown, but no one at the Black Swan noticed. The *rione* of Pozzo Bianco—the White Well where cheap love could be bought for a few *soldi*—was alive. Suddenly and quite abruptly, the dance was over. Berti bathed in sweat, thick rivulets streaming down his ripped shirt into his britches.

"Don Diego, how about some dessert now?" Adrien shouted across the hall.

"We have some almond cakes and raisin pastries." Don Diego pushed back through the crowd. "Sugared fruit, but if you prefer it natural, we have lovely peaches and plums and melons, as ripe and soft as you like them," he explained and pointed to the row of señoritas vying with each other for the rich visitors' favors.

"These ugly chickens? Don't you have anything more suitable for gentlemen?"

"My lord, there is my wife." The crowd exploded in laughter. "And my daughter."

"Don Diego, go and roast them for your dinner! That's all they're good for," the drunken Pascuale yelled. "How about Isabella, your pretty ward?"

"*La Bella,* we want *la Bella,* the white flower of Castiglia," the men chanted in unison.

Don Diego hesitated. "But she's so young and pure."

Adrien threw a full purse at his feet. Don Diego called for his ward.

"To the white swan of Black Diego." Adrien barely managed another toast as he unlaced his codpiece and relieved himself. "Or would you like to go first, my esteemed friend?"

She was young and trembled like the bird Adrien's housekeeper sacrificed for their last dinner before Berti left for San Oreste. He winced at her protests as the women tied her down on the table, but then she became resigned, like Monna Alba while he raped her.

"Music, *amici,* let's be merry!" Don Diego snapped his fingers. The gypsy men struck a lively tune as the poor girl's shrieks resounded.

"Santa Maria!" Don Diego's shocked wife whispered and crossed herself.

Even Berti, suddenly horrified, shook his head as Adrien dropped his britches.

"Adrien, please." His voice drowned in the crowd.

"To our gracious host!" The men cheered Adrien as he flipped the girl's skirt over her head and mounted her briskly. "One, two, three!" they screamed. "Bravo, *signore,* what a gentleman!" They swayed enthusiastically, applauding the merry rider, watching his freckled back flash. The shrieks subsided when Adrien finally climbed down.

Berti's gut was in his mouth.

"You're next." The merchant motioned to his queasy friend.

"Why ever not?" Berti did his duty by Lucifer, first putting his coin into Don Diego's greedy palm, and watched the other men follow him.

"Wasn't it a splendid night?" Adrien mumbled sleepily as they staggered out into the maelstrom of peasants, wagons, and animals moving about as dawn signaled a new day.

Berti could hardly face himself, feeling only emptiness.

† † †

Berti staggered across the open Borgo, in no shape to return to the Belvedere. He could not stand the sight of Adrien, although he enjoyed his company, nor could he face Maddalena, who was in mourning. The inexplicable deaths of Don Alfonso and Monna Alba consumed him. He could not face the facts. The boy was innocent.

Why did the Virgin not punish *him,* Berti? Of course, in a way, she did, by taking Alba. But suicide is a far greater sin than bearing a child out of wedlock. Why was she so stupid? He did not want to marry her—and he was glad he did not have to—but he would have done, had she asked him the right way.

A gust of wind rushed by him, bearing a foul scent. He bent down to smell his shirt and recoiled. The black gypsy's musty oil was all over him. He shuddered, remembering her biting his last coin. *Good riddance.*

He arched and spilled his dinner over the corner of a house. His knees shook, and he slid down against the dusty wall and put his head down. Damn, you old fool! He cursed silently, recalling the youth who walked the Borgo his first day in Rome. Five years had passed since he stayed at the Three Bears, and he still had not learned enough. He stood to round the corner.

"Watch where you're going!" A voice towered over him, nearly toppling him.

"Begging your pardon." Berti was about to say sir when he recognized Claudio, the owner of the Three Bears. He had not changed a bit, still the rotund man with a gray scruff of a beard who changed his clothes only with the seasons. "How's your missus?"

Messer Claudio stared at him glassily, tottering unsteadily.

"How's Signora Maria?" Berti replied in return.

"Do I know you, Excellency?" Claudio regarded the disheveled dandy with surprise.

"Bartolomeo d'Anversa. You helped me when I first came to Rome."

Claudio shot a stare of recognition. "A thousand pardons. May I be of service, sir?"

"A bit of rest would be nice," Berti muttered as the innkeeper accompanied his unexpected guest to one of his best rooms. When he awoke, it was dark. He slowly descended to the front hall where, weak from hunger, he ordered food. The respectful woman who served him brought a large tureen of steaming bean soup laced with garlic.

Berti sniffed it, and his stomach churned.

"Send it over to that table. They look like they could do with a bit of food." He pointed to a gaunt Franciscan talking to a haggard fellow who looked like a merchant. "Bring me some bread and a bowl of warm milk.

"On second thought"—he changed his mind—"why don't you invite them over here?"

The men hardly understood their sudden fortune.

"Blessed be your sweet mother." The Franciscan was about to hug Berti.

"Eat!" Berti pushed the friar away, making sure his fleas stayed home.

"Bad times befall us, sir." The humble man scratched his arm. "The pope's money feeds his fleet, and the people of Rome starve."

Berti dunked bread into the milk. "Are you both from Rome?"

"I come from the hills of Perugia, and my companion here ... I didn't hear your name."

"The people who want money from me call me Isaac. That'll do fine," the other man muttered, watching the steam rise from the soup.

The Franciscan drew back. "You wouldn't happen to be a Jew, would you?"

"What if I were? You've got as many fleas as I do, and we're even in God's eyes."

"Whose, yours or mine?" the Franciscan hissed.

"If you want to know, our god was the father of yours, and Jesus was a Jew too. And, signor *corteggiano,* what might be your calling in life?" The Jew turned to Berti.

"I am the painter for His Holiness."

Isaac drew back. "Are you an informer, sire?"

Berti laughed. "Stupid old man, I'm too busy to worry about the likes of you." He dunked another, larger piece of bread in the milk and felt the warmth spread in his gut.

The Franciscan paused between hasty mouthfuls. "You have fame and money, so what brings you here to us, the scum of the earth?"

"I don't know. I might be seeking peace and happiness," Berti joked.

"We all want that," the monk replied, "but surely Fortuna stands at your side." He fingered Berti's fine but smelly clothes. "Is it not power and fame you desire?"

"I want love—pure, immortal love." Berti often changed his mind on the topic.

"But love's cheap. It's out there, yours for the asking." The Franciscan pointed to Berti's pockets. Berti turned them out empty. "I seek a woman who'd turn me into a good person."

"Why don't you ask your God for help?" the Jew suggested. "As you papists tell me, He can arrange anything."

"Well ... " Berti was about to agree but shook his head instead. The woman he wanted had also to be rich and of fine family, bringing him a big dowry and a position at court. Alba was sweet and innocent, very pretty too, but even God could not perform miracles that great.

The Jew misunderstood his remark. "If He can destroy Ali Pasha and his fifty-thousand men, what is it to Him to give you one special woman?" he asked and belched.

"Not so many perished, but that is what the victors are saying," the monk rejoined.

"And who's to believe you, brave soldier of God?" the contented Jew snickered.

"I was there!" The friar grew livid. "I saw Ali Pasha's head mounted on a spike at the stern of his ship, and I saw his Turkish crescent descend and our cross rise up instead. We were in the bay of Naples. It was on the first day of August when the infidels took over Cyprus."

"Leave the Moslems in peace," the Jew broke in. "What makes you think your religion is better?" He sneered at the Franciscan.

"Who's talking here? For centuries you fools have been waiting for the divinely anointed one. You don't imagine that he will ever come, do you?"

"Keep your mouth shut!" the angry Jew cried. "The messiah may have descended to earth this very minute. We just don't know about it," he protested adamantly.

"My friends"—Berti filled the men's tin cups with wine—"would you leave your differences for another time? We're all made of the same dough! Your tale, padre."

"It took us two weeks to reach Messina. We loaded three-hundred ships with fresh water and provisions and sailed to Corfu," the

Franciscan explained. Happy with a full cup in front of him, the Jew sat passively, although he feigned only to pretend to listen.

"We sailed by Corinth, heading for the mouth of the Gulf of Patras. Pasha's fleet was off Lepanto, and we met the enemy on a misty morning in October three weeks later. Their masts filled the horizon, but we were ready for them, the Venetian galleys on the left, the papal and Genoese forces on the right, and Don Juan's flagship in the center with more Venetian galleys behind and the Spanish closing the rear.

"You should have seen us lined up!" the Franciscan continued. "Don Juan's galley went right to the front. His armor shimmered in the sun, the grace of God on him. We all knelt, the crew, soldiers, the humble and the rich, beseeching Our Lord for a victory. With each shot, the silver crucifixes glittered, giving us strength and shielding us against the Turks' arrows.

"When they saw the head of their leader on the poop deck, they ran with their tails tucked. We got about half their ships. For the 150 we sank, they took ten of ours. There may have been more, but our cannon killed twice the men theirs did."

Berti shuddered. "You say this battle was the will of God the Father?"

The Jew challenged him. "What makes you think that?"

"Only Our Lord could have led us to such a great a victory," the Franciscan beamed, his face illuminated with faith. "But the battle drained our dear leader's coffers. If the pope has any money left, the Jesuits take it, and we soldiers go hungry. Times are bad and getting worse by the day, while the cardinals get fatter and fatter." The monk suddenly changed his tune.

Berti lost his patience with the common lot. "Don Claudio!"—he clapped as soon as he sighted the innkeeper—"Look after these men tonight and put it on my bill.

"I bid you farewell." Exhaling the sour air, Berti left the squalid inn.

"We've been looking for you!" Surprisingly, the angry pontiff was waiting in his studio. "Don Vasari tells Us you've been wasting your time in foolishness. It makes Our heart bleed."

Berti backed away. "Forgive me, Holy Father. I've been distraught by a series of tragedies."

"Tragedies? The next time you come to see Us, We want to see your new drawings of the passion of Christ all complete, do you hear?" Pius shouted back, forgetting his calling. One look at his immoral painter clearly revealed the ugly truth.

† † †

Four men, still warm, dangled on the gallows near the bridge of Castel Sant'Angelo that morning, their blue tongues pierced and hanging from their purple faces. When Berti inquired about their crime, he learned they had not observed the Sabbath according to Pius' law.

Berti glanced at them, and fear erupted in his heart. His patron, who supported the hospital of Santo Spirito and built new quarters for sick prisoners by Tor di Nona, was merciless to sinners. His painter knew it would not take much for his body to swing on the gallows.

Back at the Vatican, Berti bowed deeply to Cardinal Montalto. Felice Pedretti, the son of a gardener from Montalto, wore his crimson robes humbly. The same age as the vigorous Alessandro, he leaned heavily on his stick, resting next to a basket of figs and olives. Berti could not understand how he tended his gardens by Santa Maria Maggiore nearly alone.

Listening to Montalto's dry cough, he watched him pick up the basket for Pius. Berti imagined the two men talking about blights and bees, lost in the world of botany while Montalto wound the frail pontiff around his fingers. Some rumors had the Vice General of the Franciscans go far, despite his enemies' slander. Berti knew that he could wear the tiara next.

Berti crossed himself. He did not fancy working for Cardinal Montalto. Should he look for another post? The *Last Judgment* was finished and had been duly blessed in a ceremony eight hours long. Berti bowed again to another cardinal.

Unlike the frail Montalto, Hugo Buoncompagni of Bologna rose on his laurels as a scholar of canon law, a man who smiled warmly to all. Berti straightened his back, following the protocol until Buoncompagni's figure reached an appropriate distance.

"Pleased be God," he muttered, "that Alessandro succeed the pope after all."

Berti knew that the richest man in Rome had faith in his money, although palace rumors also whispered of King Philip's gold and Medici scorn for the Farnese upstart. But Berti did not care. Tired of Pius' Rome where joy smacked of heresy and the new Grand Inquisitor ruled the curia with an iron hand and new gallows grew daily, Berti craved a change.

Shuffling into his workshop to clean up after Pius' huge epitaph was gone, he decided that he was sick of saints, sick of Christ's damning hand. Saints, saints, and more saints! Drawings of them, studies, color sketches, littered the whole place. It seemed like ages since the time he thought that there was more to Rome than grinding paints and cleaning brushes.

Damn them all! Studies of Christ's passion flew about and landed everywhere. He cracked his knuckles, picked up a quill, sharpened its tip with a couple of trained strokes, and dipped it vigorously into the ink.

The naked upper torso of a young woman grew on the surface, tinted brown. Full cheeks, lush lips, eyes piously thrown back—but the bosom and the hips! Full and supple, he panted, imagining how he would deflower such a pretty thing. Let's give her a dagger thrust deep into her breast and call her Lucretia! No, Marcellina's her name! He clicked his tongue, as he imagined the daughter of Monna Lena's fishmonger at the market square.

To hell with Pius! Damn the brushes! He swept them all to the floor with one stroke.

The next morning, however, reason reigned, and he crawled humbly back, hoping that Don Vasari had not heard about his latest venture. He hated his job, and the Belvedere felt like a prison.

"Yes, Holy Father"—he imagined himself muttering obligingly—"I made my confession early this morning in Santa Maria in Trastevere. She was sweet, sweeter than you can imagine, but that's strictly between me, the young lady, and the haystack that bedded us last night."

Familiar footsteps sounded down the hall.

"Hey, Maarten, where did you come from?" he called out, jumping to hug his friend. The timing was amazing. "Haven't seen you for ages! Are you passing through?"

"I'm on my way back home. Wanted to see you on my way down but couldn't."

Berti glanced at the courtyard. "When are you leaving?"

Maarten looked relaxed. "*Beh,* the coach was leaving this morning, but maestro Vasari still had some business with the Holy Father, so we'll leave at noon."

Berti faltered for a second and replied, "Is there room? I'm coming with you!"

"We'll make some." Maarten replied, excited. "But can you go?"

Pius was not pleased, but seeing that Berti's task was completed, he granted a week's leave. Berti hated to share the coach with the conceited maestro, who constantly complained to Pius about his laziness.

But Berti needed a change, tired of working hard, tripping over ancient columns, and studying new frescoes. With Pius' epitaph done, he agreed to decorate a chapel in San Luigi dei Francesi for the French padres. But he did not have to start soon. After all, the padres paid in gold, and a man was born to spend it.

† † †

All night long the carriage crossed a moonlit, wintry landscape of rolling hills and mountain towns that reminded Berti of San Oreste and Don Alfonso. The journey was long, and Berti was tired, but unlike Maarten, he could not sleep. Maestro Vasari sat in the opposite corner of the coach and complained about the misery of traveling by hired coach. But occasionally he addressed Berti with more pleasant questions.

No, Berti had no plans. Yes, he would be willing to try his luck working for the archduke and come to see the maestro's new project in the Old Palace. No, he was not hungry, and once more definitely, no, he was not planning to visit any Florentine churches the very next day.

When dawn broke and the sun streaked from behind light clouds, spring perfumed the air, and the landscape looked surprisingly lush. Florence was provincial and charming, a colorful jewel of shorn medieval towers and church steeples around Brunelleschi's dome. As the carriage rattled over Ponte Vecchio, Berti could not keep up with Maarten's pointing finger.

"That's San Miniato on the Mountain—the Old Bridge with shops— and the new corridor so that His Lordship, Archduke Francesco, will stay dry while visiting his father across the river. And, oh, the Medici offices, next to the Old Palace on the main square. And the Bargello, that big prison where the coachman will let us off."

They did not have far to walk. Maarten's quarters were just behind the prison, a minute from the City Hall and Francesco Medici's residence, and he made Berti very welcome. All next day, they toured the town without entering a single public hall or church. Florence was small, with squalid alleys housing cats and the poor but also with ostentatious yet severe palaces.

It was damp, and Berti was tired as they approached the old granary near the Guilds of the Dyers and Woolmakers, marked by large crests. Clumsy, shabby dwellings mushroomed one over the other as they had for centuries, the front shops blocked by reams of cloth, spun wool, and silk from abroad, the muddy alleys filled with an acrid stench of waste mixed with streams of wet dyes merging in colorful pools in the hollows.

The shop they entered was small and dark, and the old shopkeeper crippled with age and rheumatism. Maarten always had some unfinished business.

"This is what we agreed on, Meneer de Waal." The man peered at him nearsightedly and pulled a dirty piece of yellowed parchment from a stack of notes. "And here"—he pointed to the section headed by 'To Be Received'—"is what you still owe me."

Maarten calculated the sum. "Messer Sacchetti ... "

The old man fired a hard look. "A deal's a deal. I'm but a merchant, and I need to live."

Berti studied the shaky rows of tight ciphers of accounts receivable and payable while the two men argued about the price of silk affected by the recent troubles in the Mediterranean. The vendor's seemingly fragile demeanor hid shrewdness, and Maarten was no novice. Berti studied the old man's worn rabbit-fur coat and the molting fox cap he straightened every so often with his crooked fingers and wondered whether he had overvalued Messer Sacchetti's wit. Finally the men shook hands on the deal, and Berti was pleased to see daylight.

"You should see the mess in his warehouse! But name your cloth, chose your color and the most exotic weave, and Messer Sacchetti has it. But now we must meet your adversary." Maarten reminded Berti of his rendezvous with Archduke Francesco's first painter.

As they neared the river, the city became cleaner.

"Who's that?" Berti pointed to a sedan chair moving toward them.

"Some call her *La Bionda,* but Francesco calls her *La Mammola,*" Maarten explained. Reclined under the canopy and buried under a pile of white fur, the Venetian courtesan smiled regally, playing with a pale monkey in her lap. When nearly abreast, the woman raised her face toward Berti and blew him a coquettish kiss.

Berti turned around and gasped aloud, "*Mammola.* A mammal?"

"No, the word's a sweet endearment for a woman, like a darling, a kind of pretty violet."

Berti grinned, unsure about the name, and looked back once more.

"Venetian blondes have purple eyes, did you know that?" Maarten added.

Berti breathed in the lingering scent of violet water. "*La Mammola,* you say."

"Forget it. She belongs to the archduke!" Maarten exclaimed in feigned horror. "And say, how is your old patron? And Maddalena?"

"I don't see them as often as I used to," Berti replied, unsure whether Maarten knew about Maddalena. He felt guilty about not having seen her for a while. "I suppose they're fine—but, my friend, I'm just damn depressed. They were all innocent, the boy who wanted a father, the trusting girl, my unborn child." Berti shook his head, worried.

"Men hang for lesser offences. What's going to happen to me? Will I stew in hell?"

Maarten stopped in mid-stride. "No, you won't, and what in hell's going on?" he asked as he put his arms around Berti's shoulders, sorry to see him break down. Often away from family for months, the prosaic businessman healed Berti's fear instantly.

"Look, the Lord just took my third-born. I loved him dearly and hoped that some day he'd carry on my trade. I have four daughters left, and their dowries are expensive. But the Lord takes and He gives as well. I've closed a few exceptionally good deals, so I'm content.

"Berti, I understand how you feel about losing the cardinal's boy, I've lost a son! But Alessandro, not you, will stew in hell. And surely the Lord will find a better wife for you than that silly goose who took her own life and your son's."

Maarten was a pious man, and Berti tried to believe him, forgetting why Monna Alba took her life in the first place. Maarten's bear hug made sure he did, because he needed to go on.

They walked on until with one more turn they faced the palace in which the ambitious Medici archduke lived with his ugly Habsburg wife. It looked small compared to Alessandro's, but as they neared the stronghold with a tall bell tower, it grew to formidable proportions.

"They used to call it the Palazzo della Signoria, but since the old duke moved across the river, it's the Palazzo Vecchio, the Old Palace," Maarten told him, summarizing a rather more complex history.

"Isn't that where the elders preside?" Berti asked Maarten.

"The Medici family *is* the government," Maarten replied. A favored merchant, he entered with his guest unhindered.

Passing through the Audience Hall, a room before which even the Hall of the Farnese Deeds paled, Berti finally understood GiorgioVasari's fame. "Not even princes live like this," Berti sighed, amazed that one mind could have invented such splendid fresco decorations.

"But the Medicis are more than princes. Francesco's wife is the daughter of one Emperor and sister of another. And did you know that Francesco was born on March twenty-fifth, the Florentine new year. Only gods are privileged to be born on such fortunate days."

Berti was impressed and loved the rest of his Florentine visit, but his search for a job was a failure. The archduke did not want an extra hand, and the snob Vasari did not help to change Francesco's mind. And so Berti returned to Rome, disappointed. Relieved to be back after a long ride with a noblewoman who never stopped chattering, he found the atmosphere in the Vatican much altered. The pontiff his benefactor lay on his deathbed.

Pius' tomb in his native Bosco, decorated with Berti's copy of Fra Angelico's *Last Judgment,* was complete. All Romans walking the Via Alessandrina and Bonelli toward St. Peter's Basilica remembered the good pope for building those streets and praised him for fortifying the city walls against Turkish raids. After the feast of Christ's Resurrection, Pius summoned Berti and spoke to him once more, asking Signor Cirillo to open the chest and pay his painter all he owed to the last *baiocco.* But no more.

"Remember me by this," he said, pressing a plain crucifix into his hand. "For with this, the Lord will also remember you and guide you."

The ungrateful Berti grumbled to his friends that he was given crumbs. Three days later, on the first day of May in the year of Our Lord 1572, Pius' saintly soul ascended to heaven.

Only then did Berti realize how little he appreciated his enviable post, for less than two weeks later the new successor to St. Peter's throne no longer smiled at Pius' painter in the halls. Gregory XIII, the plump Buoncompagni pontiff, was too busy enjoying his new dignity to worry about the likes of Berti. Excluded by the new pontiff's supporters, advisors, and hangers-on, Berti felt unwanted, whether he coveted his old post or not.

Excelsior

After the iron age of Pius came the silver age of Gregory, and to Berti's surprise, his sun shone brighter than he anticipated. Although his post vanished with Pius' death, he felt secure because of his investments with Adrien to move in with his friend, ready for a new life.

"My lord, there is *someone* to see you," Gertgen announced gingerly one warm summer day. With time, Adrien's young valet had grown wiser, and both Adrien and Berti depended on his judgment. This time the self-made servant looked serious but offered no clues.

"Which one of us?" Adrien raised himself sleepily from his chair, sunk in the courtyard's deep shade. He could not imagine anyone moving around that hot summer afternoon.

"A gentleman by the name of Pietro Portinari desires to speak with Master Berti."

Reluctantly, Berti raised himself on one elbow.

"A gentleman. What the devil about?" Somewhat concerned, he put down his goblet and slipped off the hammock. Those days many gentle and not-so-gentle men wanted a word with him, mostly about his debts or their daughters. But Messer Portinari might be a new tailor in town, and Berti's good taste was well known in the Roman haberdashers' district.

"Do I know this distinguished gentleman?"

Gertgen forced a smile. "He says that you've met his wife."

Marginally interested, Adrien yawned and stretched back on his chair. Berti raked his mind but without success. "Pietro Portinari ... What does he want?"

"Meneer Portinari did say something about you decorating his wife's bathroom with new frescoes," Gertgen offered.

Berti glanced at Adrien, but his friend appeared to be dozing. Puzzled but no longer worried, Berti checked himself and straightened his clothes. "Show Messer Portinari in," Berti commanded in Italian, since the sound of the name suggested no one from their northern circle.

The gentleman was rotund, prosperous, and sweating profusely in the heat.

"How did I earn the pleasure of your acquaintance, sir?" Berti gestured broadly toward the stone bench in the alcove. The visitor responded in broken Flemish, muttering about a family mercantile business in Bruges.

"So you belong to the Roman branch of the family?" Berti asked, confused. For the next few moments, Messer Portinari took Berti's breath away with a torrent of words.

"I understand now," Berti said. "Your family's fortune bought you a young, noble wife who traveled with me recently."

"Just so, master painter," Pietro Portinari beamed.

Berti needed a moment to reconsider. "And your business, is it in Bruges?"

"The Portinari family's fortune is in Florence, where I reside."

Berti would not return there just to paint a bathroom. "Your business here in Rome?"

"How can I explain. My wife, the honorable Madonna Isabella, her blood noble although her family's fortunes are not the way they used to be." He lost his thread completely as he continued in Flemish. "Madonna Isabella was born in Rome, and this is her world."

"*Ja?*" Berti replied impatiently, hoping Meneer Portinari would come to the point.

"The Roman Counts of Della Valle are proud men, and my wife bears their blood."

"*Signore,* might it not be easier to explain yourself in the language of your land?"

"By God, yes. But it's sometimes pleasant to speak the tongue I learned when my father's affairs were in Bruges." The gentleman mopped his forehead and opened the top buttons of his fashionable but uncomfortable vest.

Adrien, recovering wakefulness, rang the bell, and Gertgen appeared.

"Some refreshment for Meneer Portinari," he ordered in Flemish. "I shall now leave you to yourselves, gentlemen."

Relieved not to have to confess the foolishness of his mission to two strangers, Pietro Portinari quickly opened up. "Master painter, here in Rome, my wife stays in her family's town palazzo"—Messer Portinari now shifted to Italian—"but it's old and needs restyling. You, Signor Bartolomeo, impressed her, and I wonder if you could decorate her *stuffetta da bagno*."

Little serious business crowded Berti's schedule during the summer as Rome slept. "I'd be delighted." Berti shook the man's sticky hand.

"Would ten florins bind our contract?"

"That's a fortune," Berti thought. "*Ja!*" he fired back.

"I am so overjoyed," Pietro continued, still pumping Berti's hand. "Perhaps now my young wife will be happy in her Roman abode and favor me with sons."

Berti raised his eyebrows. The Florentine merchant looked older than Alessandro.

So that was what was really troubling Messer Portinari, he thought, amused. "I'm sure we'll reach a mutual understanding," he said, smiling knowingly. "My warmest regards to your honorable lady wife."

While Gertgen accompanied the guest to the back garden gate opening on Via Giulia, Adrien returned and sat in his chair.

"Berti, some people know how to marry," he joked. "He's old and rich. She's young, idle, and poor. But her blood is blue!"

Berti stared blankly. "What do you mean, idle? You haven't even met the lady."

"When a wife can't give a merchant a son, what else do you call her but lazy?"

"Adrien, be serious. He's an old goat, and she ... " Berti began whistling.

"Stay out of trouble, that's all. Remember that now you must earn your keep," Adrien joshed, for their investments in the silver mines in Peru were making them richer than they had ever hoped. "I'm taking a short rest!" Adrien examined his buffed nails and turned on his heel.

Berti remained in the shade a while longer but without solving the mystery of Madonna Isabella. The sharp tongue he remembered but not much else. His recollections of the fair sex in those days were often fuzzy, as women had become a new mission in the young lothario's life.

† † †

At twenty-six, Berti was a mature man with dark curls lining a face so virile it could be read like an open book. Ever since he joined Adrien's household in Via dei Banchi Vecchii, helping his friend enjoy the palace of the absentee prince-bishop, the book opened even more as the muses of pleasure guided the painter's life decisively.

But obstacles remained. One was his friend Hans, who preached and practiced natural piety and humility, seeking others to follow. Back from Venice and content in his little house by the Trevi fountain, Hans enjoyed a quiet life with his new wife. Berti, however, was his own enemy, for women looked at him and fell into his path.

Dashingly handsome, his magnetism, not his looks, made ladies swoon into his arms, a power and masculinity that turned the heads of even the most devout matrons.

For all her dignity, Madonna Isabella was but a grown child. At fourteen she understood little of Pietro Portinari's frantic ways of begetting a son, which neither of his two deceased wives gave him. She suffered her husband with the distinction bestowed by her noble blood and the position his prosperous mercantile business supported.

But the childish Isabella tired of him, turning to the protective arms of her nanny and to silly amusements with a blackamoor page and a foundling girl from the convent of the Innocents. She linked her misfortune with her need for easy gratification, and the dashing painter was but another toy, one she hardly remembered from the trip with him. She meant to use him for her purposes and satisfy her impotent husband with an heir.

Dressed plainly without the colorful decorations of current fashion, his chest draped in the softest Flemish linen, his featherless biretta decorated with Alessandro's diamond pin, Berti rang at her palace behind the Church of the Holy Apostles to discuss his new contract.

Madonna Isabella sat in the garden, roasting in the sun's heat, her long hair arrayed in a golden cascade over the broad straw hat that kept it off her face and pretty dimpled shoulders.

"Are you sure that the potion is fresh?" the contessina fretted underneath the hat that protected her creamy complexion but did nothing about the nauseating fumes from the dye her nanny used to paint her hair.

"Little lamb, stay still," the nanny clucked, checking the last spots to be touched up. "You may go." She motioned two servants to remove the clay pot with the brew of saffron, walnut oil, and poppy seeds simmered with a sorrel mare's droppings.

"I am sorry, little mistress." She bent and kissed the hem of Isabella's cotton robe. "Monna Lena did not have the flowers of Glaucus with her last order. You know, my precious, the troubles in Syria … "

"This is awful!" Isabella stamped her little foot as the foul odor drifted by her nose. "Am I not dry yet? Freckles are popping under my hat!"

"A few minutes more, my lamb. Think how pretty you'll be for the gentleman."

Isabella wagged her finger. "Nanny, if you can't get those flowers and you have to use that awful muck from my Vixen, I want more lime and licorice in the brew! This stinks!"

"My pet, this brew is stronger than what we've used before, but the herb lady says this application will last a whole year. Think of that, and you'll feel better." The nanny motioned to the page to move his feathers faster. "This recipe comes from Signor Nostradamo's book, and he served greater princesses than you, Madonna Isabella."

The nanny soon spirited her mistress to her chambers while Messer Portinari discussed the project with Berti. "Should you have any questions about the decorations, I'm sure my wife's *bambinaia* will be at your service," he said. "When I return, I'd like to see progress in your decorations and a happy wife in the bargain!"

Pietro Portinari was scarcely back in Florence when the mistress of the house made her presence well known in her *stuffetta*, appearing at all hours of the day, endangering her beauty by skipping her accustomed nap, making Berti's life difficult and slowing his work.

"Madonna Isabella, if you want a stucco fountain in the corner of your bath, you must speak to your noble husband to find you a plasterer," he told her. "I paint frescoes."

The lady pursed her lips and batted her charcoal eyelashes. She made a particularly enticing picture, her golden hair freshly washed with lye and rinsed with lemon water. But all the Flemish painter could do was work on the little birds that flew over the imaginary Roman landscape by her bath!

"Come, Peppina," she commanded her nanny as she purposely dropped her flimsy veil.

"I beg you to forgive me," he apologized, "but if I pick up your veil, my dirty hands might soil it." He always tried to discourage Isabella by stressing the lowly status of his profession.

"What a brute," the girl mumbled ungraciously, though not deterred.

"Little lamb, you're playing with fire," her nursemaid warned. But when Berti arrived the following morning, it was to find Madonna Isabella splashing unabashedly in her bath right in the middle of the room. "Peppina, fetch me more rose petals from the garden. The white ones!" she said, knowing that they grew high above the briar hedge that went rampant in the summer heat. Never before had Berti desired a woman less than that spoiled brat, despite her cherubic beauty, and never before had a young lady wished more to be conquered.

"Maestro, would you fetch my soap?" She let the aromatic ball slide away. "And wash my back!" Berti reluctantly obliged the child tyrant. "But I think my skin has had too much water today," she announced, stepping out brazenly, holding her hair up to let Berti admire her. At that point, no one, not even the determined painter, could resist Isabella's plump girlhood. So he loved her long and willingly under the bright canopy of vines and birds he painted for her, until she was sure that he gave her a son.

Never did the brazen girl make her bald husband happier than when she showed him her new pretty *stuffetta,* except the day his messenger brought Berti another, unexpected leather purse heavy with gold. "Pietro Portinari is going to be a father, and judging from the weight of this pouch, he must expect a son. Is that right, Berti?" Adrien inquired slyly.

"How should I know?" Berti responded, trying not to laugh. It was hard to keep his face straight. "Would you invest this for me wisely, more wisely than I earned it?"

Not all Berti's commissions were as interesting, as delightful, or as rewarding as that one. His job at San Luigi dei Francesi started rather more modestly but was made more pleasant by the company of Hans painting the chapel vault above him. Mindful of his promise, especially now that Hans' family was growing, Berti persuaded the French padres to include his friend in the chapel decorations. "We make a good team," Hans said. "I have ideas and you paint. I'll do the drawings and you put them on the walls."

When the chapel was finished, the French padres were happy with its bright colors and clean lines, and when the New Year came they also admired Hans' new daughter Berta, named after her Flemish godfather. Frau Klara, who felt her German roots strongly, controlled her house so utterly that Berti wondered how she also managed to make Hans so happy. He was jealous of the newlyweds and visited his godchild often, looking for the secret of Hans' marital bliss.

Cornelis was back in Rome. Scorning matrimony, he became a natural companion in Adrien's and Berti's merry outings, albeit his taste was more particular than theirs. When one day he attracted the prince-bishop's special attention, his fellows understood the meaning of the name he had among northerners. '*Wipsgoy*' some called him. His appetite raised eyebrows here and there, but the palace was big and the prince's pockets full—so no one cared.

Manus Domini

Alessandro was no longer the man Monna Lena playfully married in the gardens of Caprarola, but she still loved him. Frustrated that his gold could not bribe his fellow cardinals to elect another Farnese pope, he grew to hate many. The new Buoncompagni pope enjoyed good health, and unless Alessandro reverted to the Borgias' tried methods, his enemy would rule too long. But it never dawned on him that his mistress stood in the way.

Monna Lena felt acutely for *ecclesia romana's* rejected suitor, lamented his ill luck, feeling him closer. Grieving for Alfonso, she with a woman's sentiment and he with a prelate's reserve, they sought each other's company more often, as though each other's only true friends.

He visited often, ostensibly bringing papers to read while she watched him working, sitting quietly across the room with her sewing. When they first met, Alessandro was a god incarnate, but now she loved him as he was, honoring and serving him while preserving her own dignity, a quality he quickly learned to appreciate.

She tried to find the light of God and her new faith in him, but soon she realized that for Alessandro, the grandson of the worldly Paul III, religion was a habit, like his wealth and power, and reciting the Lord's Prayer was peer to enjoying his *prima collazione* every morning.

She tried to change him, to humble him and bring him down to earth, not for herself but for the people of Rome, hoping to cultivate the same kind of fervent religion that dominated her life since her conversion, but she did not succeed. Of all her failures, that was hardest to bear.

Yet as time went by, and they grew closer, Maddalena was able to understand his ideas better, and their talk grew longer and ran deeper. While she did not always find the right words, her acumen easily made up for her unpolished rhetoric.

"Alessandro, you should be more careful about coming here," she said and offered her warm cheek when he stopped by one morning on his way to the Vatican. After he settled in his cozy spot by the hearth, she spilled her worries.

"Look what's happening on the continent," she said. "The French queen rules triumphant, Coligny is dead, the Huguenots are slaughtered, and Gregory is jubilant."

"You're right," Alessandro agreed half-heartedly. "Gregory couldn't wait to have a medal struck to commemorate the massacre as if he had contributed to it personally."

"Such slaughter of innocent people! Such terror and confusion!" Maddalena envisioned the streams of French fugitives fleeing to Geneva and Strasbourg. "At least some survived. But you must think of your own position. You have enemies, even if they smile in your face."

Alessandro winced. "Don't preach to me about politics. I don't want to hear what Alba's doing right now or about the Dutch pirates attacking coastal towns in Holland and Zeeland."

Monna Lena remained silent for a few seconds. "But dearest," her mind painting pictures worse than reality, "what if the Protestants rise up here, taking over churches, looting them, destroying images, running the clergy away? What will you do then?"

"There are no Protestants in the papal states, my pet. The Holy Office makes sure of that, whether by sword or fire. And the Farnese are like the rock from which they are hewn."

Monna Lena sharpened the tone of her voice. "Think about Cardinal Carranza. That holy man never imagined that he'd be behind bars for nearly twenty years!"

Alessandro shrugged her suggestion off. "Stupidity was his downfall."

"Not stupidity," Monna Lena corrected him. "Enemies. The Grand Inquisitor Valdez. And do you know why, Your Grace? You rich people, blinded by money and power! There are some in Rome who envy *your* position and covet *your* wealth!"

"Have you read the heretical manuscripts Carrara wrote as a student?"

Monna Lena replied with urgency. "And how about the holy commentary he also wrote?"

"This woman knows more than is good for her," Alessandro thought. It occurred to him that she, not he, could make enemies. But Maddalena held her own.

"Be careful what you say in public these days, especially around Gregory."

"Anything else, my inquisitive lady? Because if not, may I fill your goblet again?"

Maddalena paused and lit the oil lamp, making sure the shutters were closed.

"*Carissimo,*" she pled, "do be more careful about coming here! Sometimes I think even the walls have ears, and when you are comfortable in bed you tell me things that no one, absolutely no one else, should ever know."

He took a long sip from her goblet. "Have you any reason to suspect Beltraffio?"

"None. Just a feeling."

"A feeling? Then all's fine. Stop fidgeting, woman, and sit here by me." He patted the familiar spot next to him. "*Subito, amore.*" She checked the lock on the street doors. "Have I told you lately how I love you and how much I need you?" He kissed the tip of her nose.

"You have." She rolled his head into her lap and stroked his hair slowly. Now that the election was over, Alessandro cared little to dye his hair, and silver once again graced his crown.

"I can't stay longer." He rose suddenly. "But I'll see you soon, my sweet angel." Indeed, she looked heavenly, from a world beyond, her face neither feminine nor masculine. "God be with you, my sugar plum, and guard you always." Her eyes shimmered like an oasis.

He kissed them slowly, one at a time, and was gone.

† † †

Maddalena should have been more careful. She had friends but also enemies. None were worth mentioning, folk that delivered the hay for her donkey, doing the hard work that Beltraffio could not manage, people envious of her apparent wealth.

But Monna Lena was heartbroken, walking by the room where Don Alfonso once sat by the open window with his tutor. She closed the door to his bedchamber, letting Crispina dust it, never wanting to see it again, holding herself responsible. Keeping the memory of his suffocating face alive, she struggled to learn more about a child's anatomy, hoping to discover the cause.

The presence of any woman in the surgical hall of the hospital of Santo Spirito was unthinkable. There, even learned doctors proceeded cautiously, worried about the prickly brows of the Inquisition. And the bodies of convicts were hard to get.

But Rome was a city of eternal movement. Visitors came and went, keeping the brothels buzzing. Many dead babes were thrown into the Cloaca Massima or left to die at the doors of foundling houses. Don Alfonso was once a baby, and one day an idea sprang into Lena's mind.

Dressed as a man, with her breasts bound and her hair tucked under a biretta, she walked the streets at night, looking for dead babies, a dangerous pursuit. And Lena had competition.

Every so often, luck smiled on her, and she returned to her house, taking her small bag to the wooden shed in the back. After sealing the windows with moss and covering them with dark cloth, she put the tiny bodies on the plain wooden table.

"In the name of the Lord." She always commenced with a prayer, hoping he would understand and forgive. Those nights the candles sputtered away quickly, and Lena sliced and poked, each time learning a bit more about the working of the little human body, although nothing about the disease that destroyed Don Alfonso. The infants she used were as healthy as their mothers, sick only in their abandoned virtue, and the little bodies were small indeed.

But she was patient. Her inquisitive mind searched into the night, oblivious to the danger. When Alessandro did not come, she retired to her dusky den, studying her anatomical books, comparing them with her drawings. He did not understand her fatigue, but having learned patience, he was certain that time would heal her deep mourning.

As summer came to its close, Berti and Monna Lena found grief drawing them together. She was his first model, and he captured her from life, uncharacteristic for the time. He liked drawing her sewing, bundled up by the fire, or looking out the window, bare-shouldered on a summer morning, her spine—once proudly arched—bent in humility.

There was neither sense nor purpose to his exercise, only the desire to keep his fingers busy while he visited the cardinal's woman. He did not covet her. Wise women curbed his roguish inclinations. Her beauty, her kindness, and her gift of bringing joy drew him to her.

Berti often wondered whether Lena would not be happier with her own people, for she seemed alone with God and her wisdom. Feeling sorry for her, he visited from time to time, leaving tokens of his favor. After Alessandro, botany was her greatest passion, so when Adrien's galley returned from Turkey, he brought her bulbs which blossomed and died in the spring.

"I'm glad you like them." Berti examined her drawing of a tulip, amazed at her deft hand.

"I wish they'd last longer," she replied as she squinted in the light, shading her tanned face, and pointed to a row of pointed yellowing leaves.

"They will," Berti assured her. "Remember what Adrien said: leave the onions in the ground and dress them with the waste from your kitchen; and come next spring, they'll all come back. Like Persephone." Lena nodded skeptically.

With great interest Berti studied the pages of her new herbarium of bulbous plants. "Let me see the rest," he demanded. Only a precious six sprouted in her garden. She drew them all—each different—one especially low, with silvery striped leaves and a full white blossom.

"And look over here," he called spiritedly. "This one has little baby flowers. Lena," he winked, "what if these grow more, and you have more bulbs?"

She smiled. "That's simple. My garden will be prettier for it."

"Lena," he hesitated momentarily. "Why don't you marry and have children?"

Maddalena did not answer. Although she was no longer *in love* with Alessandro, she still loved him. Perhaps her blind admiration first began to pale when he lost the papal chair and began to change, imperceptibly at first; and then ... Well, Maddalena preferred not to think.

Still, she could not imagine betraying him by choosing another man.

Berti paused. "Look, I leave you now. I'm going to Monna Piacenza's for my lesson."

Lena laughed the first good laugh since Don Alfonso died. "Don't tease me!"

"But it's true! She's teaching me the stories from Ovid. Do you know them?"

She did. She read the charming tales in the original Latin.

"Which one did you learn last time?"

"The story of Cupid and Psyche. Want to see?" He pulled out a crumpled drawing of the nude Cupid sprawled across a canopied bed and a maiden holding a lamp high over him."

She wanted to show it to Alessandro. "Can I keep that?"

"It's poor, only a sketch." Berti analyzed the scribble more critically than was warranted.

"I'll trade you." She offered a rose from her garden. "Give it to your teacher. And now go!" She pushed him out, eager to walk the streets of Rome in search of another stillborn babe.

After the house was deep asleep, she checked her reflection in the Venetian glass, having completed her own transformation sedulously. "Who can that be so late?" she wondered as she pulled the biretta low over her brow, hearing sleepy Crispina's voice talking to a man.

"Your Grace," the voice pleaded, "she's asleep and ... "

Falling objects clattered tinnily, the racket reverberating through the house as Alessandro pushed toward her bedchamber's locked door. He could not imagine why Crispina would keep him away from Maddalena, available to him day or night. Furious, he kicked the door, and as it flew open he beheld a young man's back against the wardrobe.

"You'll pay for this," screamed the jealous lover as he ran toward the bed, expecting to find Maddalena under the covers. Instead he found the bed empty. "Where is she?" The rotund cardinal leaped to the stranger's side and gripping his shoulder, spun it around.

"Maddalena! *Could that be you?*" He pulled the biretta off and saw her face transformed, her hair pulled into a tight bun at the base of her neck. "You look stunning, *amore,* as I've never seen you before," he whispered, overcome, still gathering his wits.

Monna Lena froze, unsure what to do next.

"Turn for me!" he commanded, spinning her around. "Ravishing," he mumbled not waiting for an explanation of her charade. "Undress, but not completely. I want you like that."

KLARA

Berti rose feeling restless. Or was it a sense of unfounded gloom? He went to bed early, but his sleep was shallow, thanks to Adrien's rowdy friends.

All night long, he listened to glasses clinking and cards slapping the table, but the game of *trionfetti* was innocuous. The hour was late when the main gate opened and he heard Gertgen talking to a latecomer. Finally the cardsharpers quieted as the men retired, but then the noise grew louder, and he was too annoyed to sleep.

Berti scratched his head and rang the bell.

Could he possibly have fleas? Horrified, he examined his dirty fingernails. Gertgen appeared at the door. "Where's my clean water?" Berti demanded, pointing to the basin.

"Master, please forgive me. I thought you were out last night."

Berti felt little urge and even less obligation to explain. Dressing himself hastily, he left the palace without breakfast to find the streets drying after a thunderstorm. Finally, after a dry August which had cracked the baked land with jagged gaps, the Lord blessed the city with water.

And then the rains came day after day, as though there were no end. The land blossomed again, and even the chipped mortar between the stones turned solid green. As Berti followed the river's wide curve past the Angel's bridge toward Monna Lena's house, he gathered a bunch of wild flowers for her. She could spare him but a few moments, so he walked on toward Platea Colonna, stopping first by the little church next to the Trevi fountain.

"And God be with you," Berti answered Hans' greeting from the high scaffold. He was working on another vault in a chapel with a miraculous icon of the Virgin, painting scenes from the Virgin's life in four triangular compartments.

"Did you take your midday *collazione?*" Hans called down.

"No," Berti laughed. "I didn't even eat breakfast!" He pointed to his stomach.

"Why don't you stop at my house," Hans offered. "Klara baked a nice potato pie with onions and lots of good drippings."

Berti preferred meat to potatoes, but the Speckaerts had no money to spare.

"It's nice of you. I'll surely do that," Berti thanked his friend. "How's that coming along?" He pointed to the figure of the Virgin walking up the steep temple steps.

Hans paused and straightened for a moment. "Slowly. My back hurts when I twist it, looking up for hours. I'm so tired when I get home. But did you see my little Berta? She has her first tooth!" Hans turned his back and concentrated again on his work. "Why don't you stop to chat more often? Where have you been these days? We see you less and less often."

"I work here and there," Berti answered truthfully. With his mercantile investments, he worked only when his expensive pastimes required it.

"Lucky man. Look, I must get on. The plaster is drying too fast in this heat."

Berti found the small church moist and the air cool. Had their camaraderie grown chilly since Berti began to resent Hans' complaints about his long nights out? Fortunately, Hans knew nothing about Cornelis and the prince-bishop. Since Hans and Cornelis met in Venice and Hans painted a portrait of the engraver, they were inseparable.

"Hans would never believe Cornelis' new life; it's better he doesn't know," Berti thought as he took his leave.

A boy, a bit older than Don Alfonso would have been, was selling wild asters around the corner from the church, and Berti bought a bunch and let himself into Hans' cluttered home.

"How nice," exclaimed the buxom Klara, her babe at her breast glistening in the raking light. "Thank you." She fussed pleasantly, plopping the swaddled infant in Berti's arms.

At ease around Klara, he felt awkward with baby Berta. "How sweet." He praised his godchild as she displayed her one, lonely tooth and exclaimed, "And mommy, too!"

He liked watching Klara move about. She seemed so sensible for a young bride.

Suddenly, Klara's expression clouded. "I wish Hans would join the painters' guild. He says the fees are high, and we can't afford them. One of these days they'll catch him, and then what? Who's going to buy me a new dress?" She leaned toward Berti with her skirt spread wide.

"I will," he laughed, "for a nice piece of potato pie."

Taking the sleeping baby from Berti's arms, she laid her in a basket by the window. Without knowing why, Berti liked the way Klara walked, her full hips moving in a resolute yet sensuous way. Her feet, chubby and pink, looked almost erotic in her slippers.

"Berti, I couldn't!" Bashfully she pushed away the coin that appeared on the table.

"Think nothing of it." He pushed it back. "I won't tell Hans," he whispered in her ear and pulled her closer to smell the milk on her skin. "Tell him you saved your house money."

Klara blushed. "I couldn't." She inspected her plain cotton dress, still unsure.

"But I want you to." He caught her hand and with a trained movement fanned her skirt and pulled her even closer. "A little kiss, *Liebchen*." He watched her eyelids flutter before letting her go.

"You scoundrel," she laughed. "I thought you were serious!"

"*Liebchen,* how about a flask of your good beer?" He encouraged her with a low pat, resting his hand on her soft seat a moment longer than appropriate.

"*Mein lieber Gott,* I have to feed you quickly," she gasped as she saw a stout lady walking toward the door. "Frau Pecham and I have some spinning to do, and I nearly forgot!"

"*Grüss Gott!*" Berti jumped up gallantly to kiss the baker's wife's plump hand.

"My goodness," the lady giggled and squirmed happily, for Berti had a way with all women. She turned to little Berta, prattling and babbling. Seeing himself outnumbered by the German women, Berti thanked Klara for the meal and parted with another gallant kiss on Frau Pecham's chubby hand and a soft one on Klara's cheek.

"What a nice man!" Frau Pecham clasped her hands. "Why is he without a wife?"

"He's younger than my Hansi and says he wants to do great things."

"*Um Gottes Lieben!* How much higher can a man climb than being a painter for a pope?"

"You mean a dead pope?" Klara put Berti's affairs into the right perspective.

"*Ach, mein lieber Gott,* it's all the same to me," the estimable lady prattled on. For a moment Klara wondered why her husband was less successful than his friend, but Berta demanded a meal, and the talk turned to other, far less interesting gossip.

Berti drew Lucretia.

(Page 156)

Klara's breast glistened in the raking light.

(Page 181)

Maddalena feared the jury.

(Page 186)

The fire caught at Maddalena's feet.

(Page 199)

Berti admired Florence.

(Page 205)

People came to Maddalena.

(Page 218)

Berti and Hans crashed to the floor.

(Page 246)

Maddalena's figure grew distant over St. Peter's.

(Page 268)

Nemesis

One church, one faith, and one shepherd. Thus ran the motto of the Roman curia.

While Moslem swords spread fear on earth, the Inquisition rekindled God's wrath and purged the city with holy fire. A century after the most Catholic Kings of Spain, Ferdinand and Isabella, rid their peninsula of Jews, Moors, and Saracens, the name of the Inquisition burned as strongly in Italy as in Spain, even more after the Council of Trent.

Maddalena was not alarmed, but in power struggles news travels through hidden channels, and before long, the new pontiff's ears were full of stories about her, some true, some false.

He cared naught for Pius' healer but feared his rivals; and the Farnese cardinal remained powerful even after the election. No wonder that Gregory, himself the father of a bastard son, was sensitive how old, lax habits might influence members of his new curia.

"This woman, you say," the pope said, raising his hand in a sign of welcome, "is she like Medea steeped in witchcraft and magic powers? Did you mention blasphemy and contriving to join forces with the devil? And what's your proof, Felice?" the pontiff asked his visitor.

In the holy curia, even dead saints had ears, so Cardinal Peretti pushed his seat closer, leaned to Gregory, and whispered hoarsely, "She is the daughter of a Jew."

"Come, Felice, you know better than that!" The disappointed pontiff reached for a bowl of figs. They were juicy, and their ruby centers stained his lips red. "She is also a *conversa*, but if the saintly Pius did not doubt her faith, on whose word can I rely?"

Felice's mind remained focused. "It has come to our attention that on some nights the woman has been seen dressed as a man going to a shed where she stays alone for hours."

"And on what authority do we have this information?" Gregory was more interested in his figs and wine than in Felice's news.

"Two peasants came to my bishop. They work for this woman, delivering food for her animals, and they have been watching her and her household for quite some time."

"And will they swear to their statement, even under torture?"

Felice exhaled and lowered his voice. "Naturally. The matter is not to be trifled with. The accusations of the peasant Pardo and his wife Gerolama have already been examined by the district office. Their deposition is ready."

Gregory reached for the bowl of rose water. He washed his hands deliberately, paying attention to the stray seeds caught under his manicured nails, brought them closer to his short-sighted gaze for his approval, until he was ready for discussion. "Is this report trustworthy?"

Felice's eyes rolled in disbelief. "Gregory, you should know me better by now!"

The pontiff folded his hands, turned them inside out and stretched them. "The charge?"

"Heresy." Felice shifted his cane to the other hand, ready to rise. "Disputing the supremacy of God over the Holy Virgin. Fornicating with Lucifer in the form of a man."

"What do you mean by that?" Gregory exclaimed, his interest finally engaged.

"Rather complicated, my friend," Felice announced, already up but not meeting Gregory's gaze, busy thinking that if he were to succeed him, he must weaken Alessandro.

"Holiness," he added with unnecessary formality, "you may wish to read the scribe's notes."

"Anything else?" Gregory demanded and cracked his knuckles. He had other matters to worry about. "No? Then God's will be done!" But first he picked the last seed from his front teeth, smelled it, examined his pink nails again, and finally raised his fat body to his scriptorium.

Dipping his quill into the ink impassively but with the certainty of his power, he wrote, dusted, and sealed his letter. When Felice Pedretti kissed Gregory's hand more submissively than befitted his status, the coveted warrant for Monna Lena's arrest lay on his bosom.

To bypass the channels of the Holy Office directed by the zealous Cardinal Sanseverina, the Grand Inquisitor, was extraordinary. Gregory's writ suddenly made Alessandro's woman a bit of bait in Rome's greater ecclesiastical game.

That same afternoon Adrien rushed home to give Berti dreadful news, his ruddy moustache limp in a face marked by fear. "Maddalena was arrested," he said hoarsely.

A wave of horror gripped Berti. "What! How do you know? Did you talk to Crispina?"

"They took them all but the children."

Berti stumbled, dumbstruck. "Are they in Tor di Nona?"

"Beltraffio and his wife are. Maddalena they took directly to the Vatican."

"That's peculiar," Berti muttered, confused. "I guess you know about her?"

Berti and Adrien never spoke about that topic. "*Ja.* I do. Strange."

"There must be more to the story," Berti wondered aloud. "But what? Let me change, and we'll go see Alessandro." But the cardinal was no help, in shock himself, absorbed in wondering what Gregory's reign held next, feeling personally the dogged hand of the Inquisition.

And Gregory fumed. Curious to meet Maddalena, hoping for useful information, the pontiff encountered a wall more invincible than the fortress of Sant'Angelo. She answered questions, clearly willing to please, but saying little, nothing incriminating he wanted to hear.

"Then God's will be done!" He gritted his teeth and let the Swiss Guard remove the obstinate bitch from his sight.

When Maddalena found herself in the darkest corner of the prison, she feared that she might never see the walls of her house again. Her cubicle was so tiny that she found comfort only sitting down, and she, who dissected tiny bodies in her garden shed without flinching, vomited when the stench of human excrement rose up to encircle her tighter and tighter.

But she was strong, worrying more about Beltraffio's family than herself, wondering how much of the little they knew they would divulge under torture. She entered the courtroom with her chin up. "I am entitled to a lawyer to represent me," she reminded the clerk as he swore her in. But quickly she found her fury rising.

"No," she answered defiantly to the statement identifying her as Monna Rebecca, the daughter of Ephrahim Ben Shuham of Ferrara. "I am Maddalena da Venezia. I am a baptized Christian and the humble daughter of Our Lord and God Almighty."

She swallowed hard. She feared the jury. Rarely did the governor preside over cases himself, accustomed to delegating those duties to a lieutenant, but this time even the governor sat on one side. At the center of the magisterial table sat Giulio Antonio Santoro, Cardinal Sanseverina himself. Although they met one day when she was waiting for Pius, the Grand Inquisitor showed no recognition.

Why was she to be tried by members of both courts? She looked at the Grand Inquisitor. If he were here, she did not care who else was next to him. But when the trial commenced, his secretary stepped down from the podium and asked her whether she knew why she found herself under the judgment of God and His vicar on earth.

"No, sir. I haven't the faintest idea why I'm here," she replied. Asked her profession and age, she stated, "I'm thirty-one years of age, and I help sick people." About her education, she added, "I learned from my father, who was an apothecary in *platea judea,* and from the people."

The secretary motioned the clerk to approach. "Messer Giovanni, can you tell the honored members of the tribunal to whom these belong?"

"They are mine, sir," Maddalena replied, recognizing the bindings of Alessandro's books.

The Grand Inquisitor stepped down to take charge. "And you say that you learned only from your father and the people. How about these?" he said and pointed to the books. "These heretical writings, forbidden by order of the Roman curia and the Holy Father himself?"

Maddalena's confidence ebbed. She did not want to implicate Alessandro. She would not tell; she would take the blame herself. She fumbled an answer but kept clearly to her chosen path. Soon the Grand Inquisitor lost patience and changed the direction of the interrogation.

"Daughter, your lawyer, Ser Domenico here, produced references of your good conduct, from your own priest, certifying your attendance and confession at San Salvatore, as well as testimony from others to the power of your religious conviction. That pleases the Holy Office. I also understand that Cardinal Farnese baptized you when Holy Mother Church accepted your plea to leave the path of darkness and embrace the one and only true faith."

Maddalena waited. The chains on her hands were heavy but not so heavy as her thoughts. She knew Cardinal Sanseverina did not come to flatter her. Her eyes were glued on him as he traveled the length of the room to stare into her face.

"Maddalena, why did you become a Christian?" he demanded. "I understand from people who have fallen prey to darkness that anyone born a Jew would not want to become Christian, no more than any man born infidel would voluntarily consent to accept the true faith."

Maddalena felt a chill. "I believe in God the Father and the Lord of the Universe."

"Isn't it true, though, that all men born Jews or Moslems believe in God but deny that He was born of the Virgin Mary? Do you believe in the Mother of God, Maddalena?"

"I do, Your Grace."

"How do you know she was virgin?"

Fear began to choke Maddalena's throat. "Where's he heading?" she asked herself silently as she replied in full voice, trying to keep her chin stiff. "The gospels teach us that, Eminence."

"This one?" The Grand Inquisitor pulled out Maddalena's vernacular Bible. The tribunal was silent, poised on the answer.

"No," she replied. "I read Latin. I bought that book for my servants so they could learn Our Lord's word more easily."

The Grand Inquisitor grabbed Maddalena's shoulder and shook her. "Do you realize that it is blasphemy to spread God's word other than in the language prescribed by Holy Mother Church?"

A cold sweat broke on her brow. "I think so," she managed finally to reply.

"You think so?" he thundered. "Do you claim to understand the scriptures better than the church fathers?"

"I don't. But I believe they were human, like all of us, men who erred in their ways and saw the light of God and followed it. That is why they became saints and we value their word."

"Umm. Have you ever visited the church of St. Gregory, Maddalena?"

A slow sinking sensation gripped her. "I have, Monsignor," she breathed.

A smile faded behind Santoro's steely eyes. "You have also undoubtedly shown your faith by venerating his holy relic that we are blessed to possess here in the city of Rome."

"Your Eminence, when the saints died, their souls went to heaven and dwell with Jesus Christ. Here on earth, they leave but the human shell which is no different from yours or mine. I do not believe in venerating the bones of men who only spoke and recorded the word of God. Only He alone, He who created heaven and earth, is worthy of our undivided love and devotion."

"I see," came the Inquisitor's wry answer. Ignoring Ser Domenico's anxious appeal, he begged the tribunal to consider the feebleness of his client's mind, the weakness and frailty of her sex, her dedication to a totally insignificant calling in life.

"Tell me," the cardinal's dry voice came back, "who is God?"

Maddalena's voice faltered for a moment, and then it colored strong. "The greatest and noblest spirit in the universe."

Santoro feasted on her fear. "What does He look like?"

Maddalena shivered, realizing he wanted to trap her. "I don't know," she replied finally.

"Try!"

"The priests tell us all men were created in His image, but I think that He is only air. If you look up into heaven, you see nothing but clouds and air."

Santoro's voice sounded victorious. "Is Jesus the Son of God also only air?"

The chamber was stifling as Maddalena answered. "Jesus Christ is the son of Mary, born like me."

Santoro's face clouded. He would get that obstinate bitch, he told himself, gritting his teeth. "So you say that when the spirit of God descended on Mary, her flesh transformed that spirit into human form?"

The questioning grew demanding. Maddalena searched her mind furiously for the right answer. "I believe so."

"And so when you receive Holy Communion, is it air? Or what else might it be that you receive in the form of the host?" The question jarred her thoughts until an answer appeared.

"I believe it is the Holy Spirit."

"I see," Santoro's scoffed. "But I know for a fact that your parish priest teaches you that it is the Body of Christ which is present in the most holy of all sacraments."

Wearily, Maddalena settled her eyes on her enemy and spoke her mind. "That's what he says, Excellency. But is the Holy Spirit not greater than Christ, who was a son of a woman, whereas the Holy Spirit came from God himself?"

"Your Holiness, may I be heard?" Horrified, Ser Domenico asked to brief his client.

"Granted," the cardinal answered. Although the Grand Inquisitor had heard enough to have Lena dismembered and burned at the stake, there was more he hoped to learn from this woman who thought she was born as a man and likely sprang from the seed of Lucifer. That is what her lawyer told her when he got her transferred to a cell fitter for a man of his ilk to enter.

"Ser Domenico, we are all born in sin. Isn't our origin sinful, and isn't that why Christ died for us on the cross? Isn't it because He understood our frailty? He also pardoned the harlot Magdalen and opened her eyes to the true light of His teaching."

"Forget what you believe! When they ask you questions, if you are lucky enough to get another chance, say what your parish priest told you. How would he answer the question?"

Lena struck to the plain truth. "I believe in the Ten Commandments, and I try to follow them to the best of my ability. As for the priests, they preach to us in Latin, saying things they scarcely understand, and their congregation not at all. Many priests live not to teach the word of Our Lord but to fatten up their bellies!"

"Maddalena, *think* before you answer. Don't volunteer anything, and for the love of the Virgin Mary, pay her the honor she deserves. Don't ever say she was born a Jewess or anything stupid that will convict you of agnostic thoughts."

Maddalena nodded. She understood only that she must not implicate Alessandro.

"In the name of Our Lord Jesus," she prayed. "Great and holy God, I beg Thy mercy, if I have offended Thee. Please teach me how to speak but without ruining my beloved. If I have spoken the wrong word or acted against my conscience, punish me, for I accept my lot; but I beg Thee, do not let Alessandro suffer for my foolishness. Amen."

† † †

The pain of uncertainty filled the days. Only once was Berti permitted to visit Maddalena, and he trembled, seeing a ghost of the woman he once met in *platea judea.*

"How's Beltraffio, and how fares Crispina?" she inquired warmly about her servants.

He could not bear to tell her about Crispina's pitiful state. Instead he tried to divert her.

"Cheer up! Beltraffio's back home again. Those devils found him too weak to torture."

Maddalena smiled, but without conviction. Her inner vision was dark.

"Don't worry, Lena! At least he's with his children now, looking forward to seeing you home. Why don't you eat now, and I'll be back with more food as soon as they'll let me."

She clenched her hands behind her back so he would not see them and shook her head.

"I'm not hungry. My faith keeps me. Berti, how is Alessandro? Have you seen him?"

"He's praying for your safe deliverance. And do you know what? He has a new friend!"

"How ... Who?" she muttered, confused.

"Jacopo, Beltraffio's eldest. I was there a few days ago, making sure the children were looked after. Don't be afraid, Lena. Your neighbors are good people, and the cardinal came too."

Lena hung on his words. "Well?"

"He asked me who the boy was and stood looking at him. Finally he called him."

"What do you mean?" Lena knew Alessandro.

"The boy went to see him the next day at the palace. I think Alessandro wants to see him educated. He was impressed with what you have already taught him and his zest for learning."

"How strange are the Lord's ways," Lena whispered. "He taketh and He giveth back."

They both thought of Don Alfonso.

"Here, I brought you something." He produced a handful of sheets of paper and a box of chalk. "I know there is little light"—he glanced up at the small barred window high above their heads—"but you have the fire."

"And I've something for you." Maddalena felt around her neck for the chain Alessandro gave her. Even in the cell's murky light, the heavy golden cross gleamed.

"Lena, you must not think that way. You will come back. Please."

"Keep it for me, will you? And should I ... " She turned away. "Give it to your wife some day to remember me," she said and kissed him on the cheek.

Berti found himself sobbing. "Lena, I really cannot. It's from Alessandro, I'm sure. Isn't it?" Finally he took the cross and hid it. Maddalena suddenly looked weary as they parted. "Take care, and remember that the Lord's ways are just and that He loves us all."

Days passed, and Berti soon learned that once Crispina could tell her relentless tormentors no more, Monna Lena became their main victim. Forbidden to enter the prison, he often paced by the gates, lost in thought. When he saw Alessandro's litter-chair nearby he figured that all that could be done would be done, not knowing that even men as powerful as Alessandro bowed to the Inquisition.

Maddalena's interrogation was long, Sanseverina's henchmen growing more determined each day, but no more than their master. They did not ask to see her undressed to see if she were fit to undergo torture. The customary procedure was no longer necessary. They only knew she must survive for her final punishment.

The *strappado* lay limp on Lena's wrists for the moment, as Giulio Antonio Santoro reentered the chamber, ready to challenge her anew. "In these letters," he said, pointing to a pile on the table, "there is enough evidence for you to burn in everlasting hell."

The Grand Inquisitor stared her directly in the eye.

"Wretched woman, if you care not for your own salvation, you must at the very least protect the soul of the person who put these heretical thoughts into your head. Was it Cardinal Farnese?" As he pulled her hair until her chin pointed to the ceiling, she almost panicked.

"No. My thoughts came into my head by themselves, from the writings of St. Augustine."

Santoro laughed. "What double blasphemy! How dare you insinuate that the venerable saint would think, let alone write, that men and women were created equal. Tighten the ropes!"

Maddalena saw her letters. How had they left Alessandro's desk? Who betrayed him?

"I ask you again." Santoro gripped her face in his steely fingertips until the blood drained away. "Did you ever discuss the things you wrote to him in these letters with Cardinal Farnese?"

"I couldn't have! I was locked away in the convent at Assisi."

"Pull!"

Maddalena hung from her wrists tied behind her, her body twitching in agony.

"I care not when, whether before or after or at any other time! Did you or did you not?"

Maddalena could barely answer, but finally she managed, "Monsignor, I did not."

"Higher!"

The rope groaned under Lena's weight but no more than she who shrieked, "Jesus, deliver me! Have mercy!" She prayed but revealed nothing.

"Higher!"

"Monsignor, I believe she fainted again," one of the men grunted.

"Down and water!" Santoro was not finished, but the body, torn by pain, twitched.

"Maddalena," he said grimly, "for the last time I ask you if Alessandro Farnese gave you this and if he led you astray from Christ?" He pointed to the uncensored edition of Bocaccio's *Decameron* atop the stack of books and the *Legends of the Lives of the Saints* and an unauthorized translation of Jacopo da Voragine's *Golden Legend*.

"No!" she gasped with her last bit of stamina.

The men eyed each other. "Monsignor, should we try the torch again?"

Cardinal Sanseverina glanced at the charred blisters on Lena's feet and hands. "We are done with her," he snarled, knowing that any one of the charges against her would seal her death warrant, though without obtaining the desired evidence against Alessandro Farnese. "Take her! She'll burn at the stake, and We'll provide her learned friend with the finest seat on the stage."

"And the servant woman?"

"She's useless. Give ten lashes as a warning to all."

When Berti heard the news the following morning he was numb. It did not help matters when Pietro Portinari chose that moment of all times to present his portly self at the palace gate.

"Adrien's not here," Berti informed the Florentine, thinking he came on business.

"It is you I seek, Meneer Spranger," the man said acidly.

Portinari being the last person on Berti's mind, he grumbled, "Won't you come in?"

"On the contrary. Will you give me the satisfaction of stepping out?" The Florentine pointed to a covered carriage, his hand on the hilt of his sword.

Perplexed, Berti obliged the fuming man. The door opened, and he saw a small bundle in the nanny's arms. "Congratulations, my good man! I hope that is a fine son I behold."

"Yours or mine?"

"You must be joking!"

"See for yourself!" Pietro took the swaddled child from the nanny's arms. A sleeping porcelain face peeked out at them, the pale skin enhanced by a shock of curly black hair.

"Sir, are you joking?" He looked at the balding man. "Your son looks like nobody but his fine, tiny self. May I congratulate you and your esteemed wife on the blessed event?"

"You may not, Meneer Spranger. You have a birthmark on your left shoulder blade?"

"What does that have to do with your son? Does he have a similar mark?"

"No, but you certainly do!" Pietro ripped Berti's shirt out of his pants. Furious, Berti leaned forward and hissed, "And, pray, how do you know that?"

"My wife's slave woman spied on the two of you together in my wife's bathroom."

"Of course she did," Berti roared with contempt. "You fool! How else was she to direct my work except by guiding me in person while I worked? How else was I to satisfy her whim? Isn't that what you instructed me to do in the first place, upon pain of forfeiting my fee?"

"And your birthmark, sir?"

"*Signore,* now you insult me with your slave's gossip. She may have seen it, many a time. Have you ever worked in the heat of the Roman summer the way we artists do, high on a scaffold with a shirt on?"

It was not the first time Berti navigated the channels of a cuckolded husband's ire.

"Look, my good fellow, your little son is but a few months old. I am certain that when his first hair comes out, he will be endowed with your wife's golden tresses."

Pietro scratched his head, recalling that Madonna Isabella's flaxen hair was not given by God but rather by something her *bambinaia* helped her apply.

"I see," he said. "If you're sure, Meneer Spranger ... " Pietro's hand dropped from the hilt of his sword. He looked at the little boy's pretty sleeping face.

"Would it help if I swore by the Blessed Virgin?" Berti crossed himself theatrically. "Or do you believe the word of a slave over that of a gentleman?"

"I'll have her whipped!" the embarrassed merchant cried, retreating to his carriage.

"Do no such thing, honorable sir. Treasure your fine wife and your adorable son."

When Berti regained the palace, exhausted, he thought the day's evil sufficient unto itself, but only hours later came news that Adrien and his ship had foundered off the coast of Crete, its cargo filched by Turkish pirates and his friend murdered.

If that were not bad news enough, a personal invitation from the Holy Office to Monna Lena's public execution assured him that if any surviving tincture of faith remained in Berti's veins, it died poisoned that day. He had to go. The invitation was not a suggestion. Hard to imagine, he also needed to see Maddalena one last time.

Inferno

The day sagged under a sudden heat wave.

Berti's first thought belonged to Maddalena, wondering whether the whole world had gone backward into the Dark Ages. He wished Adrien were there. His carefree friend would tell him that his misery was only a nightmare.

But Berti was not dreaming. Standing barefoot and unshaved by the window, staring at the river, listening to the roar of its swollen current, occasionally his eyes focused, searching for passing boats as if expecting to find Adrien's spirit on one of them. When an occasional gust brought fetid air from the river bank, he shuddered, picturing Maddalena's cell. He had no idea how long he had been standing there when Gertgen tapped his shoulder.

"It's time to go," the loyal servant whispered.

The place of Maddalena's ordeal was not far, a short walk by the old banking houses and through the Street of the Pilgrims. Had Gertgen not stopped him, Berti would have passed the market square, despite its noisy confusion. A few empty stalls gaped. The whole city seemed to be gathered around the south end, forming a tight noose around Gregory's Swiss Guard and the Inquisition's armed militia. In the time of Gregory's pious predecessor, hardly a handful guarded the pontiff. Now a forest of spiky halberds glittered above men's heads, reaching the temporary stage backed up to the podium built for the members of the Holy Office to enjoy the spectacle.

Time crept and then ran as Berti and Gertgen moved forward, pushed by the currents of the agitated but peaceful crowd, for a few of the customary hecklers incited the people's animosity. Many who loved Maddalena now stood in a daze, incredulous.

Finally they stopped by a group of Netherlanders, near the guards.

"*Morgen, Meneer Cort.*" Gertgen acknowledged the engraver with a nod and stepped aside as befitted his position.

"Cornelis," Berti whispered hoarsely. As the time of execution neared, he grew limp. How could anyone think that Maddalena of all people, the gentle woman who helped everyone but herself, who woke and slept thinking of others, was culpable of treason, heresy, or whatever ridiculous, trumped-up charges the Inquisition brought against her? He could not or perhaps would not see the obvious link to Alessandro.

"Berti!" Cornelis replied with compassion.

"God bless," Berti muttered back through his tears. He wondered about Cornelis' liberal opinions, letting people choose their god and religion while following none himself.

Maybe there was no God, only Lucifer. No just being would condemn Maddalena. Not Maddalena! He could not live without her. He had not realized how much she meant to him—taking her for granted—a compassionate soul, a mother, a sister, a friend, all in one.

Everything in him raged. Tears blinded him as he shook his fist at the podium.

"Berti!" Cornelis pointed to two men elbowing toward them through the crowd.

"Anthonis." Berti acknowledged the young innkeeper. The crowd now swayed in angry waves. A few more fists flashed, fingers pointing at the podium, at the Grand Inquisitor. Berti breathed heavily, fearing the sight of the procession with the condemned.

"Berti, I know it's a bad time to introduce my new lodger, but this is Meneer Van Mander." Anthonis nodded to a lean man next to him. "He just arrived and is visiting with us."

"Karl is my Christian name, and you must be Bartolomeo." The newcomer looked at Berti's blotched face. "I'm sorry, compeer. Anthonis told me about you and about Maddalena. I am so sorry indeed."

His Flemish was melodious, but Berti only stared back. Yet despite his despair, he was drawn to the fellow, a year or two younger. His reaction was instinctive, an uncalculated response at the worst moment in his life. Perhaps wanting to avoid the reality of the day, he shook Karl's extended hand.

"What wind brings you to this wretched part of the world?"

"Just visiting. I left Kortryjk earlier this year, and I'm staying in Florence."

"Continuing to Naples?"

"Not now. Maarten told me you have a fine brotherhood here. I'd like to meet the men."

"Maarten? You know Maarten de Waal?" Thinking of Maarten and a place other than godforsaken Rome almost cheered Berti up, forgetting why he was there, surrounded by a mob.

"You're looking for a job here? That's funny. I just went to Florence thinking about working there. I'm beginning to hate it here. But the Vatican is swirling with activity. The new pope wants to be remembered for his good works. I thought … "

The harsh rattle of drums filled the air, resonating with authority in every corner of the square, and the halberdiers adjusted their weapons. Berti shuddered back to reality. He moved away, afraid to face the podium or the stake. Karl nodded with understanding. He, likewise without knowing why, was drawn to the man he had just met.

Berti scanned the podium, looking for Alessandro.

He was there, his face blanched, an unearthly power keeping him upright. The cardinal sat oblivious of his surroundings in a chair reserved for a servant of God expected to rejoice at a fair punishment. From his high vantage point, he spotted the head of the procession and began to tremble, his heart racing, taking away his breath, his vestments fused with his flesh, choking him.

Life without Maddalena was unthinkable.

The crowd parted to make way for the condemned. The heat rose, and the onlookers' bodies reeked. Berti tried to look through and past the dense row of guards with matchlock arquebuses over their shoulders, but he had to wait until the procession came closer. The crowd continually shifted and reformed in disorganized waves. An open hay wagon neared. Berti saw two men tied against the open ribs in front. Two women stood facing the rear.

Pandemonium broke over the cart. The men in front tried to duck a shower of rotten figs. Clumps of foul animal innards flew, and the warm sun turned the path into a stinking rut. Berti's glance riveted on the women behind. Crispina swayed, cradling an invisible child in her bruised hands, but he did not recognize Maddalena in the other woman. Both were bare to the waist like wild mountain creatures, their matted hair flying loose. Only when the trumpets sounded again and the wagon passed could he see the cardinal's woman in the wagon behind.

She knelt barely erect in an animal cage, and if she had any pride left, her demeanor hid it. She looked wild, her head and back enveloped in a dirty mass of gray hair. Rocking from side to side, her swollen eyes searched the crowd for someone, but she appeared barely to notice Berti and his friends. Her fate had touched many hearts, and as the two donkeys pulled her cage, people reached out to touch her burnt hands, covering her with flowers and pushing sweet cakes through the bars.

Finally the long trail of guards and prisoners reached its destination, and the drums ceased their infernal clamor. The crowd hushed as the prisoners were separated into two groups. First the guards tied Monna Crispina and the other woman to a post facing each other, then the two men the same way. Maddalena they fastened alone to another stake.

The square froze as the trumpets sounded for attention. The silence intensified for a few moments, the crooked wind hissing. Several officials walked to the podium, but Berti cared little for what they said.

The midday heat continued to rise, peppering the azure with small puffy clouds from the sea. People squinted into the scorching sun and sighed with relief as the wind picked up. More words, and the clamor rose again as final judgment was pronounced. Berti awoke from a reverie of his first encounter with Maddalena, hearing the crowd hiss.

"Fiametta di Napoli, a strumpet from Ortaccio ... vulgar and forbidden books and prints ... crime of sodomy ... guilty of stealing ... "

The voice faded in and out. "Fifty lashes and exile."

Berti snorted, "Fifty lashes and death!"

The drums whirred and cut out on command. Long before her lot was finished, the whore fainted, her back ribbons of bloody flesh. The crowd grew impatient.

"The Lord is just, taking mercy on all poor sinners who repent." The bailiff spoke again, announcing Crispina's verdict. But even the ten lashes allotted left her demented. The crowd was visibly agitated and hardly listened or watched the punishment of the two men, as the wind picked up, carrying dirt and waste in broken spirals into the sky, growing more ominous.

Broken passages of Maddalena's crimes reached Berti's ears. He clenched his fists and fought the tears. A gentler and kinder spirit than Maddalena could not be found, but the list went on: poisoning an innocent boy until he suffocated, fornicating with demons at the cemetery, opening and robbing graves.

Berti had an urge to laugh hysterically. Where did all the crazy charges come from? As the list unfolded and the wind howled, Berti listened to each account without hearing Alessandro's name. The drums sounded again, and the tall executioner stepped onto the wooden platform around the stake. He removed a dagger from its scabbard.

"What is he doing?" Berti asked. When he dared look, he saw him hacking Lena's hair, whipping in the wind. The task was difficult, and after a few attempts he stopped, directing his attention to the podium. The sky was almost black as gigantic drops of rain dotted the square, threatening the spectacle. The Grand Inquisitor's voice cut through the howling wind.

"I exhort you to keep your eyes on those who speak against Holy Mother Church. May God's hand of wrath be upon you, Maddalena, to burn eternally in the fire of hell without sight!"

As if in answer, the sky exploded in a giant arc of lightning, and thunder shook the square. The crowd gasped as the executioner stepped up to Maddalena. Grasping her head in his thick hands, he pushed her eyeballs out with his thumbs. Horrified, the people saw the crushed mass trickle slowly down her face.

As a huge lighting bolt hit the church behind the tribunal, illuminating Alessandro's contorted face, another cold light in his head burst into a million red droplets and turned his lips blue. He tried to call out to Maddalena, to reach out, and bless her, but collapsed instead.

When the torches hissed, Berti covered his ears, for the fire caught instantly in the wind, shifting and dancing. Soon the entire ring of wood blazed steadily, hungrily reaching for Maddalena's legs, as the stench of singed skin flew in all directions. A burning branch caught by the wind flew through the air and struck her back. Berti could neither see her face covered by her wildly blowing hair nor hear her agonized screams. Panic ruled as the crowd ran for cover, trying to escape the wrath of God. The wind whipped debris around, but Berti remained, locked in silent prayer for Lena's quick delivery. Karl and Gertgen barely held on.

Two massive arcs lit the sky behind the square, and the roof of an ancient church by the river disappeared in a cloud of smoke. A third bolt crashed so near the high podium and with such force that it threw the entire presiding tribunal off their seats. Like mice, men scurried in all directions as the skies opened and deluged the square. Minutes later the angry Tiber responded, leaving its banks and spilling brown water into the Via Giulia and the square.

Berti gasped for air, clinging desperately to Gertgen and Karl, all three whipped in the vortex of the storm still feeding life into the burning faggots around Maddalena. Then the deluge darkened the square, and the sky hung so low Berti could hardly see his companions' faces.

The storm subsided as swiftly as it rose. Large branches littered the ground, tangled with broken beams and split shingles floating on the river of mud, engulfing stray animals scrambling helplessly in the almost deserted square. Stupefied, the trio waded through the muck toward Lena, fighting the elements with every step.

Berti ripped a piece of his shirt and covered his nose. The stench of Maddalena's burnt flesh made him sick. "Karl, help me!" He reached for his friend's dagger and cut her ropes as the other two supported her limp body.

"Careful," he shouted at Gertgen, hoping she might be alive. "Give me your shirt," he yelled at Karl and tossed the dagger to Gertgen. "And you, get Crispina! Karl, get that mule." They seated both women on the stray mule with Karl's shirt separating their raw backs.

Heavy mist clouded the air as they waded through the deserted streets toward Berti's home. "We must get them out of the city. Immediately! But where?" Berti asked, undecided.

"Take them to Florence," Gertgen suggested.

"But the archduke is Gregory's friend," Karl objected.

"Do you have a better idea? We have to get them out of papal jurisdiction," Gertgen replied. Berti laughed. "You mean there's a place the pope can't reach?"

There was little choice. Three men and a wagon soon crossed the Porta del Popolo, telling the guards that the large caskets in the wagon held Berti's tools. They headed for Florence without knowing whether the women were alive or dead.

Long before they reached the gate, Alessandro's body was lowered into his state bed and tall tapers lit around. Since Maddalena's arrest and throughout her ordeal, his soul had steeped in hell, but no angels rescued it, no caring hand brushed his forehead, for he was beyond care.

† † †

The mood at the papal table was dismal.

"The Lord's ways are mysterious," Felice Pedretti snuffled as he looked out the window. "There is little men like Us can change when His will goes contrary to Our wishes."

Gregory cut into the pheasant and took a chunk of meat into his fat, rosy hands, watching Felice poke his plain pancake into the corner of his plate.

"What else do you want me to say?" Cardinal Pedretti asked guiltily. "You were there. I was there. We both saw it. The *rione dei banchi* is still caked with mud, and the roof of St. Catherine needs repair. Even men as holy as us may be ... mistaken."

Gregory dropped his knife, took another slippery chunk in his hands, and sank his teeth into the flesh.

"More wine for the Holy Father!" Felice clapped his hands, himself desirous of none. He had weathered far worse storms.

For the next half hour, the pontiff ate until his belly smoothed the folds of his robe. He cleansed his hands in rose water with customary care and rang the bell for his litter-chair. "Pedretti, issue a proclamation. May We say ... a kind of pardon."

"Do I understand, Holy Father"—Felice always took problems seriously—"that by God's will all convicted left alive go free?"

"Yes. Whatever happened to them?" Gregory clucked in frustration.

"The men died the next day from suppurated wounds," Pedretti replied, wondering why the pontiff asked.

"And the woman?"

"That insolent painter of Pius took her body from the city. She is in God's hands."

But Lena's life depended on more than a miracle. After two weeks of agony, she nearly shared the fate of her servant who was buried in a small hamlet deep in the Sienese hills long before Berti's wagon reached Florence and Maarten's house.

"What are we going to do?" Berti asked the padre.

"Wait."

And he did, watching the Franciscan come and go, covering Lena's scorched legs with leeches. The slimy creatures squirmed over her fetid, open wounds, eating the bleeding sores corrugating her burned skin. As he sat by her bed and wiped her sightless face, he leaned closer from time to time to check her breath against his cheek.

Days went by. Maddalena shook with fever, and Berti wondered that she was alive. Maarten came and went on his business, but Karl often stopped by her bed. If someone told Berti that he and Karl came from the same womb, he would have agreed readily, for hardly ever had a stronger friendship grown under stranger circumstances.

Without food and able to accept only droplets of water on her lips, Maddalena was barely alive. But one damp morning, Berti walked into her room and sensed that something had changed.

"Gertgen!" His voice broke. "Help me turn Lena over!" Although the burns on her back where her hair caught fire had already scarred, the pink skin was angry and delicate. Then Berti removed the cover and saw that one leg had taken on the color of a corpse.

"Will she live?" he asked the barber as he examined the raw stump below her knee.

"It is God's will," the surgeon replied and packed his tools into a bag. Berti looked at the bloody saw and at Lena's mangled amputated leg, and his gut heaved. As the days passed gloomily, Berti sat by the woman who refused to die, keeping himself sane by painting.

Shortly after they arrived, he entered the Archduke Francesco's service on Maarten's recommendation, commissioned to paint those little pictures the Medici despot liked for his mistresses. As in Rome, but more quickly, Berti paved his way, making friends and enjoying rapid success.

The ducal court was full of Flemings. Some, like the tapestry designer Jan van den Straet and the archduke's sculptor Jean de Boulogne, lived a life of prestige and luxury. Of the two, Berti particularly liked the latter, now called Giovanni di Bologna, and wanted to spend more time in his workshop; but fear for Maddalena's well-being kept him away.

One day as he wiped her face with water, her lips moved, and foreign words escaped. He lifted her head and moved her higher, but still he understood only one word: Alessandro. Maddalena spoke in her native tongue.

It was a beginning. He spent more time looking into her sightless face, feeding her broth, watching her spirit return, the essence of goodness, a light not to be extinguished. Rarely did he entrust her to others. During long, damp evenings when the fire blazed to keep Lena's hands warm, they began to chat. Often he sent the servants away and read to her from the Bible. When the candle burned low, they prayed, she from the depth of conviction, he to please her.

She was unbelievably frail, her face a crescent moon, her eyes like craters.

Could he tell her the terrible stories he heard from Rome the day the surgeon amputated her leg? He was unsure then if he wanted her to live.

How would she exist without Alessandro? The first rumors said that a seizure took his life. Then as other conflicting news trickled in, Berti tried to make sense of the gossip circulating in the ducal palace among the servants and his new friends. Finally, he gathered that Alessandro survived but that the attack clouded his mind and left him stuttering. Whether he could ever resume office was uncertain, because the apoplexy paralyzed him.

The room was dark. Berti strove to know Maddalena's blindness.

"Lena, do you think about him?" he asked, unable to tell her the bad news, not until she improved. He could not even utter Alessandro's name.

"I pray for His Grace. For his peace and his well-being."

"Do you ever regret the fate that brought your paths together?"

"No," she replied, choosing each word thoughtfully, the weeks of confinement having robbed her of breath. "I thank God for the joy He gave me with Alessandro, and I bless Him for the punishment I deserved."

Berti lost his temper. "Deserved? If that old lecher hadn't tempted you! Oh, what's the use?" He patted her hand, seeing his slur agitated her. "Sorry. I get frustrated seeing you … "

"You're wrong," she broke in. "The choice was mine, and I made it regardless of what might come." Her hand reached to wipe tears, but they had dried at the stake. "You see, now that Alessandro will not want me, I am free to serve my Lord the way He deserves."

Berti clenched his fist in defiance. What God permitted such suffering? Then he opened his hand, grateful that Lena could not see the gesture. She had already fallen into the light slumber that occupied her recent days and gave her strength to recover.

† † †

On the Feast of St. Anthony in the year of Our Lord 1574, Maddalena saw Florence for the first time. The carnival was open, and people and voices filled the streets. The city sparkled with a dusting of new snow over the old towers, lightly covering the rooftops above the palaces' deep loggias.

For the first time since Santoro's guards came to arrest her, she was outside to breathe the city through her soul and Berti's voice. Once tall but now a cripple, she moved about Maarten's house on her knees, groping with her hands and dragging her stub of a leg behind. At Francesco's court, Berti met a carpenter and asked him to build a pushchair with wheels to which a donkey could be hitched.

At the end of the first day out, she was glad to return to bed, so Berti left her and joined the carnival festivities at the palace. Since Maarten left Florence long before winter made crossing the Alps impossible, Berti and Karl alone made their way toward the large square near the Arno.

"Do you ever get homesick?" Karl asked, prodding his horse past a crowd of men.

Berti had no intention of leaving the city, but he had had similar thoughts.

"No. Sometimes. Only when I'm not sure where my life's heading."

Karl threw him a glance of surprise. "What do you mean? You've already made your fame as a court painter. You live like a king. You lack nothing."

Berti turned away. Karl was right. He lacked little except a purpose in life. Looking at Karl, he answered truthfully. "I don't know where I'm going."

"Don't worry! Gregory has pardoned Lena, and I'm sure he's long forgotten you. Return to Rome and work for another cardinal or a prince!"

"I want a home," Berti confessed. "My own home. I'd like to have a wife to honor. And children to hold in my arms." He could not forget Don Alfonso's squiggly nose pressed against his cheek.

"Is that all that's bothering you?" Karl laughed incredulously as they crossed the large open courtyard toward the grand staircase. Mist rose from the Arno, trailing its customary way through the streets and alleys. The city was in disarray, littered with rubbish from days of carnival. Beggars squirmed in the chilly dampness, shifting stubbornly through the city's bowels, combing its paths for lost trinkets, begging for a bit of human warmth.

Berti became generous, especially when Maddalena started to show signs of recovery. Riding along, he suddenly enjoyed the feel of blood circulating through his veins. Women's gazes first skirted him, then invited him openly. He sat straight on the gelding. Sleeping little and enjoying a lot, he felt invigorated.

Maarten's house was a short hop from the Piazza della Signoria and the center of Florence. He and Karl wandered through the city's streets and churches, admiring the city of Brunelleschi, Ghiberti, and Michelangelo, also enjoying the fresh air and good taverns in the surrounding hills.

Berti was content in Florence, charmed by the turreted intimacy of the small city on the Arno. He had found his niche, met new friends—and yet without knowing why, he started to feel an urge to return to Rome. He nudged the gelding to speed up.

"Hey, wait for me!" Karl cried in Flemish.

"Stop daydreaming and watch where you're going!" Berti lost his patience.

"Now be fair!" Karl smoothed the creases of his handsome rabbit-lined velvet cape. "How much longer did you say before you finish the coat of arms for the School of the Affiliated?" Berti's latest project was a panel of life-size figures, elaborately carved around the outlines, of two women holding a central shield depicting the rising sun.

Berti touched his cap and smiled at two women walking by. "I have to finish the two *amorini* at the foot of the shield and glaze the entire panel. Why do you ask?"

"Don't know. Just asking. Berti, wouldn't it be fine to be in Rome after Corpus Christi?"

"You too!?" Berti wondered what suddenly made Karl so itchy.

"Florence is so small-minded, so tight-fisted, so controlled," Karl muttered unhappily. "Enjoy a little virgin now and then, and before you know it her father comes running after you with a noose. The only sure thing is a paid woman. Why don't we dine at Messer Giancarlo's?"

"If you like. But remember, my friend, Rome's no different, except bigger and perhaps easier to hide in." Berti wondered why he had not seen Pietro Portinari in Florence. But the plump merchant was easy to fool; Berti did not worry about him. He was more uncomfortable about the perfumed notes the archduke's mistress kept sending him.

"*Libero, sempre libero …* " He sang a little tune he learned in Florence about man's need to remain free and unattached.

The wind picked up over the river. Karl buttoned his doublet. "What are you mumbling?"

"Some foolish air," Berti replied as they galloped across the Old Bridge. At a butcher shop, a pack of dogs fought over the smelly remains of a lamb. "Didn't Francesco pass a law about keeping this bridge clean?" Karl unstopped his nose when they reached the other side.

"How should I know? It's mostly jewelers now," Berti replied. He pushed the gelding up the steep hill toward the ruins of an old fort. They paused there, admiring the city's skyline, broken by the large carmine round of a big dome dominating the center, the checkered façade of Santa Maria Novella on the distant left, and the earthy bulk of Santa Croce on the right. The distant blue hills of Fiesole cut the horizon softly.

"Let's go. I'm hungry." Berti's stomach made its needs known.

They pressed along the ridge toward Monte ai Croci until the familiar outline of Messer Giancarlo's tavern rose before them around a bend.

"My friend, I hope I don't have to remind you that Fioretta's mine!" Karl warned as they turned the corner around the walled terrace.

"I'll have a rabbit instead," Berti laughed, "and take whatever's left for dessert."

He jumped off the horse and let the stable boy take the animal. The distant view of the city was spectacular, its soft outline merging with sky and land. Berti liked the bucolic look. For a few moments he stared at the changing skyline, the clouds gathering rapidly over Florence. The land was gray but for the verdant patches of grass that always throve in the Florentine rain.

"Welcome, gentlemen!" Giancarlo rubbed his hands with pleasure at seeing new customers. His face, his chubby under-chin and rotund belly, even his short stubby fingers were cushioned to survive a winter without eating. The broad Neapolitan stood scarcely five palmi tall, but he knew how to please customers, particularly on a Monday afternoon when God-fearing men worked. "Taking it easy today, signori *fiamminghi?*"

Berti nodded, wondering whether to appease his stomach first. "There's little to do now, and I don't want to commit myself to a new contract," he responded.

"You wouldn't be leaving us soon, would you?" the Neapolitan lamented. He tried to wink, but his bulgy lids refused to move fast enough.

"Who knows?" Karl answered. "Our fate rests on him."

Berti laughed. Truth to tell, he did not want to return to the empty palace in Rome without Adrien there. He had said so to Karl.

"Which of my tender lamb chops would you like to taste today?" The innkeeper clucked and pointed to the back room. Berti shrugged.

"*Signore,*" the innkeeper breathed warmly, "for a round coin, you can have a lamb chop and also enjoy a nice dove. Now, she may not be as pretty as you like, but she comes nicely buttered, my noble friend. But that's for you to find out."

"What do you say, Karl?" His friend was too busy cleaning his teeth.

"Deal." Berti pulled out his pouch. "To your health and to the prosperity of your family!"

As often, she was young, with dimpled cheeks, and when Berti rode home alone at the crack of dawn, the taste in his mouth was only slightly bitter.

† † †

"This is exquisite!" Maddalena fingered the fine dress fabric and rubbed the soft velvet of the bodice against her cheeks, slowly filling out again. She moved her rolling chair into the breeze from the window to imagine what she could not see.

The morning light fell across unruly locks frosted with snow, framing her face in the laurel of her martyrdom. While her garments concealed the fading scars on her back and legs, two craters endured as the reminders of her fate.

Berti sneezed.

"Should I close the shutters?" Maddalena's hand fished through the air.

"No, the fresh air feels good." He sneezed again and blew his nose. "It's just a tickle in my nose," he offered cheerfully and sniffed the air again, suspiciously.

"Maddalena, do I smell violets? Did Gertgen bring you a bunch?"

"No, Berti. There was a fine lady here looking for you while you were gone this morning. She must have been beautiful," Maddalena sighed. "Her dress rustled across the floor with the fullness and elegance only such women can wear." She turned away, pressing the gown against her bosom, thinking of Alessandro.

Berti gave a helpless sigh. "What did she want?"

"I don't know." Maddalena steered her thoughts back. "She was cross. She said that if you don't come to see her straightaway, she will tell the archduke that you raped her."

Berti snickered. "As if he'd care," he replied, more to himself than anyone else. "It's no one, Lena. Just another of my ladies. Yes, Gertgen?"

Adrien's servant looked cheerful. "Mail, master Berti."

"From Rome?" Lena inquired.

"From Don Clovio." Berti recognized the handwriting and the seal.

"Can I feel it?" she asked eagerly. "Isn't that wonderful, a letter from Rome, from Don Clovio! You must tell me all the good news!" She clapped her hands like a little girl.

While Berti studied the old miniaturist's shaky handwriting, her thoughts flew back to Rome, to her cozy house, and to Alessandro. Berti in turn wondered how the cardinal fared, still hesitant to break the news to Maddalena. A red flush burned at the corners of her mouth and on her cheeks. Berti knelt by her chair.

"I'm so sorry." He pressed his face against her cheek, holding her tight.

Maddalena pulled away with alarm. "Is it bad news?" Her voice caught.

Berti bit his tongue. The time was not right yet. "No ... not at all! I didn't mean to upset you. I ... felt for you right now, your life gone so cruelly," he replied.

"Tell me, how's the old man?" She smiled softly.

"He's fine, as fine as an extremely venerable man like Don Clovio can be. His eyes trouble him but no more than usual." Berti did not tell Lena how shaky the handwriting was. Thank God, she could not see. He tried to imagine the frail, transparent man and added, "You'll see, Lena. He will outlive us all!"

Maddalena averted her face.

"Lena? What is it?"

She turned toward his voice. "Forgive me. I'm an ungrateful woman who doesn't deserve to be heard, but here I am like a child, depending on you and the servants for everything." She reached for her crutches and fingered their length. "Could we go home to Rome ever again? I could be much closer to … I have bad dreams about *him*. I see him laid out on a bier in the apse of his new church."

"That's preposterous." Berti tried to laugh. "*Il Gesù* is not finished yet!"

"I know," she sighed, "but it's a premonition I have as I sit here by the window day after day without knowing whether or when the sun rises or sets. In my own house I could do things alone, for I know every corner by heart. I could open my shop and be useful again. And if Alessandro ever needed me again … "

"How could you manage?" Berti asked, awed by Maddalena's courage.

"I could get Crispina's girl to help. You remember Antonella, don't you? She must be nearly twelve. She could be my eyes and legs, and I could help people the way I used to."

Berti scanned the letter and put it down, as Adrien's familiar face grew large in his mind. He was nearly paralyzed with joy.

"You can and you will." He leapt forward and grasped her hands lying curled in her lap. "Maddalena, would you be quiet and let me read you the good news about Adrien?"

But my son, I have little desire to dampen your days with sorry tales of my old age, for I bring you good tidings as well. I do not know if you remember His Grace's servant, the merchant Geronimo. Not long ago he came back from the Levant where he saw your friend, Adrien. Yes, it is true and may the Lord be blessed for his kindness! Adrien is alive and well, but weak from his days in captivity in Constantinople, so he must bide his time before he boards a ship for Ancona. I am sure that he will gladly tell you the sad tale of his long ordeal. But before I forget, son, the prior of the little church by Porta Latina came to see me the other day and wanted to know if you would consider painting an altar depicting the Martyrdom of Saint John Evangelist for his order. Perhaps His Grace, the Farnese cardinal, would take you back; he recommended you to the friars. You could cheer him up with little allegorical paintings. Ever since the great tragedy of the saintly woman Maddalena, he is melancholic. In any case, you are most welcome to stay with me again in the Cancelleria in your old room, for the prince-bishop gave up the lease on the palazzo on the street of the Old Banks where you used to live. Some ugly rumors that he was taken with the French disease came my way, but I am sure that the young man simply wishes to settle back in his homeland after finally having taken his vows.

Berti sneezed again and stopped, but Maddalena was so overwhelmed she did not notice that Don Clovio did not say much about his benefactor's health.

"Lena, what do you say? Shall we go? We can take Karl with us. I know he'd be grateful. I need only a few days to look after my affairs and say farewell to all my new friends."

He searched her face and imagined a tear trickling down by her nose.

"Maddalena, did you hear what I said?"

"Yes, Berti, and I want you to go to bed. You don't sound well."

"If that's all that's on your mind"—he tried to conceal his fatigue—"I'll see my tailor."

"I believe that visit should wait, Berti," Maddalena scolded. "The woman who came here looking for you was raving mad. 'My father's name no longer matters,' she said, 'but they call me *La Mammola*.' Is she someone's kept woman?"

"She was," Berti replied curtly. "Francesco's. And mine for a while."

No matter, for in a week he sat in the post-chaise with Karl, Maddalena, and Gertgen, eagerly looking for the familiar outline of the mountains encircling Rome. He had to tell her the truth about Alessandro before she heard it from anyone else. Having instructed everyone around her in Florence to keep quiet, he could not control matters in Rome.

Naively, he thought the blow would be lighter in the familiar air of her home, but Maddalena responded to the news unexpectedly. She sat by the chimney in the *salone,* silent.

He did not expect tears but at least some sign of grief. Instead her back went rigid, and her face set in stone so hard that she looked like a sphinx. He tried to talk with her, but she stared unblinking until he could not face her and left her in the care of Beltraffio's family.

† † †

Not far from Maddalena's house, Alessandro faced the Tiber in his moving chair, propped erect on cushions, watching boats and barges fight the current toward the harbor.

After the rain, the air smelled clean as the sun appeared and then quickly set. The western skies grew pale as the brilliant scarlet slowly dissipated among puffy clouds shifting toward the ocean, leaving the city's dark outline behind. From morning to night, his mind journeyed frantically, mostly seeking Maddalena, without knowing that she had returned to Rome.

She had become all that he could not be, but with her the great prelate became more human, learned to appreciate life from her perspective—the beggars in her home, the dust on his shoes, the clouds in the sky. He no longer hungered for the carnal knowledge between man and woman. After tragedy struck him, he reexamined his life, knowing nothing of her ghastly survival. He presumed Maddalena would come back to him some day, somehow, unchanged.

Fighting his malady with unflagging tenacity, he woke every morning before sunrise to read the Bible. The sun found him up, shuffling papers, messages, and daily tasks, but as duty occupied his mind and put him in command, there were times he could no longer imagine being tied to anyone, not even Maddalena, lost in a quandary between God, fame, and happiness.

God was a link to the world beyond, where Alessandro's life would continue unimpeded. He tried to be a good bishop but was too rich, too influential. His sermons were noble, but the nobility needed little comfort, and he thought not of the poor. Ready for a far more important mission, he considered what the world, not just Rome, thought of him.

One thing mattered, the one unfulfilled dream. He had to become Rome's new shepherd. Having lost the woman he loved through divine intervention, he was sure the Lord would finally help. Still he missed Maddalena, his other dream, and when he wanted her most, he hated his thirst for fame, knowing that without her, life was unreal.

The price was too high. More than Maddalena, Alessandro loved fame.

And so the tireless scale rocked back and forth, tipping this way and that.

When he felt strong, God was a brilliant light at the end of his privileged journey, and the nearest he could come to Him was to sit on His earthly throne. Everything around the spoiled prelate was beautiful, and the papal throne was the most attractive.

If forced to choose again, the choice was clear—to revenge his family's ordeal after his grandfather's death and Maddalena's suffering.

Already he pictured himself in St. Peter's chair, his enemy crushed at his feet. As the dream grew, he savored it. He began taking his meals alone, greedily eating the last crumb on the table, enjoying the imaginary suffering of his foes.

Was he not rich enough to win the next round?

But at the end of the day, when he was tired, Maddalena haunted him, in the darkness, over the river. "A dark girl I am," she called out, "but comely ... "

Bewildered, he answered, "Look, you are beautiful, girl companion. Your eyes are those of doves, like a lily among thorny weeds, so is my girl."

With the words of the *Song* trailing over the river and Maddalena's eyes burning brightly, he pulled himself to the window and cried, "Come back to me, come back to the land of lilies!"

Angel of Mercy

The city seemed bigger than Berti remembered, and he appreciated it more. Don Clovio's hospitality overwhelmed him, and his old room in the Cancelleria felt pleasantly familiar.

Until Adrien returned, Berti was free to help Maddalena. Since her trial and Crispina's death, Beltraffio became a burden with his first-born Jacopo gone studying in Bologna. Were it not for Antonella, the eldest daughter, her father and three young brothers would have been lost.

Everything went wrong for Beltraffio because of Alessandro, his comfortable job ending in the accident that twisted his spine, his service in Maddalena's employ causing his wife's death. Seeing the cardinal talking to his son with that display of affection clerics have for boys, he raged. Poor, crippled, and becoming feeble-minded, he was unable to affect his affairs. Without Maddalena, nothing was right, his family in chaos.

After she returned to her house, however, she comforted him and gave him back a sense of pride. On the second day, she rang the bell she kept with her, sat the hunchback by the hearth, took a lump of charcoal from her apron, and drew simple pictures on the wall. When she finished, she called him closer.

"Raffi, look," she showed him her stump. Then in the darkness of her sight she pointed to an animal drawn with two circles and stick legs and cross-hatching under its head.

"Every morning you must give the donkey fresh water and hay and change his straw. I can't do it, but you'll be a big help. I'll have a lump of sugar for you and Ettore, waiting right here in the jar. Now, come even closer. I'll tell you a secret," she whispered, knowing childish Beltraffio's liking for games. "If you do everything I tell you," she added, drawing one more picture, an oval with black dots, "you'll get a raisin pastry for being good."

Maddalena had never harmed a soul and could not understand how Santoro's men could torture Beltraffio, a broken man close to God, needing care.

"So tell me," she said, pointing again to the pastry, "what will it be for good Raffi?"

Beltraffio stuck out his tongue and pointed to his belly, as always willing to help, except when he wandered away to look for his wife.

She picked up a basket. "Now, Raffi, get some clover for our bunnies!" Grabbing the basket, he scampered out of the kitchen.

The moment he was gone, Maddalena put her head on the table, overwhelmed.

Antonella ran over in a flash. "Is it the phantom pain again?" she asked anxiously.

Maddalena raised herself. "No. I just don't know where to start. First, we'll need money. I think Santoro's men didn't find the chest hidden under the fireplace. Move the tiles, get it, and hire men to clean this hovel up and paint it. It stinks and the walls are gritty. How could you and your family live here? Didn't I teach you better?"

"Madonna, with that devil's shadow over this house, we were glad to be alive."

"Why didn't you let us know Santoro's men were badgering you?"

Fear reeled through Antonella's veins as she crossed herself. "Only one was after me."

"All is well now," Maddalena replied, feeling burdened by too much responsibility. "Why don't you talk to our neighbor? Signor Tasca is kind. He might recommend the very men we need. Maybe his wife will help with the laundry." Maddalena leaned over to touch the soiled curtain separating the kitchen table from the children's sleeping corner. It smelled of soot and wax. Just as she reassured herself that all was under control, shrieks rang through the hall.

"Madonnina, blessed mistress!" Beltraffio staggered back, like a madman, howling like one possessed. "Santoro's outside! The cardinal is here to take us again!"

Maddalena considered. The Grand Inquisitor never arrested anyone personally. Perhaps he wanted to express his regrets? Impossible. "Quiet, Raffi! *Vieni qua!*" The simpleton stood pointing to the door, through which a man's voice could be heard pleading with Antonella.

Could it really be His Eminence at last? Maddalena was unprepared for Alessandro, though she had imagined facing him many times. Suddenly, she had no idea what she would say.

When she heard footsteps and smelled an old man, she froze. As Antonella came in and pulled her whimpering father from the room, arms in rustling robes embraced Maddalena and she began to weep.

"My treasure," the shaky voice stammered. Two foreheads met, and two damaged bodies touched, lightly at first, then locked together as though they would never part again. The body in her arms struggled for composure as the horror of her condition sank into the cardinal's mind.

"Alessandro, I loved you that hot June morning I first saw you ill in bed," she murmured, "and I love you still."

The cardinal tried to reply, but only jumbled words came.

"Alessandro, my pain didn't matter then or now." Her crutch fell away, and he helped her sit on the bench. "There, why don't you sit, too?" She pushed him away and pointed across the table. Freed, she felt surprisingly relieved.

"Is there anything … What can I do to repay you?" His voice was laden with guilt.

"We both have suffered, but we still have the joy of what was before," Maddalena replied, "and the real pain comes when we realize what is and must be."

Alessandro protested. "We'll have to be careful, my angel, but I'll take you away. We could go to France. My word is law."

"You mean leave the church and your clan?" she protested. "Both would disown you. You need care, the kind I cannot give you anywhere. Only you can nurse your wounded pride and fight for the papal chair. That wouldn't be possible if you left Rome."

"What do you take me for?" Alessandro demanded. "I want to marry you."

"A Farnese through and through," she thought.

"But we are already married," Maddalena replied with a smile. "Remember?"

He remembered how happy he was that day, hopeful that love, glory, and the papal throne awaited him. Yet that same proud man sat bargaining for his honor, because his moral sense demanded it. Maddalena could not see him, but his purpose could not have been clearer if it were inscribed in stone. She admired his courage but could not accept the sacrifice. Both had already lost too much.

She heard him move around the table, desperately wanting to hold him close again, but if she did, she would become vulnerable. Instead with great effort she gripped the edge of the table to steady herself. Alessandro knelt by her, pushed his head into her lap, and embraced her knees.

"Damn it woman, can't you hear me?" He stuttered in the pain of not reaching her, and she nearly submitted. "I've cursed enough the fate that brought us together.

"Maddalena, can you possibly comprehend the anguish that has gnawed me from the moment I heard you were in prison?" he asked her. "I knew why they took you—to get at me. Forgive me, but I was afraid you would implicate me. I feared exile. I went through it once. But I'll do it again. I'll leave the bonds I've hated all my life to be free, to be happy with you."

Maddalena understood the tragedy of the fall of a man who had lived surrounded by power and wealth. Knowing that she must be strong for both of them, she pulled away.

"Alessandro, you were and still are dearer to me than my life. I thank you for all." She stretched her arms toward him, palms up and fingers wide, in a plea of understanding. "Don't make it more difficult for me. Just go *away* and let me be."

She raised her chin and turned away from his voice and heard him reply with the cold, arrogant confidence of his class, "At least take the deed for your house. It comes with a stipend. It will ease my conscience if you lack nothing."

Alessandro pushed himself up and left. The scroll burned in Maddalena's hand and spread pain through her chest. She covered her face and cried as she had not when she heard that Alessandro suffered a stroke.

"I love you, Cardinal Farnese," she whispered, "and wish you well."

† † †

Maddalena's return brought order to the house but stirred the neighborhood. Only a saint could have survived her ordeal, but there she was, alive, full of spirit. Each moment spent inside the familiar walls growing warm under her inquisitive fingers, each whiff of the river air, each crack in the walls, each rattle in the streets fed Maddalena's will so strongly that, were it not for her blindness and her lame leg, her neighbors would have found her unchanged.

The first time she went out to buy a loaf of bread, she walked the familiar street guided by the walls, groping her way on crutches. Awed, people gathered. Some watched from a distance, others welcomed her—weeping, laughing, exclaiming, touching her scars, her empty face, kissing the hem of her *gamurra* as though she were a saint.

The new Maddalena remained stoic, determined to endure. She cried with those who gathered about her and laughed with them, too. They came to her one by one or in groups, streaming in and bearing gifts as generous as they could spare. Soon the rabbit cages by the back wall were full, the chicken coop crowded. Ettore, the tired old donkey, found a young mate, and the modest larder groaned under so much generosity.

There was no place there for Berti, glad to be in his old room in the Cancelleria, waiting and thinking about Adrien, but he stopped at Lena's often, each time more amazed.

"How do you get around the house so fast? What's your secret?" he asked as he watched her moving between the table and the corner with her remedies and potions as though she could see. The house still showed the wounds Santoro's men made, but the walls were whitewashed, the floors spotless. Passion for life shone in Maddalena's face, and in her voice he heard a new kindness, as though her very femininity had mellowed in her submission to God.

"God bless you, Berti. It's not a secret, but a simple trick," she replied, hearing his footsteps. "I count. Ten paces to the front door, fifteen to the cupboard, twenty steps upstairs, and then comes the landing. I have to remember where I am. It's like a dance in which each new step becomes familiar as you approach it."

Berti shook his head in disbelief. The agonizing, tortuous months of recovery in Florence were hard on her, the sedentary life weighing her down and darkening her soul. Yet before him was a new, mysterious woman.

The front gate creaked and opened cautiously, spilling in a muddle of strangers.

"Who are those men?" Berti turned to see if he recognized anyone.

Maddalena cocked her ear toward the gate, trying to recognize the voices.

"I don't know."

"Why do they come to you here?"

She paused as if deciding whether what she was about to say made sense and crossed her hands over her chest. "They believe that even now I still can do something for them," she told him simply.

"Do something? But you're hurt."

"Men, women come to me with their families. When they are hungry, I feed them; when they despair, I pray with them. But often I help them. Not long ago a mother brought her yellow baby. Her older boy was also born saffron color. I couldn't do anything for the first one, but I told her to lay her new baby under the full moon to cancel the influence of Mars. That worked, but when Luna faded, I made a syrup from honey and the juice of hops. In no time his flesh released his blood and turned pink."

"Hops? Vrouw Santvoort makes beer with those. Wouldn't that make the baby sleepy?"

Maddalena laughed. "Yes, *humulus* does that. Its sedative powers are part of the cure. Half a dram of the powdered seed brings down the woman's curse—that is, when her womb isn't blessed by a child. It expels her urine, and … "

Berti was not convinced about the cure. "But how do you do that? How can you *see* what you do? Aren't you afraid you'll make a mistake?"

"All herbs have their scent, some strong, almost burning. I cured Pius' gout with horseradish. When I cleaned it, my nose told me what I used! I couldn't keep my eyes open. They streamed water. And Antonella helps me. I taught her to write, so she now reads the labels for me. People know I will help them. They come, kiss my hands, and leave changed."

Maddalena's voice came with the clear conviction of her true purpose on earth.

"What do you mean *changed?*"

"I don't really know. People here in the *rione Ponte* say that I perform wonders. But I just do the Lord's work."

And they came. Berti watched her fingering heads for lice, checking faces for eruptions, putting crushed leaves on eyesores, rubbing aching shoulders. He saw the aura of her faith and witnessed the impossible. A gentle stroke here, a kind word there, a bowl of warm broth, a bag of herbs, a jar with ointment, and the beggars left rich, the maimed restored, and the doubtful made believers.

Most were uneducated, but Maddalena found a few bright ones, especially the young, and encouraged them to visit her school. With each new letter, they grew in dignity. She followed her vision, sheer dedication changing the woman Alessandro once loved.

Berti wanted to ask her about him.

He saw the cardinal, hardly recognizing the man who now, although he still apparently moved with purpose, had no sparkle. Yet his figure had mushroomed into breadth that occasioned a lassitude seemingly impossible in a man once so vigorous. No matter how he tried, Berti could not persuade Maddalena to reveal her feelings about him.

With sallow skin, thinning silver hair, and a beard that did not hide the wattles drooping from his mouth and chin, Alessandro clung doggedly to his multifarious activities but with little satisfaction. Berti watched him deliver a homily, and realized that faith in God was all the aging Farnese scion had left.

For Berti the days flew, but his commissions were small, and most of his investments had gone with Adrien's ship. Before he left Florence, Berti sold his gelding, and without a rich patron his prospects were poor. He had Alessandro's diamond and Lena's cross but could part with neither.

The padres at the little church at the Via Latina gate were not rich, so their first payment bought Berti only an old mare; but they liked his sketches of the altar and wanted to see one enlarged. The figures were not quite life size, for an altar slightly bigger than eight *palmi* left no space in the apse. St. John Evangelist stood in a cauldron of boiling oil while his executioner tended the fire with a long shaft. Neither figure came easily since lately Berti had painted mostly frivolous scenes for Florentine noblemen.

As he sketched, his mental image of the executioner clarified as the giant who gouged out Maddalena's eyes. Although he never saw the man's face, he was sure it was like Lucifer's. He posed him close to the frontal plane, his thick hands gripping the shaft.

One day on the way home from Via Latina, Berti stopped at the foot of the Aventino and picked up a clay pot for Monna Klara. Now a frequent guest at the Speckaerts, he enjoyed Klara's cooking and Hans' renewed friendship. After months of caring for Maddalena, he did not miss being with her, content so long as the padres of San Giovanni in Oleo made their payments.

As for his sorrows, he drowned them at Monna Piacenza's.

† † †

"You're a lucky man. You have a comely wife, a pretty daughter, and now this!" Berti raised a lantern to admire the painting spanning the modest space Hans added behind his house.

"For Cardinal Ippolito, the story of Acteon? Is it done?"

"I still need to paint the background vignette." Hans pointed to a small hunter, about to be torn apart by his dogs. The soft curvatures of Diana's chaste nymphs had Bert's attention. He pointed questioningly to the dainty cloths covering their bodies.

"Nudes are no longer accepted by the new rules established in Trent. The Inquisition has a long reach, and Ippolito likes his job. Frankly, so do I. I like the fire in my hearth, not at my feet. So I paint a few scarves here and there," Hans explained, pointing to the creamy back of a nymph with a diaphanous cloth partially covering her plump behind.

"Is this Klara?" Berti indicated a figure with an arm curved over her head.

"Heaven spare me! Ippolito would come and steal my wife if he thought that was Klara."

"Hans, what elegance and what colors! Where did you learn to mix them?"

He gazed at the brown underpainting of the giant tree over Acteon's head and the fair-skinned Diana crouching in her bath. Acteon's red cloak merged with the neutral landscape accented by bright yellows and greens in the scarf across his chest.

Hans shifted his gaze back to the painting. "Not sure. Perhaps in Venice. The dark underpainting magnifies the colors; it brings out their luminosity."

"And what's next?" Berti asked enviously. He once helped Hans get contracts, and now Hans fared better than Berti.

"I was going to tell you about that over dinner. His Holiness wants me to show him a few designs glorifying the Catholic Church."

Berti eyes widened. "For the frescoes in the new library?"

"Not frescoes. Gregory wants to send my drawings to Brussels to have tapestries made for St. Peter's. For next year, the Golden Jubilee. I learned to draw from my father, watching him design borders for grand tapestries."

Berti sighed with a tinge of envy. "Is Gregory generous?"

"I guess he pays as well as the others. Enough for a new son."

"Are congratulations in order?" Berti spat into his palm.

"My wife is still nursing, but I hope it's God's will to give me a son."

Berti lifted the lantern again to see the figure that reminded him of Klara. She was indeed tempting, he thought when he greeted Hans' wife. Klara also made the best beer in town.

"To your health and your success." Berti clinked his beaker with Hans' and pulled him aside. "Do you ever make Klara happy with a trinket or two? And, by the way, a good draught of her beer would make her even more receptive to begetting you a son."

Hans would not consider. "My wife is too virtuous to drink beer."

The lady was also a fine cook. As Berti rode back to the Cancelleria, he carried with him the scent of her sausage and cabbage, as well as the picture of her strong arms in rolled-up sleeves. The absurdity of his vision was so frustrating that he wanted to confess it, but Adrien was not back yet and Karl had left Rome with a group of Netherlanders.

Some nights Berti had a recurrent dream about the land of Cockayne, filled with flying geese with knives stuck in their backs, large rounds of bread, and marble fountains with trickling beer, wine, and milk. He also saw flying clay pots like the one he bought for Klara, full of long sausages. Like fallen stars they landed on round tables, and each time strong hands like Klara's wildly jabbed a knife into them until their pale juices stained the white cloth.

One morning Berti woke late, tired from a nightmare, surprised when Maddalena and Antonella stopped at his studio to hear about the new painting for the padres of San Giovanni in Oleo. He was uneasy, describing the painting to her being the last thing on his mind.

She wore a new gown but not the one Berti bought her in Florence, a gown that she said was so special that she wanted to save it for the angels.

"You couldn't have made this by yourself," he argued pleasantly, admiring the pattern embroidered in the pale linen around the neckline.

"Not entirely. Antonella cut it out, and then I worked on it in the garden. Remember my tulips? Antonella says they are as beautiful as last year. Aren't they miraculous?" Maddalena marveled over many little things, but most of all she enjoyed the chatter of children in her house.

"Would you guide my finger across the outlines of your painting?" she begged.

"I haven't transferred it yet, Lena. The padres only approved the design yesterday. They were worried about how I was going to set the figures. But I could guide you through the cartoons if you like?" He freed her right hand from the crutch.

"These are the men in the foreground. They're Santoro's men. This one"—he outlined the feathered helmet on the head—"gestures toward heaven with his open palm, astonished by the grace of the dying saint. This one at the bottom is hot, and his back is bare except for the robe that has slipped off his shoulder. I think I will color it blue to blend with the sky."

Lena read the picture with her hands.

"And here are the men witnessing the martyrdom, struck by the saint's nobility."

Maddalena felt the surface of the paper. "Is the fire hot?"

"Not yet, Lena. I haven't painted it yet." Berti glanced at the scars on her palm.

"Did it hurt?" He could scarcely ask her.

"I thought of Alessandro. I was beyond pain and was ready to die for him."

"Did he … ever come back to you, Lena?" he whispered, not sure about Antonella.

"Don't worry. She's my eyes and my soul. I've nothing to hide. He came. Once, to give me the deed to the house." Her voice cracked. "That visit hurt more than the fire. As if goods could pay for loyalty and suffering! I did not suffer for gain. I did it for the love of him and his God." Lena stood up to leave without mentioning Alessandro's other offer and turned around. "There was a lot of smoke! I still smell it. The darkness was like Santoro's blackened soul."

After she left, Berti worked on the altar as her words rang in his mind. With unanswered rage, he painted the fire blazing hot with dense smoke rising to heaven.

† † †

By summer Berti's new altar was consecrated in San Giovanni by Porta Latina. The varnish was hardly dry when another proposition came for the same little church by the Trevi fountain where Hans worked, not far from Hans' house and Cornelis' *bottega*.

Although he was busy, the engraver was not well, his hands misshapen by the pressure of the burin, a small worry compared to the ravage the French sickness wrought on his health. A bit of his vitality was lost in each new copper plate, and though his fame spread far beyond Rome, Cornelis had little money to show for it.

When the olive trees bowed under a full crop, Adrien returned to Rome. Berti had new lodging behind the Piazza dei Santissimi Apostoli for them. Happy to be back, Adrien enjoyed the flurry of activity at their new home. When he appeared in a gray suit with a tall lace collar and silk stockings, he drew applause at Meneer Santvoort's.

"Stranger, looking good! What happened to your cuddly pillow?" Anthonis welcomed him back with a poke.

"Too busy with the Turkish ladies? How's the food over there?" another teased him good-naturedly. By the time he reached Rome, however, Adrien was well recovered from his trial. If anything, Berti thought that he looked fetching. A hint of silver brightened his rusty beard, and a surprising sedateness graced Berti's merchant friend.

The night was memorable like many others, and the next day Berti awoke with a familiar ache gripping his fuzzy head. All that morning the scaffolding in the chapel danced woozily before him, but Berti worked away, transferring the outlines of Mary's birth onto the canvas.

The design was handsome, and Berti was proud. "I'll paint the birth of the Virgin as a stage play." After nine years in Italy, he had seen enough religious processions and plays to illustrate the entire Bible. "Each figure will be like a character paused in the midst of her role."

The bells chimed noon when Berti climbed down from the scaffolding to view his work better. The air near the ground was cool, and his head felt more at ease.

The painting was the best he had ever designed, with God the Father hovering over a ring of clouds that looked like a string of Klara's fat sausages. He liked the young woman by the fire best. He had seen women painted in this pose in other works of art, but his was more powerful, bent over the fire with her strong arms holding the copper cauldron.

As he walked out into the sunlight, images of Klara bathing her baby, Klara cutting bread, Klara hanging Hans' shirts on the line, Klara sitting by the table and smiling, overpowered him. His head felt heavy again. He wanted to grind paint for tomorrow's *giornata*, but he could not get any work done. Maybe Klara would have a remedy.

Soon he rounded the corner and knocked on her door. "*Grüss Gott*, Frau Speckaert," he greeted her at the door. "Did Hans come home for his *Mittagsessen?*"

She shook her head. "He's working with Anthonis."

"Since when?" Anthonis liked to draw, but Hans said he had a big heart and little talent.

"Frau Santvoort found someone new to help her run the inn," Klara explained. "Anthonis was willing after his uncle died so suddenly, but he didn't find the work fulfilling."

A sharp pain closed Berti's eyes.

"Are you not well?" Klara asked. Berti adjusted his vision, and the pain eased.

"I'm fine. You mean that Anthonis is now working with Hans?"

Klara tilted her head, thinking. "I don't know," she replied. "I don't remember how long they've been together. Not long. Hans felt sorry for Anthonis and took him on."

Berti walked in and slumped down on a bench. "Is he teaching him how to paint?"

"I believe so. Otherwise Hans would be working here. What's the matter?" Klara looked at him curiously. Berti's eyes were slivers of pain.

"Ah, *mein Kopf.*" His hands went up to his head.

"Let me do that for you." She walked behind the bench and rested Berti's back against herself, cradling his head in her hands. Her fingers trailed knowingly through his thick locks, looking for knots of pain from the forehead down and across the shoulders and the broad back. Berti gave in to the tingling warmth and sank unwittingly into the cushion of her bosom.

"Frau Klara," he thanked her gallantly afterwards, "I'm a new man."

Klara smiled faintly. "Nothing to thank for. You didn't even stay for a meal."

"You're most kind." He could not resist a squeeze around the waist. "Another time?"

Hans was busy working with Anthonis and hardly ever came home at midday. Frau Klara's hospitality was tempting. Soon Berti was a frequent guest, ostensibly to see his godchild but in reality succumbing to his admiration of her able hands.

† † †

The altarpiece took shape each day. Life infused heads, shoulders, and clouds, the canvas drinking up Berti's colors like a thirsty plant. He was often at the Speckaerts', basking in the sun of Klara's attention. Although he visited often, he chose not to reflect on his feelings.

He was not in love with her, and he did not want Klara the way he wanted Monna Piacenza's whores, although the thought crossed his mind. He simply enjoyed the lack of commitment to someone who was married. Their innocent moments together took on new dimension when their hands met accidentally or their hips brushed. Berti cherished the image of Klara's warmth against his aching head.

She trusted him implicitly and put him on a pedestal, a man who could do no wrong. Although childish, Klara was faithful to her husband. Like many before her she was attracted to Berti without knowing why.

"*Klärchen,*" he said, patting the child in her arms, "what is your most secret wish?"

"How about you?" she asked, tidying up after a meal.

"I'd like to live like a king."

"But you do live like a king."

"No, not quite." Berti wondered if he should invest a small chunk of his savings in Adrien's new ventures. "Now it's your turn."

"I don't know. I think I'd like to go back to home, to Augsburg where my parents came from or to Brussels to live with Hans' family."

"Aren't you happy here?"

"It's hard to explain."

"Maybe Hans could get a job in Augsburg, with the duke. I'm sure you would also do fine in Brussels. There's always room for another painter at the Farnese court."

"Hans already tried going home to find a new job, but he came back."

"He never told me about that! When? Why did he come back?"

"He was sick and had to return to Rome. He made it only to Florence." Klara described Hans' aborted journey.

"He was in the city of the Medici and didn't come to see me?" Berti's feelings were hurt.

Klara turned cautious. "Don't tell him I told you. Hansi came back, sick in an oxcart, yellow as a mustard seed. He didn't want anyone to know, not even you."

"*Klärchen,* why don't you like it here?"

She just shrugged.

"Have to run. *Grüss Gott,* Frau Speckaert." He rushed back to his work. As it progressed, he earned great admiration for the way the figures shone through the monochrome underpainting. The heavenly aura surrounding God the Father exploded with a brilliance that spotted the supple clouds and highlighted the reds, blues, and greens in the attendants' starchy robes. Karl liked it and said so when he stopped by from time to time.

Rome bustled in preparation for the Jubilee Year, and the days had too many hours to enjoy them all. Streams of newcomers descended on the city, long processions accompanied by easy women. Near the end of each day, Berti looked forward to riding out of the city toward the hills with Karl for a breath of fresh air.

Once when they took refuge among the Roman tombs scattered along the Appian Way, Karl broached a new topic.

"What do you say we start a school of drawing? A fine draftsman never produces bad work, which is better than a good artist producing bad drawings or none. We'll apply to the pope to form a Roman academy of drawing and elect Hans leader. Is anyone better suited?"

"But do you think Hans would agree?" Berti wondered about his friend's health.

"Why not?" Karl replied. "I'd love to do it, but my drawing needs practice."

"Let's talk about it with some of the people who might join."

"We can copy Cornelis' prints. He has a mountain of them. If we make him second-in-command, I'm sure he'll agree."

Once again Berti wondered about the engraver's health, but lately Cornelis was looking well. Maddalena assured him that the treatment he was getting from the French barber was the best. Nothing worked on syphilis sores better than mercury. The warm leaves of henbane she first tried worked on the swelling but did nothing for the impotence.

"Who but the French would know best how to treat their own maladies?" Berti thought, momentarily caught by his own problem. For quite some time he had no steady woman, and the only person who caught his eye was married.

"What would we draw?" Berti asked. "Landscapes? Stories? Portraits?"

"Let's spread the word around. Ask everyone in town, including sculptors." Karl suggested. "Hey, Bart! Watch out for the pilgrims!"

"Must be Neapolitans," Berti laughed. "We'd better race down to the inn, or we'll get nothing for our trouble coming this way." Soon they settled in the inn's front room, sighing in relief, watching the dusty procession snaking toward the city gates.

Fallen Angel

Silence hung in the morning air. Berti moved about slowly, looking for a broad brush. The tools of his trade littered the church floor. He was a neat worker, but he was distracted. As he bent to search under a pile of cloth, he was shocked when a belch heaved from his gut, forcing him to confront a problem that had nagged him for far too long.

Drawn to Klara, he now considered seducing her, since staying away only gave him indigestion. No man has a right to his wife without pleasing her. He was not sure how Hans managed little Berta, but just one look at Klara told him that married life did not please her.

"Shouldn't be hard." He began to whistle. "Hans is never home."

The church portal opened with a bang.

"And blessed be the name of Jesus Christ," he answered the liveried man who walked up the aisle. "Give me a moment to cover my tools."

He did not know the servant, but his message was clear. Berti ran past him to the street.

"When did I last speak with Alessandro?" He remembered but not gladly. They met in front of Maddalena's prison. "And Alessandro assured me she would be released the next day. What went wrong? Why did the powerful man fail?"

The cardinal was waiting in a litter-chair. Berti had no idea why he did not summon him directly to his palace. A pudgy hand pushed the curtain aside as Berti stepped in.

"Eminence." He kissed the signet ring choking the fat finger.

Alessandro clapped his hands, and the chair moved jerkily in the direction of Santa Maria Rotonda and the Cancelleria; but as they came near Via Recta, it turned sharply left and wove through smaller lanes in a part of the city still a jumble of wooden houses. Peasants walking south toward the market slowed their progress to see them pass.

All that time Alessandro hardly acknowledged Berti, who sat quietly waiting for a sign, afraid of saying the wrong thing. As for the cardinal, he seemed lost in another world. Only when they stopped in front of the new church of the Jesuits, he leaned forward and announced without preface, "I cannot bear my life without her."

Berti's chin dropped. While his benefactor looked improved since the day he heard his homily at San Lorenzo, he still seemed old and heartless. Gout swelled his feet. Or was it too much sugar? Berti did not understand those things, but the idea of a crippled Maddalena and a lame Alessandro coupled in bed was absurd.

"You've always understood me." Alessandro finally picked up his thoughts. "I hope you are still my friend." Without Maddalena's tooth powder, stale breath erupted from his innards past his few remaining front teeth.

Berti found himself in a difficult position. What should he say? Alessandro helped him as thoughts unfurled, breathing heavily as he spoke.

"Maddalena and I ... We still love each other but must live apart." He remembered how Maddalena turned from him when she sent him away. He found himself regretting leaving her with cold words and the empty gesture of a gift at the moment she was prepared to sacrifice herself for him for the second time.

Alessandro spoke with his eyes closed, and Berti listened with his heart.

"I've never thanked you for what you've done for her. Although what I'm about to offer you will bring you a nice reward—I understand that your circumstances are pinched since you've returned to Rome—I hope you will appreciate the honor it confers."

Alessandro opened his eyes for a moment, and their gazes met.

"I want an altarpiece for the chapel of St. Magdalen in my new church. I leave the design to you, but you must abide strictly by the new laws governing the images of saints."

Alessandro actually smiled briefly, picturing Titian's nude Magdalen by his bed. "And, Berti, I want a smaller version for my private chapel in the palace."

He looked exhausted. His head sank into the cushions. He still had many tasks before him that day and for the rest of his life, however brief or long that was. He would complete them with Maddalena at his side. He would see her morning and at night when he knelt at her feet and admired her face in the candlelight.

As Berti accepted a pouch of gold, he realized that his true reward would come from immortalizing Maddalena in paint. Suddenly he was thrilled. He had never realized how much he admired her. In fact, he was so pleased that for the rest of the day he forgot entirely about Klara.

† † †

"Not bad," Hans mumbled as he admired Berti's masterpiece, but the praise was insincere.

The dark November morning left a heavy mist behind. The day before Berti noticed that Hans' fresco on the side wall had ugly damp spots and warned him about the consequences. Hans had little experience with fresco painting, although his errors were nothing Berti could not fix. Yet it puzzled him that Hans ignored his advice.

"He must be jealous," Berti realized suddenly, without knowing why. The petition for the new drawing school Hans would direct had been submitted for Gregory's approval. They were finishing the new decorations in time for the Jubilee, while the little church's façade was being whitewashed. "What's that fuss outside?" Berti protested the noise.

"They're moving the scaffold higher," Hans snapped back.

"Have you been drinking the lime water from your bucket?" Berti had warned his friend twice about poisoning himself drinking that water, but Hans had not listened. Berti studied his own composition, complete but for the two female figures. Finishing the tiled floor was a trifle even for a beginner like Anthonis, who already proved an eager assistant to both.

Hans threw a rag at Berti. "Do you want to be burned at the stake like Maddalena?"

"What do you mean?" Berti came to life. His wrapped figures looked more like mummies than female attendants. Should that not please that bastard Santoro?

"That!" Hans pointed to the woman tending the fire. Alone, she had bare arms. Worse yet, her bosom spilled over her draped bodice as she bent low over a large cauldron.

Berti grabbed a brush and his palette, and with a few strokes painted in sleeves to cover the arms to the elbows and drape the bodice higher toward the neck. "Better?"

"Yes. And now how about lunch?" As they passed through the gate, a large bucket of water broke off its rope and wet both men down to their hose, barely missing their heads.

Her wet guests shocked Klara. If the meal seemed less delicious, it was because she left her cooking to watch the two naked men change by the fire. The lusty maleness of her husband's shivering friend fascinated her.

While Hans fussed over his wet attire, she naively conceived the idea that she would find out once and for all exactly how she came to be blessed with little Berta. But questioning Hans would do no good, for all the pious man guided by the scriptures would tell her that evening was what she already knew. Then, too, her devout mother had told her to submit to the will of God and her husband without questions, no matter how much they puzzled her.

The next day she was out bright and early to find out the truth at Frau Schneider's.

"Ridiculous!" the women in her spinning circle laughed. "A kiss on the cheek!"

"But Hans said it came from God. He can do anything! Even put babies in a kiss."

"And what did you think about the christening of fire on your wedding night?" the feisty Frau Schneider replied. Her husband, the spindly tailor, hardly had time to keep his family clothed. "*Und meine liebe Klara*"—Frau Schneider's tongue was sharper than her husband's scissors—"I can't recall the last time my husband kissed me, and look at my belly!"

"Do you mean to say that"—Klara, suddenly seeing her humping husband in a new light, could hardly bear honing her thoughts to a finer point in front of all the merry wives—"that Adam and Eve did not eat the apple and the snake spoiled Eve?" Never having seen her naked husband, she tried hard to wipe the picture of Berti disrobing by the fire.

Klara's simplicity amused the women. "But aren't snakes poisonous?" she whispered.

"They do bite here and there." Frau Schneider patted her stomach with authority. The wheels hummed while tongues clucked.

"Frau Schneider," Klara asked, "you mean when Hans told me he must chase the devil into hell he really meant ... Oh, my, I am so confused. I thought we were pleasing God."

"But you were! Think about that!" her wise neighbor replied.

"Ladies. You've done me greater service than you can imagine," Klara exclaimed.

When Berti dropped by after lunch with pretty ribbons for little Berta's cap, Klara was all thumbs. He pretended he hoped to find Hans at home to tell him that Cardinal d'Este was recruiting men to decorate his country villa. "Do you think Hans would be interested? We could even take Anthonis along. There'll be room for novices."

"He's not interested in anything these days," Klara replied fretfully, wondering if Berti wanted refreshment. She looked like a petulant child, and Berti realized not for the first time how young she was.

"*Klärchen,* how old are you?" He pulled her closer.

She did not protest but stayed on guard.

"On the first Sunday of Advent I will be sixteen."

Berti calculated and whistled: "You were a child when you and Hans ... "

The stiff waist eased, but Klara's strong spine kept distance between them. Her cheeks were full of inner fire, begging to be kissed.

Berti stopped whistling. "Is Hans coming back soon so I can tell him the good news?"

"*Nein.*" Her red lips pursed in displeasure formed a full rose. "He left earlier than usual because the days are getting shorter, and he and Anthonis have a lot to finish."

Berti dropped the ribbons on the floor and embraced Klara. *"Bärtchen!"* she protested a bit as he tasted her lips. His were firm and demanding, and Klara's knees buckled.

"Liebling Klara, you're like a *Stopsel."* He lifted her onto the bench.

"I'm not a cork, and if you would please put me down I can show you that my legs reach the ground." Childishly, she pounded his chest as he swung her sideways into his arms.

"Don't worry, *Liebchen.* I won't hurt you," he coached her sweetly as he bent to her lips and brushed them playfully with his own.

"Hush! Be careful," she murmured as his warmth melted her breath. Berti took her to the end of the kitchen where the conjugal bed was behind a curtain. *"Bärtchen"*—she arched her back as he laid her down—"isn't this sin?"

"Don't worry, *mein Schatz.* You know Gregory has promised an indulgence to everyone who visits at least four churches in Rome next year. Are you planning to die before that?"

How skilled his fingers were as he untangled her laces!

"Ach, lieber Gott!" Reality dawned on Klara, finding her breasts bare. She tried to tighten her bodice. How often had he admired Klara nursing her babe! Never more gently than now, he moved Klara's protesting hands as he came closer, tasting each delicate morsel, unwrapping it little by little and savoring it as if time stood still.

"I'm cold." Klara protested as her skin tingled on the bleached linen.

Berti dropped his britches and knelt. Klara stared so naively that he could hardly keep himself straight. "Are we going to chase the devil into the hell?"

Berti paused, unsure how to proceed. She hugged her knees tightly.

"Well, are we?" She smiled and reached toward him impishly.

"Are you really cold?"

"Ja." She began to shiver and pulled her hand back.

"But you don't like playing the hell game, do you?"

"Not with Hans."

"Forget Hans. Now *I am* your angel." He kissed the tip of her cold nose. "And you are my heaven. Believe me. Will you let me in?"

He thrust his tongue between the shivering lips, and she met him halfway. In the old language of her kind, she locked her legs around him while her skin tingled under his breast.

"*Bärtchen!*" she cried out. "Will your snake poison me like Frau Schneider's belly?"

"Don't worry," Berti gasped in the agony of pleasure. "My angel has wings, and he'll fly away like a little birdie so he can come back again soon."

The stout matrons found Klara strangely mature when she joined them at the next spinning session, and she stopped pestering Hans to give her a son in a kiss. Advent's approach brought their pleasures to a sudden halt, though, since Berti was obliged to satisfy the touchy padres of the little church by the Trevi fountain with a finished job.

† † †

Alessandro's new commission proved more difficult than Berti expected.

He tried a number of compositions, but none pleased him. If the painting were to be memorable, it must be novel; to honor Maddalena it should also be beautiful; but above all it had to demonstrate the magnanimity of the man who built Il Gesù for Rome and his own glory.

He worked all afternoon, and when he had wasted too many precious sheets of paper on sketches, he grew impatient and drew directly on the floor with a lump of charcoal. The studio's large window overlooked a courtyard lined by the service buildings of the small *palazzo* he shared with Adrien. As he knelt on the floor, the late afternoon sun shone a beam of light through a circular opening above the window and framed the shadow of his head in an oval halo.

"Why didn't I think of that?" He smacked his forehead squarely, picked up the charcoal, and outlined his head in the oval light on the floor with the abundant hair of both the biblical woman and Alessandro's mistress.

Jumping up, he wiped the charcoal dust from his hands and grabbed a new sheet of paper. Soon he was refining the black chalk outlines with pen and ink, adding the details of a young woman whose torso pushed out of the oval frame. One hand pressed a crucifix against her bosom, while the other rested on one of two skulls supporting a smaller oval with Alessandro's portrait, her abundant hair embracing her shoulders and arms, cascading past the oval frame.

He hurried, remembering plans for a night with Adrien, although he could not quite remember the name of the new, elegant brothel his clever friend had discovered.

"What in heaven are you doing here, Klara?" Berti stood horrified in the door and pulled her in. The banging was loud enough to raise the dead. "Is everything all right?"

She smiled, so he kissed her proprietarily.

"Where's Hans?" He held her close. Still shivering from the winter dampness, she embraced him hungrily and sank her face into his doublet, seeking the bare skin under his shirt.

"Are you mad, running through the dark streets by yourself?"

"Hans is at the Anima. Some church meeting. You know those pious men and the Jubilee. And my friend's minding Berta."

Berti's jaw dropped. "Is it safe?"

"*Ja*," Klara nodded wisely. "I do the same when her husband's gone."

"Lord, you made them smarter than we like sometimes," he mused to himself, then asked Klara, forgetting his plans. "How much time do we have?"

Klara heaved a sigh. "About two hours. Then you must take me home."

"Who are you talking to?" Adrien shouted from the top of the steps, tying his collar. "Ready? Gertgen is waiting outside." He ran briskly down the stairs.

Berti hid Klara's face against him. "I'll join you later," he replied, still trying to recall the name of the new meeting place. He looked at Klara's flushed cheeks.

"That's the name of the place. The Red Hen."

Their new lodging by Santi Apostoli was nothing like the prince-bishop's palace, but Klara thought it was paradise. She ran around like a child, touching everything, reveling in the beauty of wealth. God and certainly not Berti understood how Adrien managed his business affairs, but whatever he touched turned to gold. Klara could hardly rest for a moment.

"Please!" She pushed him away impatiently as she tried the settee by the hearth. "Let me try this out." Berti heard the town crier go by as she took off her shoes.

"*Gut*," he agreed roguishly and picked her up and changed seats with her. "What pretty legs," he murmured, making her comfortable in his lap. She loved surprises. He tickled her bare toes, and she wriggled her warm nose into his beard. He scratched her back, and she quivered with delight. In no time he felt her skin against his. He kissed her pink rosebuds, and she melted with passion. When their games found the moment, she battled her foe with youthful fire.

Footsteps sounded by the front gate "Adrien! What are you doing back?" Berti grunted at his friend's timing.

"You womanizer!" Adrien retorted in Flemish. "Can't you at least go up? And what am I doing here? I *live* here. You got me so confused that I forgot my skins." He opened and closed various compartments in the tall cabinet in the front hall. Then the noise ceased abruptly.

"Is that you, Klara?" Adrien stepped back, recognizing her dress.

"Adrien! For goodness sake. Just go on!" Berti tried to capture the lost moment, but Klara was upset. "Damn fellow," he cursed, trying to soften her face with kisses. "*Liebchen,* you must have known he would eventually find out!"

"Not like this," the shamed wife whimpered into his ruffled shirt.

"Now, now. Why don't I show you the rest of the place?" Berti offered, hoping for peace. Adrien would be gone in a minute or two.

"Can you carry me upstairs?" she pled mischievously, ready to forget about Adrien.

"I can try." He flexed his muscles, for Hans' wife was substantial.

"Will you forgive me?" she whispered timidly and nuzzled his whiskers.

"Nothing to forgive," he grumbled. "It wasn't your fault." Panting under her weight, he dropped her unceremoniously on the bed.

"Please don't," Klara exclaimed, unsure of his dark face. "Can you take me home now?" Pinned under him, she fumbled for the stays of her bodice.

"Not until I'm done, *Liebchen.* Without interruptions."

He pushed her back and took a slug of spirits. After he drained the cup, he loved her crudely until she filled to the brim. When he finished, he took her home, barely sober enough to find his way to Campo Marzo and The Red Hen.

Childish Klara was sweet, and Berti soon made peace. While Rome received crowds of strangers, some of them visiting Adrien's and Berti's house, no neighbors seemed to notice her visiting him. If Berti felt uncomfortable cheating on his good friend, he worried little about it. Neglecting Maddalena bothered him more.

"Welcome, pilgrim." The lady recognized his footsteps one afternoon and offered her cheek. "You feel tired," she noted as she fingered his face.

Berti looked around the kitchen, darkened by the shutters filtering out the late afternoon heat. "It's always so neat here," he wondered. He praised Antonella, ready to filch a crumb from the almond paste she was cutting into neat slices and dipping in sugar crystals.

"Do you have guests tonight?" Berti inquired.

"No, sir." Antonella slapped his fingers stealing toward the bowl on the table. "We sell the sweets and use the money for the poor who come to us. Begging your pardon, sir, but I'm busy." She turned away and began circling the kitchen, stepping into the pantry, peeking into pots, taking dishes out of the cupboard, too preoccupied to worry about the little confit thief.

"Good morning, boys." Berti pulled out trumpets and wooden swords for Beltraffio's two youngest. "Where's Stefano? I have a present for him too."

"He went to the market with his big brother. Jacopo's back from Bologna. Why didn't you come see us?" Maddalena reproached him mildly and turned away. Her profile shadowed the wall in the rising light, and he could not help admiring the woman who once enchanted the Farnese Cardinal. Her beauty seemed more ethereal than ever.

"Is Jacopo at the palace?"

Maddalena nodded. She was happy for Beltraffio's eldest, happy that Alessandro found a replacement for his son, one he could love openly since he was not his own. She could not, however, reconcile herself to her own loss.

"Lena, you comfort so many. Can't you comfort yourself?"

Maddalena reached for her bosom and the invisible cross.

"My friend, God knows I've tried, but he does not want to help me. He chose a different fate for me." She righted herself and found her poise. "I heard about your new fresco. I so wish I could see it. One day I will, when I return on my wings."

Berti swallowed with an uneasy feeling. "Don't talk that way."

She touched his face, pulsing with fatigue. "Have you been working too hard?"

"I worked late last night." He looked at the woman whose beauty he was resurrecting on canvas. "I haven't told you about my new job. Forgive me. I've been too busy." He described his meeting with Alessandro and told her about the altarpiece and the painting of St. Magdalen.

Maddalena sat up stiffly. "He still loves me then."

Berti kissed her forehead and sat beside her.

"We all love you, we all need you. I know I do." It was his turn to cry. "Lena, I've sinned greatly." He began telling her about Klara, hoping she would not judge him too harshly.

Instead she wove her fingers through his thick hair to calm him. "The Lord is wise and forgiving." She guided him like a little boy through the tunnels of his darkness. "You must forget Klara and ask for Hans' forgiveness."

"Ask me anything but that!"

How easy it was to sin and how hard to face one's transgressions.

"Give me time!" he begged.

"It's not up to me," she replied. "Only you can make peace with Christ and with those you wronged. Understand?" She took his head, and in her palms he felt incredible power.

"I do." He kissed each and left her house a new man. Maddalena felt changed too, feeling closer to the man she still loved.

† † †

Between the eve of Christ's birth and the new year of Our Lord 1575, the Eternal City basked in the glory of being the holiest on earth. As Gregory solemnly opened the Holy Gate to St. Peter's, Berti watched among the masses. Although the pontiff forbade the carnival that customarily followed Advent, Romans found ways to get around.

Berti was of two minds. He yearned to join his friends in their nocturnal frolic, but he resolved to start the new year with the prescribed pilgrimage to the seven basilicas. As he climbed the Holy Steps on his knees he began to feel better about hurting Hans, but despite his promise to Maddalena, he could not face him. He spent a lot of time at the new drawing school at Anthonis' inn and enjoyed the companionship, but he was uncomfortable in Hans' presence.

"What will you do?" Adrien asked him, afraid that Berti had lost his pepper.

"I must find the right moment to tell him. God knows, it was hard enough to tell Klara. Damn it, women are always unreliable in a crisis. Adrien, why is it that I always catch their wrong side?"

"I think you're wrong."

Berti blinked uncertainly. "What about Alba? Then Lena. And now Klara?"

"Let me tell you something." Adrien closed his ledger, seeing that Berti was disturbed. "Alba's death was not your fault. You were so carried away that you never understood there was a full moon that night. Besides, Bart, I always said there was something strange about her."

"Don't say that!"

"As far as Maddalena is concerned," Adrien continued, "you were a servant, a pawn in Alessandro's hands."

"But I should have known!"

"Known what?"

"That he's like everybody else, no better and no worse, and that he'd discard her soon."

"From what you tell me, he didn't quite do that. By the way, have you seen the bastard ogling that young ward of his in the church?"

Berti gnashed his teeth. "Beltraffio's son? That's preposterous!"

"That's exactly what you said about the prince-bishop and Cornelis."

"Shut up!"

"What's bothering you today?" Adrien came closer, but Berti nudged him away.

"Sit." Adrien pushed him down. "What really happened?"

"Might as well tell you. Remember the night you found us? First I got mad, then I got drunk, and now it looks like I also got her with child."

"What's the problem? Hans wants a son, doesn't he? They all do!"

"Don't be vulgar, Adrien."

"He shares her bed from time to time, doesn't he?"

Berti confronted the truth, but without relief. "*Ja.* He does his best."

"Hans needn't know. Klara won't tell him, will she?"

"That goose?" Berti snorted. "She's pleased more than you know."

Adrien turned on his heel, searching for the right words.

"Look, my esteemed friend, the laws of love are stronger than all others. Think of Lot and his daughters. Haven't you heard of fathers lying with daughters and brothers with sisters? So what is it to you? Hans is just a friend. You acted only as lady love bade you."

Berti considered his words. Some of his friends had a convenient way of seeing life.

"You should blame Lady Fortune, not yourself. She's the goddess that gave Hans a fine wife like Klara whom he neglects for his mistress—art. And you? You have a soft heart, and Klara's beauty deserves to be appreciated." Adrien folded his arms across his chest. "Can't you see? With a pious husband she would have never tasted life's greatest gift?"

Berti still looked glum.

"I should stop seeing her, but she may not let me. What do I do? I'm such a wretch!"

"Save the lament! Let's cheer up. The Brill brothers are giving another party tonight. What do you say? Will you come?"

Berti cocked his head, thinking. "I can't. I promised Maddalena."

"Let's review the situation again. You've lain with your friend's wife and will make him happy with a son. How is that different from the time you put horns on Pietro Portinari and took money for it?" Adrien was exhausted. He preferred to leave his wits for business and then find pleasure in life. Everything else was immaterial.

† † †

The letter from Gianbologna was short, cheerful, and informative, but with unpleasant tidings. Stunned, Berti picked it up again, searching for the passage that stopped his blood. He always found the Fleming blunt like the hammer blows that shaped his statues. So was his letter.

> *I do not know if you have heard, but La Mammola took her life. Some rumors in the Medici circles blame Francesco's wife, but most of us believe the* principessa *would never stoop so low. Some say a young man broke her heart, and others that her heart stopped beating a long time ago, when our most gracious patron abandoned her for his noble mistress, the arts. I will cast a small bronze of the diva as a sleeping Psyche visited by Eros to immortalize her for his new* studiolo.

Berti dropped the letter to examine his hands, elegant, with finesse of touch, as reliable in trade as in the art of pleasure. Whether they held the tools of his craft, fingered a fine bolt of cloth, or pinched a lady's breast, they were skilled, efficient, and obedient.

He squinted into the light pouring through the open shutters and examined an ink stain on his index finger. For a man who used the quill with the accomplished draftsman's bravura, the stain looked clumsy. Spitting on the offending digit, he rubbed the stain. Then he took a fresh sheet of paper, sharpened his quill, dipped it into the inkwell, and began with resolute strokes.

My Esteemed Compatriot. It pleases me to hear that your career at the court of your most generous patron is blessed with nothing but success and contentment. My own career here in the Eternal City also continues to bloom under the smiling eye of Lady Fortune. So much so that I find myself at a crossroad.

He laid the quill on the table, cracked his knuckles, and walked to the window. The city's sounds rose enticingly, nudging him, enthralling him with their pulsating life. He still had to finish the two paintings of St. Magdalen, and he was not sure he felt like repairing Hans' flowering fresco as he had promised the padres at the Trevi church.

"Yes, Gertgen?" He spotted the valet's shadow from the corner of his eye.

"Master, a message for you," the servant replied with apprehension.

Berti broke the seal. The padres could wait no longer. Either he agreed to stabilize Hans' fresco, or they would hire the newcomer, Aert Mytens.

"The devil they will," he muttered, annoyed.

"Master, the padres have been after you for a week," Gertgen offered diplomatically.

"Run down," Berti replied, "and tell them I begin tomorrow at daybreak. I'm too busy now. Tomorrow we can reach a mutually satisfactory agreement."

If the padres insisted on repairing the damage before the air was suitably warm, that was not his problem, he reminded himself. Knowing that he needed to put his warning in writing, he turned back to the table. Gianbologna's letter sat on top of the pile of papers. The passage jumped out clearly:

While flattered by the generous offers of the Imperial Chancellor Wolf Rumpff, I dare not disappoint the archduke by leaving Florence. But I have been persuaded to part with my finest apprentice Hans Mont, whom I am willing to send in my stead. As for the Italian-trained painter of northern birth His Imperial Majesty the Emperor Maximilian demands, I have recommended you as someone who would satisfy his needs.

Berti stirred. The Emperor's offer seems promising, but no contract for anything of substance was offered, only piece-work. It was a long way to cross the Alps without knowing what the next day would bring.

He was not ready to leave Rome. He began writing.

My friend, although indebted to you, I must gratefully decline the Emperor's offer. Despite my increasing restlessness, I haven't reached the terminus of my journey. But, should I receive a contract as the emperor's official Kammermaler, *I would be most honored to cross the Alps to serve a new master.*

With a few flourishes Berti finished, signed, and sealed the letter with a firm hand.

The pontiff strictly forbade carnival festivities, but nothing prevented Romans from celebrating the sanctity of the year with song and dance in their homes. Having changed his mind about his promise to Maddalena, Berti dressed carefully, although he pulled up his silk hose and laced his codpiece with the insouciance of someone sure of not needing it far into the evening.

† † †

Early next morning, an exhausted Berti climbed the temporary scaffold. It was not strong, but he did not worry. Most of all, he needed good light to remove the soft sections of the fresco cleanly without damaging the solid parts. The padres were anxious to get the plaster dust out quickly, and they refused to obstruct the chapel with anything cumbersome. He had barely scraped away a section, when Karl appeared below. As usual, he looked dapper, carrying a sword at his side as did Berti, a privilege granted by the pope to a select few.

"I know you're busy, but come down and celebrate with me," Karl invited him, holding up a full basket from which a leather flask stood up prominently.

"What about?"

Karl puffed his chest. "Congratulate me! I am going to Terni, to work for Count Spada."

In his excitement, Berti turned around, forgetting the loose plaster in the ceiling, and it crashed down in a cloud of dust.

"Madman! I said celebrate, not bury me!" Karl yelled, dusting off his velvet *biretta*.

Berti climbed down, watching the thin boards arch unpleasantly.

"Thunder and lightning! When we signed our names in the Golden Grotto of Nero last year and made our wishes, I didn't think you would be famous this soon!" Berti hugged Karl with so much heartfelt enthusiasm that the plaster on Karl's clothes rose up in a cloud.

"Come and take a break. The sun's warm," Karl pleaded.

Berti hesitated. "Only for a minute. Otherwise the padres will eat me alive!"

They settled down, facing the Trevi fountain with their backs against the church.

"Tell me, your new patron, this Count Spada, where does he get his money?"

"He comes from an established family."

"And the project. Can you manage it by yourself?" Berti rubbed his back against the wall.

"Not entirely sure of the details, except that I know the frescoes I've been commissioned to paint will depict the gory story of St. Bartholomew's night."

"Good luck and farewell. Otherwise your count will have your head off!"

"That's not funny," Karl observed dryly, "because *spada* means sword. Sometimes you're obtuse, my friend. *Il Spada* is a gentleman."

Berti checked the sun. "I have to get back. When are you leaving?"

"Not until the Feast of the Lord's Ascension."

"I'll see you before then."

Karl patted his back. "Hope Maddalena is well," he yelled back across the square.

The job was messy, and Berti regretted accepting it; but Hans was working for Gregory, and he owed him more than friendship.

Not much remained of the afternoon. He filled the hole with new plaster, taking care to mix it right and attach it to the healthy foundation. The rest was easy, mechanically repainting the damaged section. He worked feverishly and was ready to quit when the boards heaved beneath him.

"Hans! You scared the wits out of me! Watch out! The boards are not strong. Not enough for two. I hope you like the way your fresco is coming along." Berti chattered, but Hans stood strangely silent. The light was dim, and the darkness accented Hans' paleness.

Berti lit a lantern and lifted it to Hans' face as the boards heaved. "Are you well?"

"Why didn't you tell me! You son of a cur."

Berti was in turmoil. He was no coward, but he did not want to hurt Hans. After all, once he was his best friend in Rome. "Hans," he mumbled but did not know what else to say.

"It's your son, not mine, isn't it?" Hans' voice echoed in the space. A few of the devout gathered below. Although they conversed in Flemish, the assembly below clearly sensed tragedy in the air.

"I wanted to tell you about it! Believe me, I wanted to. I even promised Lena."

"Bastard! Coward!" Hans stepped forward. "I welcomed you in my home like the brother you nearly could be."

"Hans, please, can we talk about it somewhere else? This is the house of the Lord."

Berti froze as Hans came nearer, his face purple with rage.

"Did you think about what the Lord would say when you lay with my wife and put the horns on me?" Hans spat across the scaffold. That insult was hard to bear.

Berti took his friend's first punch square in the face, as he deserved. They staggered on the narrow boards, the lantern swinging wildly, light dancing across the frescoes as the men struggled in the chapel vault. From the corner of his eye, Berti saw the rector running in, but Hans punched him in the stomach. The floor whirled under him.

"Hans, for the love of God, forgive me! Stop! Please!"

The boards groaned, but Hans was too furious to hear it. Pride excluded reason, and his heart forgot forgiveness. Berti put up his free arm to take the next blow. Hans lunged forward. A loud crack ripped the air as the wood suddenly splintered and the men crashed onto the stone pavement. The crowd babbled and ran to them as a spill from the lamp fueled a narrow line of fire.

"Eternal curses on you, you heathen, fighting under the Lord's roof!" The rector pulled off his heavy cloak and threw it over the fire. "Are you hurt?" Berti heard his voice and felt himself being lifted from a soft body. His vision was pricked with a thousand stars, and his ears were about to explode. Oddly, he felt only very bruised.

"I think so." He struggled to stand. Hans lay without a sign of life. Berti tried to focus, but his legs gave way.

† † †

"Karl? Adrien?"

Slowly, the faces of Berti's two friends came in and out of his limited line of focus.

"Don't move," both answered in unison.

Pain shot through Berti's neck. He then remembered what happened. "Hans! Where's Hans?"

Karl and Adrien looked at each other.

"Is he alive?" Berti blurted, awash in fear.

"Hans is in the hospital of Santo Spirito," Adrien volunteered.

"Will he live?"

"I think so." Adrien exchanged a glance with Karl.

"What are you hiding from me?" Berti tried to sit up. The hair on his arms stood.

"Bart … " Karl laid him back. "Hans is alive, but they think he broke his back."

"Merciful God! I am the lowest debaucher and no less than a murderer." Berti choked on his words and turned his face to the wall.

"Don't say that," Karl pled. "Hans will live. He has to. His talents can't be wasted."

Berti pulled the pillow over his head and broke down, sobbing.

"How can I go on knowing that I killed my best friend?"

Adrien drew a startled breath. He never saw Berti lose control so. He reached out to comfort him.

Berti recoiled. "Leave me alone!"

For three weeks the nuns of Santo Spirito fought to save Hans' life. When the Lord answered their prayers and he regained consciousness, his friends realized he might never walk.

Still badly bruised from the fall, Berti soon visited the seven prescribed churches in Rome in penance. From the last stop at St. Peter's, he went to the Santo Spirito to see Hans.

Later with Maddalena, he still could not comprehend what he saw, a living corpse propped on pillows, changed and fed like a newborn. "Lena," he said, his voice seething with anguish, "how can I begin to describe that wreck of a man who once called me friend?"

"Tell me about it," she encouraged him patiently. "You'll feel better, when you do."

"You've no idea, Lena. He looks like a bloated fish. His skin is sallow like lard, puffed up and punctured by pools of rotting blood. Something must have broken in his chest, because awful noises come out when he breathes. And his feet and hands ... " Berti trembled imagining them. "They're shapeless, full of air, like a pig's bladder. His whole body looks like that, like he could fly."

"It's not air. Probably impure liquids are trying to escape and can't. Can he speak?"

"Sometimes he rants without sense, and when he calms down, he says such awful things. Lena, I feel so horrible, so miserable. But Christ! What can *I do* to help?"

"Don't take the Lord's name in vain!" Maddalena replied and quickly reminded Berti of her own recovery. "Hans will get better, Berti, and the Lord will show him how to forgive you."

Berti hung his head. "Do you think I'm as bad as some make me out to be?"

"Would I be here with you if I did? No one who did what you did for me can be evil. Klara's charm led you astray."

Berti shook his head. "She was willing. She even came to me. She wouldn't let go."

"Men are stronger than women."

Confusion colored Berti's voice. "That's not what you said before."

"Forget what I told you. The world has changed since then."

"Not true."

"You're wrong. Look around. Pius hasn't even been buried, and Gregory, and please, don't misunderstand me, would like to see the church restored once again to its full glory and he her greatest advocate."

Berti sat down and stood, again. "What are you saying, Lena?"

"Watch the world changing back to the way it was. The priests are hungry for fame, glory, and wealth, all in the name of Christ." Maddalena's voice quivered with fear. "Ask yourself, who will have to come again and die for the second time to save us all from eternal damnation. Brother will kill brother, and parents will renounce their children. I see fires, I see dead bodies, I see men with crosses, all fighting in the name of the same God, but speaking different languages, wanting different things."

He watched the blind woman, and the future looked black. He shivered.

"But to you I want to give hope, not despair." She shook her head as if to chase the vision away. "Tell me, will Hans listen to you or anyone else? Would he see me?"

"I'm not sure," he thought. "Lena, it's horrible to look at him. I can't tell you."

"How's his wife? Could you take me to her? How did Hans find out?"

"Frau Margrethe told him. When Klara came to see me, she looked after little Berta. Klara did the same for her when she cheated on the blacksmith. And, no, I don't think Klara is sorry. If anything, she's angry with me for dropping her like hot coals."

"I don't understand why the blacksmith's wife went to Hans."

"Man's follies, Lena. They make no sense. When I swore to Klara that I would not, could not possibly see her again, Frau Margrethe thought Klara tried to steal her own lover away."

"That's rubbish," Maddalena thought. "I can't believe Klara is so perverted. She's a child. If she were crazy about you, she would not want another man on a whim."

"Klara is a child. She also likes playing with fire. But what do I know? What matters is that Frau Margrethe played a dirty game and told Hans, the only way she thought she could keep her young lover. Hans didn't take long to figure out who was father of his new child."

"So you're going to be a father."

God help him! Berti had not thought about that problem.

"That's important now, more than you think," Maddalena said.

"Maybe I should take the emperor's offer and go to Vienna."

"That would be running away. Is that what you want people to think?"

"I don't know anything any more," Berti thought. "My friends don't condemn me. People were there in the church. They saw the fight. They saw the accident. I didn't want it to happen."

"And I am not the first man to bed a friend's wife."

"Berti, you're not sorry for sharing Hans' wife, but you're sorry you were caught?"

"No, Lena!" he cried hoarsely. "I fear the wrath of God. I'm afraid I'll burn in hell."

Berti got up abruptly and left Maddalena's house, unaware that the sign of her cross would follow him to a bitter end.

St. Magdalen

Alessandro's life changed after Maddalena's return. Nothing could replace her, but Jacopo slowly displaced her. With tight curls and hazel eyes, he reminded Alessandro of Berti, although Jacopo was soft-spoken and effeminate. Bologna was far and Jacopo's studies demanding, but the cardinal spared no money to keep his ward around.

They leafed through manuscripts, studied coins and gems, and often Alessandro was not sure whether his art collection or his ward's admiration for it delighted him more. Before Jacopo realized it, he too became one of the cardinal's precious possessions, a seraph to be treasured for the joys *extraordinaires*. In his company, Alessandro continued his existence, collecting works of art, bringing *Il Gesù* to completion, and pursuing his hopeless dream.

When Berti passed Jacopo in the palace, floating on a cloud of self-importance, he wondered why Alessandro asked for a private version of St. Magdalen, when it was clear he had been unfaithful to her. In Berti's altarpiece for the newly consecrated chapel in Il Gesù, animal skins and her own hair covered the saint, but in the palace chapel, a tawny breast incited yet a different kind of adoration.

A man's taste is not to be disputed, especially not *il gran cardinale's*. He never looked at another woman, as he once promised Maddalena, praying to her image with the same breath that he next dedicated to his ward, renewed in his determination to carry the next papal election.

He traveled between Rome, Naples, Caprarola, and Capodimonte, still enjoying his palaces and villas, but less frequently. All the while sickness and age increased upon him. Growing more pious outwardly, with Jacopo he fell victim to all the depravities Maddalena abhorred.

When she heard about Alessandro's new life guided by powers greater than hers, she wept. When occasionally their paths crossed, Berti could not meet the cardinal's gaze. Yet Alessandro's money paved Rome, and Berti was not rich enough to snub the man who fed and protected him for so long.

† † †

"And then what happened?" Hans exhaled, learning again to use his lungs.

Anthony Santvoort checked his pocket for a piece of paper. "Messer Vecchi came by and left his best wishes. He also reminded me of the fine we got for working in that damned church without paying the guild's dues. I tried to explain that you were ... that you cannot pay."

"To hell with them, Toni, but thank you for the collection. How can I repay you?" Hans looked around. The modest quarters behind the inn that Anthonis provided for Hans' family were clean and his without obligation. "Maybe we can run the school together," he suggested. "If we collect a small fee, it should repay your burden."

"Don't worry, Hans. My aunt is happy to help her Christian friends and count me in too. She says God will remember her good deeds. That reminds me, I have to run. With all the pilgrims, we could hire more helpers and still not catch up!"

Hans grinned crookedly.

He had use of his chest and arms; the rest of his body he viewed with hostility. After Anthonis left, he slumped in the chair. He heard the birds chirping and wanted to enjoy their song, but resignation shrouded him. He wanted to rest, but the inn's infernal racket carried into the back rooms—wheels rattled, doors banged, and chanting pilgrims passed continuously. When the noise subsided, he heard his baby daughter whimper and wheeze. Klara was often away now, helping in the kitchen with the inn's extra guests.

Hans braced himself against the chair and wedged his back into the open spaces between the slats. The pain in his upper back contrasted with the numb chill in his legs. If he could swing himself onto the bed, he could rest and escape the nagging ache. He rolled the chair to the curtain separating the corner bed from the rest of the room and pushed his legs out toward the low straw mattress when the wheeled chair rolled from underneath him and spilled him out. He lay helpless on the floor, his face splayed against the cold boards.

Before long, the door opened and wheels hummed. He heard an unfamiliar voice soothing his daughter, frightened by the crash. Then small fingers worked to turn him over. The girl was young and he helpless, heavier than a stone. They both struggled until he managed to pull himself onto the mattress, resting his face against the coarse linen, breathing hard.

"Let him who stands beware lest he fall." An unearthly voice sounded above him. The sound of wheels stopped. He turned his head and saw nothing but an aura of light. "Do not sink into the darkness from which you came." The voice was kind but firm.

"Who are you?" Hans mumbled. A celestial warmth seem to enclose him.

"Your eyes are the lamp of the body. If your sight is clear, you'll shine with goodness. If you see evil, you'll be consumed by it."

Hans twisted his neck but could not see. The light was blinding.

"Who said that?" He scrambled up on his elbows until his face hit the wall. "Who are you? You have a girl's hands." His head spun. He pushed the greasy hair out of his face and saw a throne of majesty. Angels hovered sweetly above.

"Is it the Virgin?" Hans wondered. A figure in a mantle of heavenly blue braced herself against the throne with a foot in a golden slipper. A child in a linen shirt sat in her lap, smiling and stretching its palms toward him. The child spoke: "Father, Berta is hungry!"

Hans trembled. His mind played tricks on him.

"My child, is that you?" He tried to pull himself closer to look into a sightless face. "Maddalena, wretched sinner!" he recoiled. "What are you doing under my roof?"

He averted his face, forgetting she was blind.

She shifted the child in her lap, turning her head in the direction of his voice.

"Has *he* sent you to me?" Hans' voice gushed venom. "I told him God will judge all fornicators and adulterers alike! Get out of my house, Maddalena! Curse you and all sinners!"

Turning the chair's wheels with both hands, she came closer.

"Hans, man's wrath pleases the Lord no more than does his pride," she admonished. "Weep over your misery, and He will console you as you forgive others. Turn to Him, and you will no longer be afraid; believe in Him, and you will be blessed."

"Satan's harlot!" Hans squared his shoulders. "Who do you think you are to preach to me? I opened my house to that villain. I would have shared everything with him, everything! My life, my talent, my wisdom, my sweet child, everything but my *wife!* He stole her and defiled my house. If God chooses to pardon sinners, I can't help it, but don't you ask me to forgive *him!*"

"Help me down." Maddalena handed Berta to Antonella and reached for her crutches. "Guide me to him," she said softly. Hans recoiled as from a snake but was helpless as Lena felt her way toward him and reached for his hand.

"Hans, we are all sinners. That is why Christ died for us, so we can live on eternally in His grace. You have your child and a wife who loves you. She is a good Christian woman. I have no family, but other people love me."

Hans gazed into Lena's sightless face, and reality dawned on him. He was crippled, true, but he could see, and people did care for him. "Lena, it's been hard, the Lord testing me thus."

"How could I not know?" she whispered and clasped his hand as it met hers. "I do. But you must have faith." A brilliant light shining from Maddalena lit every corner of the dark room, as her fingers blessed his face, down his neck and his back to his lame legs.

He pushed her away, blinded by the aura of her miracle, and cried, "I believe!"

"I know, Hans, and time will help." She offered him her crutches and scrambled onto her knees. Antonella helped her into the chair, and they left.

He never saw her again to show her how well he came to walk.

† † †

The ides of March came weeping mist and warmth, and then came more rain and mud. Berti and Karl stepped out into air smelling of new growth. The grass had doubled overnight, and so had the weeds, filling every crack with their springy leaves.

"I'm glad you came to see me before you left." Berti lifted the hem of his cloak and jumped a puddle. "Rome won't be the same without you!"

"What's this melancholy?" his friend demanded. "I won't leave for a while, if I do at all. Are you going?"

"I've been thinking about Maximilian's offer."

"I'll be sorry to see *you* go, but I understand your motive."

"Do you, Karl?" Berti snapped. "How could you?"

"Wouldn't anyone grab a deal like that? I would."

"The emperor's offer is attractive enough, but as I've told you, it offers no security. Maximilian is ailing, and that son of his ... What will *he* do when his father dies?"

"Yes, the emperor is a crypto-Lutheran, and his sons are no different, even if they were brought up Catholic. But what does that have to do with art? You don't have to be Catholic to be a patron!" As Karl spoke, he wanted to recant. The Protestants looted and whitewashed all the churches during the recent religious storms in their country.

But Berti was not listening. "Can you wait for me?" He turned to Santvoort's inn and swung the gate open. "I must see Toni before we take our walk. Or if you want to, come in. I have no secrets from you."

They found Anthonis lost in his accounts at the back counter. Since Hans' accident, he could not find work as a painter, but like most people, he held no grudge against Berti. To mount a temporary scaffold bound on revenge was insanity.

"*Morgen*," he replied to Berti's and Karl's greeting. "Have you come to help me? Doing numbers is not my forte."

"Collecting coins is?"

Anthonis grinned sheepishly. There were many more guests that year, and his Aunt Anna shared generously, now that she had him back. He had not told her about his plans to open a workshop when he had enough saved.

"Toni, don't worry," he said. "You'll soon find your place. You have a few years to catch up to me, eh? And when I leave … "

"You've changed your mind again?" Anthonis' face puckered in surprise.

"Constantly," Berti laughed, "but maybe I won't this time." He pulled a small leather pouch from his doublet and emptied it. When Anthonis' candle lit the diamond pin, Karl stood back, shocked. "Bart! Is that Alessandro's gift?"

"What's this?" Anthonis gaped at the great diamond. He had never seen it so near.

"Let's get things straight. I don't want any sermons from either of you. Tony, I want you to take this to the shops by the river where you can get the best price. Invest this for Hans, and should something happen to him, God forbid, let Klara return to Augsburg with her children."

"Hans would never accept any help from you."

"For an fairly good businessman, you're plain stupid. He won't know. I'm sure you can think of something. If not, ask your clever aunt." Berti admired the pin for the last time before kissing it and laying it on the counter. "I hope it will help him more than I did. Come on, Karl, don't stand there." He laughed, feeling good for the first time in days. "This is not a funeral. Let's go for that walk! Enjoy your ledgers, Toni." Berti shook his hand and left.

Karl caught up with him outside. "I don't care what you say, *you* must be going." He stopped in the middle of the road, shimmering in the soft drizzle. "Why not now?"

"Do I have to swear to you that I don't know whether I am going or not?"

"Why the hell not?"

"If you must know, I can't leave Lena."

"Don't you be a fool! She's fine. She's happy. People will look after her. You know that. Alessandro may even love her again."

"I don't know why. I can't leave her. It's as simple as that." Berti looked up into the clouds and remembered the hot afternoon nearly eight years earlier when he first saw Lena. There had been no clouds in the sky that day. Life was grand and simple then.

The drizzle ceased, and once again azure colored the skies.

"Shall we walk down toward the *campo?*"

"Certainly. Now tell me, what will you do for the emperor if you do go?"

"How should I know? Probably paint some frescoes at the imperial court or maybe some other work. All I know is that everything must be done in the Italian style to please the old man."

"I suppose that's why we're all here. Would you be the court painter?"

"I don't think so," Berti replied gloomily.

"What's eating you today?" Too busy scolding, Adrien tripped over stone artifacts imbedded in the roadway. "Too bad it's been so wet! I've hardly sketched any of these things lately."

"You and your boring old stones." Berti grumped.

As they passed the Colosseum, Karl looked up and said, "I'll bet you have never once drawn this magnificent building!"

"You're right and you're wrong!"

"Which is it?"

"I certainly did *not* sketch it here on paper, but I did draw it from *memory* and painted it. That little piece got me started."

"You're a barbarian! I bet anything I own that you won't do any studies of antiquities when you cross the Alps," Karl muttered.

"Absolutely right."

They walked silently for a while. The fields were muddy, and they studied the ground as if it were about to disgorge a new treasure. The soft ground sported patches of new grass, and tiny daisies dotted the meadows.

"Where are we going?" Karl asked. "To San Giovanni by Porta Latina? We should have come on horseback. Why didn't you tell me?"

"Just taking the air." But contrary to his word, Berti turned into the path to the buried Golden House of Nero and followed it down into the damp cavity.

"Do you always walk around with candles?" Karl laughed at Berti.

"Sometimes," Berti replied and walked toward a dark wall. "Remember?" He pointed to Karl's signature and the date, 1574.

Karl nodded. "That was last year, and we hardly knew each other then. I was fresh from Florence and like a fool went back with you and Lena. I'm going to miss you." He clasped Berti to his bosom. "Friends for life?"

Karl nodded sadly. He could not imagine Rome without his merry compatriot.

† † †

For a few days Berti vacillated, wondering if Maximilian's offer was still open. Finally he wrote to Gianbologna asking for more time. Feeling less harried, he took his favorite walks through Rome, fighting the streams of pilgrims flooding the city for Palm Sunday. The city sparkled, polished and resplendent, welcoming them despite the heavy spring rain.

Il Gesù, the first of its kind, was the most noteworthy of Rome's splendors. No wonder the cardinal loved it most and chose it for his final resting place. Dominated by a huge, austere façade, the church rose in the new style, with a wide nave and no aisles, reverberating with the constant footsteps of the faithful.

The decoration was sparse, most of the chapels still whitewashed like the huge vault and the dome, but what it lacked in final touches was made up in temporary decorations. Festive banners competed with splendid tapestries; finely wrought chalices rested on delicately embroidered linen, all lit by rank upon rank of tall tapers.

Berti eased through the crowd toward the crossing and gazed up into the cupola. The church doctors gleamed from the four freshly painted pendentives, ready for the jubilee. The poses were old-fashioned, almost wooden, but the Holy Office wanted pious decorations. After he finished admiring the church, he fought through another flock of pilgrims proudly bearing banners with the name of Castel Gandolfo, their town in the Roman hills.

Seeing a woman who reminded him of Maddalena, he decided to visit her. Absorbed in his thoughts, he did not notice the shadow of another woman following him. She moved stealthily, ducking into the underpasses when she thought he might turn.

At Maddalena's house, the aroma of roasted garlic and pungent herbs filled the air. He shook off his wet cloak and dropped it on a bench by the portal. Starved, he followed the lingering scent to the open hearth and wrinkled his nose with pleasure. "What is it, Antonella?"

"Potato soup with lots of onions and a good helping of garlic and rosemary."

"God bless you, Nella! May I?" Berti helped himself to a thick slice of fresh bread, but not before Lena's diligent helper signed it with the cross. He sprinkled on salt and sank his teeth into its grainy goodness. "Where is your mistress?"

Maddalena was rarely far away.

"Upstairs, sewing." The long rows of neat stitches of Maddalena's sewing always amazed Berti, especially now that she could not see.

"Who is it?" Lena pretended surprise as he kissed her cheek. "Young Fleming, you should trim your moustache. You feel like an old sheep dog."

"How did you know me?" He never understood how Lena recognized visitors.

"I know your footsteps and also the smell of your clothes, and your voice gives you away. I heard you all the way from downstairs!"

Berti sniffed his shirt. It seemed fresh enough, but the lavender of his last bedmate still hung on. "Now wait a minute, Madonna!" He pushed her chair toward the window. "If you're not nice, I'll make you sit outside until you look like a wet chicken."

"How are you, Bartolomeo?"

Lena always looked graceful, and she bloomed especially when Berti came.

"Fine. And you? You look so pretty and fresh today."

"I'm fine. But you haven't forgotten your promise, have you?" She reminded Berti that he agreed to visit the holy churches during Lent.

"How could I? You'd put a spell on me if I didn't!"

"Bite your tongue." She looked around. "The walls have ears."

Even at the worst times, Lena was a good soldier, and his heart swelled with affection.

"*Tesoro mio,* my dearest and oldest friend, what would I do without you?"

Maddalena raised her face toward him as Berti knelt by the chair and embraced her, feeling her heart close, cheek against cheek. In that quiet moment of warmth, he realized that he had always loved Lena, even when she was Alessandro's. His was the passion of a child, a brother, a friend, and a lover all in one, filling and sustaining as rain does the fields.

"I love you, Lena," he said slowly. "Will you be my wife?"

Maddalena sat as if she had waited her whole life for those words.

"Berti, I love you too. I always have, even when Alessandro's, but I never knew it."

"Say yes. I will honor you and look after you."

Maddalena's face sank on his shoulder. He took it in his hands and kissed her eyebrows.

"Lena, I love you!" His lips searched her face, merged hungrily with hers.

"I'd be a burden. And Christ does not mean me to marry."

Was it possible to love two men at the same time? Probably not.

"Say yes, my beloved."

"Give me time. I cannot, not now."

"I will wait, *cara,* as long as you want, but I'll be back tomorrow."

Berti kissed her hair, watching the light play about her face. Her hair was white, but it seemed flaxen as if the holy aura that framed her sightless face had kissed it golden.

"Until tomorrow."

Berti ran down the stairs two at a time and reached for his cloak. It was sodden. He should have left it to dry by the fire. He paused, wondering what to do, when Lena appeared on the top landing. She looked regal in the cloud of gold about her head as she laid her crutches aside and sat on the top step.

He made a gallant sweep with his hat. "Your servant, madam."

She smiled as if she could see him. "You monkey."

As he admired Maddalena he scarcely felt the draft of cool air on his back as the gate opened. He listened for the customary patter of Maddalena's beggars, but the steps on the stone floor sounded cushioned. He tried to turn, but his neck caught in a twitch. With horror he saw Maddalena pull herself up against the wall without her crutches, her face frozen.

"God protect you! Look out!" She flung her arms wide.

Berti sensed movement behind his back and turned as a hand plunged a knife at his chest. The blow was weak. He struggled for seconds before he recognized the assailant.

"Klara! You! Why?" He searched the girl's livid face.

A dull thud came from above. Maddalena lost balance and tumbled down the stairs, her head striking each step with a crack that echoed down the steep incline. The muddle of her clothes followed until she crashed to a stop on the bottom landing.

Berti flung Klara against the gate and saw her flee as suddenly as she appeared. Had he not seen Maddalena at his feet, he would have thought himself in a nightmare.

"Lena, my love! Make a miracle. You can do it!" He cradled her head against his chest.

She smiled faintly.

"My life is not mine. The Lord's will be done on earth as it is in heaven."

"Amen," Berti whispered. The walls disappeared, and a heavenly glory descended.

Lena stirred.

"Promise me, whatever happens, you'll go to Vienna and be famous."

"I promise." He clung to her as Maddalena covered her face to shut out the world.

† † †

On Palm Sunday, two pilgrims moved along with the crowds of confraternities, monks and nuns of many callings but one conviction, he hoping for a miracle and she for deliverance. Berti was gaunt, Maddalena barely a shadow. Miraculously, her fall broke no bones, only bruised her; but Berti's confession and her revelation were burdens too heavy to bear. She loved him, but she did not want to be a millstone around his neck, dragging him lower with time.

That her love was pure, she had no doubt, but she also knew she was but another star in the roster of his youthful infatuations, a star that would wane quickly when his true love appeared. She also knew that would be a punishment greater than all the torments of the Inquisition or the fires of hell. And so instead of love, she sought solace in pilgrimage to the jubilee churches. Each succeeding basilica found her wearier, her strength ebbing for good.

The spring sun warmed the streams of men and women moving toward St. John Lateran, all bearing palms to be blessed in memory of Christ's triumphal entry into Jerusalem. Berti walked with the sun in his face, its warmth imbuing him with the feeling of renewing life.

"Shall we pause at the Colosseum, Lena?" He took out his water pouch. Lena's face was ethereal in the sun's glory. "A drink and a rest?"

"Thank you." She took a sip and returned the pouch. "Some shade sounds refreshing."

Berti took a long drink and began pushing Lena's chair across the road. It had not rained for days, and pilgrim feet, hooves, and wheels pulverized the thirsty ground into dust. He wiped his forehead, leaving the back of his hand gritty. The bells of San Clemente rang brightly as they passed its walled gardens. This part of Rome belonged to mother nature. Unlike the stretch to Santa Maria Maggiore, it showed no signs of dwellings.

"A bit more, Lena, and we'll rest in the shade." He checked the right wheel of Lena's chair. Not meant for rough roads, it was threatening to break.

A troop of pilgrims passed, streaming toward the Lateran. Even from a distance he could tell they were German, with jovial faces like so many he had seen in Santa Maria dell'Anima.

"And may the Lord also give you strength in your journey," he called in German. "Hold on tight, Lena. The path is rocky here," he warned as he pushed toward the Colosseum through a break in the crowd, looking for shade and a stone to rest on.

Maddalena's face was like a sheet of paper etched by the day's effort. In the morning they visited the first basilica and in the afternoon, the second. Both scaled the Holy Steps on their knees. Berti pulled her up to the pinnacle. Not having eaten for days, she struggled to stay upright while reciting the rosary.

"Lena, you must drink more." He held the pouch near her lips. "Fast if you must, but if you don't drink, we won't finish the pilgrimage."

First she sipped, then nearly drained the pouch. Berti sat down, watching her face regain color. "Better?"

"Yes." She tried to smile as a stray dog jumped into her lap. "May I?" She gave the animal the rest of the water.

"Lena, you always think of others," Berti grumbled. The pup scrambled up and licked her face. "They all love you," he whispered, "and I do too. I will never forget you standing at the top of the stairs and your arms open wide. To this day I don't know if you were blessing me or warning me." He kissed her palms. "How did you know?"

He needed not ask. That dreadful day when Klara came to Lena's house looking for him was forever imprinted on both their minds, but whatever happened, he could not fathom how. "You couldn't see Klara. You'd no idea who came in. How did you know I was in danger?"

Maddalena moistened her lips. "But I *did see* in my heart that you were in danger."

"That's impossible."

"You saved my life once. I gave it back to you." Although she was clearly too weary to explain, she suddenly raised her head like a lioness who hears her cub call and turned as a small, horse-drawn carriage pulled up.

"Lena? What is it?" Berti asked. A bulky man emerged from the carriage and shuffled toward them, leaning heavily both on his cane and the young man who accompanied him.

Berti bowed, kissed Alessandro's hand, and stepped aside. Although Alessandro did not speak, Maddalena's face lit with recognition.

"Jacopo, bless you for looking after your benefactor," she whispered. "His Grace has always been kind to your family and now to you. Return all you receive a thousandfold, but remember that when you come to be judged, the Lord may not ignore your transgressions!"

Berti was stunned. How she recognized Alessandro and his ward was beyond him. Maddalena's clairvoyance came from elsewhere, but her earthly grip on the facts put the cardinal into a rage. How dare she judge him? The insinuation was clear, even if her words were directed to his ward!

For some moments, three pairs of eyes crossed over the frail woman's head—Alessandro's, fuming at Maddalena's insolence, Jacopo's, leering with bored indifference, and Berti's, raging in sudden hatred toward both men.

"Your servant, Your Grace." Berti bowed deeper than required and whisked Maddalena away, leaving the shocked cardinal behind leaning on his cane and his ward. Seeing that the encounter had been too much for her, he tried to divert her. "We must hurry, so you can rest. How do you expect to be ready for our journey north?"

He still talked of marriage—without success.

They followed the ambulatory of the Colosseum's ancient arches and left them heading toward the church of Saint Cosmas and Damian.

Tufts of yellowing grass covered the imperial *fora,* and even the large pilgrim crowds did not scare the hungry cattle. Berti bent for a rare clump of fresh grass and put it in Lena's hand.

"It's spring. You must teach Antonella to care for your garden after we leave Rome."

She squeezed it and replied, "I ate from the tree of knowledge, and my road became thorny. I must return to walk a new road leading to eternal salvation."

"Lena, you're tired. I beg you, don't talk like that!" Berti pushed her chair carefully, searching for a smoother path. When he finally laid Lena in her bed, her life seemed to hang by a thread.

Across town, Alessandro hobbled tensely about his room. Nothing was right, nothing that mattered. He had schemed, plotted, bribed on his putative path to glory, watched his wealth rise and fall in the tumult of his artistic patronage, smiled at those who honored him, and cursed everyone who did not, all along unsure if life without Maddalena had any value. Now the insolent woman had the nerve to insult him in front of his servant!

"Damn her, who does she think she is? I am the *gran cardinale,* scion of the house of Farnese, and she—a Jewish whore!" The long soutane once lending his figure grace stuck to his bowed legs and his soft gut. He tottered toward a chair.

"Maddalena, forgive me," he said aloud. "I didn't mean that. We have hardly ever quarreled. Now I can never feel you in my arms, know the warmth of your body."

An unspeakable sadness enveloped him, gripped him, and pulled him down.

"Lord forgive me," he cried as darkness closed about him and buckled his ungainly body against the desk.

† † †

"Maddalena, wake up!" Berti rubbed her hands, his own face drawn with fatigue. For most of a week, he sat near Lena's bed as her life ebbed.

"Maddalena, His Grace is here."

Berti could hardly look into Alessandro's face. He had no idea how news of Maddalena's condition reached him, but he hardly recognized the corpulent man, so greatly had he changed since their last brief encounter.

"*Carissima*," Alessandro mumbled, dragging one leg behind as he came to sink by Maddalena's bed, heedless of Berti. "You were my inspiration, my tree of life, my power and vitality," he said in a voice that broke. "When I watched you burn, my breath died. But I wanted to live, to complete the tasks we talked of so often. I couldn't do it alone. There at the stake I forfeited my right to you. I lost my son, but God gave me Jacopo in his stead.

"Maddalena, that boy is like me—bright, determined, and as willing to please as I was when I was made cardinal at fourteen. In Jacopo's face, I see myself again, and as I love myself, I also came to love him." Alessandro flushed with the effort of what was to come.

"Maddalena, I Alessandro, Cardinal Farnese, confess to you and beg you to intercede for me. Before your saintly face, I admit that our union was a great sin, but my transgression with Jacopo was worse, because I not only defiled my sacred vows but also those I made to you.

"I have wronged you and I am sorry. Will you, can you ever forgive me?" Alessandro hid his face in the folds under Lena's transparent hands. Her lips twitched, but she lay inert.

"Lena," the proud old man wept so unashamedly that Berti could hardly bear to watch. "I still love you and always will. Can you ever *forgive* me?"

Maddalena's hand rested on Alessandro's silken cap. Her fingers read his tall forehead, feeling for his once-luxuriant hair. She whispered, "Dearest, what happened to your locks? Are they now covered with snow?"

"My noblest wife, we all grow old." He covered her hands with gentle kisses.

The room filled with rivulets of light that streamed through the window and joined hands in a dance over Maddalena's and Alessandro's heads. She breathed in sharply as she recalled the precious moment when they married under the moon. The presence of the man for whom she gave up her family gave her new meaning, and all else sank into oblivion.

"Till death us do part," she whispered.

Alessandro gasped, convulsed in grief.

"Don't cry. It was not your fault. There was nothing you or I could do. We know the ways of men, but the Lord's ways tower above us, and they are mysterious. I have nothing but gratitude for the passion in your heart, and I have only compassion for your soul."

Alessandro sobbed silently.

"There is nothing to forgive, much to be thankful for, Alessandro. You baptized me with these hands. Will they also give me the last rites?" She brought his hand to her heart. The old man felt reborn that she should ask that of him. It was not why he came.

"Lena, my life!" he cried, dampening her face with his tears as he clasped her weak body close. "Please try for us. The Lord saved you once, and I know he will again."

"Alessandro, I beg you, don't deny my last request."

The cardinal raised himself, composed once again. He looked at the plain crucifix above Maddalena's head, crossed himself, and drew the sign of the cross over her:

"*Domine Fili unigenite, Jesu Christe* ... Lord, the only begotten Son, Jesus Christ," he began in a thin voice that grew fuller and steadier as his prayers drifted over the dying woman and his fingers anointed her with holy oil. Maddalena grew more peaceful with each stroke.

Berti could not watch. Quietly, he went below to the kitchen.

Before long Alessandro joined him and took one last look around. He stood erect, his voice firm. "She is sleeping. May the Lord grant her peace. She loved me until the end," he whispered as he headed toward the portal.

For a long while Berti could not make himself climb the steps. Now that Alessandro had been with her, he felt he would be an intruder in Lena's room.

She did not die that night or the following morning, and on the eve of the Lord's Resurrection she appeared remarkably recovered. Though wasted and gaunt, she radiated a new kind of energy as if Alessandro's visit had shown her the final leg of her terrestrial journey.

"Shall we go to St. Peter's?" Maddalena asked almost cheerfully, propped up in bed.

"You're still weak," Berti replied cautiously. He and Antonella exchanged worried looks, not knowing what to think of her recovery.

"You promised."

"Then go we shall."

† † †

The following morning, as they crossed the bridge by Castel Sant'Angelo, a rich tapestry of pilgrims unfolded along the river bank.

"We'll be there soon." Berti patted Maddalena's shoulders. She looked fresh in the lovely velvet dress she saved for the angels. "At the end of your pilgrimage to the holy basilicas," he added cheerfully. "Oh Lord, please make her live," he prayed silently.

Halfway through Via Alexandrina the road became more and more congested, and they had to fight through a maze of riders, carriages, and pedestrians converging on St. Peter's. At the end of the street in front of St. Catherine's, the last of Berti's strength ebbed from his limbs. His back throbbed from days of pushing Lena's chair through the jubilant city, and the ache in his wrists made him wonder if he would ever paint again.

"Shall we pause by the fountain?" he asked.

Maddalena nodded, hearing the weariness in his voice. He gripped her chair and pushed again. The last few paces into the densely packed square were exhausting, but when they came to the fountain in the center, the pilgrims opened a passageway for the crippled woman.

Berti filled his hand with the sparkling water cascading from the fountain. He washed his face with soothing strokes. The cool water lightened his exhaustion.

"Would you like some?"

Maddalena's face brightened briefly as the water ran down her face, trickling through her dusty hair and dropping into her lap in little muddy tears.

"More?" Berti bent for another handful. She nodded, feeling the water on her forehead, feeling Alessandro's fingers of so long ago making the sign of the cross.

"I baptize thee Maddalena," the cardinal had said, aware of a sense of infinite goodness.

Goodness filled her face as she raised herself in her chair, listening intently as the waves of singing pilgrims moved toward St. Peter's. Leaning on her crutches, she turned her face toward the familiar façade, the image of which remained clear in her mind despite her blindness.

A soft breeze toyed with her hair. The belfries tolled Angelus, and the joyous clamor from nearby churches fused with the hymn of the Lord's Resurrection. As if He wanted to join His people in their joy, the leaden clouds locked over the city during the night began to disperse.

Mesmerized, Berti watched the heaven open in a sea of divine light, filtering onto the unfinished dome of St. Peter's and spreading rapidly toward them in a carpet of fluffy clouds. A heavenly mist fell and settled gently on Lena's brow, touched her face and shoulders, her scarred legs, and she became transfigured within it. As the bells echoed in the air, she seemed to grow taller, her face blossoming with the beauty that once enchanted Alessandro.

As if in a dream, Berti stared at her as though she were an apparition, until she embraced him tenderly and gave him her crutches.

"Thank you for all you've done, and may the Lord bless you always."

The cardinal's woman stood firmly as she smiled at him for the last time.

"Don't leave me!" Berti cried. "What will I do without you? How will I know when the sun rises and when it sets? How can I face tomorrow?"

Maddalena's eyes reflected the wisdom of her Moorish ancestors.

"But you don't have to, Berti. Don't worry about tomorrow when you have today. When the next day comes, you'll know what to do."

"I won't. I'm afraid."

"Don't be. You must walk alone now, and only so will you achieve all the great things you have always desired."

Berti did not want to understand. He knew only that she was leaving, and he grieved for himself and the world around him.

"*Quo vadis,* Rebecca?"

"Back to my only master, to serve Him faithfully as I did here on earth."

She paused a moment, waiting for the mist to subside, then began to rise through it, slowly treading the soft cushion of clouds that folded obediently under her feet into a heavenly path. With her, little by little, went the loving goodness that filled Berti's life for so many of his days in Rome, a gift he took for granted until he lost it forever with her.

Watching her go, he thought of the tall ladder in Jacopo Bertoia's fresco on the ceiling of Alessandro's winter bedroom in Caprarola. The passage of time and the sudden birth of his own wisdom awed him. As Maddalena's figure grew distant, Jacob's *Dream* played in his mind.

> *After Isaac blessed his younger son and Jacob parted with his mother Rebecca, he set out for the land of Laban. When the night took over, he found a stone and set his head against it. And he began to dream, seeing a ladder growing out of the earth and reaching toward heaven, and behold, there were God's angels ascending and descending on it.*

At the top of the young woman's path stood the Lord, surrounded by angels, and when she reached Him, His arms opened wide. He smiled and spoke.

"Welcome, Rebecca, my child. I am the God of Abraham, your father, and Sarah, your mother. But I am also your Lord and God, Maddalena. In this promised land which you now tread all creatures are equal, as I made them on earth at the very beginning."

A gust of wind blew from the hills, dispelling the clouds and the golden light that filled the streets of Rome on the day of the Lord's Resurrection in the year 1575. A great current of air swirled over St. Peter's Square, joining the crowds moving through the open gates. Caught in its embrace, Berti moved on in a daze, the vision burning brightly in his head. When he reached the basilica steps, the saint's face shone brighter than ever. He knelt and kissed the holy ground.

As he straightened his back, he sighed from the bottom of his heart, *"Blessed are thou, forever, St. Magdalen."*

Author's Notes

The story of *Maddalena* is inspired by Titian's *Penitent Magdalen*, painted for the historical Cardinal Farnese and now in the Pitti Palace in Florence. The heroine Maddalena is entirely imagined, a spirit to touch humanity. Set in post-Tridentine Rome in the 1560s and based on years of research and writing, this first book of *The Golden Tripolis* trilogy rises from the nucleus of a broader tale of northern artists in Rome, whose journeys to the Italian penninsula eventually included Peter Paul Rubens. His is but one name in the second book *Bartholomæus*, set in Rudolfine Prague. *Christina*, the third book, centers around the Protestant Queen whose armies devastated the imperial capital, a monarch who gave her heart and wealth to Rome.

Care has been taken to depict the historical setting with verisimilitude, but *Maddalena* is fiction, in which prose emulates reality with an ulterior motif. As such, it is just another tale in which serious academic discourse of the historic fabric and documents is discouraged.

The cover painting, illustrations, and map are inspired by period material.

The plot unfolds during the Italian journey of the Flemish-born artist Bartholomæus Spranger (1546-1611) who served Cardinal Farnese (1520-1589) and Pope Pius V (1504-1572), and who later became the favorite artist of Emperor Rudolf II Habsburg (1552-1612). Berti, as he is known to the reader, is an important link between the fictional but compelling Cardinal Farnese and his Jewish-born mistress. Berti's picaresque character is inspired by a biographical reference written by his friend, fellow artist, and important Netherlandish biographer, Karel van Mander, in his *Schilderboeck* of 1604, that at some point of Berti's stay in Rome the young artist worked only to support a life of pleasure in the company of an unknown Netherlandish merchant, the fictional Adrian Floris.

Apropos other characters in *Maddalena* who are historical figures, Hans Speckaert died in 1577, likely from paralysis, and the ailing Cornelis Cort followed him withing a year, the same year as did Don Giulio Clovio, Cardinal Farnese's miniaturist. Alessandro Farnese pursued his dreams for more than a decade, most of which were realized, except for the papal throne. He likely died from apoplexy and was buried in *Il Gesù*, in a simple tomb in front of the high altar. After a brief period in Vienna, great fortune smiled at Berti Spranger in the service of one of the greatest and most peculiar patrons of art.

Since this story has gestated for the better part of a decade, in fear that I would forget to mention the name of a colleague, editor, family member, or friend, to all of you who have supported the dream of seeing *Maddalena* born, who have read the manuscript, made invaluable suggestions, and provided much appreciated support, a most profoundly felt thanks. Beyond, all remaining blunders and mistakes are entirely mine.

About the Author

European-born and educated in the United States, Eva Jana Siroka has also lived in Canada. An art historian and artist, she forged her interests at Hunter College and Princeton University. *Maddalena,* the author's first novel, is based on years of research. A professional painter with works in private and public collections in North America and Europe, the author is working on *Bartholomæus,* the second book of *The Golden Tripolis* trilogy, set in imperial Prague.